Cataca: the door

L.A.T.D-K

Cataca: the door

Vanguard Press

VANGUARD PAPERBACK

A CIP catalogue record for this title is
available from the British Library.

ISBN 978 1 80016 829 9

Vanguard Press is an imprint of
Pegasus Elliot Mackenzie Publishers Ltd.
www.pegasuspublishers.com

First Published in 2024

Vanguard Press
Sheraton House Castle Park
Cambridge England

Printed & Bound in Great Britain

Dedication

To E Diana Bubb-Dasent, my mother, my biggest influencer both positive and negative. I miss you and thank you for all the support, pens, papers, and books given to me to write.

Acknowledgements

To my legacy, Khaila and Kalila, sisters, Dianne, Avonella and Keisha, brother, Natakki, niece, Titanja. Victor, daddy. Thank you for your ears, your eyes and your patience with me. I love you all.

CHAPTER ONE

I was terrified, quick shallow breaths. Pulse thumping through my ears, liquefied across my forehead. Consumed by the memory of last night. It's still warm, new and stained in my brain forever. I sealed my eyes. I couldn't make sense of this.

Everything jumbled up all at once flooding me, as the lump in my throat grows harder. My eyes filling by the seconds. My whole life seems to be laid on a scale: my marriage, my career, my child's life and my life.

I froze, creasing my sweaty palms at the edge of the wooden table, shuddering at the prosecutor's seat. I opened my eyes shuffling manila folders of papers, pictures and statements of evidence. Laying it out, as my life placed before me to decide. A puzzle I don't know how to put together.

I don't know what to do.

Am I ignorant and blind? I torture myself.

My eyes shut trying to envision the details of my life. Attempting to recapture some small sign.

There must have been something, something not blinded by me trusting.

Is trusting so wrong?

I will myself to remember, blocking everything else out.

Ten, nine, eight, seven, six, five, four, three, two, one...

I count circumspectly, my nose began to flare. Flowing like a common cold instead of my eyes. Breathing unbearably louder and louder.

I don't know how long again I can hold it in...

I try to convince myself as I exhale deep and long. Relieving those feelings.

I can't do this now, not here. I scolded myself again.

Awakened by the hammering sound of the bailiff's hands slamming into the wooden bench as I avulse to the task at hand;

"Order in the court, come to order…"

His voice echoes and my eyes open. The tall, slender, black man. Clean-shaven, tidy, well-groomed low hair. His khaki uniform, a white T-shirt poking at the top of his shirt. Finishes the concealment of his chest hair which bulges below. Seamed straight pants with a green cord at the seam. A gold shield shining underneath his name tag, 'Officer James Talend' with a green webbed belt and a gold buckle.

The rustling of chairs and footsteps echoed through the silence behind me. Rising tentatively, sliding the black webbed chair on its wheels with the back of my thighs, whilst gliding my hands towards my sides. Across the glossy black table covered in folders. I came to my feet cautiously blinking hard and opening my eyes, relieved.

The middle-aged bailiff continued screaming, "… Case number 8639210 is now in session. The state county of Divinish verses Mr Adam Jolee, representing the state, Mrs Shannan Davis-Hall and representing the defendant Mrs Jennings Gibbs, Judge Franklin Ligmore presiding."

He recited as if practised.

The judge was as big as he was tall. Broad shoulders, towering over the bench as he walked with his chest up towards his chair. Contrasting chestnut skin and light white hair yet he seemed to be in his early fifties.

His black gown flows, the seams revealed as he quickens towards his chair. Grabbing a handkerchief he saps the gloss from his forehead, pausing in front of the massive black leather chair. It looks custom-made and adjusted just for him. He smooths the strayed pleats, stared into the crowd leaned over his desk and sat. Pulling the chair closer to the bench.

"You may be seated…"

He exposes the manila folder hidden by the partition whilst opening it quickly. He glanced at the content then he stared right at me.

"… Mrs Hall, your opening statement."

His voice thundered and echoed throughout the bursting courtroom.

"Thank you, your honour."

I whispered then cleared my throat.

Six months ago.

My husband will never understand.

I didn't quite tell him the truth about the interview, for a good reason. For him, he'd prefer I don't work at all. He seems to think I am this fragile thing that needs protection though he taught me to fight. I left police training at the top of my class, though I trained really, really hard for D.P.F. Daver Police Force.

I had to quit because of…

Uh… personal issues…

I really hope they don't ask why, but at least I got the training, which can be a plus!

I begin to unravel my foundation. This would be a better use of my degree in law and psychology and with a minor in administration.

Yes, being the head of S.D.A.F. personal assistant?

Internalising, stepping swiftly, my black swede court shoes struck the floor with a deep echoing sound. Striding to the width of my polyester, over-the-knee aubergine pencil skirt suit, with a small slit behind. Giving me enough room to step the stride of my size: four-and-a-half-sized feet. Clearly, not room to move as I would like to. The skirt stretched to its capacity tightening above my calves.

Gosh, I hope it wasn't a mistake wearing a modest-length skirt without a stretch.

My criticism began at the second interview. The vacancy for an executive assistant to the director in command, of this newly formed law enforcement organisation. Special Daver Armed Federal Force or S.D.A.F. It is not quite where I want to be, but it is a foot in.

Did they leave out the last F for effect?

I began second-guessing my research again.

Gosh, I hope that isn't one of their questions.

I'm sure to get *that* wrong.

I internally slapped myself on the forehead.

Oh my!

My shoes squeaked with a subtle stumble, as I raced through the foyer. The speed, not generating enough air to keep the sweat forming on my forehead, pooling in my armpits and increasing my heartbeat. The heat, building underneath my jacket.

I straightened my dark, curly, hair so it flows on my back past my bra. Swinging my black leather briefcase balancing my high heels. My bronze skin and hazel eyes look green now that I'm edgy, but I felt lucky.

My eyes always catch interest and, if nothing else is, that is always a great icebreaker.

The receptionist, alert with a smile, was standing at the end of the open floor spaced ground floor, her bright blue eyes piercing through me. My heartrate increased further as I close the gap between us.

"Shannan Davis-Hall."

My mouth opened and the words flew with my bag across the countertop. She put her hands up stopping it from throwing her pens on the ground. Her grin widened with my eyes as I apologised instantly. Folding my lips, crunched my eyebrows, shutting my eyes to scold myself, for that second.

Taking up a clipboard from the table below the partition, she turned the paper holding it behind the board. They fluttered with each page she turned. I reminded myself of the advertisement squeezing my lips tighter together. The moisture gathered on my palms while she turned another page.

Times were changing and the government reformed all defence organisations, in an attempt of eliminating corruption, and promoting transparency and accountability.

Opening this new law enforcement group is the final stage of the government's plan. To have an independent federal organisation to be the highest form of policing, to attack crime and terrorism in specific forms, against national security.

A lot of opportunities were opened and a lot of other divisions of crime fighting were closed or in the process of restructuring.

She inhaled at the same time as me.

"Aha, Mrs Davis-Hall, yes, you're at ten."

I nodded unable to exhale. My eyes bulged at the clock behind her says nine-forty-five.

"... Your waiting room is at the end of this hall. One of my colleagues will let you know when they're ready."

She grinned widely. I exhaled, and turned at ninety degrees with a squeak and a cringe at the sound. But keeping my head up as I prepare internally once more.

I have passed the bar.

I can navigate well around the computer.

So ready to help clean up the thriving crime in my beloved country. I have never been able to prove my worth with other employment that is. *Fast food cashier and a grocery store assistant?* I rolled my eyes at the refresher.

And being the directors P.A. is?

Yes. I answered myself.

Law and enforcement are where I thrive to be. I was eager for this change. To be a part of the process to make the transformation. If I couldn't be directly involved in law or enforcement, at least I'll be closest to the place where justice was served.

Hum... and besides if nothing else, my husband made sure I can fight...

... Not that I should need it here, but...

Five women sat waiting, their ages seemed to range between thirty and fifty. Arriving at the receptionist's directions, a woman exited a wooden door opposite the chairs behind the seats.

I must be the youngest sitting here.

Taking the last vacant seat, legs crossed by the ankles. Shaking my foot as I wait against a wall on the light-coloured sofa gazing at the paintings of dark cultural men, I think. Long limbs and bright yellow and orange pants. Their faces blend with the dark background of the oil paints and seemed like ancient Zemand. I was drawn to it dazing into the soul of this painting, which is like ataraxic, narcosis. The tap of my feet seized. The movement in the room wakes me. A woman was called into the room behind the receptionist's desk, shutting the door behind her.

I am sure I've seen at least two of these women dressed as police officers, or at some event with my husband.

My observation further increases my nerves. They all appeared so mature and each dressed very professionally in pantsuits.

Their resumes must be longer than mine.

My husband is the lieutenant of the Special Crimes Unit in the Daver Police Force, one of the most commended officers and probably their boss.

Oh gosh, I hope they don't tell him I was here...

Or maybe they won't because I've seen them here...

Smiling at my naughty thoughts for a moment. Then, I began tapping my feet again, uncrossing my ankle and caressing my wet palms next to my thighs. Anxious for my name to be called.

The only thing anyone could have over me is experience...

... The only thing they have over me is experience.

I consciously repeated to convince myself. Then.

"Mrs Mall..."

My heart reached my throat and all my movement seized. I cannot exhale, her singsong voice calling me by the wrong name. Raised my hand as though at school with anticipation and caution answering modestly.

"That's Mrs Hall." I exhale slowly.

"Sure, sorry!" the receptionist responded singing again. "... This way..."

She pointed pleasantly. Her grin looked as if it had been painted on with her lipstick and contrasted with her bright teeth.

Her appearance was polished, pretty and perfect. My insecurities piqued self-conscious about my conservative feminine attire. Slowly, I rise from the chair throwing my black leather shoulder bag over my shoulder. Trying to keep it from swaying, straddling carefully towards the biggest door I have ever seen.

Shana, you can do this!

I give myself another pep talk. I pounced from side to side, shaking my arms loose at my sides. Twisting and cracking my neck, straightened my crooked jacket. Changing my expression as I went through.

One hour and twenty gruelling minutes later I was one of the first agents hired by the newly formed S.D.A.F. I was proud. Not the job I went for but better! The hard work and sacrifices finally paid off.

I was right, my husband didn't understand.

"Shana! What, were you thinking?"

His tone was deep and serious with two feet between us whilst I sat on the edge of our bed, next to a suitcase piled with unfolded laundry next to it. My hands clasp in pause, folding a shirt with a twist, tilting my head. Squinting eyes as his voice reverberated through me knowing how he'd react.

His gleaming brown eyes squinted. Full unshaved beard, and curly, dark, silky hair in his what-should-be loose boxers, gripping his muscular hairy thighs. White socks pulled as high as they could go, close to his calves. And, my favourite article of clothing; a white vest. Complimenting his broad, muscular chest and buffed biceps. His dark chest hair peeked through the top of the vest. One hand on his hip and the other wagging his index finger pointed at me.

"It is not as bad as you're making it Eric."

I argued with my head down avoiding his beaming gaze.

"Really, really…" His voice went up a couple of octaves on each 'really', "… I can't believe you did this! I thought we'd dealt with this after you quit."

You made me quit!

I frown in my head outward, I pout. "… Honey, those organizations claim transparency but are moulded in corruption, shaped by lies and cooked in conspiracies.

"I don't want you spending your whole career chasing after conspiracies. Trying to find the root of corruption and ending up a part of the whole scandal. Why would you put yourself through that?"

He sighed. Came to me, stooped, looking up at my bowed head. Engulfed my hands with his pleading. The disappointment covered my expression. I dazed at his large hands folded over mine. Finding courage filling my lungs. I slipped my hands out of his, and waved it around as if painting the picture.

"Eric, first of all, I am not going to chase any conspiracies of any sort. And secondly, my job comprises of collecting and analysing data… writing reports… advising if and when needed… it's *not* to chase after criminals." My voice getting softer, "… Nor making arrests… no policing of any sort. I'm in the office… completing administration, paperwork."

I couldn't hide the disappointment in my voice. I stood up. His hands fell and he off balance, I walked across the side of the bed to our black laminated chest of draws, opened the second draw wide, placed the shirt, I held it inside then, took another one out.

"Shana... That makes no sense!"

His exasperation was absurd as he then sat on the bed where I was. I took a deep inhale trying not to roll my eyes at his ridiculous attempt to allure me then exhaled.

"And what you said does? Would it make sense if I told you *this* is what I want?"

Bundling shirts out of the draw and adding to the pile next to him trying to avoid eye contact.

"What about our family?"

"What about it?"

Shrugging my shoulders in apprehension.

I know where this conversation is headed.

I made my way back to the chest of drawers. Comfortably placing my ass, on the edge of the draws, crossing my arms in anticipation.

"We discussed this before. Danielle would suffer."

Oh... there it goes!

He leaned forward crisscrossing his fingers together then clasping his hands as if praying.

"What are you talking about?" I blurted out, almost laughing, but hoping he won't notice and continued. "... Danielle's ten and goes to boarding school. It's not like she needs my twenty-four-hour care... she has a mother." I waved my arms again.

"Yea, you."

I couldn't control the need. I rolled my eyes. He strolled next to me, putting his huge hands over my shoulders, and caressing the knots with his thumbs.

"... You're intelligent, talented and one of the best women I know. Baby, why would you put yourself in danger like this... again there are safer jobs within... that organisation. Besides the one you lied about applying for."

"I didn't lie. They offered." I shrug.

He hummed with a sigh.

His fresh breath touches my face. My eyes closed as he lowers his head to my shoulder. Every hair on my body raises and I calm accepting his caress.

What is he doing?

No!

I snap to myself before his lips made contact.

"Don't do this Eric," I whispered then shrugged his hands off me moving to the bed.

"Don't!" I am more forceful.

"What?"

He threw his arms up surrendering pretending he wasn't trying to work one over on me.

"Don't taint this for me. Don't make me feel guilty about D.P.F. training and…"

The memories are still fresh and my emotions sway. I moved beside the dressing table stool at the foot of the bed looking at him through the mirror.

I can't look at him!

"If I wasn't there, who knows what would have happened… to you… to Danielle."

The incident flooded me. The ball grew in my throat, my eyes redden, and my nose pulsated. Filling me with instant regret. I recalled my arrogance and his response. Inhaling deeply then exhaling.

"Danielle is fine and I'll be fine… It's because you do *this*… that's why that happened…" I turned around and shouted, "… Look I'm not asking for much, just your support."

His eyes went down, he folded his lips exposing his gorgeous dimples through his unshaven beard. Nothing was said for a few seconds. The silence brewed as we both gazed at everything else but each other.

"I can't," he eventually said softly. My heart sank, my face fell and I can't breathe. Pressing my eyes together and placing both hands over my face.

Ten, nine, eight, seven, six, five, four, three…

"It is what it is Eric." I removed my hands and shook my head in disapproval.

"What does that mean?" He is attentive.

"I'm leaving for Divinish in the morning, my first case."

I walked to the bed and zipped the suitcase placing it in the closet.

"*What!*" he shouted.

We both weren't backing down. Getting louder, words exchanged back and forth. Arguing for about an hour until Danielle poked her dark-brown curly head hair into our room. Rubbing her eyes asking us to shut up, so she can sleep. She is quite grown sometimes more grown than me, or her dad most of the time.

Danielle is my stepdaughter. Eric's daughter from his first marriage. Cute, a mane of dark-brown, big curls. Light brown-skinned with blue eyes. She is a smaller, darker version of her mum.

His divorce was more of a resurrection. The short version was his wife and child supposedly died in an IED explosion.

It was left as a present under his car from one of his cases. Danielle was three years old at the time. He was devastated, of course, and self-loathing. Pretty much drank himself to sleep almost every day. A total mess.

No more than I was anyway. Ten years ago…

On edge and confused. Roaming the cold streets of the capital Ceda with an urgent need for sanctuary. There was nothing clear but my name: Shannan Christine Davis. Anything more was a fog, hidden in darkness. I need to go, but I can't remember.

It was winter and the sun has set early, the cold snap was coming fast. The chill seeps through the dirty brown jacket. The holes near my chest are getting bigger, the webbing lining leaks out. And it stinks. I stink.

'You need to remain hidden.'

The hairs on every part of my body stand. They're close. I sense his stare.

I have to remain hidden.

The echoed words of a ghost. The words are my voice and the face in the deep abyss of my memories. The sounds around me amplify with my breathing and heartbeat. Dashed into an alleyway and stooped behind a large dumpster. My heart has to catch up with me. It's still pounding at a rate that I cannot calm. I quickly peeked around it.

I think they saw me!

My heart races faster. I waited a few minutes. The puddles are freezing at the edges. My breath is steaming in the light. I have to go further into the darkness so that I won't be seen. Keeping low and ducking between dumpsters, I found a pile of newspapers and a box half as tall as me.

I scrunched a few sheets of paper into the holes by my chest. I Tear the box in the centre and lined the paper along the box, crunching a whole newspaper one after the other for a pillow. It was perfect for the night. Somehow, I managed to rest.

Bang! The metal door opened. A man was thrown out. He landed meters from me. Wild, curly, silky hair, a beard, dark-brown eyes, glassy, reddened. Our eyes locked briefly, my hazels to his dark-brown. I have reflected in his eyes and that second, my thoughts shift.

He got up, shrugging at his alcohol-drenched sweater as if that will somehow make him look any less unkept. Staggering past me without deliberation. I watched him drift along the walls and dumpster while I nestled pulling more newspapers into me and fluffing the makeshift headrest. Calming back to sleep.

Then, that damn banging again!

Another drunken idiot!

The second man landed as though laying along the side of the dumpster close to my face. His alcohol-inundated breath puffed, blowing my curly hair out my face. His light blue eyes flicker and glow when our eyes meet.

Breathing shallowly, to my quickened heart, the urgency returns. My throat instantaneously dried and my saliva thickens. I turned my face away from his gaze hoping he does exactly as the first. This one paused. I cautiously rose to the plank position taking my left foot back then my left arm, my right foot and my right arm crawling out of the makeshift boxed tent.

His aspect sobered, awaked in a gawk, full of concupiscence intent. I stood, slightly passed his face wrapping the newspaper-isolated coat over my chest. I am suddenly aware of my lack of bra and wished he would just move on.

He sat up, his arms reaching for me. Like a deer in headlights, I leapt over him in an attempt to escape. He gripped me by both ankles, and with no time to brace, my face slammed, burned and echoed aloud with the impact. I tasted the blood in my mouth. The initial pain and shock paused my reaction. The cold, wet concrete drenched with garbage spills, urine and vomit only intensified my burning face.

Mopping the floor with my face and wild hair, he reeled my feet back next to the box. Bringing a mix of liquids with me. I grasp for anything within my reach collapsing the box. Groaning with a yell. My legs open to his waiting thighs. Pushing my head down, his hand made a way through my thick mane steadying my head to the concrete leaning over me. I am trapped.

"*No!*"

Blaring to the top of my voice until it hurt. With one swoop, his other hand grabs the stretchy waistband of my pants exposing me. Breeze skims my backside. A zipping sound thrilled through the air.

"Please…" My voice was sore from screaming.

"Chacáyione!"

He growled laying his lower body over mine. I heard footsteps and a thud. His warmth was removed. I didn't wait, pulled on my lower clothing, dressing fast. Running towards the main street, I paused at the end of the alley to see what had happened.

The man kicked out before he stood volleying him on the ground. He sees me looking on and calls for me. He takes out his phone, makes a call and walks towards me. The open doesn't feel safe but there is something about this man I trust. He met me.

"It's OK. I am a police officer. My name is Eric Hall. I can help you."

My body is still in shock. The adrenalin has subsided, but the cold has come shivering for something else.

He saved me.

I nod understanding staring into those brown eyes reflecting me. His height and broad shoulders thankfully block my view of my attacker. Looking instead at Eric's significant features.

Full beard, chocolate skin and a confusing afro that is both smooth and curly, a bit like mine. Eric peeks every few minutes at the man that is still on the floor. My breath steams and I shiver.

"Are you OK?"

Reminding me I need to hide. My eyes dilate and I move towards the dumpster. My forehead and face sting, and I taste blood in my mouth.

"It's OK… what is your name?"

I said it to him. He didn't understand or maybe I confused him. He tilted his head to one side taking a step closer. The alcohol is strong. I shook my head and he stopped.

"Can you tell me your name again?"

"Shannan," I repeated.

"Shannan, OK," he says understanding.

Sirens blared as he walks into the streets and waved to the police. I whimper behind a dumpster. He points down the alley and the ambulance came. He walked me straight in. I don't want him to leave me with them.

"They will take good care of you. I just need to talk to my friends at the police for a bit, OK?"

My eyes widened and I shook my head arguing. The paramedics stared oddly. There was a low rumble and car alarms began blasting. "Eric." Everyone else moved their heads around looking for the source.

I closed my eyes and my feet warms. Heat has touched my feet coiling around and making its way up. It is warm moving up my knees and the inside of my thighs, rising from my hips to my stomach surfacing, slowly, growing inside.

"Shannan," Eric calls me. He is standing in my way. The feeling subsided.

"Can I ride with her to the hospital?" Eric then asks the EMT.

"Are you family?" one paramedic questioned.

"I am the cop that has questions." He showed her his badge.

She nodded.

Apprehensive to leave the alley with a man claiming to be the police dressed in dirty stained clothes. There was something about him. He convinced me to go into the hospital to get the bruises checked. The ride was short. We moved through to a side room. He paced back and forth.

My clothes were torn and smelly but so was he. Nothing about his decorum was shining and *I can* say. I didn't realise it at the time, but we both saved each other.

… Another story that is on the rise.
Two of the most challenging years of our relationship. I did some things I am not particularly proud of. On some level, I do understand why he was angry with me for taking this job. But I never lied to him.

CHAPTER TWO

Punctual as usual,

    … Even more so, because of Eric, I cringed at the memory.

After Eric took referee Danielle to bed, I took the two packed bags downstairs. Where I slept in the day bed of the study of our two-bed house. As the sun rose, so did I.

Got ready quickly, and I avoided confrontation or delays. Though I would like us to be on the same page with this, I'd rather ask for forgiveness than permission. I went for my joining instructions.

Hoping to make a good impression, I arrived early to the brief. But also, to meet the team of specialists before we made our way to Divinish by flight. This new building in Ceda, the capital of Daver was a modest five-floor constructed a few years ago but recently opened in time for the interviews.

This time, armed with my letter of confirmation, I perused the HR department and collected and signed most of my starter documents, inclusive of my firearms license. The weight of the semi-automatic pistol sealed the affirmation of my position. I smiled.

This is really happening!

Doing cartwheels inside my head. Eager to get started, I clipped my issued hip holster and weapon on the right side of my waistband hip. Rushed to the conference room on the other side of the floor. The glass wall was frosted with an open door and a shadow of someone waiting inside. My grin grew.

I bolted through, filled with optimism and anticipation. My eyes widened and my heart jolted at the sight. I froze.

Surprise, surprise there she was, gnawing loudly on a bubble gum. Her mouth exposing her molars opening and closing making a squishing sound as she chews. The bones along her jaw strained with her loud, disgusting habit. Urgh!

A freshly cut bob, black, straightened hair, piercing-blue eyes and an innocent face, waiting in my conference room. Dirty blue, cut-up boyfriend jeans, tight white T-shirt tucked in, beneath a biker leather jacket. Her construction boots are black, and perched on the glossy, new, oval table that bounces her reflection off it.

Gingerly, I walked in trying not to portray intimidation. Lifting my chest confidently, flicking my straightened, glossy, dark-brown hair on my back. My navy pencil skirt, this time with a slight stretch, jacket well seamed and tucked yellow patterned blouse. Carrying my leather briefcase in my ruby-polished fingers.

Is she lost?

"What happened to your hair?" cockily I asked.

Evading the obvious question, sauntering towards the head of the table near a TV monitor to gain distance, and avoid an argument.

… She can be so frustrating!

Settling at the head avoiding her daze. I wheeled the chair back and set my briefcase on the table just then she popped her gum with a slight grin.

"The long, brown, curly hair makes me look like a mother."

Caught off guard, stunned in a short pause by her response. I try to recover my countenance swiftly, with a rehearsed smile, inwardly.

I deserved that. I reminded myself.

We exploited each other's agony and gloom these past two and a half years. So, I understand Samanther Martinez's hostility towards me. In reversed I don't think I would have behaved differently. I pondered, however, to how to approach this matter at hand.

"Look!"

Her rustic voice was clear. Taking me from an oncoming reminiscence as to her reasoning. She slid an A4 brown envelope across the polished table towards me, moving her feet from the table to the floor. It swivelled with a light swish to me. I stopped it as I pulled my chair back standing in front of it.

I hope this isn't what I think it is…

As it reached my hands, they instantly became clammy, sweaty, trembling almost. Simpering with my face in a painted smile. I placed my index finger between the seal and a space at the top of the envelope, pulled upwards and opened it with precaution and hope.

Please say no…

I quiver inside and I pulled up three pages. The S.D.A.F. headed paper with a letter of acceptance, at a quick glance.

"Is this document for this assignment?"

She heard the panic and disbelief in my voice. My breath hitched, trying not to let my lips part for too long. I don't want her to see me traumatized. Her face is glowing, knowing she's savouring the sight of me squirming.

I really hope that it's just a 'rookie' joke.

I blanched. My behind reached the chair and I bounced. Feeling a little queasy about the genuine signature and seal of confirmation. I try settling on the chair, my breathing shallow and my mouth dries.

… Breathe Shana breathe!

Attempting slow shallow breaths, my pulse amplified in my temples. Oh… my…

A verification letter from the secretary of defence. She unzipped her biker jacket exposing the chest holster with two P224 Sig Sauers pistols poking out. Just to advertise that they're, there. Her badge was on a chain around her neck, showing off her recent promotion to sergeant.

Am I dreaming?

Wake me, please!

She puts her feet back up and is really relishing this. I can tell by the creases forming in her cheeks, she's never pleasant. Her eyes are glowing and I prayed a small prayer closing my eyes and clasping my hands together.

God, please! Wake me if this is a dream!

I heard movements in the room.

Is she gone?

I peeked. Aaliyah Faith Paul just walked in.

"Oh, Lord!"

Her deep distinct voice snapped as she entered the room throwing her hands in the air. I shut my eyes again, frightened to open them as *that* sounds genuine. She slapped her long firm thighs, forcing my eyes open by the sudden sound but still continued in.

Samanther tilted to the side sliding her chair. Her feet fell to the floor rather unladylike tumbling, as she steadies her chair. Samanther's eyes widened, and jaw loosen following Aaliyah with her eyes as she stalks in.

Please say you've got the wrong room.

Please say you've got the wrong room…

A woman of her stature can find herself in a place like this, from time to time…

… Yeah, that could be it.

I am convincing myself following her graceful and confident stalk towards the chair to my right. Intentionally opposite Sam, I think. Her forearms were adequately moist with a well-nourished glow propped on the table. Polished glossy gel nail polish.

The shade matches her playsuit exactly. Always in her favourite colour of course, black. Which grabs her firm protruding ass. It smooths around her curvaceous hips, making her walnut skin tone bright and gleaming.

With an intense icy-blue evil daze, pouty full lips and straight nose, everything was so meticulously smooth and in place, for her age. Including her natural darkest brown hair. It is naturally curly like mine, but she keeps it open and straight. Accents of expensive, chunky gold and dangly jewellery. I just might be a tad jealous.

Of *her!* Maybe…

Settling in her seat, she tugs the smooth white bodice of her exclusively designed black and white playsuit, from under a sophisticatedly smooth genuine leather jacket. It has the fresh-from-the-store smell of newness mixed with a sweeter-than-sweet perfume filling the room.

I can tell an actual cow died to give her that to wear!

I wonder why she bothers to work.

Forcing my mouth from a frown, hoping the terror in my eyes doesn't give me away. Whilst trying to take some tension away from the gleam in their eyes as they began a staring competition.

I try to articulate my position and rationalise the situation without sarcasm or insult. Just then, my cell phone rang a welcoming sound to break the tenseness.

I hope this is Eric!

Scrambling for it from out of my jacket pocket, I popped up and moved towards the door facing out with optimism. That maybe *I* got the wrong room, or, this is the exit to this nightmare that is, Samanther Gabriel Martinez and Aaliyah Faith Paul in one room. Politely I answered, "Hello, Davis."

I really pray it is the president calling to tell me this is a joke, a cruel one, but still, a joke. Instead, a woman babbled.

"Hi, I'm Paula Torrez from Daver Police Force."

"Hi… um… yes," I squeaked then cleared my throat.

"I'm supposed to be at a briefing with you for nine today. I had been assigned to a case with S.D.A.F. as the forensic analyst. I know I'm late but I'll be there in five minutes. I am just caught in traffic."

She didn't even breathe!

The call ended just as abruptly as it started.

I don't want to turn around, please…

I cry inwardly and cannot move. Fringed at the door with my phone frozen to my face which is ghostlike now. The sweat from my palms creases down the phone onto my face.

Ten, nine, eight, seven, six, five…

"Why oh, why."

Did I say that out loud?

The muscles in my neck tenses a migraine coming. I wobbled around and managed to motion my legs one after the other jell-O-like. I shivered back into the room and slumped into the chair in horror and disbelief.

Barely able to loosen the grip, sweat from my phone into my bag. Samanther and Aaliyah sat opposite each other quiet, measuring, scrutinising anticipating with their eyes in a fixed gaze. Strong squinted saying so many things without a word.

Thank God, they're not talking.

The door knocked breaking my trance for a moment. A delivery man came, bearing a large twenty by twenty box, strolling in, not affecting their stare.

"Agent Davis-Hall," he asked.

Agent… Me? I like the sound of that!

He rescued me from the convergent boundaries, Sam and Lia, reminding me of my achievement. I waved him to come in. He rests the box on the table and gave me his electronic device to sign. My heart raced as I stroked the stylus. He took it and left.

This is not what was expected when I woke up this morning!

… Not even in the slightest!

Did I wake up this morning?

Am I really here?

I pinched the inside of my arm under my jacket sleeve.

Ouch, shit!

Oh, it can't possibly get worse than it already is.

At that moment I missed Eric's wise counsel even more. He always manages to calm things as if it would always work out. Not too sure that he could calm this brewing eruption though.

Funny, this tension is partially his fault.

My thoughts sobered.

I chuckle inwardly though it is not funny… he has a footing over us women.

Shana, you wanted this, you can do this.

I reminded myself and inhaled.

One, two, three…

… And exhale with a new approach.

Right then and there I drew a line, between personal and professional.

My shoulders went back and my chest pressed forward rising off my chair. Taking my house keys from my jacket pocket. I pierced the cello tape seal, pulling the keys toward me creating a zipping sound to reveal the content. Chucking my keys into my handbag.

Folding the flaps at each side, I exposed a simple typed letter flush over the contents with the S.D.A.F. letterhead. The shield was shaped of a bear head with the letters and the word at the bottom of each letter. Behind the letters a bear, his mouth opened and a red star shone contrasting the gold shield.

The minister of national security confirmed the members of the team with an overview and instructions for this case. I skimmed the letter following the main instructions there are several folders in here.

Hum… this is really happening.

Taking out the folders and placing them with care on the table next to the box. I counted four. There were also three temporary security clearance authorising letters and badges with each ladies names.

This confirms it.

I sighed, and dangled the badges from their metal-dotted chains placing them carefully on the table. Each lady's, on their corresponding folders based on their specification. There was one permanent pass with a level-one security clearance with a larger folder letter and details with my name on it. I put the folder close to me.

A brief grin reaches my face, I feel their stare. Prudently, I unbuttoned my jacket, took the chain off and placed the badge on the folder meant for me. Pulled the hook with my index finger and thumb, sliding it onto the left side of the waistband of my skirt, making it official.

The pleased expression grew as I placed my hand on the highest curve of my hip exposing the gold and red badge. A stray thought of the argument with Eric yesterday.

What did he mean by corruption and chasing my tail?

I snickered pausing at the moment. Then, Paula Torrez clambered into the room. The silence shattered and the eruption began as she curses.

"Fuck!"

Her voice was high pitched, her mouth opened wide. Their faces whipped towards her in unanimity, and facial expressions changed. The sense of accomplishment faded with one foul word. The smile became a nervous one. Forcefully waving her to join the madness.

… Be cool, be cool.

Their faces were more stunned as I almost forgot she was joining the party. Her never tidy, cheap pantsuit, grey pin-stripe with matching jacket, and a man's cotton vest underneath. Black, unpolished wedge shoes, green eyes with bags beneath them.

… Has she slept?

Her light complexion only highlights the dark circles as it contrasts with her natural dark-chocolate wavy hair. Bundled with a clip, which looks like it belongs in a museum. Untidy tendrils, dripping on every side.

What was she thinking?

Oh, I hope that's water and not sweat.

She dragged her feet in and fell into the chair at the end of the table opposite me. Her back to the door. At least she's the smartest sitting closely to the exit.

Who was the genius behind the assembly of the most disobedient, disrespectful, destructive, and distracting women in all the armed forces of the entire country?

… That was just the understatement of the century!

I screamed inwardly. This lot who's tolerated because they produce results but by what means?

Oh… and we hate each other.

CHAPTER THREE

Hum, so much history between us.

Let's start with Paula, she's the least complicated.

Paula Gabriella Torrez and Aaliyah Faith Paul are sisters, well half-sisters anyway, they share a famous father, whose made his money as an actor. Then, some sort of investment. He was also the governor of Ceda at one time.

Paula is the product of an affair, on their father's part. Paula's mother, Caroline was an extreme aficionado of their father. Henry Paul was a famous actor. As the rumours go, she was his 'out of town' girlfriend. Their father had always taken care of her... discreetly.

Her existence only became public when their farther ran for governor. Paperwork came to light as a political blow. Exposing his gifting to Paula's mother, the bar she worked at. Paula's mother was an addict, then later died from an overdose.

The bar later became a hob for illicit drugs. Paula had children for the man who took care of her after her mother died. He exposed her to drugs and she carried on with the life she grew up with.

She was always very clever though, but a plague of her own happiness. Stories are, Paula was the best 'chemist', which was her alleged alias. All of course are rumours, nothing solid has ever tied back to her.

Aaliyah was a victim of a scandalous kidnapping when she was a baby. She was an adult when she ran into her identical twin, literally.

Yes... unfortunately there are two of them with that perfect ass. I cringed at myself for thinking.

Their father confessed to the affair around the same time Lia reunited with her birth family. Paula's existence was overshadowed. The potential governor's illegitimate offspring and confession of infidelity, were moot after Aaliyah's reunion, pushing him to win elections.

A lifetime of having a substandard relationship with their father, to now being publicly acknowledged and meeting her older twin sisters weren't any different.

Knowing especially, as her father's emphasis shifted completely to making up for the lost time with his kidnapped adult child, didn't help either. Paula grew angrier and Zeliah, Aaliyah's identical twin became jealous.

After an alleged unsuccessful attempt on Lia's life, she accused her sisters. It caused an obvious rift in their less-than-awkward non-existent relationship.

To be fair, Paula was probably high and wouldn't remember if it was true.

To add insult to injury, Aaliyah's identical twin slept with Aaliyah's husband and she blamed the two sisters for her failed marriage and all other unfortunate events which followed.

Their father died and Lia inherited seventy-five percent of her father's wealth. Paula shared the remaining twenty-five percent with Zeliah.

That's rough!

Paula kept the sleazy bar running with the remainder of her inheritance, and became qualified in her field. Paula tried to apologise to Aaliyah.

… That bitch can sure keep a grudge.

Well, they don't even acknowledge they are related.

Professionally, I met Paula near the end of my D.P.F. training. She was a mentor, the only friend I had there. I was sidelined into a ride-along that led to the separation of her long-term relationship, and abusive boyfriend. He got arrested and she faced disciplinary charges. The bar was tossed and damaged during the arrest.

The bar has been known to be the drug hob. Sam, a member of the drug enforcement unit, as a regular, enjoys a violent raid on Paula's place causing unbelievable and non-refundable damage, though she has stopped dealing drugs.

Sam can be quite a dick!

Not too sure if Paula has stopped dealing though…

Sam, of course, doesn't care and the Paul women, hold grievances really well. I guess that's why the sisters are still enemies.

Aaliyah Faith Paul has known Eric for almost twenty years. There are so many rumours about the golden duo undercover team. Together they are a legend of the Daver Police Force, with a high number of convictions, three serial criminals including her stalker and taking down a drug cartel from the inside at the top of their career as a unit.

They were best friends, very close, until Eric met me and became a lieutenant. They had to be... they were the star undercover couple. Sometimes when things are repeated enough, they become habits. Gossip spread like wildfire after Eric and I got married.

Some of which I believe she started!

Eric never confirmed or denied any truth to the whispers between them. It almost ended us right as we began. But he assured me that I am the one he wants. I had no compulsion to doubt his commitment to me.

The distance, tension and energy between them when they talk; how often and long, she grabs his biceps laughing loudly and intentionally when I'm around.

Ugh! Sometimes too long and too often

... Her behaviour disgusts me.

I know Lia had a miscarriage sometime after Eric enrolled me in boarding school. She was in a horrible car accident. I was with Emily when she saw the news. Aaliyah's ex-husband used that as his escape, to file for divorce.

Yeah, Aaliyah is kind of famous, because of her father.

... And her miracle story.

Lia claimed that her baby was a result of the attempted reconciliation with her husband. The media reported a secret wedding between Eric and Lia, after a drunken one-night stand. I am compelled to believe the one-night stand over the marriage.

Another famous Hall and Paul tale.

Their relationship is uncomfortable and sometimes painful for me to witness. I asked him once to be honest with their relationship, then, I had nothing to lose. After his evasive reply, I never pressed him. I choose to trust him. He says they're just friends. He's my husband and I know he doesn't want to lose me.

Straight after that pregnancy thing, Eric and I gave into our desires. We became more than friends and were married not too long after.

Samanther Gabriel Martinez is Eric's first wife and the mother of his daughter, Danielle. Though wife and mother are a loose term in their situation. The wife and ex-wife have their reasons on their own other than Eric to hate each other.

Being Sam's first daughter's best friend and the legal mother of her younger child doesn't help. Not that Eric makes it any easier for her as well.

Before I was in the picture there was the famous Paul and Hall duo. A legend pair: with the highest closing record in the D.P.F. under their belt his working partner and their uncomfortable status of 'best friend' since they were in D.P.F. training. In short, they have a long history.

Aaliyah was really ticked off, when Sam, being a nurse and nursing her back to health after a big case. And, Aaliyah's first girlfriend started dating her partner and then, eventually married him.

… Although Lia was also married at the time!

I shook my head inwardly at the nerve.

Obviously, I wasn't in the picture at that time.

… But it still makes me *mad.*

Sam was really thorough with her cover. A stray thought filtered.

Needless to say, Lia and Sam's friendship went sour soon after. Not to mention Lia's marriage had run its course and was at an end.

Her endless meddling in Eric and Sam's relationship, made things difficult for everyone involved. The pinnacle of her true zodiac sign, 'Leo' (bold), and Samanther's 'Scorpio' (intense). Eric and Sam's marriage weren't in the best place either.

Before it went into a full-on blow session; take down and countdown between them, Sam was out of the picture. Loads of rumours surfaced that Lia may have been behind Sam's death.

I don't know if there's any truth to this.

When Sam resurrected, she had no friends, especially Aaliyah who isn't known best for forgiving. Eric's grief for his family changed him into something on the opposite side of the spectrum. Or so I was told. Which caused a greater riff between Sam and Lia, leaning towards Aaliyah.

Lia, one… Sam, zero!

After our encounter in the alley, Eric possibly felt obligated to help me. One, because I have no one else, and two, because I don't know anyone else. The day we met was the first memory I have.

I have amnesia, from the trauma, or so I was told.

He offered me a place and got me off the streets. Arrangements were made for me to attend boarding school. It was better for us both than the awkward encounters of being under the same roof.

He's got quite some numbers on my age. I didn't want to be taken care of neither did I want a repeat of the alley with him.

With a part-time job in a store, I helped pay my way as he subsidised my boarding school. I finished school, graduating earlier than my peers and moved back temporarily after graduation. Our relationship shifted after my nineteenth birthday. A year after finishing university, we were married and… Sam showed up with Danielle.

Awkward!

Every time we met.

Painful.

I still carry some scars.

Two years of turmoil.

My subconscious describes it best. After all, she was at rock bottom, broken and alone.

We were all broken…

hurt…

Sam submerged as the head of the drugs department of Ceda Offices Police Service, C.O.P.S. the capital's unique police force, after the reform restructured the intelligence office.

… Amazing how the system works for some.

We all had our own reasons to be nasty in the past and present. Being thrown into a team most certainly is no help.

CHAPTER FOUR

Paula sat relatively quiet for a chatty woman.

I observed while continued to empty the contents of the box, escaping the staring competition and distracting myself from their presence. There, a folder with a picture of a beautiful hazel-eyed woman was.

… Funny, she looks a bit like me.

Twangy skin tone, naturally curly hair a soft demeanour. Underneath several gruesome pictures of her gagged, feet and hands bound with duct tape, covered in dry blood naked in the trunk of a car in a pool of blood.

A closer picture of her rope burns hands and feet with threads of rope oozing from the indentations. Her back was discoloured and bruised a huge gash on her head swollen and pictures of a foetus in the trunk in a pool of blood.

I can't look any more.

What kind of beast would do this to a person?

My stomach knotted, my breakfast at the back of my throat. I squeezed my eyes for a moment.

Dear, I continue to look.

There was a brown envelope with two keys and instructions for the office in Divinish. At the very bottom was a white letter envelope with my name handwritten in blue pen. For a moment I was there with this woman. Breathing the tinge… I rubbed my wrist seeing a dark place with red all over, confused and petrified.

The sound of crinkling paper avulsing me from my engrossed thoughts. I looked at the women in the room and the tension was like tectonic plates. Trying not to accomplish eye contact, I leaned across to my handbag and placed the letter inside. I managed to stand pushing the chair back on its wheels with my thighs and placing my hands on the table for support.

Walking intensely apathetically around the table of inarticulate distributing folders, notepads and reports. Lightly placing in reach but avoiding physical contact, keeping the master copy making sure they receive only at their clearance status.

The best way is professional.

Clearing my throat, I reached to my chair standing with the back of my knees up against the chair leaning forward for the support of the table. My heartbeat intensified at my temples and my head is really starting to pound. The words softly came out:

"Thank you all for, accepting the invitation to join this task force, and working on this case with me. As you all know I am Special Agent Shannan Davis-Hall of S.D.A.F. assigned to assist you as an analyst and field manager.

"My job is not to tell you how to do your jobs. I know you all have enough experience to work on your own… but to see that we get the best results for all stakeholders… occasionally I may intervene… to oversee the processing is done as per regulations… and that procedures are being followed… correctly.

"Part of my job is also to make sure that all alternatives are explored… before … decisions are made… and assist in any area as best as I can.

"You are all supposed to be experts in your field… the best at what you do… so…"

"What's your point, Davis?"

Aaliyah rudely interrupted and anger overthrows me.

Did that bitch cut my speech?

I was almost at the end.

Breathe, breathe.

Suffocating a squint in an attempt to avoid showing the words with my hands.

"My point Ms Paul is… we are all professionals and we've got a job to do, and we should do it regardless of how we feel about each other," I snapped.

"What is that supposed to mean?" Aaliyah stupidly asked.

"Take it however you'd like Paul."

Oh, I hate stupid questions!

I began gathering and stuffing the folders, reports and everything that came out of the box rapidly, into my briefcase. Placing the box on the table and sorting through my purse for my plane tickets relishing no eye contact with that lot.

"I don't have anything against you Davis."

Paula staked her claim clearly. Her face was passive giving me a pleasant smile. I paused, raising my head slightly, tucking the cascade of hair behind my ears. Lia and Sam swivelled their chair towards her facing the entrance of the room.

I hope they are not going to say anything.

Their eyes fixed on her intensely bringing the tectonic plates tighter now forming a curve, even I wanted to hide from their gaze. Part of me wanted to smack Lia and the other was touched by her sister.

"Well... don't you?" I stuttered. "I was a key to the arrest of you and your boyfriend," I said forgetting the filter.

"So... you helped me end a twenty-year relationship of drugs, alcohol and abuse. You single handily changed my life and helped me become a better person."

Paula, still with a pleasant demeanour.

"Aw... that's sweet," Lia mocked.

"Shut up Lia!" Paula shouted aggressively as the tectonic plates got even tighter.

"She squealed on my ass too but nothing good came out of that," Sam added firstly pointing at me, then moving her head in a circle sitting up and closing in on Paula's face.

"Thanks to *me* you were reinstated as an officer."

I began pointing at Sam, "... *And* put into the drug department."

I continued by painting the words as they came out, "... on *my* word *you* got promoted and could *now* come into here smiling and flashing your shiny new promotion... then to mouth off at me," I said indignantly.

Shit! My filter!

She swivelled in my direction. Her face had an obvious twitch as she placed both her hands on the table, using it as a support to grow to her five-foot-seven inches. She began correcting my statements to her view.

"First of all, *you* didn't get me reinstated... I was never fired! Secondly, I worked hard and busted my ass to get where I am. My success has nothing to do with *you*."

She was not as loud as I thought she would have been.

"I gave a word for your promotion," I pointed out.

Again, filter!

"Who asked you?"

She's getting louder as I feel the earthquake as the tectonic plates begin to buckle.

"... I don't need your charity."

She waved her hands and her guns played peek-a-boo.

"Charity... look forget it, Sam." I was defeated.

Damn – filter!

My stomach cringed, and I am a little light-headed I tried to stabilize and she continued, "Even if *you* did anything for me, Shana, I didn't ask you. You did it because of your guilty conscience. So... *don't you dare*, stand on a high horse patting yourself on the back for *my* achievements."

Sam was up without support with her index finger towards me scolding me in a very tense tone. The saliva filled my mouth with a bad taste as I swallowed. Sweat glistened on my forehead with a funny feeling at the back of my throat.

I'm going to be sick.

"Excuse me."

I can't hold it in. With a deep inhale I rushed out the door holding my mouth. Sweat gathered on my forehead as my head began to spin. I fled to the lady's room, down the hall and around the corner.

Pouring in quickly shuffling my feet into a stall. Slamming the door behind and lifting the new toilet seat. Falling to my knees, doubling over the bowl. I threw up the coffee I drank this morning and, some of what looks like last night's dinner.

I hope it's not a bug!

Although a headache grows, I felt slightly better taking deep breaths over the toilet.

The horrid smell and aftertaste!

I flushed and went to the sink, rinsing my mouth several times. Sam probably felt that I was running away from the conversation but I wasn't.

I had no need to.

I poured water over my face cooling my head with a quick glance in the mirror before I returned to the conference room.

The door was closed but their muffled voices were heard from outside the door.

The lava is spilt.

Oh, for crying out loud…

I was appalled at the ladies' lack of respect and restraint.

… Then again.

The language was restricted to at least four, four-letter words they used as verbs, some creative adjectives and lots of the four ws: who did what, when, and why, they even threw in some hows.

They can use this passion in a number of positive ways if they try.

I entered the room, their voices blasted at me. They didn't notice my arrival, even when I closed the door behind me. Amazed and partially admiring their passion and the effort to insult each other. They were in each other's faces pointing and shouting over each other. Each one trying to get their point across.

They didn't even notice me.

I gait by.

Irritated by their bad behaviour, but too nauseated to say anything. I took the box to recycle and they still haven't noticed my movement. Even after I returned twice, retained my things and even located my plane tickets.

This is my dream job. I was not about to let their grievances make it a nightmare. Nor stand in the way. Especially after risking my relationship. I will be doing my job regardless of them.

I sigh, ready to leave them behind but paused with a thought. Inhaling deeply, I screamed at the top of my lungs, "*Hey*…" High-pitched and harsh. My voice silenced them as they all looked in my direction. "… Whenever you're all ready to forget all this bullshit and start doing your job, I'll be on a plane doing mine."

I jaunt out of the room with a sense of accomplishment, as a load lifted from my chest. I needed that more than I realised. I called a taxi to take me to the airport.

They got to the airport before I did. They were all quiet going through the gates and on the plane. Even whilst sitting relatively close to one another. It appears my words took effect, and it was over in Ceda.

Obviously, I was wrong.

After the two and a half hour flight, one would think they would be tired.

I whined inwardly. Their voices ricochet through terminals while they were arguing. About everything, but about nothing in particular. Jabbering added to my jetlag and gave me a bigger headache.

The heat builds as we trotted for the exit. At the exit an overhead monitor displays a picture of the woman in my folder, subtly prompting me of my purpose.

I need to 'lose them' somewhere in the luggage collection.

CHAPTER FIVE

The past six months flooded back to me as I stared into space searching for the sign I missed somewhere at the beginning. Words fail me, but I need to get through my opening statement before I deal with the welting in my throat or the oncoming tears.

"Mrs Davis-Hall."

It was strange, Sharron's face, there was no expression as her gaze fixed to the judge's bench, it seemed like her mind was stuck someplace else. I had dejection for her, now and even when I first saw her pictures after she was first attacked.

Six months earlier.

We landed in the same pugnacious tone we left clinging to disapprovals of the past.

I am not sure how much more of this I can take!

Silence was my solution but by me not saying anything may not be helpful either. Trotting ahead of the three, regretting my choice of footwear, I keep my head down at some distance. I see an opening through the bustling airport and chased a waiting taxi.

Rats!

They caught me running towards the van. The hired driver waved a placard of our names drawing the irascible women to me. Highly annoyed, I rolled my eyes rankling, outwardly frowning at their loud mouths and embarrassing behaviour.

Speedily taking my bags to the trunk and pouting, crossed arms in the front passenger seat. Paula tucked her bags in the back. Lia stood; her arms crossed next to her suitcase with her handbag on her forearm.

Extending my palm over the side of my face, I waited. Paula was the first in the van. There was a thud at the back, and the car shook. Sam secured her things and then clambered next to Paula.

Surely for a raise which she got from Paula who argued from inside the car echoing in my head. Sam slid inside shifting Paula to the other side. They both groaned, displeased.

Ugh! How long would this take?

Lia poised on the pavement, wildly gazing. Rolling my eyes, and audibly letting out my breath, Sam shouted at her knocking the glass. Eventually, the driver packed her suitcase into the back of the van.

Entitled bitch!

Only then, she proceeded around the van behind me where he opened her door and she perched into the vehicle squeezing Paula in the middle. The federal powers that be sent a specialist team that truly loathed each other.

This was my first visit to the contrasting county of Divinish; it touched the very top and bottom of the island, to the top of the protected ancient cities built in rocks and caves. Natives of the island still live there practically untouched and uninterrupted by the advances, of the rest of the world.

At the bottom, is a lively city built by the sea. To the right, farmers and country life thrive and to the left suburban and town life thrive, each with their own charm on this island. Daver is a little more than two hundred thousand and twenty miles around. This county feels like it's the beginning and end of every sort of life.

I couldn't even appreciate this.

The taxi drove through the bustling city in midday traffic. The heat building, though the air condition is blasting. After forty minutes, the traffic eased and the buildings became further apart.

The quiet main street with shops looked rural, and some cobbled streets marked the entrances to malls. We passed the end of a lonely street to a large, fenced area with large containers lined up and, huge open-spaced buildings with big signs on them.

The entrance of an industrial estate.

I sigh, aware of the ladies' cantankerous behaviour. Luckily the first building with two levels was our stop. The maisonette, a local shop with news and the basic food needs at the bottom. The top is not really seen from the streets.

This has quieted them.

Ah…

I clamber out unable to finish the sentence in my head. The remaining warehouses and factories as the blazing sun scorched down with no shade from the building. Unloading the taxi silently, they hopped out one after the other measuring the building with their eyes. The driver pointed to the left side of the store, as I paid the fee.

I hope this is not where we're staying.

A rusted brown iron gate with no lock in front of a glass. A double-glazed tinted door and a deadlock. I sense their eyes on me and hear the smacking of lips. The intense sucking sound of Lia's teeth was a deep tone from Sam's husky voice with a word beginning to form.

Oh shit!

Scampering in my handbag for the instructions. I recovered keys and a brown envelope with the name and directions to our apartments.

Phew!

Relieved by the find but anxious about the two keys.

Please work! Please work!

Pulling the iron gate aside, I placed the key in the deadlock, and it unlocked.

Yes! First try!

A victory danced inside as I pulled the door open, turning to them. The discourteous women tumbled passed me going up the dark stairway. Their bags dragged by the wheels thump up the stairs.

"Please go in!"

My sarcastic remarks were spoken to their backs. None of them reacted. With a frown again, I grasped my two suitcases one by one to the top of the stairs and the box with the file case on another step. My hand grazed against the wall. There was a light one the right at the landing switch at the entrance.

Shaking my head at their impoliteness, I touched the switch. The halogen lights flickered as they illuminated the path. With a scramble, I pull the door in and lock it behind me. I left the bags below and followed them up the grey work-tiled stairs with the box.

To the top right of the stairway, there was a larger landing and a door with a keypad and reception button. Lia pressed it and paused. Quick on the tongue, "We're all out here!"

Sam obviously pointed that out.

Oh, please don't argue.

I silently prayed.

I still have that slight headache and jetlag.

Cited, I hoped to get a clue as to how to open the door. Reaching for the envelope again, thankfully there was a note on the display in digital blue glowing; S.D.A.F. badge number. I blocked the keypad and punched it in.

Then the keypad displayed 'change code'. I paused. What should I put that they won't argue about? I punched in 4786.

"Is that your *pin?*" Sam teased. Before I can reply,

"Why would she do that Sam?"

Paula tried to help. I cringe. Sam and Lia, both gave her evil eyes.

"It's our last initials!"

Agitated, I resisted adding 'idiot' to avoid further confrontation. It would be ideal if when those doors open, they will leave their shitty attitude at the door and concentrate on the task ahead.

This rape drew a lot of media attention. Stealth should be necessary, but hard to achieve with four disruptive women. I verified the code. The door opened to a small reception area, grey floors, a desk and a small hall behind the desk.

It was musty and smelt of oil paint. The furnishings looked fairly new or refurbished like everything else. There was a door at the end of the reception table. Lia headed right for it and we followed.

She paused, squinting at the lock, squeezing her full lips together. We piled in range of age: Lia, Paula, Sam then me. A grin grew as I understood her pause. The fourth door needed an S.D.A.F. badge number for entrance.

"After you." I snickered.

She snared, pivoted towards the desks, flicking her thick, black hair near my face. I stepped back only just avoiding it as she dashed for the closest desk. I frowned with a deep breath.

Rustling in the background; Paula and Sam whooshed passed me. Two grown women fighting for desks. I circled my eyes and punched in the number. To my surprise, behind the door, we uncover a lab.

"I guess this is for you, Paula."

She stuck her tongue out behind my back and followed me. I changed the pass code to our first initials, 7277.

"It's beautiful!"

Paula claimed a desk by putting her bags inside on a chair close to the entrance. I wondered if we were looking at the same thing. It looked chaotic to me. I left her in her element.

One less to start a pointless argument.

Satisfied with separating them.

And reducing a chance of a headache.

Continuing my tour, to the left, there was a hall with two toilet stalls and a small walkway to a tiny kitchen. Completed with a breakfast table, a mini fridge and two chairs.

Straight from the reception, a door leads to two interview rooms complete with intercoms and cameras.

An open-plan office with four desks and chairs, two on either side. One small conference glass room to host up to six persons. Opposite that, next to the open desks, an office just big enough for a table, an office chair and two other chairs.

I finally lay the box to rest, making two more trips for my bags there. There wasn't much said. So, my best guess is they approve or are still in shock. Whichever was the case, I am glad they finally shut up.

This back office appears to have never been used, or a reappropriated asset. File cabinets, copiers, printers, stationery, everything we need to start work. It was already past two. We paused for lunch, later unpacked, set up the office for us and collected the keys to the assigned rented apartment complex.

A twenty-minute drive from our office and twenty minutes from the city or so the brochure says. Most of our day was wasted travelling, setting up and quarrelling. The evidence was three days old and the victim was at the hospital recovering.

With nothing more to do, exhausted from the heat and the echoes of their voices, I was ready to leave. The wall clock read six and the ladies of course went back to their apartments. The excitement of this job drained from the arguments.

At least I can have a fresh start tomorrow. Sorting the files according to skill set, noting assignments and packing the folders together for another hour. Finished resting them on a side table along a wall in my office. Slouching behind the desk, my eyes burned.

I should go…

My head lowered to the desk with a sigh, and my phone buzzed. I popped up and glanced at it. My eyes dilated seeing several messages from Eric throughout the day and two missed calls:

Hey, have you landed… Call me when you can…

Did you reach safely?

Have you settled? Call me if you can.

Shit!

I cursed inwardly screwing my eyes tightly that second debating.

Do I really want to deal with him after today?

My tiredness increased but instantly I missed him. I held the phone looking at his name.

I really do…

Our fight last night comes first to mind, after breaking the news of my new job.

I hope he's still not mad.

I don't think I could handle that right now.

Then travelling across the country.

I literally ran away!

The guilt fills me. Internalising with a debate, closing my hands to the phone pressing the call button on his number.

Shit!

The second ring he picks up. "Shana… are you OK?"

His voice is soft and calm.

Something I didn't expect, especially after three missed calls. Exasperated unexpectedly with a yawn.

"Hey, I got your messages." I am wavering.

"Just wanted to know if you landed…"

A second past. He cracked first.

"… How was your, um, flight?"

This is a change of pace, but I'll roll with it.

"All right, I guess… Did you know that Lia is here?"

I began my grievance.

"She told me," he answered without hesitation.

Of course, she did.

I rolled my eyes.

… Did she complain about me?

I frowned at the phone.

"… Is she giving you a hard time?"

He stated the obvious.

Really? I gasped at the phone with a tightened grip. *You know she is!*

But I don't want to talk about her…

"Are you still mad?"

I cut to the chase cringing for the answer. He exhaled.

"Not as much…" He grinds through his teeth. "… Just, missing you. Are you still angry?"

"Honestly Eric, I'm missing you." *I should explain.* "… But I have been so busy…"

"I know you are." He cuts me off, understanding, it seems.

Is he really, OK?

"… Talk to you later?" His way of apologising, and finally accepting my decision.

I grinned with a glimpse of hope. "Sure, love you."

"I love you too, baby."

I hung up before anything more begins, or him changing his mind. Holding the phone close to my chest. This is the best way to end this horrible day.

Eric and I have been married for just about two years. In Daver, marriages follow the Zemand tradition. Some are prearranged from birth. It's all about having the right linage and depends on the family's view of tradition or the adoptive measure of progress.

The marriage ceremony consists of two parts, Shabráda and Cáhilt. Shabráda happens as an intent to combine lives with the meaning in Zemand. Similar to an engagement, but legally binding for two years, after which a Cáhilt happens, a marriage.

The couple does what is known as putting up the bands. It is worn on the upper arms men on the left and women on the right. They also keep rings on their left hands. The father of the bride traditionally gives the wife to the husband and transfers all power from a rise ceremony this happens at a Cáhilt.

A Chbáhlit is a covenant of a lifetime partner, meaning in Zeman, happens only if the couple is sure or prearranged from birth as divorces are infrequent, and a difficult process that takes years. Many ceremonies and trials stand before this happens, which are complicated.

The settlers skip the Shabráda and Cáhilt to be married. This has been a growing trend among the Zemand, who do not want to fall under the Chbáhlit, which can only be broken by a deathly ceremony agreement.

If there isn't a prearranged wedding, dating traditionally lasts for up to six months. Once then, the couple either Shabráda or move on. Settlers usually date and would have both ceremonies at once wearing a ring instead of the traditional upper arm band that Zemand would wear. Dating usually happens three times for a Zemand before marriage, but tradition have been fading.

If after two years, a Shabráda couple doesn't complete the ceremony, it is dissolved. They forfeit their marriage and will be considered under the law of infidelity.

Eric and I got married three months after I passed my bar exam. But it has been one thing after another since I put on this ring. We've always managed to make it through to the other side.

****

I struggled to get both suitcases up the stairs at the same time. Considering our marriage, I managed to throw everything into my one-room apartment. I blew in exhaustion.

It's all spread across the floor space or sitting on the double sofa. I had hoped Ms Fancy would spend her own riches but she painfully accepted the open plan flat, denting my budget.

Thankfully our apartments are not linked by walls. We could, however, shout across the courtyard, standing outside the long-railed hallway overlooking the courtyard.

Those women are the most capable. I aggravate myself for even thinking.

It's a really beautiful and quiet view. Quite the opposite of Ceda's city life. Inside, an open plan room with no walls separating anything besides the toilet and bath. Just a double bed with two wooden side tables and lamps.

A double sofa, small kitchen two cupboards basic laminate worktop and breakfast bar. A stove, under-counter fridge-freezer, and two stools at the breakfast bar. An overhead wardrobe enclosing the bed, next to the toilet door with a full mirror.

Conjoining the toilet and bath with white tiles. A small TV is perched on a basic wooden stand, next to the balcony entrance along the entrance by a window.

This resembles my short-lived apartment during university and my room at boarding school. The only difference was the kitchen and the porch with sliding doors to the back. Besides the side table, two outdoor plastic chairs and a glass coffee table were present. The balcony overlooked the parking area. Behind that, was the highway and rocky hills, beyond the busy road leading to the entrance of the canyons, with an amazing view of the sunset.

The autumn sunset which would be crisp in Ceda, is warm here. I took a few moments to appreciate this as I couldn't earlier with the yelling. I was just happy to be away from those dreadful women.

What would be the best approach to this job?

The understandable tension between the four of us exchanging profanities and hating each other. I so badly want the opportunity to start my dream job, not stay in this nightmare that I thought I'd escaped in Ceda. At that moment, I stare harder at the fading pink skies, wished for that, the dream job without the nightmare as the sunset and the skies darken.

CHAPTER SIX

A natural early riser filled with the hopes from last night and needing to gain some footing. The bags blocking the limited footpath, I unzipped hanging my ten conservative skirts and dress suits into the wardrobe. Wrapped in a towel after my shower, I began tidying.

Folded my underwear and bras into the top of the three draws inside the wardrobe. I emptied the first bag. T-shirts, shorts and casual trousers in the next draw. Work shoes, sneakers, flip flops and sandals on the shoe rack and store the bag inside the other. I was ready.

Not quite to satisfaction but practical.

Taking out a grey skirt suit, with a light shirt was a smart choice. Slipping on the jacket. Not so much, we arrived in the middle of a September heat wave. It was not even eight in the morning, but the sweat was building.

It's too hot for a shirt…

The thought tortures me. I swap the shirt for a cotton vest below my polyester grey jacket. Flat-ironed my hair adding some foundation and lip gloss glancing into the full-length mirror next to the bed.

I hope this looks professional.

I should have done more research before I entered the hottest county of the country with full cotton suits. Wrestled myself pulling my hair back from my shoulders into a bun.

Reaching the office at nine, it was empty as anticipated. On one hand, I am grateful for the peace, especially after yesterday.

My headache isn't quite gone.

At the same time, I'm irritated that they would purposefully disregard the reasoning for their paid presents in Divinish.

Then again… Ugh! I grunt at my disappointed expectation.

Why was I chosen for this job?

Wondering about my credentials and comparing them to these three professionally endowed, mature women. It seems senseless that I would be the lead of this group.

Or maybe it's because no one wants them around.

I began to unravel. From my limited knowledge, these women have made a reputation for being disrespectful, disobedient and unprofessional.

There was a sudden ringing that sounded like an intercom, it startled me. I looked around. The buzz happened again.

Did they forget the passcode already?

Aggravated I stomp to the reception. A delivery man stood outside with several boxes balancing on a wheeled trolley.

"Delivery of laptops," he shouted like a question through the intercom waving his ID.

He can't see me, right?

I was not expecting anyone and I am questioning if I should have. I let him in and he went about his business setting up the equipment.

The ladies' ones were left on their desks. I quickly occupied my time setting up my email and other intranet connections. Passwords and replying to several waiting emails marked as urgent. I opened the first one:

'Congratulations Mrs Davis-Hall on your assignment. As a field manager, there are several learning tasks to be completed by the end of this week.

Attached is a copy of the immediate regulations and rules to be studied. Each one requires a pass mark of 80%.

Weapons training commences weekly for all staff. Further details will follow. Details of other requirements and policies will follow.

Your reporting will be daily and sent to the director. They will make contact following the chain of command. Emails will follow with further instructions or requirements.

Kind regards,

Amy Welch

Senior Personal Associate

S.D.A.F. Director Assistant'.

Crap!

Attached were three documents and instructions on how to set-up my inbox and e-signature. My assignment, besides overseeing this process in this case and being the main authority in this area to the S.D.A.F. was to increase the federal presence, but also recruiting local officers. Feed the media updates. To keep my directors happy without allowing these women's egos to get the better of my anger. The instructions were a bit overwhelming.

Knowing these women.

Urgent policies and intranet set up were the first completed via telephone calls from my cell phone. I busy myself with getting up-to-date and putting together the daily report from our first meeting to the director.

Who by the way, hasn't given me his or her name for me to address the email to? Idly, I fantasised about being the one who wrote this letter and was surprisingly pleased it was not me.

This is frustrating! I viewed the report on a Word document complaining to myself.

If only I can add those, favourite four-letter words they throw around so often, all the points on my report would be filled!

Finally finished the report after an hour and a half, I emailed the director. I hadn't realised the complexity of this job. Astonished by the diplomacy I exuberated in the email.

Maybe it was my qualifications.

Doubting myself again, I finished what I can. Completing some background research, on the three confirming suspects. I arm myself. Afterwards compiled manila folders with the basic work start for the ladies.

I went into the conference room and laid out assignments including a 'to-do' list. They strolled in after eleven, one after the other. Aaliyah as per usual immaculately dressed.

I can tell maybe that's why she's late.

Sam, her usual jeans and T-shirt with her chest holster showing off her pistols casually, through her open leather jacket. Paula, still as if there wasn't an iron in her room. My eyes followed them through the glass wall of the conference room. I placed the final folder on the table, waiting.

Their curiosity will get the better of them and they will enter.

The thought not too long passed, and Sam's and my eyes met. I was making my way around the table returning to the top.

My chair. I turned my eyes towards her.

Then, they poured into the room; Sam, Lia followed then Paula last, in that order.

No 'hello', 'hi'?

Frustrated, I exhaled and sat. Without any greeting or excuses, not that they should have any. I eyed their movements.

Do I expect them to?

I leaned back into the chair slightly rocking my annoyance at their audacity. They moved around and as before; Sam was at the end of the table opposite me inspecting me. Aaliyah enters to my left, bathing the room with her perfume. She stands behind the chair in a pose; one hand on her hip, the other luminously hanging over the back of the webbed chair. Moisturised, I supposed with an expensive glimmer lotion highlighting her even copper tone. Paula opposite her sister, tugs on her wrinkled jacket before she daintily sits on the chair that's left.

"Ladies we've got a lot to do," Aaliyah opens her mouth. My eyes widened.

Really!

Always the entitled one.

I propped my face in my palm, one hand across my chest bracing my elbow, observing their attitudes. Narrowing my eyes at her notion, sensing the explosion of personalities.

"Really Lia," Sam interjected quickly, as usual, one eyebrow higher than the other. Then she, jolted the chair out from under the table. She's always ready for a confrontation. I spectate curiously.

I am surprised those two haven't fisted it out yet.

Maybe they have and I don't know about it.

I snicker inward visualising it for a second and pay no attention to their prelude argument. Sam shrugs putting her feet on the folder I prepared earlier. She crossed her legs at her ankles dirtying the new tabletop and leaning into the chair. My jaw drops and anger kindles.

Did she just...

Aaliyah picked up the folder, the sound forces me to turn. Only to view her open it, flicking the pages as if it was a fan, not looking. Barely acknowledging the work I've done compiling the correspondences.

I've seen that dick move before in training.

I shudder at the memory.

Does she do that on purpose?

After she has skimmed the materials, she slaps it on the table palming her manicured, white French tips over the manila folder.

"Yeah Lia, you're not in charge," Paula protests timidly,

Horrified I look on. Aaliyah's two-second intense grey stares and Paula turns away.

Wow! Still intimidated by her older sister.

I shook my head. And Aaliyah continues, "I will talk to the victim Sam..."

"Don't talk to me, Lia..."

Sam says as a matter-of-fact, rolling her eyes and head at Lia. She will not back down. I groan in memory of the pre-op meeting. The tectonic plates lift. The pointless pissing contest continues. Their volume increases and their vocabulary is limited to their preferable four, four letter words with their short temperament.

I don't know how much more of this I can take.

Deep breaths, eyes shut, meditating on counting down from twenty and twirled in my chair. The room quiets the sound has been sucked out of my concentration. My heartbeat is all I can hear as it increases its rhythm through my ears.

... Nineteen, eighteen...

Aaliyah's instructions seep through returning sound to my bubble. She points and syllabifies as if she's talking to a child.

"Again... I'll talk to the victim..." She points to herself.

I screwed my eyes trying to calm.

Fifteen...

"… Sam, you get information on the pendant…" She points at Sam, who pushes back her chair sliding her feet with the folder to the floor with a thud in protest.

I gasp! My folder!

"What did I just say?"

Sam points back with all her fingers fluttering her blue eyes and crinkling her face.

Count Shana! I remind myself.

Fourteen, thirteen, twelve…

Some noises fade again.

"… Paula you, do… what do you do anyway?" Aaliyah's voice seeps again teasing her sister who jumps to her feet, objecting.

I twitch.

"… Shana you…"

My name in her mouth…

All voices return. I erupt, "Who the fuck put you in charge, Paul?" I've shocked myself.

I'm standing.

My voice echoed over theirs.

The room is silenced and a hint of a smile grows on Sam's face. Their heads whip to me. I can't calm my breathing.

"I *am* the most experienced," she pointed out adding to my irritation. My eyes are burning at her arrogance.

"*And,*" I somewhat agree.

"Yeah right!" Sam disputes loudly and they began arguing again,

"*Shut up!*" I screeched loud and high-pitched shattering the noise again. "… Since you've accepted this assignment all you've done is argued about shit…" My voice strained to the loudest it's ever been, my face grim.

Paula sits.

"… Why are you here? For two days all you've done is whine, argue and fucking measure whose dick is the biggest. *The answer is none!*"

I screamed at the complaining women using all of their four favourite words.

Reel it back, Shana! "… You are supposed to be professionals. For once in your career fucking act like one!

"We've been here two days and the victim has been in the hospital for five. We're already behind and you know what happens to evidence in a rape case after several days. This is time-sensitive."

My voice is softer and less strained.

Sam sits.

"... The director's crawling up my ass and the media are up theirs. And you all should know that shit rolls downhill. All you've done is behave like cunts... fucking wasting time. There's a reason I alone had access to all the information and there's a reason we were chosen to take this case."

"A typo," Aaliyah swanked.

My gape intensifies to her. I resist the yearning to slap her.

Still think this is a joke?

"You think you can do this Paul? Why?" I am curious. I cross my arms.

"Not only that I am the more experienced." Raising both my hands at both Sam and Paula and narrowing my eyes at them, who shift in their chairs to let her finish her egotistical statement.

"... But I am the oldest," she replied cockily twisting her head, first to Sam, Paula, then to me.

"Damn right, *you are* the oldest," I added crossing my arm and twisting my head to her shifting my weight to the left and raising a brow. Sam and Paula chuckle quietly rocking back into their chairs.

"I'll pretend I didn't hear that." Aaliyah caught out and attempt to recover her pride.

"And that supposed to mean what?" I shrug narrowing my eyes at her. "... You think that your experience surpasses all?"

You are nothing without my husband!

Happy I didn't lose my filter with that sentence. It partly makes me uneasy that it is true.

"Well, I have..." Her third try to recover, I cut her.

That's enough!

"Nothing more than consultancy's badge." I finished her off. She stills in the realisation, I believe. I give her a few seconds to sponge it. Savouring and silencing her arrogance.

Satisfying...

"You have no idea what you're doing," she barks her last words like a defeated mongrel before submission. Yanking her chair from under the table, she drops to the seat and slouches in a pout.

Good girl.

The initial frown at the start of this impromptu meet has smoothed to a small grin as I bid my composure of a victory dance.

"That may be true Lia, but the complexity of my job is beyond the tact, age and experience of someone like you..."

I show more teeth than I intend. Paula and Sam spectate attentively.

"What!"

She shrieks and the wrinkles squinted with her eyes.

Too far.

I contemplate and rake in my triumph and finally sat. Taking the folder and opening it. I settle into my chair pulling it so I'm comfortable. Their eyes peered at me.

The task ahead.

"Anyone of you who has as much as my age in experience and yet none of you was offered my position.

"... Each of you has something in your past that can taint the reputation of what S.D.A.F. stands to build; some conviction, disciplinary action, assault, battering witnesses, questionable interrogation methods, the missing and slash or altered evidence. You do get the job done but at what cost?

"How many of your solo cases actually made it to trial Paul? Your conviction count is what, Sam?" I squint at her and she shifts in her chair. "... Any cases dismissed without prejudice, Torrez? Please correct me if I'm wrong, tell me different, anyone?"

Now that I have their attention.

"... This is a sensitive case it requires astute, amenity and poise. Everything is monitored, we are being scrutinized by the country. What we do here will build a reputation for all of us and a second chance for all of you. This here is bigger than either one of us. You may not like me but you are going to respect my rank."

That is the least you can do ladies.

Damn!

I exhaled.

"… So, here's what's going to happen; I'm not accepting any excuses. If it's not the case, then leave it at the door before you get into this office. You can pick it up when you leave or take it on your way back to Ceda."

I gave them an ultimatum. They are quiet. Paula is visually considering. Sam has an unfamiliar expression and is surprisingly unassuming.

"… If you don't respect each other, respect the skill and accept you cannot perform each other's duties. You *will* report everything to me, don't act on your impulses, if you have an idea let me know first and *I'll* decide."

Aaliyah is unsettled in her chair.

I wait for her.

She says nothing.

I resumed, "… Torrez, collect all the evidence and medical reports from the local police and hospital. Examine it as you're the first one to see it.

"Martinez, get a background check on the victim. Her family and friends including juvenile records. I can get them if they exist.

"Paul, research everything you can on the jewellery found around the victim's neck. All that you can on the religion of the Zemand, and all their ceremonies etcetera."

"And you'll…" Aaliyah questioned.

I should have put you down… I say to myself disappointed I didn't before, but ready to rise.

"Do what I have to." My eyes alight to her quizzing.

Why is she always such an asshole?

Should have ignored her… My reasoning kicked in listening to the wounded mutt.

"And if we don't." She chuckled solo and dry scanning the room for support.

The others disregard her.

"Goodbye then."

Enough!

"You have got to be kidding me. Who do you think you are? Oh, I'm so scared." Aaliyah scorned.

Forget her! I ignored my inner thoughts voicing, "This is not a holiday. You either get on or fuck off!" Speaking as plainly as they do.

I took the folder under my arm and slid the chair back then proceed to drive to the point. "It is now…"

I reached for my phone and pressed the home button. The displayed time. "Twelve thirty pm. I want my reports typed, emailed, finished, filed and waiting on my desk at two pm tomorrow.

Then, we will discuss further proceedings. As a matter-of-fact, we will meet every day at two pm. Time starts now…"

I flicked the tendrils of hair around my ear. Then regarded them as I amble to the door. Stepping on the mess of papers Sam made earlier. I squint at them, then at her, lifting my shoes off them.

She fidgeted. I tilted my head regarding her reaction slightly stunned. Their expression as though I had just lost my mind.

Maybe I did?

I shrug to myself.

I need to cement that, especially to Lia.

"I know you like challenges Aaliyah, dare to venture?"

I winked at her. My chest up striding to the exit. Aaliyah loves to taunt her authority figures. The fact that she has challenged me reinforces her view of me. I am both thrilled and cautious about my new position of power. A part of me looks forward to being the opponent she couldn't gain.

Do I really?

I think for a millisecond.

Absolutely!

I look forward to packing her ass out of here. Pivoting at the door with a wicked thought of Aaliyah being thrown out of my office, I smile. Wagging my finger. "… And ladies, no tardiness."

Too much… Maybe.

They sat in silence and I went into my office. Place the folder on the table, exhaled the adrenalin from the encounter and walked around to my chair. I see movements through the glass window and frosted conference glass wall. Sam bends retrieving the scattered paper. I am shocked.

… Maybe sinking it in…

I nod to myself peeping at their reaction.

They are either quiet or whispering.

Paula was the first to leave. I opened my laptop pretending to work. She peeked through my office window, slowing I think, to catch my gaze. Instead, I kept my face serious, typing my password. When I glanced, she was out of sight. I supposed she must have gone to the lab.

Then Sam stomped out of the room. The folder was scarcely secured under her arm. She went around to a table, slapped the folder on the desk, turned on the computer threw her weight on the chair, and then adjusted it.

Aaliyah was the last to go, stubborn as ever. She put the folder on a free desk, took her bag with her phone in hand stepping out of my sight.

She may have gone for a cigarette!

Internalising.

Or quit, one would hope.

One of the limited things Eric says about her is that Aaliyah can be a bit challenging.

His words, not mine!

Unfortunately for her I always rise to every occasion.

CHAPTER SEVEN

After I gave them the stipulation for working with me, I researched the three.

Paula once told me after meeting her older sister, she was inspired, like me, to become a police officer. She quickly realised a field officer was not her calling. A natural in the lab, she is good.

One of the best forensic analysts, but there are few internal investigations against her name. It all involves Ian and Suzanne's father, her drug-abusive boyfriend, or their associates. Some questionable chain of evidence and tampering allegations keeps her at the same rank, for the nearly ten-year career.

After *Sam* returned, she went into the drug department. Knocking down walls and destroying property is her thing.

Battering witnesses, they all share.

Sam has so many complaints about police brutality. She has to attend a monthly anger management therapy session as mandatory.

Maybe that's why they promoted her, to get her off the field.

I shook my head, my assumption.

Lia didn't have an effect on her work without Eric. Each time he moved up or moved on there were issues. He has done this three times before and each time she struggled. Somehow, she managed to join him or pull her back in with her. Except when Danielle came back, that time was different, so she used her fist... a lot.

The difference is she has the money.

And fame...

... A power team to make those things go away.

My eyes were a bit tired after an added seven hours of intense work. I am now up-to-date with my online training. Booked my weapons training and of course, kept those rebels at bay.

Not bad for my first day as a field agent.

I pat myself on the back. They added to my actual job. That, coupled with the heat totally exhausted me.

After planning tomorrow's diary pushing another hour. I mapped our next move based on a review of the ladies' initial report. Two email alerts pinged one after the other.

… Way to go ladies!

Just in time for me to submit my eight p.m. deadline. I skimmed through.

From: Detective Sergeant Martinez
To: Agent Davis
Subject: Background check

The victim (Sharron Mall) was found by a recovery truck employee on the hard shoulder of the Divinish S12 alongside a cornfield three days ago.

Witness Victor Walters from Walters' tow truck saw the car on the side of the road, as a freelance tow engineer is paid by the county to pick up abandoned vehicles around the town.

He attempted to move the car, noticed blood inside the car and heard something loose as he was about to leave. He detached the vehicle and opened the trunk discovering Ms Mall.

Mr Walters is fifty-three years old, and has a wife and two teenage daughters in university and a son who works with him. Owns two tow trucks; his son works in one area both men have no connection to Ms Mall.

➢ Sharron Mall, age twenty-five
Address: Apt five, seventeen Bilstine Close, Shadeyah, Divinish
Mother: Catharine Mall deceased – information restricted
Father: Michael Mall – information restricted
Next of Kin: Restricted
Siblings: Darline Shianne Brown – restricted
   Brian Kumal Mall – restricted
➢ Occupation: Bartender, Jonopus Bar and Social Club
Work Address: Twelve Driver's Avenue Shadeyah, Divinish

- ➢ No known boyfriend and friends.
- ➢ Co-workers – still looking into them.
- ➢ Social life – still looking into that.

Det. S. G. Martinez
Consultant S.D.A.F.

Though basic, I shrug.

Sam at least completed it.

One observation though.

There are restricted events on her name.

Interesting... My curiosity was piqued.

Challenge accepted!

With a grin, I opened the S.D.A.F. database to begin my search typing my username and password. There, staring at me, a picture of Sharron Mall. She is beautiful, hazel eyes. More, green than mine, curly, tamer hair and not shy to show any skin.

I searched social media. There are a lot of selfies with her at various clubs as recent as one month ago. She is never seen in a photo with another girlfriend, unlike me. There is someone behind the photo but never next to her.

Her life fascinated me. Tabbing back to the report she made given to us by the Local Divinish Officers L.D.O. she was not reported as missing according to the initial report.

Didn't anyone miss her?

An initial timeline suggests she may have been missing for about a week.

Hum... Why does this report feel like it's... lacking?

No post-interview was recorded.

I find that hard to believe.

A thought of my own incident comes to mind and the invasive hours of questioning that followed.

Was she comatose?

Horror overthrew me.

Don't go there!

I pushed the thought aside reading more. There they were again, pictures up close, gruesome and invasive ones, of the violence and pain. Forced upon, the once vibrant and stunning Sharron Mall. The worst ones were of her laying in a pool of her own blood, and a foetus fully formed human, below her still attached to her.

The saliva thickened and my eyes are in disbelief. I can't stop looking.

Why would someone do this to her?

The more I ponder, the angrier and sickened I got. The more driven I became. Moving further along the report, she was taken to the Divinish General Hospital to recover from her injuries. There, she is in a stable condition, cognitive, but weak.

So why has no one interviewed her?

I searched for her location.

Maybe I can get an interview.

Alerted by the reading, she was moved into a private room at the hospital.

Curious.

Her car was impounded.

By whom!

And why not taken into evidence?

Conspiracy! I gasped mocking myself.

Maybe Sam should follow up, although I know she would think of far more than me. I am forced to think of her again and it irritates me.

Move on to the next email.

I edged myself then clicked on the next email.

Paula's report.

From: Officer Torrez

To: Agent Davis

Subject: Evidence

Car: Audi A3, black, taken from the impound at a cost of 200.

Front driver window glass broken glass inside, blood, glasses with blood, trunk lock broken as a result of her rescue; car undamaged otherwise.

Hospital report: The victim was cut five times on her torso, with small incisions approximately 5cm in width; the victim was bleeding from her abdomen, private area front and back passage. Other evidence and reports are in the progress of re-examination.

Officer Torrez, P.G.
Consultant S.D.A.F.

See, they can be professionals, when they need to be...
I closed off the email looking for a third. Nothing, I exhaled long.
Does she really want to play this game?
I am peeved!
Email sent to the director with the details of the reports omitting Aaliyah's lack of report. I included copies of Sam and Paula's report with mine being sure of true transparency.

On to Aaliyah, researching how best to deal with her insubordination. I am pleased with the effort of the two, though unexpected, who may have taken me seriously.

Not too sure if that's a good thing knowing the methods of those ladies.

It didn't pan out. I am tied to giving her warnings before taking action. It's not the answer I hoped for.

Great!

I have to stare at her pale-blue eyes a bit longer.

I huffed and looked into leadership methods. After reading two articles and more about the HR role I play. I drool from boredom.

Focus on the wins!

I huffed at myself quoting one article. Behind the open policy I closed, the window to shut down and retire for the night the pictures of Sharron Mall's attack faced me once again. It nauseated me. Saddens me and takes me to a memory I don't want to regurgitate. Distracted, I inspect the room. The wall clock displayed eight. I peeked out the window. The office was empty.

How long have they been gone?

I have already stayed here longer than expected. My eyes burn and my shoulders ached.

I should be going to the apartment.

I think of the way it was left suitcases on the floor and no food.

Do I chase a taxi or call one?

I confused myself.

I may also need to get some food.

There are a couple of pamphlets in the box from our briefing. I shuffle through them for food and a way back, but my focus is on Sharron Mall. I couldn't stop thinking about her. The way she was brutally attacked and the information from the L.D.O. A lot of things didn't make much sense to me. I have lost my appetite.

I packed the few folders, and my laptop and turned off the lights in the office. I walked down the stairs to the local shop below the office it was closed and the streets were empty. I find myself walking down an unfamiliar street with little recollection besides the bickering of A.P.S. Aaliyah, Paula and Sam.

Would she be up to visitors?

The thought filled with enthusiasm and anguish for the victim.

Is this a good idea?

CHAPTER EIGHT

Not what I expected at all for a small town, compared to Ceda. This hospital was huge! The taxi let me out at the main entrance. Gazing at the height of the main building and the connecting roads and signs displayed to my left and to my right. The sun was setting and dusk began on this autumn evening. There weren't many people around coming or leaving.

There weren't any reporters in sight.

A stray thought filtered and I cased looking out after. It seemed as though shifts were changing, and not many care assistants were on site. A main desk to the left of the entrance and a single lady behind it, security was out of sight.

The elevators near the desk with signs. Unable to make sense of the room numbers and named conditions on the digital display directions, I approached the desk.

Everything is white, clean and hand sanitisers are near the elevator. My workbag with my laptop balanced on one shoulder and my handbag on the other. Skilfully, I fasten my jacket concealing my gun and badge. When meeting the front desk for help.

"Good evening, I am looking for Sharon Mall. Can you tell me which ward she is staying in?"

"Are you another reporter?"

The pleasantly plump receptionist in white raised her head peeping over her tiny no-frame reading spectacles.

I should have expected this.

"Hi, sorry I should have introduced myself."

I paused and stretched to shake her hands.

"Are you family?" she grunts in her strong Divinish accent.

"Um, no but..."

"She is not open to any visitors."

Did she just cut me?

She instantly dismissed and went on writing her notes. I understood her position but am a bit offended by her manner. I folded my lips instantly eating my automatic reaction and breathing.

OK… finish introducing then…

I squinted and unfolded my lips, stepped back, unbuttoned my jacket took out my badge with my identification.

Maybe she needs something visual.

"I am Agent Shannan Davis-Hall with the Special Daver Armed Federal Force. I would like to see Ms Mall thank you," I added manners.

"Never heard of it." She's brief and pouted at my disturbance of her work.

"S.D.A.F. the newly formed Federal Force."

I try explaining however my patience is leaving quickly.

"Oh, I'll get right on that then."

She raised her index finger with her pen, shook her head then went on with her writing.

Is she serious?

How rude!

Lucky for her I just had practice.

With a simper, I replaced my badge closing my jacket with one button. Amused by her effort which is nothing compared to Aaliyah, Paula and Samanther, A.P.S. I stepped forward with conviction.

"I understand you're doing your job ma'am. Well done for holding the press off by the way, but I am trying to do mine."

My patronising tone caught her attention. She stopped, looked over her spectacles then replied,

"Oh, she still isn't open to visitors."

Chuckling at her further attempt to be unpleasant. To ignore my position and to aggravate me.

Challenge accepted…

"Are you a doctor?"

"Excuse me?" She leaned into her chair finally with some eye contact.

"Of course not, you're a receptionist. I only approached you because your signs confused me. As a courtesy, I introduced myself.

"Have you ever heard of an obstruction charge? Of course not! You're neither a lawyer nor, does your job require you to execute the law. You are a receptionist."

"No, but..." she tries explaining.

"Oh, well if you heard of it, I presume you will know by preventing me from seeing Ms Mall today, I can return with a court order tomorrow. In which, you can be arrested and charged with knowingly hindering the course of justice. This can carry a few years of imprisonment. I am sure you don't want that."

"No." She stood up, her brown eyes fixated on me growing to below my eye level.

I looked down at her. She picked up the phone from her desk and began strumming the keypad.

Cute.

"I do hope it is Ms Mall's doctor you're calling, if it's not, I hope it's your lawyer. You've got exactly five seconds, to hang up that phone and direct me to her room before I arrest you." I bring my hand to view my watch.

"... Four... three... two..."

"It's second floor 101 room G."

She said briskly, pressing the flash button.

"Thank you for your cooperation!"

Turning on my heels, my dark hair flicked out the bun with the motion stomping towards the elevator exhaling my rage.

Why did she have to force my hand like that?

She has added to my irritation. Reminding me of Aaliyah's missing report and the fact that I cannot just get rid of her. I noted her name marching along the halls.

What was her problem?

I shrugged to myself pounding the call knob for the lift to come down. The hallways suddenly became busy. I repeatedly strike the button as my patience is not what it was, at the entrance.

Finally.

The door opened and a janitor stood inside with his mop and bucket. Our eyes meet and we froze momentarily.

"Going up," he calls unexpectedly, with a clear and deep voice. It caught my attention and I hesitate at his familiar appearance.

Where have I seen him before?

I trace my limited memory crossing the threshold. Turning away from his reflective eyes to stare at his reflection through the mirror as the door closes. His grin, partly mischievous, mine is curious at his smirk behind me.

He must recognise me…

There was nothing much in the past I can remember, that pegs him to me. Yet, his small smile alarms me as his eyes pierce at me all big and blue, lively. The hairs on my body prickled and I am suddenly aware of my heavy breathing.

Ping!

Relieved by the door that couldn't have opened sooner. I leapt out, turning briskly to have a better look at him. He's disappeared.

The old dude is quick.

He must have scurried away.

The explanation was not comforting. It was odd. Gaining my bearings, I am on the wrong floor. I pressed the elevator again for a short ride to the next floor.

Greeted by two men in black suits, standing on either side of the elevator doors. They appeared to be private security. Black suits, white shirts, black, glossy polished shoes and sunglasses indoors.

Not subtle at all.

Saying nothing I walked past them.

The nurse's station was vacant and I followed the sequence of the room numbers. The floor was almost deserted and the men shadowed me.

This may be the welcoming party.

I snickered pooling what energy was left for a fight. Their footsteps echo on the empty floors, the blood rushes through my body. My heartbeat picked up the pace but I purposefully didn't.

This must be on my terms.

Assessing the width of my skirt, I unbuttoned my jacket keeping my hand closed for a draw. Settling in room 101 I was so ready for a third challenge. They walked past me. I review the door eyeing their movements at the side and waited a few minutes. They were out of sight.

Carefully examining the wall for her name, with an exhale I am once again flooded with the memory of her condition.

There was an eerie chime and an echo of a distant, steady, thump. I pass through the doorframe with anticipation to the lightly lit room. She had been mummified and connected to monitors. Her face was swollen, colourful and glossy.

This is worse!

I couldn't tell if she was asleep or awake. Her eyes were slits, glistened and moist. This was nearly a week after being attacked. On her finger, there was a clip. Her wrists were circled with plasters. There was a bandage around her head and covered plasters along her jaw.

Though she was covered over the waist, part of the hospital gown exposed her bandaged torso. From the report, this was the part of her body that was the centre of her attacker's attention cutting her. My throat ached with the unbelievable vision before me. I swallowed hard.

Sympathising, my eyes are filled. I felt responsible, motivated and driven to seek this viper that prey misery on this unsuspecting woman. Cleansing my lungs again holding a rising ball about to open my mouth, she whispered.

"Hello."

Her voice was husky brimming with pain.

Hold it in Shana!

I took a moment.

"Hi, I am Agent Shannan Davis-Hall from S.D.A.F. I was sent here to investigate your attack."

I spilt the words as fast as I could, to contain the breaking of my voice.

"I… I already sp… spoke to someone."

She slowly aching her words in slurs.

Barely grasping a pleasant demeanour as empathy chokes me. Every sore and emotion hit me. I cannot find my own, baffling me all at once. My nose began to flare, the words falling out.

"I understand you did…" I exhaled inhaling sharply. "… And I know that you're in a lot… of pain…" *I can feel it.* "… But I need you to please… as best… and as slowly if you like… please help me… to help you."

What is going on with you Shana?

I am overthrown, pinned by her sadness, fear, aches, embarrassment and something else. The hairs on my skin alert me.

Get a grip!

Her breathing became shallow as mine did. It is hard to look at her, weeping through the tiny space of her engorged eyes. I count.

Ten, nine, eight, seven, six, five, four, three, two, one.

Gaining some control of my breath her emotions are her's again. Struggling to remain professional, I try to complete my visit.

"It is important that we go through the events."

I paused and the pain rises again.

"… Whilst it's still fresh in your memory. I really want to help you, Miss Mall." Her confusion, panic and vengeance came out with my tone. "We can do it in parts… or you can do it all today… once you feel up to it."

Blood seeps through her sheets as her heartbeat increased setting the monitors off. The mixed emotions are gone.

A nurse appeared to the blearing monitors. She eyed me.

I stepped outside.

I needed to clear my head, anyways.

What is going on with you? I scolded myself.

I need a moment.

I leaned against the wall outside her room. Covering my mouth with my hand, I bent my head to the floor. My tummy stirred and a sickening feeling grew. Almost doubling over to stifle the erupting wail, breathing and counting.

The need to help her overthrows all logic. I sense a connection to her, unable to deviate my emotions from consumption of her empathic despondency. Control seemed to flee as I am reminded of my own ordeal.

Why do I feel this way?

This is not about you Shana.

You're here to help her, not to cry…

The two men from earlier interrupted my reviver stomping in my direction.

Again.

I lifted my head fully leaning back on the wall. One man was bald the other with a low haircut. They looked military. I straighten up giving them room for them to pass. Hidden behind them, another man walked with them.

He was well-aged tall and dark, with dark brown and grey hair wearing a grey pin-stripe suit. Under the jacket, a light blue shirt with a gold brace draped around his shoulders to the bottom of his chest.

There were links of gold that were sun-shaped with blue stones inside. Three medals under the pocket with a matching handkerchief and tie. As the men pass, he drifted towards me with his hand stretched for an embrace. Unexpected, I stretched to receive.

"Good night, I am Mayor Michael Mall of Shayeda," he introduced himself with a broad simper.

This is a bit weird, but I'll bite.

"Hi, I am Agent Davis-Hall, nice to meet you. What a lovely town you've got here."

How did I keep a straight face with that lie?

It is unbelievably hot here!

I grinned at my wayward thought.

His tough hands hold firm to mine for too long. I want it back.

"It's nice that you're here with us for how long?" His voice was steady, and firm and he got straight to the point.

OK! I accepted his forwardness. My eyes widened a second bewildered by him, then I squint with a stolid grin.

"Oh yes." I try emitting diplomacy and not mechanically. "... I see..."

My eyes stuck into his and he enfolded his other hand over my one trapping it firmly.

Let go!

"Well, I know that you're visiting... and our customs can seem to be strange to guests..."

I find the people primordial and their customs more archaic!

I smile a bit more contemplating.

His polished, political smile vexes me. With a slight quiver to his rosy cheeks with only a small bit of his teeth showing, his face appeared to be stuck.

Ugh! Reminds me of Aaliyah's.

"Sorry I don't follow…" I stipulated, baffled again.

I know those grins come with an agenda and I want him to say.

"I hope by the end of your time here, you might see change?" His face returned to the plastered mouth slightly opened, teeth showing a smirk.

I stilled my eyes from circling. *I don't want to get involved in politics.* "… Change, to what sir?" I breathe out forcefully through my nose.

"To your understanding." I try taking my hand again but he held on fast.

Of what! I gritted inwardly, outwardly speaking. "… I accept what I can't change and change the things that I can."

Quoting a random memory, something from many years ago.

"Oh, I am happy you're willing to accept things… the things you can't change."

What is that supposed to mean?

Oh, I hate these games. "Is there a reason for this conversation sir?"

I slid my hand out his as my filter left. His workman's hands bruised mine. I wince momentarily thinking of Lia's diplomatic games.

Not so good at those too…

I crossed my arms across my chest to keep them away from his.

"… Because I can't help but wonder, why an esteemed member of Shayeda has come to greet me in the hospital of a publicised victim's room at this late hour questioning my motives?"

Ahh, filter! I shout inwardly at myself.

"Which agency did you say you were with?" He changed direction and again, I forced my eyes to be still.

"I didn't. Special. Daver. Armed. Federal. Force." I twisted my jacket letting my badge peek through. "… A part of the government's initiative reform for transparency. The Defence Secretary assigned me here." I ended as a matter-of-fact.

I unintentionally blinked too many times narrowing my eyes and looking up at him.

"Great!" His appearance became visibly relaxed though his voice is far from genuine. "… This is family, my daughter…"

What!

My eyes widened and my face was surprised for a second but indifferent afterwards.

"It would be best our relationship be absent from this investigation," he says, but I know it is a command. "Show your sister phenomenal, and give her time to restore."

Unable to decipher if his language is of the natives or just cryptic. "I understand," I reply only as a sign of respect. He lingers and I know.

But that is not why he's here... I wish he'd just get to the damn point!

A political grin covered his mouth irritating me further. "... Just as a courtesy while you're in town. I do hope you enjoy your stay, but I will be sure that my officers are as considerate as you are, you know, while you're here."

Is he threatening me?

I nodded and squinched at his gesture.

Do I have the energy for this tonight?

"Have a good night, Agent Davis." He ends our conversation before I could gear up for the fight. With his hands at his side he nods with his eyes on mine staring uncomfortably.

"Goodnight, Mayor Mall."

I returned the nod sceptical of his role in this tragedy.

Seeing her injuries in person is more heart-wrenching than the photos. I didn't want to disturb her further. It was late, and she needed rest. At least one mystery in this case was solved, her family was listed as restricted. Observing her from afar, I wondered how she was identified at all.

CHAPTER NINE

A lot of appointments today.

I viewed my calendar which filled overnight. The landlines weren't connected so all calls came through my mobile.

Annoying, yes very annoying.

I can't scan my calls. Only because the one person I really want to call hasn't. I quarrelled with myself.

He must have been called away. I sulk excusing his distance. Being the second-in-command of the Ceda branch of the D.P.F. going undercover was not viable as his face could be recognised and...

Aaliyah is here. I noted unpleasantly.

... That can't be it. I argue with myself again.

Or he's still mad at me? I folded thinking of the words said in our brief call.

... Maybe he is with Danielle, it is the half-term holiday. I consider it without knowledge.

Shana focus! I scream at myself.

There were so many things required for the office. My list got longer by the hour and my nervousness was piqued by the growing list.

I hoped my inexperience doesn't get the better of me.

I unravelled again.

Focus on one task Shana! The reminder was necessary.

I opened my laptop and began completing tasks. Before I knew it, two in the afternoon and my calendar popped up with the reminder.

Shit!

I was late for my own deadline. At least the notes I made last night can be useful today.

Not the one from the hospital.

The overwhelming emotions are a harsh and confusing reminder that lingers.

After last night, I don't know what I expected from this lot. I strolled into a silent conference room with Lia and Sam, Paula was missing. Surprisingly, Sam sat with her feet below the table for once. But I seem to have interrupted a staring competition, again. They sat opposite each other glaring.

Silent, but glaring.

I am happy for one thing, behaviour, which is an improvement.

Better than bickering!

A disturbing déjà vu especially Paula wasn't absent. For the last one I expected to miss my deadline, but, she did. Wayfaring cautiously to my chair I squinted at them.

"Is there something on my chair?"

It was aloud and not inwardly as I'd hoped. Placed my laptop, notepad and pen on the table, Sam slid a manila folder to me holding one for herself. I stopped it right before it fell off. Inspected the chair before I sat gingerly, pausing for a reaction. Sam began, "The victim Sharron Haley Mall; born April 23rd, child of the sitting mayor, Michael Mall. I guess that's why a special team has been assigned."

Here she goes.

"Sam!" I warned.

"Sorry!" She belted as a reflex. Then, turning her head towards Lia. "… She is of course spoiled rotten like every rich kid we know, always in search of her daddy's attention. I guess you'd know a bit about that umm, Lia?"

She winked at Aaliyah chewing loud. In turn, Aaliyah strikes the table with her hand. Gliding her chair backwards. I pounced to my feet before they did. Pointed at them both on either side.

"Can we do this without teasing?"

"I can…" Sam began chewing with her mouth opened and squinted hard at her. "… But it won't be much fun." She leered. Aaliyah inhaled but I was quick.

"Are you five?" I directed at Samanther.

Aaliyah crossed her leg, shaking. Then, pulled her chair under the table, perched her elbow on top propping her chin opening the folder flicking the pages loudly. Bobbing her body with the movement under the table, carrying on the staring game. I rolled my eyes seating cautiously.

"All right, I'm sorry..."

Sam apologises. Her husky voice seemed genuine this time.

Sam apologising!

Twice!

Wow!

Inside my jaw drops outwardly into an impassive pose. Sam continued with a wide grin as if she was enjoying an inside joke.

"There are three miscellaneous reports of her: running away, soliciting her father and fake kidnapping. Two assault charges from her, both dropped.

"She was charged with wasting police time after she faked kidnapping and served six months which was five years ago. She has kept a low profile since then."

Wait. "How did you get that information?"

The material from the juvenile court should be sealed. Her mouth goes and her eyes went up to the left.

"I have my ways." Sam shrugged with a sly grin.

"Sam!" I cautioned.

"The L.D.O..." She shrugged whining in her alto tone.

I hope she didn't.

"Legally? Wait, don't answer that. I don't want to know but this is your second warning."

I lay out the repercussion of her actions.

She huffed; rolling her eyes intently and went on with a crinkle between her brows.

"Native of Divinish which means she is a Zemand."

"Because she is a local automatically makes her Zemand?" I cut her annoyed.

I hate baseless assumptions.

"Her profile, saying she is a Zemand makes her Zemand."

Sam rolled her head at me opening her bright blue eyes, I'm sure keeping score.

OK.

I ignore the reaction browsing through her report.

"Her apartment lease is in her father's name. Besides that, they have no contact with each other. I know. I've checked her phone records for the past six months. I also tried having a chat with him and never got past his secretary." Sam dragged her voice rolling her eyes.

"Don't worry I had an interesting chat with him last night," I confessed shruggingly, reading through the report she just explained.

"OK then…" Sam sat up straight looking at me in anticipation. "… Care to elaborate?" Sam demanded leaning into her chair, and scrutinising me.

"No!" I peeked through my lashes a second lifting my head briefly, then back to the report taking notes. I know she's rolling her eyes at me again and I don't care.

"Well, not many people may know about his estranged daughter." She put the folder down and focused her displeasure my way.

Again assumptions! "They do," I rectified short not wanting to detail the not-so-subtle threat and my lies about liking it here.

"Well, he does *not* want them to know." She rolled her head at me and I still didn't pay her much attention.

She is presuming again but this time. "That is true," I agreed, writing my sentence, taking notes for the report tonight. There was a moment of silence in the room, which was unusual. I looked up to be sure they were still there. Both women eye me and I try to avoid the connection.

"So, what's the next move boss?"

Sam popped the gum catching my attention then sucked it back into her mouth as she reclined horizontally. Putting her hands behind her head and her feet found the table.

Ugh, why!

My face changes from impassive at her disgusting habit.

Upside… she actually didn't fight me on her assignment and finished it on time.

Way to go Sam!

Of course, I could only think that and *never* say that aloud.

"Don't call me that." I changed to nonchalant. "… What do you think?"

I passed it back to her knowing she has thought of a way forward. My nose is deep into prewriting tonight's report.

"I don't know it's all your call." Still smug.

I knew there had to be some catch.

I closed the folder putting it to one side, sitting up crisscrossing my fingers over the table.

"After almost twenty years of detective work, you have no clue what to do? Don't waste my time Martinez." I am annoyed.

"I do apologise Agent Davis." She singsongs my name, "... I would like to speak to the mayor in person, can you make that happen?"

She is mocking but I know she has her big eyes set on Mayor Mall.

"Don't irritate me Sam I'm not in the mood... For now, he is off-limits. Trace her steps before she was taken. I don't think she's up for an interview, yet. Can you get whatever case files from L.D.O? I have a feeling they haven't been completely forthcoming."

"I wouldn't either if I was told to hand over my investigation."

Her wit is irritating sometimes.

I squint at her and she pierces me with those innocent eyes.

"Establish a timeline. Try not to ruffle any feathers whilst you're getting there, please. The first sign of resistance, call. And please be nice. You have the rest of the week for this assignment and a report is due at two p.m. on Friday."

"Thanks, but I work alone."

"Aww, that's sweet!" I mocked tilting my head to one side. "... Still not in the mood Sam! Please don't beat anyone, the public is watching and your warnings are running out."

She made a funny face just then, Paula walked in breaking an uprising. My eyes fell on the spots of funny colours across her lab coat and my anger was redirected.

"You're late, this better be good!"

Could I be any moodier?

"I'll try."

Sam simpered closing her folder.

Then relaxes deeper horizontally into the chair.

Why does she think she must get the last word? "Thank you."

My manners kicked despite her phoney gesture.

"I am sorry Shana. I lost track of time."

So, did I.

Paula explained pulling the chair back on the wheels. She rests her folder on the table, Sam passed a copy of her report to Paula.

Hum, they're sharing... I observed. Paula slowly read through the folder.

"Don't make me guess." I'm directed to Paula, still irritated.

My eyes fell on a brown stain below Paula's white lab coat pocket, her reading glasses on a silver chain around her neck bumping above the stain partially hiding F cups.

I wonder if she was here the whole time.

She pulled the chair in further. Her breasts rested on the table. She distributed the folders evenly. Opened her folder with excitement,

"There are multiple semen samples taken from Ms Mall after her attack. Six to be exact, and get this, two of the samples share twenty-three chromosomes which means they're related."

Good, I flipped my page and began to write.

"... She also had some epidermis under her nails... skin. It matches one of the semen samples not the relatives though."

She is beginning to lose me.

"... This is going to be fun to analyse and map..."

I don't get it! But her voice filled with anticipation and we were all not amused. "... Anyways... She was bound with what appears to be gold rope."

"Real gold," I questioned.

"Still have to determine whether it's real or not. At first glance, I will say it is. I got a piece from the wound in her arm at least that's what the label says. So, she must have been tugging on her restraints."

I recalled the bandages around her wrists. I agree. She carried on,

"... Here's the funny thing, it was dowsed with some kind of sticky-based substance. The sample wasn't the biggest. At first, I thought it was dried blood but it is the same colour as blood which piqued my interest and I was like 'wow'..."

She is losing me again with her babble.

Sam and my faces grim, Lia looks like she's slowly falling asleep. Paula's voice fades into the background with technical terms. Then she concluded, "... Still have a few tests to do, you know... analysed.

"... Oh, and she was cut as if they were about to have a keyhole surgery. The muscles were not breached, and no organs were removed at least that is what I read in the hospital report.

"... I can't say for certain without examining her myself but I think she has been through enough already."

I remember her swollen sad, face.

"I agree Paula."

Her face lights up and she flicked her dark-brown hair.

"The cuts were enough for her to almost bleed out in the car. Whosoever did this, knew exactly what they were doing, it was artful."

Her gaze is disturbing.

"Glad to see at least you're enjoying this job."

I'm trying to be enthusiastic with my little understanding and exposure to her work.

"Oh, this is so fascinating..."

"Just to you Paula, but continue."

"There was sand in her hair, not the type found on the beach but a red stone – like maybe from a cave, there was also guano in her hair."

What!

"What?"

Her explanation has my head spinning.

"Oh, seabirds or bat droppings."

Gross! I frown deciphering her scribbled writing.

"... So, my best guess, she was held in a cave or somewhere close to the sea at some point. Further evaluation of this fertilizer is required.

"There was also a red fabric found... very odd material. She wasn't wearing anything so... can't yet determine its origin. The foetus."

I swallowed hard as my stomach stirs.

"... In the trunk with her is hers and also matches one of the semen samples one of the relatives... so, it had to be someone she was very familiar with. The foetus was around fourteen weeks, give or take. I have reason to believe she knew about the pregnancy for a while, maybe even showing."

This is awful!

A vengeful desire rises as Paula explains.

"… I haven't finished processing the car. The secondary crime scene has been open for five days I'm not sure we can find anything more there. I would have to rely on the photos. But I'll still have a look. If you want me to…"

She looks at me in anticipation.

"Well, you have your task then, finish processing and let me know after, you have one week. Seven days Paula whatever you finished by Friday you can forward that report to me."

She nodded and we turned our focus to Aaliyah. A bit surprised she tilted her head exposing a red mark along her neck. Our eyes met and she grew that I-am-politically-correct-smile she wears right before she gets her way with her crap.

"I did not get enough time to complete my assignment."

"I didn't ask what you don't have."

I'm trying to be calm, and not show my petulance from before.

"I didn't have time to start."

She corrected herself shifting on her seat.

"So, what have you been doing for the past two days?"

I am curious. She knows we all spotted the hickey and know her promiscuous tendency.

"If you only knew," she whispered almost daring me then voiced clearly.

"… I had to go get the nugget from L.D.O. they didn't have it."

"What do you mean?" I questioned. She crossed her legs under the table and began shaking.

"… It was collected by someone claiming to be the rightful owner. They claimed he had paperwork. A purchase invoice and insurance certificate. And a crime report of its burglar."

"What!"

I didn't mean to shout! "… Didn't you tell the officer that he had no right to release evidence from an active investigation?" I paused to adjust my tone. "… Did you at least find the alleged owner?"

"I did not have enough time I had to return *here* for *this* meeting."

Oh, I want to smack her!

My gape deepened…

She does things intentionally to infuriate me.

I breathe deep, in and out.

"Please track down the alleged owner nicely. Don't break any laws doing it, thank you. You've got three days to do this.

"Find that officer. I want a written copy by six tonight. No one leaves this office until each person hands in their reports. I will try to uncomplicate some of the blockages for you."

I need their report and my notes for another detailed email to my director. Another thing added to my ever-growing 'to-do' list.

Damn it!

"You all have your assignments. Go, follow up. And six ladies, on time Torrez." I pointed at my wrist.

They all scattered busying themselves. I hear the rustling and tension outside the conference room. I am not used to it, strange. Somehow, I am unusually tense this afternoon and actively struggling to reach calm. It was twenty-to-five.

Counting the time isn't helpful.

Reminded again, of my eight o'clock deadline.

Crap!

The prewrite is twenty senseless words on my screen and the cursor mocks me blinking. A reminder of application reviews tomorrow just popped up. This is followed by one ten-minute statement with the press.

Shit! Shit! Shit!

I am not about to have another night of fast food, my stomach can't take it.

I rubbed it gaggling and tensing.

I need to go shopping.

I sighed starting with the notes to fill the reports.

Rubbing my shoulders from yet another long day the ladies pulled through once again. I barely made it; attaching the three ladies' report this time, to mine. I haven't left the conference room except for toilet breaks which have somehow increased though my water intake seems about the same.

Today's reports are still scattered across the large table. I quickly viewed the time in the corner of my laptop. Finally, I emailed my director right before the cut-off and am the last one to leave again. Their desks are cleared and they haven't had the courtesy to announce their exit.

Do you think they would announce their exit?

I reprimanded myself for expecting it. Once again, I have to leave this place at a late hour though the autumn is bright and very disconcerting coming from a county with seasonal change into this hot and constant light evening that feel like summer. I tidied the room and locked away some things exiting with my laptop and handbag swung across me trotting down the stairs.

I need to rent a car.

Standing outside at the closed shop downstairs as this time I was hungry and tetchy. Making the mistake of wearing a skirt suit with a white blouse below, the heat adds to my annoyance.

I need to be calm!

Walking about a mile into the Divinish shopping centre, the warm evening air forces me to unbutton my jacket to catch the breeze. I strolled into the first grocery I spot. There are so many unfamiliar foods. I noted pushing the trolley.

Things for the local gullet that I would not envision putting into my mouth.

The fresh meat is unlike anything I have ever seen. It is a small mammal I think, and its sternum is spread open over ice. My stomach turned.

This may be the culture Mayor Mall warned me about.

Things like that would never be displayed in Ceda. I compared the capital and my home city feeling slightly homesick after three days.

It might had well been another country.

I huffed and opened a pack of chips fresh from the hot counter. Anything to quench this craving. I also picked up a burger and lemonade crawling through the isles, shopping.

I don't know what I feel like!

Munching pretzels next through the store my small trolley was almost full. I couldn't figure out why but, the prices were amazing. So, the shop for quick breakfast items coffee, bread, eggs, cereal and fruits became four bags of I'm-not-sure-I-need-all this.

I stumbled up the stairs, two bags in my hands and two in my arms after a taxi dropped me off. Across the shared hallway the bags towered almost blocking my vision dangling my workbag and laptop on my shoulder.

I shouldn't have bought all this.

The keys were the next challenge. I reached for the door balancing the bags and shaking my jacket to fish them out, attempting to avoid a spill. Beaming at the thought of coming home; Danielle would grab a bag or two, to peak at my acquisitions. Eric would free me of the rest, easing my struggle and greeting me with a kiss and asking me about my day.

Eric and Danielle were in Ceda.

Finally, unlocking I kicked open the door. Spilling everything over the back of the sofa. Then, turned to close the door and retrieve my keys. There was a shadow passing into the toilet behind me.

I still. The blood pumping to my head, palms begin to sweat. Slowly sliding my left hand to unbutton my jacket, right across my hip. I reach for my sidearm and flicked the fastener to free my weapon safely.

Skulking cautiously towards the shadow, I pulled my Glock. Holding it firmly with both hands pointing it upwards. My heart was pounding through my chest. I opened the bathroom door. I felt the presence behind me. With one swift movement I straightened my elbows and cocked the hammer, holding my breath. The light flicked on.

"Whoa, Shana."

CHAPTER TEN

"Shit! Eric." I exhale.

There was no hint of surprise from him. My gun was in his face. Instead, Eric wears a bright grin matching his white T-shirt, fine-trimmed dark beard lined straight almost as if it was drawn in place, dark blue jeans and feet bare.

The adrenalin spike still fresh, runs through me. My hands froze in place, and my chest maintained its rise and fall. I tried to catch my breath. He pushed the gun aside as his lips meet mine, his tongue passed mine. Instinctively my hands soften and my eyes closed kissing him in relief. He pulls me into him caressing my head and back.

Oh, I missed him.

His touch soothes me. Exactly what I need. His lips trailed my neck my breathing escalated.

"I could have…"

The thought scares me. He took my head in his huge hands with a lusty beautiful smile on full display.

"I could have…"

Words fail me he shook his head agreeing. His hands stroked my neck and shoulders. The feeling of regret fills me and sorrow gathers choking at me. He is calm, and in control heaving my head up to gaze into his gleaming dark brown eyes.

I am limply bereft of the horrors of 'what if'. His thumbs wipe my cheeks as the adrenalin fades. Slipping his strong arms around my small waist.

Wait a minute.

How is he here…

My senses reach me. Finally, he replies.

"Na! You don't have the look."

Coming in to spoon me again. *Oh, he smells divine…* I conceded.

He nuzzled my neck placing light kisses on a trail. From shoulder to neck to shoulder. Underneath his touch, my skin tingled and my senses awake. I was almost distracted until his tongue flicked around my earlobe and his mouth closed and he sucked. I still. It was different. Delayed, I shrugged him off stepping back. He grinned at my action, and immediately I knew something was off.

"Where's Danielle?"

Hesitantly stepping back, he swizzles his hands. Then, he clasps them as though he was about to beg, sucking through his teeth and showing me them. A silly laugh escaped. He moved his clasped hands to his lips, and step back again.

I'm not going to like this!

"Uh, she's at Dave's," he mumbled under his breath.

I was right, it is the school holidays. I glow at my accuracy in remembering.

Then registering whom he said, "Honey…" I whined at the choice.

"Baby I know. But he was the only one available. Anyway, Liz's going to her in two days."

"You could have left her with Sue," I question his choice of a flake to babysit.

"Suzanne is busy!" he grunts.

"… or Sam," I say softer.

"Sam!" he blew an exhale.

"Yes, her m-oth-er!" I stressed singsong.

"You're her mother," he argues and I know this will end as it always does, in a stalemate.

Wait a minute… I squinted at him only just realizing…

"H-how… when… Why are you here?" I question his presents and odd behaviour.

"So, what are you saying, can't come by to see my wife?" He dodges coming closer to me.

"I didn't say that." I took a deep breath then folded my lips to solicit the right words. "… I said what-what are you… doing *here*? In Divinish." I squint. "… And how did you find my apartment? Where did you get a key?" I lift and drop my shoulders.

"Well, I took some time off, five days and thought, I should spend it here with you. Since we didn't really celebrate our anniversary this year."

One step, towards me with a lecherous face. I step back.

Oh no!

Not this time!

"Are you going to answer my question?" I squeak.

"Would you get mad?" he says almost in the same tone that made me weary.

"Depends." *Lia...* Exasperated, crossing my arms with the nasty echo of her name in my thoughts.

"I called in a favour."

"From Lia." My tone was deep and my words sharp as I waved my arms around.

"*No!*" he looks wounded, turned to the sofa hissing through his teeth.

"I see." I just spoiled the mood!

"... Thought we would have saved our days to take it together, somewhere away from work, maybe after this case? To plan Cáhilt and... talk... and..." I trailed, reminding him of what he promised before he had his last undercover operation.

"Baby, maybe I might get a case or you will..." He yanked the bags off the sofa and set them on the breakfast bar. "... Let's just seize the moment all right."

Shit, he is mad. But is it about Lia or my questioning?

OK.

... How will I recover?

"How can I seize the moment when I'm on-call?"

I secure my gun in its holster and shut the door. He stalked behind me and snaked his strong arms around my waist breathing against my neck. I smiled as he pulled me onto his erection poking at my back.

The moment is saved!

Twirling me around gracefully, his lips meet mine parting them, as his tongue fills my mouth. We walk in a dance. One hand kept my head in place, the other wrapped around my waist. Leading me towards the bed.

Laying me lightly on the bed, he's flush, over me. Our hips and lips met with enraged breathing, wanting. I sit up, stripping my jacket and tossing it aside as my shoes plopped off.

A small giggle left me as I reached down to the hem of his white T-shirt pulling it over his head. Exposing the beautiful, chocolate, sculpted washboard abs. Shaded with dark hair lightly over them. I threw it. Then smooth my hands over his warm, ripped chest and soft hair. He tensed and unclipped my holster coming off the bed. Put the gun into the side-table drawer.

Up on my forearms, I admire the view of him standing at the edge of the bed without a shirt. The way I like. Catching my breath, he kneels over me his eyes engaged in mine. Unbuttoning my blouse each one with care as his smile grew wickedly kissing me where he exposed and descends. Between my breasts, the top of my abs, my belly button to the waistband of my skirt.

He eyes my shield unclipping it from my waistband. Moved it to the side table and unzipped my skirt at the side, gliding it off. He disappears for a moment taking my feet out.

Carefully he's making his way up nipping and sucking my inner thighs. I moan folding my lips, sealing my eyes responding… craving… he comes into cachet a kiss when… I groan… held my mouth, and pushed him aside, legging it to the bathroom.

Lifting the toilet seat vomiting the cheeseburger, fries and pretzels I ate after craving a home-cooked meal a half hour ago. Some of my lunch and something I didn't even remember having. Barely able to catch my breath the tenseness retching from the deepest pit of my belly tingling from my toes, with tear-filled eyes.

Oh, shit the smell!

I throw up again. He rushed in after me completely bewildered holding my hair back as I flop over the toilet bowl releasing the content of my stomach.

"Are you alright?" he asks knelt next to me on the cold, tiled floor. One hand twined with my hair and the other made small circles on my back. A complimentary flush, the colours swirled my head over the bowl welcoming the breeze of the water flow. My knees were on the floor my arms fluttered, bracing for the urge to fall in. I feel faint.

"Shana…" he demands a response.

"It must be something I ate." Divulging tiredly.

"Are you sure? If it's food poisoning, I can take you to the hospital."

I passed the back of my hand across my mouth took a breath and flushed again.

"I think… I'll be fine."

The ease of my stomach forces me to taste the remains in my mouth. Gross!

I cringe.

The aftertaste is not fun.

An urgent need to brush my teeth is overwhelming. He released my hair. I slinked to the sink, opened the pipe and rinse my mouth washing some remains from my hands. The odours are suddenly overpowering, the soap, the vomit, his aftershave, it's like my sense of smell was on steroids.

"I think I need a shower."

Maybe showering might solve this.

"Are you sure you'll be all right alone in there?"

Almost forgot about him. He's standing behind me. I gape through the mirror. His bare back, the first button of his jeans undone, and it's hanging on his sculpted hips.

"Yes, I'll be fine and no, you can't join me." I grin coyly. "… You hug all the warm water."

I turned to him shaking my blouse off and eyeing him. My breast was full, merely contained by the bra. Suddenly, it's sensitive and sore. Eric's eyes zoned in.

"Period's close," I felt to explain.

"Alright."

He acknowledged and I know he sees his first target. This conversation isn't over.

I don't want an argument.

"I need a moment."

I called a retreat. My hands went up intending to move him out of the bathroom. Instead, I partially concealed his smooth pecs flattening the light hairs and steady heartbeat. I exhale.

"I *have* seen you naked, just saying."

His playfulness is so intoxicating. I bow shy and my eyes caught the exposed trail of dark hair under his navel travelling to his...

Um.

All the blood travels to my... Um.

I can't concentrate. My hands went limp.

"I promise not to hug the water..."

His begging is difficult to resist. Especially standing a foot apart, wearing black lace, briefs and a gold trim daisy lace bra.

Sauntering to me wasting no time he undoes my bra my nipples harden, instantly sensitive to the air. He's going straight for them.

Hiss...

The sound escapes through my teeth as his warm mouth covers my sore nipples, but he's sucking and tweaking. I grabbed his head he ravaged them, one then the other. The pain is overtaken by pleasure. I let go. He heads south running his tongue along my torso and nibbling.

Then, falls to his knees. Reaching the top of my lace underwear, his fingers grip the sides in a fist. Stretching the waistband of my panties, with a stroke dragging it to my knees, letting it fall with gravity.

Grabbing my hips closer I inhale hard. His breath shifts me. I throw my head back as his skilful kissing takes me deep and hard. Grabbing a handful of his short hair. My body begins to shake coming intensely quick with a muffled shriek.

I am astounded and a little embarrassed after one deep kiss and a quick release.

He stood up, with a triumphant grin. I am still tingling everywhere removing his jeans. Pleasantly surprised to learn he wasn't wearing underwear, curious but aroused. I went for him greedily exploring his mouth and tasting myself after he enjoyed it.

He's schlepped me into the rectangular frost glass shower our lips fastened. He jaunts backwards. I followed the lead my eyes closed, trapped in the desire, our tongues in a dance.

He's pinned me on the cold glass wall. It wobbles with an echo as he closes the door. One palm on the glass his knees between mine squatting making his opening. I grabbed his head running my fingers through his huge curls. He turns the shower on, distracting me.

Cold!

It's wide and flows over his head. My mouth opened from the shock. In that swift movement, his hand lifts me from the waist his body secures me shrilling as I go up against the glass. Lifting from his squat, sitting me on his erection. I moan loudly. He put his hand over my mouth, his eyes intense into mine. I am surprised by this move and aroused.

This is different but sexy as hell!

"Shush, baby," his voice deep and cold.

I wrapped my legs around his hips. He released my mouth and pulls me down by the hips filling me. I wince balancing my arms on his firm shoulders, my mouth an O, he squints at me pausing. I grind my teeth and he pulls me on again.

My ass squeaked as I slid down and he bangs hard into me rattling the glass as we go up. Slowly thrilling down squeaking, and banging as he fills me. The rhythm is unsettling in my conscious, but satisfying as his breath raises every pore on my body.

The water heated up, filling the room with steam. My heartbeat increases, tensing as we go faster and reach the high. He really pounds into me and banging and squeaking the glass door with every thrust. I climax he muffled my shouting, right before him, and he quietly released breathless on my shoulder.

The water cascades over us as we slid to the floor drenching my hair. He knows I hate wetting my hair if I'm not washing it, it frizzles. He combed my hair with his fingers gauging my reaction. We burst into laughter snuggling in the shower.

CHAPTER ELEVEN

The next morning; Bang, bang, bang, bang! There was an impatient banging on the door. I ignored it. *What time is it... ugh!* Exhausted, I rolled over covering Eric's head with the sheet.

Bang, bang, bang, bang! Rapid thumps on the front door. I groaned. Go away!

My eyes are too tired to care. Then, it stopped and the door burst open. Three women poured into the apartment. Aaliyah, Paula and Samanther, all dressed for work in their own way but rudely barging in.

"What the fuck!" I snarled at them sitting up a little, not sorry for my outbursts.

The beams of sunlight flood the apartment and I squint. Aaliyah marched towards me with intent whilst the other two stood back viewing me curiously. She reached her polished claws to me.

"Aha!" She gasped as she snatched the sheet off me.

"Ah!" Eric screamed and I protest.

"Fuck Lia!" Gathering the sheets to cover up my now exposed double Ds. "... *What!*" I snarled. Uncomfortable she looked. I blinked at her adjusting my eyes to the sunlight they let in.

Eric sat up rubbing his eyes with one hand balancing on the other. The sheet slithers down his firm, smooth, tense bare chest, abs and biceps to his waist distracting everyone. I paused taking in the view of my fine man sat naked next to me. Then turning back to Lia, I said.

"Who did you expect?" I frowned at her. "... The gardener?" I grinned. *Bitch!* Aaliyah's face grew serious. The wrinkles around her icy-blues became prominent with her squint and she crossed her arms below her chest. "... Maybe that's your style." I'm smug.

Sam leers a questioning expression. Paula immobilized in her steady eyes on my husband's exposed upper half. Then, the moment became more awkward. Only then, I am realising all three women staring at my husband.

"I'll go to the bathroom."

Eric asks to excuse himself sitting up further and the single sheet bundles at his groin. Their attention moved with the sheets. We're both naked under the cover. I blush at the memory of last night's events. After the third time, we made it here and did it again before falling asleep. I palmed his chest to break their ogling and stopped him from exiting at the risk of exposing more to their drooling.

"Turn around," I commanded the intrusive ladies, drawing a circle in the air and signalling the movement they should take. Securing the sheet around my breast with my other hand. Eric puts his feet out silently watching on.

"You know, you're not the only one that ever saw him naked," Lia boasted, completing her unwelcoming attitude and rolling her head on her neck. I rolled my eyes.

Ugh!

Sam squinted at her taken aback at me almost as a question, I think. Paula standing between the two slowly raised her hand.

"I haven't, but I want to."

I am astonished by her admission bulging my eyes momentarily. *Really?* Whilst Sam and Lia pivot towards her narrowing their eyes and tilting their heads.

What the... "Then just get out," I yell angrily.

They all turned their backs on us. Eric crawled intentionally over me, being sure I felt his morning glory with a grin and licked his lips. The blood rushes to my cheeks, I folded my lips stifling a grin and he exhales slowly over my face inches from my lips.

Then, he slid his pillow over his front, his back to the ladies and pulled mine from my back covering his behind. Tiptoeing from under the cover, I readjusted the sheet. Eric beams as the sun shines inside the room.

Pecking my lips gently, staying long to brush his tongue on my tight lower lips then clicked his tongue. Creating a loud smacking sound, delayed before leaving for the bathroom. Accidentally dropping a pillow, I think, before shutting the door behind him. On cue, the women turned.

I folded my lips fantasising about the possibilities. Wearily, our clothes are scattered.

They need to leave!

The shower went on. I remembered last night and crossed my legs under the cover. Annoyed, I turned to the waiting irritating women, arguing for them to leave.

"It's not Friday. Why are you here?"

"It's midday." Sam turned her wrist up to view her watch. "… And you're not in the office." Sam says in ambiguity.

"And?" I questioned them, questioning me.

"Plus, there was, a lot of, um, thumping, um, last night," Paula hesitantly spoke her cheeks brightened just as mine did.

Folding my lips in pleasant memory of our activities. Avoiding eye contact, looking down at the sheets cocking my knees up.

I lean into the bedhead. I should not be ashamed!

"Uh, I have a report."

Lia flicked a folder from underneath her crossed arms resting it on the side table before putting her arms up in retreat, shaking her annoying large bangles and crossing them again as if displeased.

I am married to him… I gathered my composure.

"I'm fine ladies." Still bowing… *A better sentence, more words?* I cleared my throat. "Having a late start, worked late. Anything else?"

My stomach stirs suddenly, and I groan. The nauseousness hits me, I gather the saliva in my mouth fisting my lips breathing slowly through my nose. The morning breath taste is making it worse.

"I have requested the initial report from L.D.O. but I haven't heard anything from them," Sam complained, an annoyed alto tone dragging her voice.

"How long ago was this request?" I asked forcing the unfavourable taste down upsetting my stomach more.

"We should have had this already Shana!" She says as a matter-of-fact.

Is she mad at me? She shifted my thinking briefly. "I will look into it."

I ate the words still trying to breathe picking up on a strong odour, possibly Aaliyah's perfume.

"I can go talk to Ms Mall myself," she demands rolling her eyes.

"Uh, can you try asking again…" I direct her elsewhere. "Probably nicely if you didn't before?" I point out her curt ways.

"*I have!* I believe." She gritted at me.

I blink a couple of times at her. *Excuse me?* My eyebrows meet and crinkle. *She is mad…*

Do I care? My subconscious shakes her head. *No!*

"Sharron Mall is off limits, for now. I will call the L.D.O. later to accelerate things, OK?" I try pacifying her but in true Samanther Martinez's response, she rolled her eyes giving me a woman's version of 'fuck you'.

"*Fine!*" Slapping her folder on top of Lia's before turning around and stomping out the door.

She is not fighting me? I noted with a shrug trying to expedite the others' exit, quickly.

"Anything else?"

I swallowed hard after those words as my stomach is doing all sorts of gymnastics lay outs. I try subtly inhaling and exhaling through my nose but it was noisily. So, folded my lips to hold in the excessive spit. *I don't know how long I can hold it in…* The late-night delivery of pepper wings Eric and I had, near my uvula, Paula followed Sam. *Yes!* I celebrate the exit without flak. But Aaliyah lingered as if she was owed an explanation.

Why! "What?" I whined my eyes at her. She stared for a few seconds at me, hard. Then, turned to click her stiletto heels with a huff slamming the door as she exited.

OK… Concerned fractionally, the immediate urge to vomit left with her, and I was right. Examining their confusing bedside manner this morning and concluding, *they are ridiculous.*

Though some part of me is moved by their version of caring, I am baffled by their gesture. This, I guess, is their way of caring or complying. Either way, this is one heck of an alarm. Lia's words however loitered in thought.

Seeing Eric naked.

It played with my mind. She's got a gift for that. I didn't understand her brazen statement: 'You know you're not the only one that ever saw him naked… ' They don't know each other in that intimate way, I don't think.

Ugh! She is such a bitch!

They have been co-workers for nearly twenty years, at least before he got promoted two years ago. Sam's face appeared to be as astonished by that statement as I was. I questioned Aaliyah's claim.

Eric's usually a vault when it comes to tales between Hall and Paul. I hate that their names rhyme and the sound of them together. They have a long history that sits uneasily with me. They have been policing partners for well over fifteen years, their unknown bugs me. I chew at the corners of my bottom lip nerve-racking myself as she probably planned. It could be something so insignificant, that she's blowing up just to whine me up.

It's working!

My subconscious annoyed me and I beat her down slipping on my silk dressing gown. Entering the bathroom, Eric's towel is on his shoulder, as he brushes his teeth. Nothing else, leaving everything hanging out in my view. A second to appreciate the view, I lick my lips, libido awake. He spits rinsing his mouth with words of temptation.

"Do you mind sharing?" His baritone is low and hoarse calling the parts that thump at his voice.

He knows I want to, and I hummed low. "This is déjà vu Hall." Grinning at him twitching in response.

"Fine with me, given the last outcome." He dawdles by the sink and I fully enter, sharing a full fresh smile that sinks the indentations through his dark beard.

"The neighbours complained!" My smile is lecherous reflecting his and he perches the towel on the countertop conjoining the sink slyly. My grin grows.

"That's because you're loud," he whispered and I gasp.

He is getting dangerously close. There's nothing under my silk dressing gown and he knows it. I eye my naked man's head to um, nakedness taking a quick look before returning my eyes to his. I am reminded of Lia's claim to fame.

He reaches to me and releases the knot tied to the front of my gown, slides his hands inside it on my shoulders. Sliding it down my arms and to the floor, my eyes followed its path before returning to his soulful brown eyes.

My once flat torso caught in my peripheral, I shook the thought quick. He leans down, I sucked in the air while his fresh breath blows over my face and he closes the space. Every hair on my body stands to his touch. He draws his face inch by inch and my eyes begin to close but the stupid question popped into my head and came out my mouth.

"Baby, when did Lia see you naked?"

He stilled nearly at my lips, the mood instantly changed.

"Why do you let her mess with you like that?" his tone foul, standing straight before sighing.

Shit! I blinked long to recover. "I don't. Its jus…"

I admonished myself for asking bowing my head and moved from his grasp. Twisting my mouth, ashamed I let those words out. He came to me, clasped my face in his palms, tilting my head, forcing me to look at him. The despair on his face gives me a glimpse of something I almost never see on his face, and he stares blankly as if drenching a dark fixed memory.

"When I thought my family died," he began unexpectedly and shortly, standing straight facing me. I wait but there was silence.

"Oh," my reply was shorter piercing the discomfort between us and filled with disbelief.

"I was beside myself…" he goes on saying carefully turning his eyes away but staring blankly. "… I stopped caring for anything… everything. Aaliyah checked on me… One day whilst in the shower, she walked in…"

"Mistakenly," I pointed out prematurely cutting his explanation and watching him.

"Yeah…" he laughed drily. "… Mistakenly." He became still then his mouth moved. "… she saw me." He exhales long and frustrated, I think.

"So, she never saw you naked before that?"

His eyes are fixed on something on the countertop before he answers quietly and deeply, "No."

"All the years you've been partners, undercover assignments?" I questioned.

"Shana!" He warns playfully, calling my name for me to stop.

Wow! That's the most he's ever revealed of their relationship. Should I push for more?

"All right." I shrug, surrendering for now somewhat reassured he shared this with me, but I couldn't hide the doubt in my voice.

"You don't believe me?" He finally moves looking at me with a small quiver around his lips teasing me with the view of his deep dimples.

"No!" I scoffed honestly without a filter. His face became impassive in a flash. *Shit, he caught that!* Quickly correcting. "Yes," I squeaked, *too high-pitched!* Yelling at myself inwardly for doing that.

"Well to tell you the truth." He reaches for me. "… She screamed."

"Why?" My inner self spits for more honesty fishing. *Would he say more?*

"With all this." He gestured spanning his arms open exposing sculpted arms, muscular pecs, rock abs and his bare body. I gawk in agreement, at his carved structure and well-endowed bits twitching as I tilted my head and hummed in appreciation. "… She was screaming." He imitated my voice mocking, "… Oh yes, baby yes."

"You *are* a ridiculous imitation of a female voice." I rolled my eyes shaking my head at his gull though deserved. He somehow shifted the tone of our conversation and I giggled.

"Yeah." He closed his arms across my back pulling me into him. "… Well, that's a good thing."

Bending to peck my lips softly, my eyes closed, breath shortened. Opening my mouth allowing our tongues to dance as the mirror gathered condensation.

I guess talk time is over.

He moves his warm hands over my left breast cupping, filling his hands and kneading. I smiled, gazing into his brown eyes and my hazels into his. Then, his hand heads south. I inhale sharp. My eyes close, head tilted back inhaling absorbing his caress and pores in tune with his palms. He skimmed my tummy, pausing below my navel, a moment too long. I open my eyes. He notices the curve I have and couldn't resist saying with excitement.

"I know you are."

Sinking my arousal to zero, and my anger to ten. I exhaled exasperated, and frowned moving away from his hands and turning my back to him. *Why?* I ask myself holding either side of the face basin my heart pounded. His statement raises a thousand thoughts and I questioned.

Why?

Mixed emotions wave hit me, too many to focus on one altogether drowning me. We are finally in a good place. *After...* The pain tormented me. *I can't go there.* I turned around my back on the cold ceramic and put my palm up not looking directly at him.

"Stop."

A moment passed between us and I closed my eyes willing the time back into the fog but holding on to the strongest emotion at my throat. "... Don't... just... don't..." Anger wins!

I stomp my feet to the entrance of the shower and swung the glass door open with force, slamming it behind me. The glass walls wobbled with the thrust. I opened the cold water on me.

The truth is, I knew but was scared of what it might mean. I could see and feel my body changing. Dismissing all possible thoughts. Convinced that it was my period-changing cycle. Although, I haven't had one for two months. Eric has been busy with his work after finishing his last case. I'm sure he hadn't noticed. However, knowing Eric's suspicious nature he wouldn't dismiss this, as easily as I did.

CHAPTER TWELVE

The dialogue Eric and I exchanged this morning still bugs me. I hate it. Strolling in after one, carrying a walk of shame across my face. Thankfully, Lia and Sam were not at their desk to witness, my tiptoeing and surveying.

Which one was that again? I try clarifying to myself.

Ugh!

Both of them!

I frown at myself distracted by everything about that man.

He sometimes makes me so mad.

I slinked to my office. The regret circles me. An increasingly more, sore topic, is my husband, Eric Hall.

There is so much to be done.

I have missed nearly the entire morning. I began to worry.

Although it has cooled a fraction in Divinish, the swap of professional choice from court shoes to stilettoes still echoed on the tiles. It is definitely not made for sneaking.

I don't know how Lia does it!

Somehow, I managed to think of that annoying woman again. After I lectured the women the day before, about their lateness and here I am, doing the same damned thing.

I blame Eric!

My inner self agrees.

Their morning invasion of my apartment.

Complaining about the noise, I grinned thinking… and their ogling at my husband! I frown again.

Eric is my husband! I claim him in celebration of our late-night activities and my heartbeat increased. Remembering his hands, and lips. Everything responds to the memory of his touch. I crossed my legs intentionally to ease the wanton that Eric induces, moving across the empty office space.

I should not be ashamed!

I moped.

They had to come in and ruined it.

My nipples pointed through the white polyester shirt. I pulled the navy jacket together forcing the button to close just like the skirt zip this morning.

What is going on with me?

Heaving the chair and sat. The list hasn't shrunk.

Why do I have to do this?

I complain to myself. This secondary task has swamped my desk and deviated me from Sharron Mall, splitting my attention. Then Eric, who surprised me with an impromptu visit has further diverted my thinking.

Eric didn't say anything!

He just watched me leave.

My foul mood grows with the unpicking of our talks.

Which one is that again? Ugh!

Eyeing the pile again with a squint the reports for later below. Luckily though, Aaliyah, Sam and Paula brought their reports to me.

They don't witness my flushing and squirming.

The empty office also aggravates me.

Saves me chasing them tonight!

Flicking the pages of each applicant sitting in one pile. My laptop opened, doing background checks. My diary on the other side split open in view of today's worklist. Adding the interviews for my Thursdays. I cringe.

I should have started on time today!

Yet, Eric and Lia's claim is all I could think of.

'You know you're not the only one that ever saw him naked... ' Her words echo in my mind like an annoying record on a loop.

Don't let her mess with you!

I emailed the director for approvals of the interviews, finished reading through the reports which didn't help much either. I quickly swing by the range for my mandatory weapon training. Squeezed off a couple of rounds, I am still a marksman. The thoughts just won't leave me.

Why does he have to be so stubborn?

To clear my head, I walked. The streets are foreign to me but the scenery of this suburb is a beautiful mixture of buildings, trees and red rocks. One of the few things untouched and ancient in this country. It is fascinating. My laptop sits across my workbag, making an x across my chest. I stroll debating.

We're one ceremony from being legally married.

I should text him.

I searched my pocket for the phone.

No, I don't want to fight!

The ugly thought submerged. The evening is cool. The heatwave has passed and the sun is making its way over the rocks. I walk through the car park, cross the path and up the stairs, to the dreaded door. I breathe deep, only realising I am here. Turning the key with disinclination, my palms sweat turning the knob. The apartment was dark and empty.

Where is he?

I flicked on the light with a sigh, closing it behind me. Slump my bag onto the sofa. Searching in the only other room, the bathroom. Eric went missing. Though slightly relieved, I am also worried.

His coping mechanism is not what we need right now. The empty room reminds me of my loneliness.

Should I call him?

I cowered once again. I tried his mobile, straight to voicemail. Then texted angrily.

Seizing the moment huh!

I am instantly maddened. I frowned at the phone. Resting it at the bedside then put my gun into the vault and began undressing.

Where could he have gone?

His travel bag was on the floor, I kicked it. Things were still around the apartment. I moved it to the wardrobe and began tidying. The laptop stared at me, and I cannot resist being prepared.

I convinced myself.

Finding a comfortable spot on the sofa, snacking on a turkey sandwich. My stomach wouldn't settle. I was still starving. The risk of puking everywhere far outweighed the need for food.

What is it with the food here?

I taxed my brain.

Did I buy any antacids?

The thought of leaving the apartment at nine was not a pleasant one.

A quick shower may help.

Popping on my shorts and vest and got into bed, hoping it'll pass.

****

Frightened by Eric's weight on the bed, I had fallen asleep. Blinking to adjust, my heart drums through my chest. Eric crawled under the covers, letting the cold air under the sheet.

His cold limbs tangling with mine. He is undressed and hovered over me. Tugging the sheets over him. I swallowed hard unable to see him through the dark. He's pinned me, propped on his forearms, digging his hardened erection restrained by the boxers, enfolding his cold hands around me.

"E-Eric."

I recoil, at his hands greedily groping my body, and tugging at my shorts. My heartbeat hasn't slowed to his aggression. I can't move. A drunken snicker breathing his scotch breath over my face, faltered by his coping.

Ugh! "E-Eric," I called his attention, reminding myself that it is him and no one else. It smells like him, but more, something I don't recognise. And the alcohol rich breath, turned my stomach sour.

I'm going to be sick!

I held my breath. Flush on his elbows, he played with the tiny buttons on the sleep vest. Slurping inaudibly, as his breath blew across my face. He giggles. Closing his face for a kiss. I whinge. He paused, blinking at my reaction. My body shook in fear, breathing shallowly.

"Eric!" I whimper.

He does it again. I asked, "Have you been drinking?" The obvious leaves me.

He eases off, freeing my hands. I shield my mouth and nose, trying not to breathe. He sighs deep, kneeling with me between his legs. Taking the covers off us, and waits two seconds. He leans over me again. Tugging from the hem of my vest up exposing my belly. I quailed underneath my palm blocking my nose and mouth.

"Please… The smell…"

It's the strong fragrance, alcohol and something else… I don't recognise it.

He groans loudly. Then, shrugs the covers off the bed. I shudder, closing my eyes. I still, holding my breath as my heart increased beats anticipating his next action.

His footsteps stomped away. I heard him, slapped the light switch. The light beamed through the shape of the door, into the apartment. I heard him brushing hard, spitting and gaggling loudly. The loud click. The light came off. He marched back to the bed.

"Happy!"

His baritone echoed in the dark. Then, he clambers over me into bed. My disposition is unchanged as I acquiesce to his mood. He pulled the covers over us, turn his back and within moments, fell asleep. I go stiff next to him, while he is snoring. Wary that his memory would be lost to what he has done tonight, fuelled by his coping and the hurt he has exposed me to.

****

The sizzling and odours filled my nose. Pancakes and eggs, I think woke me. Stirring, I turned towards fragrances in the kitchen. Eric stood in navy-blue boxers and a white vest, cooking. With a tea towel over his shoulder, he's holding the pan with one hand and the spatula with the other.

His white vest was stained with splatters of batter. His concentration zeroed in on his flipping skills. He's so domesticated that sometimes I forget. He's done it by shaking the pan. Suddenly, he turns and sees me staring at the corner of his view. I startle at his brown eyes catching my gaping. I still as my heart fluttered. He moved the pan off the electric hob and comes towards me. I look away fiddling with the sheets.

"Are you hungry?" His baritone hits me, tone impassive. He sits on the edge near my breasts I bowed, my view limited to his dark blue boxers.

"I'm OK."

My voice timid crackled from waking. I brace myself for his mood.

"Maybe you can, after a shower?"

His words are soft but commanding. I am sure it's a directive. I folded my lips.

"Sure." I obey scarcely audible fleeing to the other side of the bed, near the wall. Crawling from under the sheet, I placed my feet on the floor circling the bed.

I don't want to fight...

I just want to go to work...

I repeated in my head. I ambled between the bed foot and the chest of draws. Around the passageway, I pass him through the bathroom doors. My head is in view of the floor. Swiftly making my way into the bathroom for a shower. He said nothing. I undressed in the bathroom jumping into the shower. I heard him moving.

Please don't come in here!

He is inside here stirring. The toilet seat went up and I hear him peeing.

What is he doing?

He washed his hands and flushed. I rolled my eyes at his manners. I see his shadow through the frosted glass hovering at the shower door. I waited a few minutes, and his shadow disappeared.

I turned off the shower and came out. Began to straighten my hair and moisturise my skin. Wishing I took some underwear when I came in.

I exited wearing my towel. Opening the wardrobe doors blocking his view, dressing quickly. Slipping on my underwear, bra, grey trousers and white cotton shirt.

Hanging the jacket on the hanger on the door. I closed it and there he was. Standing with a plate of pancakes and scrambled eggs. I folded my lips, blinking hard as I know he will not accept 'no' for an answer.

"Can you leave it on the breakfast bar? I am looking for shoes." I try diverting his focus. He said nothing, moving with the plate and eyeing me.

I don't want to fight…

I just want to go to work…

I repeated again. Taking my court shoes in my hands, moving to the stools for my meal. He is still silent. Only his eyes were fixed on my movements. A tense disposition. It is awkward and unnerving.

He has set my plate on a placemat and a fork on a napkin. The pancake is evenly brown and in a perfect circle. At the side, a spiral of syrup and the eggs fluffed. Placing a fork on my plate, he turned to tidying the kitchen.

The eggs were fluffy and salted perfectly. It melted in my mouth. He poured me a cup of tea. I am eating my breakfast silently. He visibly relaxed, placed the tea towel away, sauntering to the toilet again. When I heard the shower go on it was my signal to leave.

CHAPTER THIRTEEN

It was a long, demanding day. Exactly what I needed to forget the distracting Eric Hall. The interviews were the first finishing at lunch. Then the daily reports. I went through the applications and felt only one of them was suitable to take up the position as my personal assistant and junior agent.

I sent a long proposition to her. Sarah Noel was local, eager, and frank with experience. All the prospects were vetted before they were sent to me, I think. So I sent the request to the director for approval. After lunch, I had the approval to hire immediately. It was strange but I didn't question my luck. Doing victory dances in my head, I called her to start the next day.

I can't wait to get rid of this infamous 'to-do' list!

There was too much paperwork overseeing this team, so I put it away for my assistant tomorrow, with the excess time, I rented a car and pulled out the file for Sharron Mall. Finally, I had time to put real work into this investigation. I took the time to read through some of the pieces the team put together so far. I scan through Sam's report. She is still stuck at the interview. I send a request again for this piece of evidence from the L.D.O. if it exists.

I did warn her about her coot ways.

Peeping through the office window, Sam and Aaliyah had left already. It was after five. All other pre-work paperwork was sent to my new personal assistant's email which I even had time left over to set up. My report was prepared for the meeting at the end of the week. I grinned, pleased again.

I should be leaving… on time today!

Unsure if Eric's mood had improved, I would be avoiding an early return to my apartment.

Plus, I am a bit peckish.

This morning, I'm sure was a version of an apology. He really scared me last night. I packed my things away ready to leave the office.

Does he even remember what he did?

I shook the thought, checking my phone. He hasn't called or texted. Neither did I...

I whined at myself making my way through the halls and turning the lights off. I strolled down to the town in search of food. Downstairs, the office, the store has weird meat and strange sandwiches on display. My stomach churned and I walked out as quickly as I went in.

Like Ceda, there were vending vans and one with hotdogs. Recalling many memories of hotdogs when I was in training, ones with Eric and others with... I feel home sick. I miss the food, and my stomach agrees. I miss my friends and I miss... him. Finding my memory drifting to training. The night we overlooked the city of Ceda when Sam miraculously reappeared. It was the first time we shared an in-depth talk.

Would Eric ever have one of those about Aaliyah? A shiver went through me and I am unsure if I would want to know.

Changing directions of my thoughts towards ideas of tomorrow's workload and particularly, Sharron Mall. I feel drawn to her somehow. Her story and everything about her interest me. She lived most of her life here, in Divinish. I was especially curious since her father mentioned their religion. This was the current and most controversial topic in parliament these days.

Did they actually take a statement from her?

The sunshine dimmed and a chilly breeze whooshed. Suddenly, I am aware of my surroundings.

Crap! I left the car at the office, I sighed, thinking I should turn around.

Wait, where am I?

I'm gobsmacked, gazing at the tall glasses shining in the afternoon's sunset. I am at the Divinish General Hospital standing on the sidewalk measuring the building cluelessly.

How did I get here?

Apprehensive of the next right move I stare. My feet have betrayed me, the journey was vague, my appetite was almost gone and my stomach clenched.

What am I doing here?

An unexplained pull moves me towards the building. I have no control over my limbs. The hospital was livelier than before. More people moving in and out.

It must be visiting time.

Going past reception, the bustling quieted or my ears were blocked. An unfamiliar worrying overcame me. I gape for a sight of the receptionist. My feet glided me, up the elevators, to the ward which had been staffed not as before. Everyone's busy with their own world. I can't stop myself. There wasn't anyone to stop me.

There wasn't any problem with the receptionist this time.

I smirk to myself.

The once lonely dampness of this place felt filled. I peeked from the hallway leaning against the wall. A doctor is examining Sharron Mall. She is receptive moving to his request. Curious about her life, it had been a week, since I saw her.

She isn't as covered with bandages, and not as swollen but her face is still colourful from bruises. Her eyes weren't puffy but still covered in dark, red and pink blotches. She wore the hospital gown with a clip on her finger and strung by machinery. Her wrist was still wrapped and seemed clean. She gave a final nod as the doctor left.

The middle-aged doctor walked right past me. A patient assistant brought her a tray with food. She sat up. Her curly hair puffed out. The wrappings around her head were replaced with a plaster holding the cut on the left side of her forehead. She had a wheeled table over her lap while she ate supper.

Some of her hair near the wound on her head was shaved. I could see stubble. Oddly, she appeared physically intact for such a horrible fate. My mind strayed from my near miss the night Eric and I met. I shudder, as this could have been me.

Is that what's pulling me to her? I asked myself, sensing this is a bad idea, I shook my head, ready to leave. Our eyes meet.

Shit! I cursed with a palpitation.

Her indistinct gaze stuck on me and I am caught like a child's hand in a cookie jar. I have shown up twice in a few days and by my creepy inspection of her eating and being examined by the doctor it appears to

114

be stalking her. I freeze and moisture grew on my palms. I am compelled to do something but at this moment, I am confused about the lines of professionalism.

Maybe if we talked, my curiosity would be satisfied and I could move on.

I swallowed hard, convincing myself not to become obsessed with her.

A conversation wouldn't hurt.

I shakingly shifted and her eyes remain, keeping my heart rate high. Sharron's alert and her hazels are glued to mine. I came off the wall walked to the doorway, and knocked before walking through.

"Miss Mall," I called her as I cautiously step towards her and my heart raced, gathering additional heat in the already warm room. "... I am Special Agent Davis-Hall, I visited you a couple of days ago," I explained, shifting my jacket to display the brass shield that shifted my purpose slightly.

"Yes, I know you."

She croaks, piercing her hazels at me with an enthusiastic undertone in her voice, the pain seems to be gone. The medicine the doctor gave to her is working. The emotions rise subtly, sorrow, anxiety, shame, it's not quite choking me but it's there, I sense it from her. Some blotches in her eyes, I guess from her trauma. She follows me with her eyes.

I feel it.

I shrugged inwardly, taking hold of my thoughts. Spinning my wedding ring unconsciously.

Eric.

His name shifts my focus.

"Are you up to speaking today?"

Fully into her room, I found my place at the foot of her bed where we can both look at each other without her straining or agitating her wounds.

Should I embrace her? A crazy thought enters my head. I flinch, eyeing her.

"I am. Thanks."

Her mouth quivers a slightly painful smile. Clumsily putting her cutlery on the empty plate. She looks up at me and I am caught again, pinned by her eyes. Curious or anticipation? I walked next to the bed nodding and slid the table aside.

I should stop the foolish nodding like a buffoon.

I try impassively rebuking my thoughts.

"How do you feel today?"

"Good," She instantly answers.

"In any pain?" *What am I? Her doctor?* My expression shifts slightly, raking in anxiousness.

"The pain medication works." She is pleasant.

I nod again then rolled my eyes at myself inwardly, spotting a chair.

"I am going to ask you about your attack, is that OK with you?"

She nodded.

"Some of the questions would be difficult. A bit intrusive but please understand that I have to," I repeat the words that Eric said to me, hearing his voice echoing in memory. "… If at any time you don't feel you want to continue, we can stop. Do you understand?"

I dragged the chair from the top of the bed to the bottom. Settling in the seat, unsure if I should continue.

"Yes," her soft consent is confident and clear, ready, as I wasn't.

I slid my workbag onto my lap and fished a push point ballpoint pen and writing pad, using the bag as a prop to write.

"Good, I need to know if you spoke to any police officers." I listened, ready to write so I could point Sam in the right direction. She hesitates.

"Yes." I looked up and her eyes are empty watching through me, "… Ah, um, a detective from Shadeyah." Her voice cracked, and then she cleared her throat. I tilted my head at her to catch her eyes.

"Do you remember his or her name?"

That was a long shot seeing the trauma she has been through physically.

"I'm, I'm sorry, no!" she shook her head quickly saying softly.

Expected but. "Did he or she leave a card?" They should at least do that.

"No." She surprised me.

What officer would not leave his card? She may have been confused. I excuse them both. But…

"OK, I will look into that," saying my thoughts aloud. I searched my bag after writing almost ready to begin. My hands landed on exactly what I needed. "… I am going to record our conversation as my penmanship will not keep up with your words."

My hazels met hers. She chuckled and then winced from the pain. I felt the sharp tug in my torso. I tried not to show any expression. I placed the recording device in my hand, pointing it at her with my left hand. With my right, I wrote the question.

"Can you tell me what happened to you, anything you can remember?"

She frowned at the bandages around her wrists and stuttered, "I-I…"

"Please." I stopped her. "… I'm not in a hurry. It's OK… Please… take your time."

I drew the chair closer to her head. She inhaled deeply and became tense. She exhaled deeply and hard blowing some torment away, I think.

"I left work early. I had a falling out with my boss, stormed out assuming I was fired."

I cut her short. "Where do you work?"

"I am a bartender at Jonopus part-time. I drove to the grocery picked up a few things then went home." Her eyes were dark, staring down at the sheets.

"Do you know what time that was?"

"I don't know, could be around ten…" She shrugged her shoulders and clasped the sheet in a fist on her lap. "… I parked outside my apartment. I was about to take the things out of the car… there was a motorbike parked in my neighbour's parking."

"Do you remember what kind of motorbike?"

"No!" She was a bit petulant. "… I remembered because I thought that was a bit strange. But my neighbour is a strange man, so I didn't give it much thought at first. I was still sitting in my car when someone knocked on my window with his riding gloves." Tears flowed down her cheeks.

"Can you describe him?"

"It, it was dark… I, I smiled thinking of something sassy to tell him."

She smirked at first, looking at me, suddenly her eyes darken, her face transformed and she bowed her head. Wrapping the sheet round her finger, from one hand to the other, her eyes grew glossy, red and full, her voice cracked almost apologetic and soft,

"… Then he punched through the window breaking it. I was pulled through the window and I remembered being on the ground."

She's in full sobs. I moved to sit at her foot. Rubbing her shin, my head tilted towards the door, away from her view, choking the rising sadness, with folded lips. Resisting the urge to hug her and comfort her beyond the physical contact that I'd already crossed.

My heart galloped and my saliva thickened, there are no words that could be of comfort.

"It's OK!" I said to her. "It's OK!" I repeated to myself. "… Take your time," my voice cracked as I reassured both of us.

Hold it together Shana.

I cleared my throat, clearing the fragments of the breaking ball, hinting for both of us to continue. A small knot and curve around my lips with a cleansing breath, she lifted her head her eyes going to the right as she recalled. Her tears were constant, streaming without effort down her rosy cheeks beneath her twangy tone.

"He, he covered my mouth with something." Her hand went up to her mouth mimicking but then dropped. "… I woke up with something covering my head. I-I couldn't breathe." She strained a harsh breath in. "… It-it was dark, c-cold and I felt something, t-tied around my a-a-arms and l-legs opened. I was on a hard surface naked. I c-couldn't see anyone. They were speaking a strange language. I-was, just foggy. I couldn't focus. I-I-I just felt them t-touching."

Her face streamed with tears. Pausing the recorder was the best choice. I gave her a moment to sob and me a moment to compose. She coughs loudly as her mouth gathered spit. Her face distended with tears. The moisture from her nose runs into her mouth without a reaction from her.

I feel it coming again. A waver of her agony, humiliation and distress penetrated me shifting my professional stance. Unable to stop, she covered her face with both her hands. So, did I, for a second, swiping whatever this emotion may be, then it slowed but did not stop.

I shift away from her, breaking contact, resting the recorder on the bed for a moment. Fetching a packet of tissues from my handbag, gave her one, and held another in my hands. Turning away I breathe shallowly.

"It's OK," assuring us both.

My nose flared.

Don't Shana! I told myself raking in whatever control I could find, reciting the one thing that raked me in. Taking a slow, deep breath with a long blink.

Ten, nine, eight, seven, six, five, four, three, two, one.

I counted to calm down.

Exhaling unhurried through my mouth. My heartbeat slowed and my thoughts cleared, the emotions subsided, pulling back to where they came from.

We both calmed.

Minutes passed.

I turned to her, my blue eyes meet her now green.

It changed.

I am partly curious but dismissing it as the lighting.

Finish this, Shana!

I cautioned myself taking another breath, and holding the recorder again.

"... It's really important that you tell me everything you remembered even if it may be embarrassing or silly, any little detail just might be useful."

Pressing record again, she covered her mouth as if it would help her change the repugnant events she lived. Squeezing her eyes for a moment glimpsing the monitors her voice broken husky and hoarse.

"After a while, I stopped feeling anything, but being wet as if I was lying in some sort of liquid... I was in and out of consciousness. When I came to it again, I remembered being taken out of my car and then waking up in the hospital."

Her voice lingered in the room louder than the chiming of the equipment she was hooked up to. I looked at her sensing something beneath and the build of her emotions crashed. I clicked the tape to stop. Her eyes flow dripping fluently from her face to the bed. It wouldn't stop.

I couldn't swallow, my insides clenched, disgusted by the events and growing empathy for her.

I am not sure how long I could keep an impassive face. My subconscious warned as the crash of an emotion shivered through me.

"If there's anything more you remember please." My voice was rusty as my insides began to crack. I gave her my card. "… Call me."

My feet shook struggling to leave with an upright posture but I managed.

Once out of her sight, I brace on the wall. My legs weaken. The snack surfaced to my throat. Blocking my mouth, I retreat for the closest toilet letting all my meals out.

CHAPTER FOURTEEN

Incapable of recalling my journey to the apartment, I stood at the door. My chest was tight, and my head spun while I was searching my pockets for the keys. The words said, still echoes in my ears, increasing the pain flowing to my head. Overwhelmed by the gruesome detail of Sharron Mall's attack straight from her mouth.

It was more than I imagined.

More than I can stand.

The more I thought about it the more I felt it.

The overpowering sensation of her emotions hang in my memory and tingled through every fibre of myself. My skin crawled from the description and bile rose remembering the act. It has shaken me to the core.

Scared, I unlocked the door, entering quickly, shutting it, hoping the barrier would seal it. The noise and the feeling of helplessness on Sharron's behalf. With my back up against the door, hyperventilating, I summarised my feelings by counting down from ten.

Ten, nine, eight, seven, six, five, four, three, two, one.

The dirty words whispered in my ear as I listen in the quiet. I couldn't drown her out even after covering my ears.

Her emotion collapses me to the ground.

Tears came, gushing out of me, paralysed by the emotions, hearing Sharron's aching voice again. My breathing increased in gusts and shook my body wallowing in pain that I wasn't sure was mine. I exhaled sniffling once more, wiping the liquids from my face and nose with the back of my hand, and taking a deep breath again.

I closed my eyes counting once more. Legs stretched out breathing harshly and then, I saw his shoes at the doors of the wardrobe.

A fraction of comfort, only now he is missing. Both pleased and saddened by Eric's absence, I try thinking of him as a distraction; he usually is.

Where has he disappeared?

Straying back to last night's experience, I am shaken again. He has never made me scared of his touch, scared of his drinking or scared that he could become violent. I try to sway my focus from the latter.

Why was he drunk anyway?

The question only raises suspicions.

The answer scares me referencing experience.

Is he hiding something?

Can he be scared of something?

Eric is never scared.

The questions and some answers came flooding ebbing emotions that were never mine. The discomfort of the hardwood and realisation of my present disposition came.

You can't stay here all night!

I screamed at myself. Scraping from the floors, I slump the bags on the sofa, stripping from there to the showers. Washing away what is left of this feeling. I clean every part I believed was touched by that monster. Part of me was brought back to that night Eric and I met. His blue eyes haunting and I am forced to remind myself of the outcome of another. The tears banked again.

How could I believe I was over that?

… And last night…

I began crying, putting my face under the water. Then without thinking my head went under as my body shakes in fear. The warm water caresses my scalp, falling over my face, the drips hiding my crying. The silky dark locks bounce into barrels and the frizz begins.

It is time to get out.

Changed into a light blue camisole and cotton shorts, I lay in bed, restless. Each time I closed my eyes, I see him, Vincent Cage, what he did to me and how much he has taken from my life. My throat tightens and begins to work, and my face crinkles.

I covered my face with my hands. The first memory I have, is seeing his light-blue gaze coming towards me, his cold hand on my exposed ass and the zipping sound after he's exposed me. I jolted from a nod for the last time sitting up. Inside I clench in shiver and disgust shaking my head.

I need to stop this!

The open space of this apartment reflects me. There is no place I can go in this hot and dusty county for comfort or normalcy. All my friends are several hours away, the silence is eerie. Stomping onto the sofa, I got my phone from my workbag and began scrolling. Sighing at the lack of calls from him, I refused to cave. Phoning my voice of reason and comfort.

"Hel-lo," she answers in a singsong tone warming me alone from sound other than my breathing. More than five hundred miles between us and her voice gives me hope, but I try masking the residual emotions and reservations. Perceptive about how well she knows me.

"H-hey Liz." My voice is still broken but thankful for her amenity.

"Shana?" she questions with a pause.

A tone that comes with layers.

I cleared my throat, exhaling, bracing for her quarrelsome nature fully aware she has picked up on my wavery tone.

"Yes, um, Liz…"

"Dani's fine," she huffs argumentatively.

Shit forgot about her.

Picking another estranged topic, "… Your first call since you've landed, you call to check up on Danielle," she argues.

Shit. How long has she been there?

Bad mum!

My inner self wags a finger teasing me with the one word, Danielle calls me with the blessing of her father but it annoys me. Elizabeth successfully brought me back to my reality only the way she always does.

"I *can* look after my baby sister." She sings. "… Besides, good practice," she mumbled an afterthought, I believe.

Practice?

I scrunch my face, holding the phone away from my ears to be sure I dialled the right best friend. Elizabeth Martinez moved across my phone and I squint pulling it back to my ear.

Ugh!

What for…

Assured confusingly, I addressed the part that she will harp on about.

"I know you can Liz." I acknowledge their relationship, grateful for what it is. "... Thanks for..."

"Don't be ridiculous." She cuts me and I paused delaying.

"Can I talk to her?"

I stay there, taking in the welcomed heated conversation we usually share and not the fact that I have been crying for the past hour after an interview with a victim similar to my case. Eric is missing. Possibly drunk and hiding something, I wallow in trust issues.

"It's five past ten, no!" Her tone was assertive, plopping me back to the conversation. "... She's asleep."

She carries on and her tone suggests she's gearing up for an argument. Once she latches onto a topic she stays there. Pleased and displeased about her voice filling the apartment, I follow her lead, refocusing on the child rather than the parents.

"How is she getting along?"

You only just remembered her, and that's what you're asking?

My subconscious reared her ugly head. I am mortified slapping my forehead, exasperated at her. Elizabeth takes a deep breath and I squint bracing for her voice to be elevated on the other end.

"Fine," she says level and short.

Disappointing.

There was a lingered pause.

It's coming...

"... What's wrong?"

Only able to be diverted twice, her direct personality is what makes her a great reporter, friend and the only one besides Eric who can see right through me.

Shit! I think, panicking.

I cannot tell her about the case or how it made me feel.

I question if that fear was actually mine as it is completely gone after a few words with Liz.

I am definitely not going to speak about Eric's drunken moment last night as I don't quite understand it.

Shaking my head at that thought I edit my words to her.

Half-truth!

"Uh, work… rough night." I was exasperated, vaguely fully aware she can if she wanted to pick my mouth. "… I miss you." That was all true.

"Umm." Liz hums with a pause.

The other half of my concern is Eric. Elizabeth always senses the disharmony and usually calls me out on it. She has a strange love-hate relationship with Eric and they both annoy me with their constant banter. I know her, she will soon ask the question that would force me to confess. "… That heavy breathing sounds like it's about Eric?"

I exhaled loud rolling my eyes.

Why can't she just… "*No!* We're good," I squeak the lie squeezing it out my throat. *My pitch was a bit too high.* "… Good," I grunt clearing my throat again. *Now too low.*

"Really? Well, where is he?"

The door handle moved and the door shook. My eyes popped and my heart skipped a beat. I cannot remember if I locked it. Keeping quiet and assessing.

My weapon is in the vault.

I noted frightened, tilted to hide behind the couch. It opened.

"Hi."

Eric entered, twisting his head eyeing my odd behaviour and closed the door. Throwing his keys on the side table near the door. I shift to the single chair, masking my actions. He flowed through holding two bags in one hand.

Two white carrier bags encasing a brown paper bag cried when he bent over and kissed my forehead as I leaned back the phone at my ear. Liz's rants are ignored by this beautiful, distracting man. I smile drinking in his fit form and straight white smile.

I can smell the…

Chinese…

The odour blessed my nostrils and salivates my tongue.

"He went out for dinner," I boasted. My eyes are filled with appreciating his telltale muscles under the light T-shirt.

He laid the bags on the countertops, mouthing the question, 'Liz'?

I nodded and he went into the bathroom. I hear his curses, loud from the bathroom. Turning in that direction, I blinked, confused and heard a groan from her.

Ugh!

"Is that him?"

Shit! She questions and I need to get her off the phone, fast.

"Yes, Liz," I say flatly.

"Does he need my foot to make a connection with a lower part of his body?"

Why is she so...

"No, Liz!" I grunt at her and she said nothing for a while.

"All right Shana..." she concedes but not hiding the doubt in her tone. "... But we need to talk, hopefully soon."

I circled my optics at the phone, hating that she knows me to the core.

"Yea sure." I ended the call with a wagged head at her accurate assumption, but become distracted by my husband's return from the bathroom.

His jeans are removed, his naked chest and he's gliding through the kitchen. His shorts were tight, defining all the right sculpted places, by the hips and between his thighs. His offensive white socks are tall and have a grin.

"Good night," I greeted him with my full attention flushed, gauging his mood.

"Hungry?"

He grins wolfish, with the suggestion that isn't missed. I fully agree, sucking on my lips. Unpacking the bags and retrieving plates from the cupboards, he moves into the tiny kitchen sightly raised on a wooden platform. His feet with no sound padded from the offensive white socks.

"I could eat," I added to the unsaid conversation filling my eyes with his form. My body hummed for his touch missed by the days of the separation for work.

You, on that plate... yum!

My thoughts send blood tingling to one place as my nipples are visible below the camisole. I sauntered to the bar stool squeezing my thighs as they cross in the short stride to sit, excited to see what he's got and knowing what is below.

Anxious to touch him, I perch on the stool, waiting to see which way is up for him today. My saliva thickens thinking of feeding both appetites. I placed my chin in my palm and elbow on the counter taking in the view of Eric Hall's physique, shirtless, the way I like.

"Great, because I got something…"

He trailed coming next to me, fidgeting through a tall brown paper bag, hiding something behind his back.

A surprise! I beam inside.

"… Now, I don't want you to take this too seriously…" His eyes gleam with the words but the tension in his shoulders holding whatever he hides behind him.

"OK…" I am sceptical and nod with a small smile.

He exhaled and slapped a rectangular box on the countertop, covering it with his huge hand. I squint, my mood shifting.

I hope it's not…

He moves his hand, a pregnancy test. Sitting up quickly at the sight, my hands fell on my lap. He's still wearing a smile, mine's dim. Squinting hard at him, I boil inside. The urge to slap the grin off his face grows.

"Are you trying to be offensive, or sarcastic?" Words fail me.

I cannot understand what would lead him to this. His face grew grim, he steps back putting his palm up with a false surrender.

He knows I am on the pill… Reasoning interrupts and I shake doubt … *mostly.*

His tone deepens and becomes rough when his hands met his hips. "Are you serious?"

My eyes widened and my mouth slacked from his astonishment.

"Your clothes have vomit all over them, Shana."

He is considerably louder narrowing his eyes at me, shocking me.

"Were you going through the dirty laundry?" I interrogate his source, defending his possible invasion.

"It smells in there!" He pointed to the toilet door.

Does it? I vaguely remember the thought but not the action. I bowed my head avoiding his gleam in case it is true.

"… You have been sick, every day I have been here. And your mood…" He paused and my mouth opened again. "… I don't know which way is up any more."

The reference to the roller coaster has my head light and I am suddenly unwell, but I maintain my position.

"*My* mood!"

I gasped pointing at myself matching his volume hopping out of the bar stool and chasing to the balcony. I need fresh air.

"What!" he says wounded, but I don't care. "… Take the test!" he chases me grabbing my arm.

"Let. Go."

My voice is soft my eyes piercing his handling me. He shows retreat removing his hand but stands to block my way. I stopped and measured him with my eyes, from toes stopping at his face.

"Thank you. Move." I grunt.

"No." His refused unapologetically blocking my way.

"Move please." I try manners but went up a decibel, and the contents of my stomach bob at my throat.

"Why?" He gets louder.

"I need fresh air." I grind the words through my teeth, locking the sickness if it were to come into my mouth. I filled my mouth with air gagging as the food climbs up my throat.

"Because you want to throw up again?"

My stare intensified. "*No!*" I defend, *yes*… I squirm inside.

"Then why?"

"Ugh, I don't have the energy to fight Eric," I say strong, *that too*… My inner thoughts fought my outer actions.

"Then, take the test, prove me wrong."

What?

I squint at him in disbelief at the words exiting his mouth. Anger floods every muscle and I tense, crossing my arms tight across my body.

Prove him wrong?

Taking the test would not prove me wrong or him right.

There was nothing to prove.

Positive or negative. There are no winners.

It is not for my benefit, only his.

128

"What then?" I argue. "… If it's negative, are you going to fall into another self-pity phase or has that already begun by evidence of your drinking last night?"

His mouth dropped, and I see the wound caused by my words the second they left me in anger.

Shit! Filter! My inner thoughts warned. My hand met my mouth too late.

Fuck!

… Low blow, shouldn't have gone there…

"I-I'm s-sorry Eric," immediately I apologised shaking my fist at myself inwardly holding myself tighter.

He blinked long and the bones along his jaw worked even through his unshaven beard. His muscles taunt, flexing from his shoulders, tightening down his body. All his abs became deliciously defined, casting shadows on his evenly brown form. I reached for him, but he stepped back and his hands went up away from my grasp.

Shit!

Working his jaw, a second time, his eyes opened lit with rage.

"Fucking take the test, Shana! Or so help me, the next time you are sick, you are going to the hospital. *And I will* call your directors."

Eric growled his words hanging long in the apartment with his eyes blazing flames at me. I sucked in air loudly, eyes widened at him and my mouth fell open with a gasp.

"I can't believe you just said that Eric!"

His lips tightened and he breathed a pant as he eyes my actions. With anger, I pivot a one-eighty, and swipe the box from the countertop. Stormed into the bathroom and slammed the door behind me. Propping behind the door, swallowing my grief, my nose pulsing and my face transformed. The sobs fled louder than expected.

Panic fills me. He threatened my career. My heart broke and what-ifs spread before me. Then my subconscious sang.

Shouldn't have said that!

For a few minutes, I let my frustrations out and all other sediments of the emotional evening seeped out with it. Then the odours of my undigested meals filled the room and stank.

He's right, it does reek in here.

With a silent protest, I walked to the toilet, swept my underwear and shorts off, took the test out, throwing the box on the floor. Holding it up, I pull off the cap positioning it between my legs as I sat on the toilet releasing my filled bladder.

What if I'm not, is he going to continue to drop hints of babies again?

The thought annoys me.

Do I even want kids?

Am I ready now?

Humm, not that we've been safe by any measure…

I reminded myself.

Shit, shit, shit!

What if I am? I frightened myself.

Would he be happy?

Would I be happy?

What about my career?

This sucks!

I begin to unravel then, got some pee on my hand.

Eww.

Shaking the excess pee off my hands, I examined the used test.

… Is this supposed to be soggy?

This is disgusting!

Resting it on the floor next to the toilet for a moment. I got some toilet paper to wipe. Dressing first, then returned the cap and place it on the sink top. Washed my hands and wait a few minutes arms crossed leaning against the sink. I got bored so, I read the instructions. Afterwards tossing that into the bin noting I should have done that first.

I saw my shirt peeking through the top of the laundry basket. The front of my shirt has red stains as if I vomited down my chest and reeked. After the disturbing interview, I was sure I made it to the bathroom. But there are some moments blanked from my memory, not that that by any means is unusual for me, it has increased in frequency.

I may have to throw this blouse.

I gagged moving it fully into the basket.

How long should this take?

There was no sound outside the door. I put my ear up against it. Eric was rather quiet outside.

I wonder if he left.

Wishful thinking, a bit pleasing but felt wrong. I turned the handle and gently pushed the door cautiously looking out.

"And…"

He startled and irritated me at the same time. Standing at the door his face plastered with a white grin. I fluttered my gape at him, confidently strolled to the bed and sat. Crossing my arms emphasising my pout.

He wagged his head at my deportment then, bolting into the bathroom with delight in his eyes. No longer nervous about the 'what ifs' but eager to get this part over with, I restrain dwelling hearing his pattering in the bathroom. Before long I heard a groan from the bathroom.

"Aw, Shana…" He's fretting.

"What now?" I whined shouting aloud. *What, did I do wrong this time?*

"You peed all over the test," he continued his complaint, baffling me, walking out the door with the urine-dowsed, plastic rectangular test in his hand his eyes bulging in contempt.

"Isn't that what I'm supposed to do?" I shrug sitting on the bed.

"Ugh, you're supposed to, for a few seconds. Now, the test is inconclusive."

I rolled my eyes not seeing an issue. "So?"

"It *means* we don't know."

I lay back on the bed sighing loud but his tone is one of complaining and defeat. The sound makes me burst into laughter. For a brief moment his ego bruised then he joined me in giggles.

CHAPTER FIFTEEN

The apartment phone ringing woke me, it's morning. After laughing for a few minutes, Eric turned to me, and kissed me. One thing led to the other and after the third time, we must have fallen asleep. Smiling at his stamina, watching his face crinkle from the ringing, he is beautiful. I groaned, reaching for my phone and glanced at it.

Crap!

Twenty-three past midday, eight missed calls. My eyes widened. I overslept… again! There was roughly an hour before my meeting.

"Shit!" I voiced my irritancy.

Two days in a row?

Because of him!

Sated and embarrassed, I scolded myself jumping off the bed as the apartment phone went off again.

"… Would you get that for me?" instructing Eric, I rushed into the bathroom, who jumped just as I have. It was Friday, the meeting was finally here. I missed the morning.

Sarah's orientation. Shit!

I skipped in and out of the shower in a short amount of time worried about the possible consequences of missing that appointment.

Wrapped in a towel after the shower, I stand at the bathroom sink glancing at my natural hair. Silked and curled in barrels over my head, gaining me a few inches from the volume.

Not a good day to have wet my hair the night before. I scold myself for the error.

It's going to take forever to straighten out!

I stood in the mirror moaning at myself.

Panicked, I grabbed some conditioner and a brush beginning the tiring task. Working around my head, brushing smooth my hair, leaving the knots on the inside and holding it tight into a lumpy bunny-tail.

This will have to do!

I fished from the basket with hair products, for a hair bobble to calm the shoulder-length mane on my head. Rolling it into a large curly, lumpy bun breathing out from the task. Eric's voice mumbled through the doors. His baritone cracking ever so often, whispers in an argument.

Is he still on the phone?

I couldn't distinguish anything. I ceased all movement and crept to the door concentrating on his voice. Still, no clear words.

Who is he talking to?

I cracked the door.

"Yes... uh-huh... bye!" He squeezed the button hanging up, hissing through his teeth in frustration.

Do I dear ask?

'*Don't*' is written across his face with fury.

Our eyes meet, catching me. I hesitate as I exit, frozen in that second. He's standing in the kitchen at the stairs next to the bathroom door. Turning one-eighty, he slammed the phone on the charging station on the countertop and began opening the cupboards his back to me.

Briefly startled, I pant waiting for him to make a move and say anything, but he doesn't. His mood has moved south. I walked to the cupboard door and pulled it towards me, unloosing the towel, patting it against my skin carefully, standing naked gauging him. Cautious to ask, willing his attention, but he didn't acknowledge me. I pulled on a lace bra and panties edging to catch his glimpse.

What's eating him?

I took the towel to the bathroom, hung it behind the door and slid into a navy-blue sleeveless body-con dress even as it stumbled over my hips and the double-D's. He continued to busy himself in the kitchen. I played with the zip until I got it up then drapes a grey jacket over my shoulders and my navy blue, court shoes.

I give up!

I packed my folders and laptop, delaying my meeting, and checking his bad temperament.

"W-was that the office?" I stutter.

He didn't answer.

OK then! I should give him space.

Checking my bag slowly, technically, I am ready for the day. I only need something quick to eat. He has fixed himself in the corner of the kitchen blocking the fridge and all the cupboards I want, everything.

I needed coffee.

I screwed my eyes shut viewing his position with a sigh. Prudently, I gait up the two steps to the counter evading contact with his naked chest. His eyes caught me as I came out of his peripheral view his lips twitched at the corner.

The cups are on the other side of him. I reached around him. Stretching on the tip of my toes, he moved slightly tipping me over and swooping me with a quick turn. Clipping me in the corner and gyrating his midsection into mine.

I am winded. He gawks at me. His hands cup my waist lifting me slowly to the countertop. Meeting my lips with his as I go up, fusing us, inhaling me, taking my breath.

My hands automatically grabbed his bulging biceps, accepting him. Pushing my tongue into his mouth twisting, prolonging, wanting. He seats me.

Then, his hands slid down my thighs to my knees. He pulls my opened thighs into him, at the edge of the counter. And up again to the hem of my dress and between my legs. I lose focus. I broke the connection with his lips, catching my breath still in his hold.

His eyes are licentious, one hand still creeping up my dress finds his target. Moving the lace panties aside, he slips one finger into me, his thumb massaging the right place, I groan. Then he slides in another.

My legs are tied around him and the dress rolls up. He gapes my reaction and I want more, reeling him in. My phone rings, his onslaught increases velocity, and my hips move to his rhythm. The ringing continues, I grip his naked back sinking my nails in throwing my head back rocking my hips. Bringing my head down to his forehead, I can't stop myself.

"Oh…" *Fuck!* "… Eric."

His forehead against mine, my green eyes into his brown. Releasing, quivering to climax; slowing my breath, my phone rings again breaking my thoughts.

"Shit!" I cursed.

He lifted me off the counter.

I dart to the phone straightening my dress and fixing my underwear. I don't want to leave like this.

The ringing stopped. I eyed him. Then glanced briefly but looked at the time and four more missed calls. The office and I have less than fifteen minutes to be there. I pout.

Fuck, fuck, fuck! "I should be back around six."

I strolled towards him. He's leaned in that corner again brooding and puts his hand up. Unsure if it's meant to be 'stop or goodbye', I stop. He says nothing, I forced a smile.

I shouldn't leave him like this!

My eyes were on him, balancing my bag on my shoulder. I took the keys and head out for work.

****

I hustled towards the reception. Her straight, brunette mid-length hair and bright-blue eyes reflect the computer screen and are alight with expectation. Sarah Noel my new assistant, sat diligently behind the front desk. The keyboard clicked on a desktop, and to the right, an office phone and three tiers desk organiser, stacked with sheets of paper. Behind her a palm tree and two drawers, filing cabinet with a printer at the top.

When did this happen?

The overnight set up further declares that I made the right choice for an assistant. At sight of me, she jumped to her feet.

"Good afternoon, Agent Davis-Hall."

Her pleasant greeting is a sore reminder of my tardy start.

I am not that late! I grew a pout.

"Good day."

I greeted her and by instinct, lifted my left hand to see the time whooshing past her. I am not wearing a watch forgotten by rushing and being um, distracted.

Disappointing!

I ridicule myself, wagging my finger at myself inwardly. She hurried behind my brisk footsteps, shoving pieces of paper at me and giving me my diary. I squint at her slowing.

Why does she have my diary?

She began explaining,

"The phones have been installed today and the Wi-Fi is up."

Oh, my 'to-do' list. I soften my expression, picking up the pace.

"Thank you, Noel."

I avoid eye contact.

I should have been here!

Sidetracked again by Eric thinking up an excuse but she went on.

"Detective Sergeant Martinez and Lieutenant Paul are waiting in the conference room."

As they should, but voluntarily?

She successfully shifted my thoughts.

"Where is Torrez?"

I checked another box and paused only just noticing her dress is similar to mine. Grey with sleeves accentuating her straight figure. Unintentionally, I eyed her from toe to head. She didn't shift, and I wondered if it was because of her professionalism. Sensing only the desire to please me, from her, she answers, "Officer Torrez has been in the lab..." She is hesitant. "... I had um, problems getting in this morning."

Shit! Internally cursing and processing the pretext. I face her.

"Yes, your orientation..."

"It was fine." She belted quickly shaking her head to assure me, "... Um, the director called Sergeant Martinez. She gave me a tour, but didn't have the code on my um, joining letter."

"The director." I swallowed hard with hesitation.

Should I be worried?

"Uh yes." Sarah breaks my thoughts or confirms me.

Don't be ridiculous, Shana! I shook myself quickly thinking. "Oh, remind me later."

The director, I am unravelling.

Oh shit! I marched towards my office in a daze.

Did APS rat me out?

Did she, rat me out?

Did I make a mistake on her acceptance letter?

They must have known I was late.

Shit.

Shit.

Shit!

"Ah… Agent Hall…"

Instant acrimony hearing Eric's name directed at me plops me back quickly. My gaze zipped to her blinking one too many times at the sound of his legendary name. I love my husband, but for far too long being known as only his. Shadowed by his achievements and his personality. Mrs Hall, like I am only an extension of his greatness and not an individual.

Uh, "Agent Davis-Hall or Davis thanks," I corrected her immediately, nodding to mask my offence.

This is his fault anyway! I mean, being late…

"Agent Davis-Hall, uh," she stutters and my name sounds like a mouthful. "… There are a few emails from the directors, uh, things that may be pressing." She trips over her words.

I don't remember her stutter in the interview.

Her statement is pregnant. I grow anxious.

What did they say to her?

Maybe, I should *be worried,* I pale inward.

The thoughts are discomforting and my assumptions are making them worse.

Remember no baseless accusations.

I am biting my bottom lip from end to end and she gawps at me.

Don't unravel Shana! I released my lip.

You need to keep it together!

I began making an internal list with a poker face.

There are some things I cannot change but some that I can.

Reciting the words from a deep hole in my memory.

I said the same thing to the mayor.

The coincidence has me uneasy. For eight years, nothing, no hits of my past but twice in one week? The effort to recall its origin. Then it was gone again and my focus changed direction.

First thing's first.

"OK, please remind me before I leave today. We should have had a meeting this morning to discuss these things but I have a meeting in a few minutes. Anything else?"

"Ah…"

It was rhetorical but. "… Will have to wait until this meeting has finished, all right?" I stopped her before she could further derail me.

She nodded.

I took the bits of Post-it from her along with my diary into my arms. The laptop bag and handbag shifted on my shoulders. She eyed my movements and I squinted intensely at her.

She turned to pace her loud heels in the direction we came. I briskly made my way to the conference room.

From the outside, I see people in the room. I never know what to presume from this bunch. Inhaling long, then exhaling my personal opinions at the glass door, I entered cautiously.

The room heat was first to hit following the soundlessness. Aaliyah, Samanther and Paula were sitting in a room, I don't want to imagine how long without a word was exchanged.

Sam was at the bottom of the table; her feet were actually on the floor. Paula still in her lab coat and her glasses which sat in her greasy dark hair. Aaliyah was wearing a silk grey top, black pencil skirt, black and silver chunky bangles on her wrists and sat opposite Paula on the left with a vacant chair right opposite Sam.

What is going on?

They aren't giving each other evil eyes. They sat civilised in silence. I sprint to my chair, shed my jacket and hung it behind my chair before I sat. Waiting for me are three folders stacked one on the other. Their eyes sprung to me when I sat.

Hauling a folder to use as a fan, Aaliyah opened a folder in front of her. She clicks a remote turning the large screen on with pictures, behind me. I slid my chair from the front, to sit close to Paula. Lia started without a cue, "The owner of the serpent pendent is Mr Adam Jolee."

She displayed a picture of an older man, with grey hair and eyes, well dressed on the screen.

"… I was unsuccessful in attaining an interview with him but I, however, had an audience with his lawyer, Mrs Jennings who read a statement on his behalf quoting:

… 'Mr Jolee lost the necklace two weeks before it was found on our victim, Miss Sharron Mall. It was misplaced during a temple visit after attending a special Zemand ceremony'. That is the Zeman religion by the way."

"Burglar report." I flipped through the folder, she answered fast, "Yes, there is one dated two weeks before Ms Mall's attack." She added with a hit of attitude before carrying on, "… The necklace was described by the news to help identify Miss Mall as her face was unrecognisable after her attack."

I pause recalling her face on my first visit to her, remorse fills me. I cleared my throat and the feeling.

"Was there such a news report?" They all moved their heads to me and I sense some annoyance.

"There is a copy…" she replied swiftly.

OK, I'll save my questions for last!

I fished out a notepad from my bag and Lia continued,

"'… He went as he learnt of its recovery collecting it, as soon as he could. It was given to him by Officer Riley of the L.D.O. He has no intention of returning it without a subpoena. He also offers his condolences to Miss Mall'. End quote. Those are his lawyer's words, not mine. A copy of this statement is attached.

"However, it is a very expensive piece. The insurance to keep this jewellery matches that. This is classed as an artefact. It is extremely old and very costly. He claims his insurance demanded the security of this piece. It is worth a lot and the unfounded nonsense about thieves in the police station.

"Officer Riley said Mr Jolee presented proof the serpent belongs to him and he was under no obligations to with-hold the owner's property."

I raised my hand.

"Stay calm Shana. I got the court order we now have the relic, of course, it has been cleaned and polished so any potential evidence may have been destroyed.

Officer Riley is fresh from training he did not know he had to keep evidence until the case was over. He's new and suspended. No harm came to anyone whilst I carried out my investigation so you can relax. What's next?"

She closed her folder her face businesslike waiting.

"Good work Paul."

Did I just say that out loud?

I admit I was a bit impressed. She remained expressionless passing copies of her report around the room, then, as she sat Sam commenced our eyes turned to her. Lia slid the remote across the table to her.

"Sharron Mall was a bartender, a place called Jonopus. It isn't too far from her place. She was not an exemplary employee. She showed up as and when she felt like it. Her boss never reported her missing because of that.

"Plus, he thought she had finally quit when she didn't answer her phone. She threatens to quit regularly; especially after a heated conversation they had earlier that week.

"The boss however saw her cosy with someone. He is rumoured to be an associate of the alleged gang leader, Valentine. They call him Sam-Sam. Her boss also thinks she has money problems, as she often gambles with him.

"Her landlord backs that statement, he said she was avoiding him. Her rent was three months late. Then, the week she went missing she paid up her arrears and six months in advance. He does not know her to have any problems with money except for the last three months.

"I'd asked Mayor Mall *nicely*..." She twisted her head to me as she expressed nicely.

I rolled my eyes.

"... If he gave her the money. I even made an appointment and waited... and waited..." she says galling.

Don't fall for it! "Find another way Sam," I ordered.

"I have. No thanks to you."

Why is she such a... a dick!

I narrowed my eyes at her breathing hard.

Don't fall for it. I exhaled growing the impassive deportment, slowly.

She continued, "... I got a court order for her bank statements. Her father cut her off three months ago, hence the money issues.

He has been supporting her for many years and suddenly stopped. He has not paid any of her bills. I'd like to know more about what went on with those two."

I rubbed my temples. "Oh, move on!" I whined.

They turned their heads to me.

Shit, I said that aloud! "We get it Sam." I rolled my eyes.

She paused a beat.

I huffed taking notes. The quiet hung for a few minutes.

She continued, "Her rent being paid doesn't make sense. Her work doesn't cover much and her boss didn't give her an advance on her salary. An advance in any case, will not cover her rent for a month."

"Where did she get the cash?"

"Ran out of time to know why."

She squinted at me.

Breathe Shana, breathe!

"I am still trying to find this Sam-Sam character the guy she was cosy with at work." Sam paused and I want her to stop.

"Good, that's your assignment then!" I finished.

Without missing a beat Paula initiated while Sam passed around her report.

"Most of the physical evidence collected had been analysed though, this wasn't the actual scene of the crime. *That* may take some time to establish.

"I did analyse the dust though found in Mall's hair. They are found in the boundless canyons of the Zeman's land and almost everywhere in Divinish. There are so many caves it's a bit of a challenge narrowing it as well as restrictions. As well as there may have been the scene of the crime.

"Semen samples," she flicked through her many pages then put her eyeglass on the edge of her nose. "... Can anyone guess how many? Rhetorical question." She cackled.

Lia crinkled her eyebrows together creasing wrinkles and staring intensely at her sister. I folded my lips together stifling the thought of Lia's age finally showing in her face.

Sam as usual in a state of boredom.

"… Seven!" Paula startled the silent pause, "… Amazingly, I tested samples to the new S.D.A.F. data base. Thank you by the way Shana. I found three convicted criminals, Christopher Bailey, John Sommers and Valentine Jason."

The repeated name piqued our attention. I wrote his name. She continued her fast babbling, "Yes Valentine, the second time that name has popped up today, right. Anyway, get this, the father of the foetus is related to Valentine. His brother, although he is not on the crime data base but, I checked medical records his name is Terrance Jason. Three samples unaccounted for. Not a criminal or just not on file yet. Though it is good we were able to find those men, bad, most of them have a criminal record.

"Her car, though glass had been broken from inside out and the bits recovered from her hair and forehead was consistent with the glass from the broken window."

I froze remembering my interview with her. '… Then he punched through the window, breaking it. I was pulled through the window.'

Maybe she was confused.

Containing my doubt, I tuned in for more information.

"… Her tyres are also covered in the same dirt that was found in her hair. My best guess is that someone entered her car without force."

"She may have known her attacker." I lost my filter thinking out loud.

Like a true professional Paula shook her head further explaining.

Briefly huffed exhale and a soft stueps, left the other two.

"There was no evidence that proves otherwise. The trusted person may have smashed her head through the glass. The bruises behind her neck suggest that. Her car was taken somewhere near in or around the caves.

"She was force-fed some of whatever hallucinogen that is still in her system. She was tied legs and arms apart. There are deeper bruises on the inside of her arms and legs. She tugged on the restrains. Cuts on her torso happened at different times.

"Some are healed and others were fresh. Her child was aborted in the process, not sure how."

My food rose in my throat. I felt sickened and appalled at the same time. Flooded by many thoughts, the one thing was abundantly clear; Sharron Mall lied. I couldn't wrap my head around why.

Maybe she was ashamed.

She could have been threatened.

There are so many excuses I can make for her behaviour but...

What would make her lie about the details?

Pondering, while they were occupied reading through the reports. My heart began to race as I thought of Sharron and my conversation.

This can give them a place to start.

It can help speed things up.

What good is this tape sitting in my handbag,

"Guys." Their eyes rose to me.

With a frown, I fished the recorder from my laptop bag holding it up for their view.

Sam leaned into her chair and Lia squinted.

"... You might need to hear this ..."

"Is that the recording of Sharron Mall?"

Sam's condemnatory tone rose as she crossed her arms, piercing her bright blue eyes at me, tilting her chair further. I exhaled attempting to get her pre-empted tone out from my head.

"Not exactly, but yes." I should explain.

"How long have you sat on that one?" Aaliyah questioned, with a squint before I could explain. I narrowed my eyes at her.

"This is not from the L.D.O. I had an opportunity to talk to her."

"And you took it?" Paula asked.

Not her too? "Please, just listen..."

Carefully putting the recorder in the centre of the table. I pressed play. Sam scowled as she listened in. Paula narrowed her eyes, tilting her ear in the direction of the recording device and a gleam radiated from Aaliyah.

They listened and intently wrote notes. Aaliyah's mischievous grin never ceased during the playback. Growing ever more as it ends. At the moment, it felt like hours, played in fifteen minutes. The emotions felt then aren't the same though, they are still mixed. My heartbeat raced throughout the playback as before. The play button popped out and the room was quiet. Paula was writing while Aaliyah opened the folders comparing, I think. I avoided eye contact.

"You shouldn't have Shana." Sam was the first to say it out loud, shaking her head almost in disgust and disapproval.

Partly insulted, I narrowed my eyes at her. She intensifies her blues at my hazels.

Paula says as a matter-of-fact, "You know she's lying?"

Always stating the obvious breaking our stance. Lia just grinned wagging her head as she writes, but says nothing.

"Figured that out after your report Paula." My voice soft, I trusted they will follow suit.

"Is this what you fear *we* would do? Ha!"

Lia finally opened and leered.

I closed my eyes for a second contemplating how true that statement is. Though, she would never get that admission from me.

Oh, sometimes I really hate her.

Not helpful. I sang.

Phew, I didn't say it aloud!

Should I be worried?

Sam and Paula faces, disillusion by my lapse but expressed nothing further. I hunched peeking up marginally folding my lips inside eating the words. Before I unravel, I should explain my motivation.

"With the missing interview and time passing in our time-sensitive case, we needed this. I will take responsibility for this one and get the initial interview from the L.D.O. myself. Someone needs to interview Ms Mall and all these new suspects."

There was a stretch of silence across the room. Everyone leaned into their chair waiting. They are back to their disrespect and defiant.

Don't let that lapse define you, Shana.

You need to take hold of them.

"Move on."

My filter was lost surprising me and them.

Good, you caught their attention, now drive it in.

Gaining traction, I added, "… The most popular name today was Valentine."

"I dealt with Valentine before. Rape is not part of his M.O. He has women at his beckoning call. They may be afraid of him but her story, doesn't add, Shana." Sam's face emotionless is defending him and not quite regarding me.

I pale, "Well can I leave that task in your capable hands?"

I am begging for a response; her impassive sedateness remains.

Don't beg.

Why do you need her approval?

Professional Shana.

A spittle snicker raises from Lia, "That would be the best, a good idea, he knows her all right." Lia's mouth quivered with humour enjoying some memory or a joke. Sam squints at Lia waving her hands as she talks. "... And we've had minimum issues, so far. Besides, you know..." she trails and gestured the recording. "... If he sees her, it won't be so much." Lia bursts into laughter.

Sam tenses.

"Great! Just great!"

Is she trying, to tick me off?

"Can you do that for me Paul..." I signalled with my hand.

"Aye aye..." She saluted, chuckling.

Fuck!

Don't say it out loud!

"... Discretely. There best be no issues. Interview anyone connected to him." My annoyance level increased. "... Torrez, I need that sticky stuff analysed and a crime scene as close as you can. Sam, you've got your name's sake."

I cannot ask her to bring Sharron Mall in though, I wish to.

"Is that all, Davis." Sam standing ready to go.

I cast my eyes away from her. "That's all."

They all dragged their chairs leaving on cue.

Why do I feel like a child who's disappointed a mother?

Liz has never felt that way about anything she says, so why do I?

We barely tolerate each other, why do I care about her approval?

I began feeling hungry and unwell at the same time.

Maybe Eric is on to something.

Or do I need a doctor?

Both outcomes are unwelcoming.

"Davis!"

Sarah knocked, lingering by the door breaking my chain of thought. Carrying newspapers, a writing pad and a pen, my heart raced at the shock.

"Oh, yes."

I didn't hide my startling. Expecting Sam and reminding myself the staffing is increasing.

"Sorry if I frightened you."

She apologised walked in, pushing the chairs that were left out for the meeting. I wheeled the chair back. Stacking the folders and laptop into my hands and pulling it to my chest. Slipping the recording device into my jacket pocket. Balancing my bag on my shoulder exiting towards my office. Sarah shadows me around the other side of the table walking through the doors.

All I could think of is how I messed up.

What to do to make this right.

"That's OK Noel, how can I help?"

Looking at my court shoes engrossed in the singular event. Sarah struggles to keep up.

"Whilst you were in the meeting, the director called."

She informs me in a shout, my footsteps ceased and the singular word left me pre-empting doom.

"Oh." This does not sound good.

Internalising the reasoning, I began a fast pace.

"He wants a meeting with you on Monday. I booked it in."

"Monday?" *Shit!* "… Do you know why?"

Some panic in my voice as she tried to keep up. Observing the floor, Sam busy typing and taking notes, Lia was out of sight hopefully on her assignment and I presume Paula was back in the lab.

"There's the other thing."

Simple words that spoke my doom; she rustled the newspaper from under her notepad unfolding it wide to display a picture of me yesterday at the hospital headlines: *Officer Interviews Catacá Victim*

My heart sank.

Officer Interviews Catacá Victim.

'Five days after Sharron Mall has been hospitalised, mysterious officer visits.

Ms Mall found in the trunk of her car, clinging to life in what was described as Catacá. To date, there has been no updates.

Authorities, policing and the government are tight lipped on their role in this investigation as the newly formed federal office at this time, are unreachable for comment.'

CHAPTER SIXTEEN

"What the…" *Fuck!* I covered my mouth to stop myself from saying it out loud.

This cannot be happening,

The day of my press statement!

Mouth and eyes widened. The picture of me leaving the hospital wearing a grey skirt suit, yesterday. I was holding my briefcase and my badge flashing with my stride, hooked in the waistband of the skirt. An enlarge picture and a circle around the badge. Underneath the heading. My mouth opened and words stuck.

"H-How?" I stuttered.

"Because you went someplace you shouldn't. And introduced yourself, when you shouldn't have, Shana."

Sam's angry voice husks and her soft blue eyes burned through me as she hoists from the chair. I am stationary to her oncoming rant.

"Sam, I…"

I want to hurt someone! My anger builds.

"You told me this investigation was under scrutiny, you didn't expect this?" Sam pointed out.

I screwed my eyes shut. Searching for an answer. Sarah froze, uncertain of protocols. Our volumes elevate and we face off.

"You are so lucky it wasn't one of us!" Sam challenged.

"This is a conversation, recorded. We needed this Sam, don't deny it." I showed her the recorder justifying my position gaining some footing.

"You lecture me about procedures, and doing things professional, you're a hypocrite." She twisted her neck rolling her head to me and pointing at the device.

Her words echoed through me and I'm contemplating counting. Inwardly acknowledging my error but re-evaluating Sam's authority and gaining a hold of mine.

"Don't, Sam."

That's the final straw! Her edge of disrespect drew me back.

"I came here to do a job. I have to fill more than one role here. I am human just like you are. I recorded a conversation between me and Miss Mall, with her knowledge and permission.

"In the absence of the official report, which, is delayed in making its way to us. This is an important part of our investigation.

"Though, we can prove some of what she said are lies. There are some pieces of information that is true in this conversation. Don't push me."

I stepped to her face.

"You can justify your actions if you'd like. This is the first slide in a slippery slope. The beginning of a bad path. And I know bad paths Shana. This will bite you in the ass sooner than later and *I will,* be there saying, 'I told you so'."

She stood her ground closing the distance between us.

"Ah." Sarah whimper between us and I reassert my authority narrowing my eyes at Sam.

"Thank you for your input, Sergeant Martinez. I will take your concerns under advisement. Is there anything else I can help you with?"

She huffed screwing her face at me, slumped into her chair, hitting the keyboard, typing.

Bitch!

With an exhale, I continued to my office as Sarah followed me inside closing the door behind.

****

We finished our diary watch booking more appointments and sending my original press release. Reviewed by the director.

I cannot comment on anything in our active investigation.

Those words are littered in my first official statement, after, the news article. I was supposed to be the one initiating the narrative, now, it only seems as if I am responding and defending.

Fuck!

The anger at the article increased and I have been resisting my counting mantra convincing myself that this does not require a calm to a panic attack. On the opposite end of my emotions, is the upcoming meeting with the director. Inside I toil officially worried, livid from the news.

I need to fix this!

Sarah and I finished a few bits before she left the office around six. I stayed in to finish reports and have a plan of action as Saturday is our day off. My eyes were really tired an hour later. Barely able to concentrate or recognise the screen any more.

There are so many things I need to finish.

I reminded myself as I glanced at the wall clock it was after seven, and I have submitted the reports to the director an hour earlier.

I should leave.

Ready to make my way back to the apartment, I think of Eric. Suddenly, my memory strayed on how I left him.

Crap!

****

Eric was surprisingly in bed, asleep. I drink in his beauty admiring his physique from afar. He's lying on the sheets, a white vest his hands under the pillow under his head. Accentuating his trapezius, deltoids, infraspinatus and triceps. His boxers, gripping tight his hamstrings and glutes.

I forget at times how dreamy he looks when he's sleeping. The argument last night faded with his adorable physic he stirred and smile.

I am in love with this man.

I marvelled at his professionalism and his ability to balance everything through his investigations. How it never appears to affect us, and his work never leave his office. This is my first and I was not sure how to deal with it.

I yearned to converse his experience and ideas. His diplomacy alone can make a huge difference. But I control my urges hoping that it wouldn't drive me insane. I only then, realised he really hasn't answered me when I asked why he came to Divinish.

He can be so maddening at times!

I flicked the switch for the night-lamp, taking my gun and holster from my waist. He blinks adjusting his eyes to the light.

"Did you just get in?" he whispered low, cracks in his baritone as he spoke.

"Yes... sorry, didn't mean to wake you." I shimmied out of my jacket putting it into the closet.

"That's OK." He turned on his back his eyes on me. He is unusually early in bed, laying back observing, I think.

"What," I smile. His gawking is unnerving, looking at my every motion.

"You are beautiful, you know that?" he says after a while.

I folded my lips. "... OK." My cheeks redden turning from his eyes.

I place my bag on the floor next to the side table then securing my gun in the vault. His eyes moved with me and mine on him. The lecherous tension builds. For a moment as we gaped at each other. My pores visible and the humidity thickens in the room.

He must be over his foul mood this morning.

Or ready to finish what he started...

Both thoughts are ecstatic. He sits up and moves to the edge of the bed, taking my right hand in his, knitting our fingers. My lips part as I wait. A groan leaves my throat blinking long, flashes of this morning.

I glance, his shadow over my shoulder he stands behind me, close but not quite touching me. The hairs on my body stand at attention absorbing the current between us. He runs his left fingers up my arm tickling. I release his right hand ready to fade rigidities of today with his caress.

He's cupped my shoulders, reeling me leisurely to his erection, poking against my back. Projecting his expectation over me with a soft flowing breath. Fresh and blowing through my hair, over my neck and tickling my shoulders.

Gasping sharply, his lips contacted feathered kisses along my neck sucking and biting. My heart flutters and I lean into his proficient hands. He takes my left hand, rolling my fingers into his right, lifting it and bringing it to cross my panting chest, pausing, a second.

Then, twists me swiftly in a twirl, my breast meets his chest. Groping one hand around my waist, moving to my ass. The other snaking up my thigh as I balance on one leg, quivering waiting, licentious.

Wasting no time, he injects his tongue and mine answered. Parting my lips dancing a deep and wonton fill dance. His hand continues its journey north, reaches the top of my sternum. His fingers curl around my neck tilting. His mouth makes contact with a firm grip, not painful but uncanny.

What is this?

I cease all movement, he noticed, balances us holding me adjacent. His hand drags the zip down the back of my dress. Slips it down my shoulders, to the floor. Our lips fastened. His hands swoop across my back pulling me deeper into his mouth. The sparks edifice south, with his hands.

The lamp flickers like a spotlight on us through the darkness. I melt to his nature. Ravenously I lifted his vest stepping backwards out my dress. He unclips my bra, it falls. Disconnecting us for an instant and fusing once again.

Waltzing forward he gently dips me onto the bed. I hang off his neck our lips welded. His hands propped at my sides. My head touch the bed as we kissed enraged with sensual need. He released my now bruised lips. His dark brown eyes twinkled in the light, soaking me in. I gaped, blushing like a teenager.

He is taking his time.

A stray thought crosses. I am so ready to feel him inside me. He beamed pleased with himself trailed kisses down from my tilted chin, neck, southwards down my body to the top of my lace underwear. His bright teeth glowing in the dim light. He curls his fingers into the top of my underwear sliding as he exhales his lips an inch away from my pubic area, plunging.

My mouth dry and inhale sharply closing my eyes anticipating his next move. He continued languid. I closed my eyes licking my lips impatiently as it slipped off with his hands. My eyes flickered and I propped on my elbows looking for him.

He's standing back gawking at my bare body in his birthday suit with his hands on his hips his erection pointed to its destination. Unsure if he's admiring or planning, I crinkled my brows at him. The grin across his face gives away his naughtiness.

He strode to me leaning forward, lifting his both hands and takes me by the ankles, I smile. He rotated me. I am surprised by his move, lingering, keeping me on the edge. I begin to shake in wait.

He's crawling over my back, his breath tickling me from bottom up. All the way to my shoulders. I turned my head to him as I feel his warm sweetness. He kneels between my legs, parting my knees with his, forcing my hips upwards. Then he leans over, I feel him.

Ahh...

My breath pauses, his hands on both my hips reeling, fulling me slowly. I have never felt him so deep before, filling me completely, grinding everything into me, and he pauses. I hear his breathing laboured as he punctured my insides. It was uncomfortable, hard and a bit painful.

I arched upwards reacting automatically, breathless, wincing with my hands reaching for his hips to ease. Pushing my back down with his palm in the centre of my back.

"No baby," he growled.

Holding my arms reaching for him and bending my elbow behind my back, then he takes the other repeating. His hand midback securing my both arms in position with one hand, planting my face into the mattress, ass cocked high, into the air surprising an terrifying me.

"Eric," I pant wearingly.

He lets go, I propped on my elbows as he crawls up my back, his lips gently nibbling and kissing. When he reaches my shoulders, he kisses the nape of my neck, then behind my ears.

"I love you," he whispers. Easing out then slowly, entering all into me again. I gasp, arched again and began to shiver. He's running his hands gently around my sides drawing the curves of my bust to waist to hips, tickling. Halting at my hips partly coming out securing his hold then thrusts fulling me again.

I yield to my body, moaning unexpectedly loud as he hung on to my hips and increased his movements in and out. I melted in his hands losing control with a shout. Shaking consistently, effortlessly and unrequitedly coming fast. Lost in him, pulsating as waves crash over and over again. Then, he comes soon after. Fully inside me grinding and rolling his hips, growling through his tight jaw riding me until he has emptied himself completely.

We catch our breath momentarily as he collapsed over me. Then, we made love again. His touch gentle and patient waiting together. Anticipating connecting then overflowing over and over again. It felt so different, erotic, honest, innocent and special. We were connected deeper than we have ever been before. Our souls were completing the circle balancing each other.

CHAPTER SEVENTEEN

I woke to his beautiful white beam, his head propped on his hand his gawping at me. His energy and playfulness is contagious.

"Good morning." His grin wide but bad breath.

I pulled the covers up hiding my nose breathing in the scent of sex beneath the sheets before replying muffled. "Good morning," I say under the sheet. My eyes fluttered at him and I grin wide.

"You know morning breath doesn't faze me." He reminds me and my stomach flipped at the view of this man.

I know.

I feel the heat growing at my cheeks. I am so shy with him at times folding my lips stifling the grin, regarding the sheets and avoiding eye contact. He brings out so many emotions at once. After three years to still feel the way I do, about him is amazing.

"Are you sick?" He's calmly excited.

Instantly rolling my eyes.

Ah, he's never going to let it go?

Don't ruin the moment Shana it's the last weekend of his vacation, truth!

I am sucking my teeth at myself.

"No, you know I don't like to talk to anyone before brushing my teeth." My tummy begins a strange sickly stir.

"I know," Eric sings factually, his eyes are assessing.

I try raking in the annoyance saying to myself. *Then why the third-degree, Hall!* "I'm going to the bathroom."

Excusing myself to hopefully brush my teeth and hold the upset feeling at bay. Naked, I walk there. Pulled the robe from the hooks behind the door, brushed my teeth, putting my hair in a shower cap before hanging the robe and started my day with a shower. I somewhat expected his frequent disappearing act yesterday but I am glad he didn't.

I guessed that the office didn't need him as urgent as they usually do.

I come out, wiped the condensation from the mirror and began to straighten my hair. The smell of his cooking seeped under the doors. He is much more domesticated than I am. I enjoy eating his meals as I am sure he loves preparing them.

I came out wrapped in a towel as he dished up the turkey bacon and eggs on the plate. The smell has not affected me today. I am relieved. He's eyeing me. I dropped my towel artfully shimmering into my camisole. I hear his swallowing.

"I-I'm gonna have a shower." He's leaning on the wardrobe door breathing over my shoulder.

"Do you want me to join you?" I licked my lips, initiating.

He grins, peck my forehead, and I held my breath.

"Eat first you need your strength."

Disappointed, I frown knowing it is not a request and it is true. I slipped on my underwear, shorts stomping with an emphasised pout to the breakfast bar. He goes into the toilet shutting the door behind him.

Nibbling at the edge of the sandwich at first, I was hungrier than I expected. My bites became bigger, I began consuming the meal. The thoughts of yesterday's headlines began to fill me piquing anxiousness reflecting on the plate. I would ask Eric what he thinks but I don't want him to think I am second-guessing my career choice or that I am giving it up.

I cannot fail my first case.

Worried about the meeting with the director and the headline, I popped to the sofa with my computer in my lap. A copy of the article electronically in a file sent by Noel. Opening the document to prepare, I read it again. News headline read, *Officer Interviews Catacá Victim.*

Why are they calling her a 'Catacá Victim'?

What does it mean, what is Catacá?

Opening a browser, I typed.

There was an image of a gold king cobra statue, all the ridges of the scales defined, its eyes sapphire and gold tongue sticking out splitting at the furthest extend. The hoods puffed out and flattened with circles inserted with rubies towards the ventricle scales.

It resembles the necklace found on Sharron Mall, claimed and taken by Adam Jolee. There were three pictures of three poses of the snake a front view, side left and side right but the image was not of the full serpent.

'Catacá: according to the Zeman legend is a cleansing ceremony performed by Cedérus the creature of sacrifice, war and revival, the third most powerful creature of the Zemand religion.

Cedérus, the eldest child of Berána and Sevínah is the only Zemand creatures with the most blood ceremonies. Catacá one of the three Cedérus' blood ceremonies. This focuses on the adulterous women of the Zeman who's never repented their promiscuous behaviour.

Details of the ceremony are kept secret and has only to be known by Cedérus worshipers and high priests whom are also rear.

The Zemand blood ceremonies are all under review by human rights laws and the Zeman has willingly abolished most practices. Catacá has not been practiced in Zeman society for over twenty-five years so, has not been included in the written law.'

Wow! I gaped at the computer in awe. This was not what I expected when I typed in the Zeman word.

Something was familiar about this, as I zoned into the study, Eric came with his plate turning on the TV. I shifted. He settles into the chair as the semi-final football match begins. He has been talking about this game for a while, and he's all geared up to cheer loudly. He knows I could care less. His silence says volumes about me having my work laptop out to avoid issues, I asked.

"You OK for me to finish up a report?"

He exhales displeased, I explained, lacing the guilt.

"I got in late yesterday, remember?"

Prompting him. It is his fault, two days in a row I was late, after late night activities that usually does not just stop at once.

"I know you have no interest in this game." His face zones into mine and our eyes line up when he tilted down. "… But it will be nice if you finish with the game." He issues his instructions. I raised my brow. "… I would like us to go out later." He grins sweetly and I relax, without a need to defend myself.

Yes! "Of course!"

I celebrate, leaning over pulling his pouted lips to mine. Holding his mouth a few seconds long. His eyes widened, distracted by the kick off.

With my legs across his, leaned into the chair arms, my laptop on my thighs, I start typing notes and copying reference as I reread the definitions.

This case may be a bit more politically motivated than I first expected.

I noted with a sigh thinking.

If this is part of the government reform, there must be something in the database.

Typing my access code, I logged on the S.D.A.F. crime data base referencing the headline going back five years, the computer beeped, no match.

Hmmmm... why does it feel familiar?

I cannot shake the familiarity. I've always heard Eric talk about a hunch but never experienced it. He also always says, 'go with your gut'. I went back ten years, no luck either.

This is a new system as well, so maybe there's missing data. I excused the resource.

Or maybe you're wrong! My ugly subconscious reared her head.

I squinted at myself even more so determined. Eric at the edge of his seat, his team is rearing for a goal, I peeked at him focused on the game giving me authorisation to continue. His wriggling however, is a bit annoying. I turned, placed my feet to the floor, intensified on my search.

Pizza arrived, on the coffee table. He's opened a beer and got some bowls with savoury snacks and some biscuits. His moving around distracts my concentrating. I peeked over my screen, he's gestured to eat. I grabbed a slice as my search deepens with my report. My fingers working and tapping the keyboard.

The attack was too methodical to be random, added with the politics, insistent of discretion and a special team. Some of Eric's warnings are beginning to rear its nasty head echoing in displeasing ways. I try to ignore his cautions from resonating in my thoughts.

Still, I widen my search to articles with the keyword Catacá. The computer starts to fill up with hits. Twenty-five years ago, just like the article says. I found a newspaper report about a local woman from Divinish they called the survivor. I read aloud,

"Missing Woman Found…"

I brought my laptop closer and continued reading.

'Missing Woman Found

After seven days searching for local waitress Camielle Charles was found in a ditch, in a pool of blood hands and feet were bound. Some witnesses claimed she was naked and bleeding from the abdomen area.

Details about who discovered her and what happened are still sketchy, and police are not giving much detail about her recovery or the circumstances surrounding her disappearance.

She was first believed to be a runaway, as relatives believed had escaped from an alleged abusive relationship, with her boyfriend, John Sommers. Her discovery turned out to be, what locals describe as the fifth victim of the Zemand 'cleansing ceremony' Catacá.

The community stands divided on the ethics of this religious ceremony, while the law stands on either corner of this fight.

If she as a victim of this ceremony she stands as the only survivor according to local sources. Weather victim of Catacá or a victim of something else, Charles is nursing wounds. The public awaits to see, if she'll be the key to end these murders but her family is lucky to have found her alive.

By Christine Davis.'

Crap! It is hard to swallow.

Five more victims.

Both bemused and horrified by my finding. So many questions filled me, a chill surged through the air and I repeat the number in my head.

Five deaths?

Shit!

I covered my mouth feeling the pizza about to erupt.

There must be some record of them.

Widening my search to any report on previous victims or articles about them. There was nothing.

Damn!

I slammed the laptop. Thinking.

The reporter.

The author of the article. Christine Davis. The name, it's eerie. But I cannot seem to keep the name to memory long enough before becoming distracted.

I copied and paste the name into my search engine. Basic information of her age, address and the fact that she's retired journalist but nothing further. Either she has lived and worked in the same place all her life, or the data is possibly fabricated.

… Conspiracy!

Eric's words are haunting me again. There was another article she wrote about Catacá and Camielle Charles.

'Catacá Survivor Gives Birth

After surviving the brutal Zemand ceremony Catacá, only known survivor Camielle Charles gave birth to her attacker's child; a daughter born from her horrifying experience.

Charles who discovered she had been made pregnant from her attack, chose to keep the child and says, 'out of evil can come good' and 'I couldn't be happier'.

There are no clues to what happened to Charles during the ceremony and the Zeman community are denying any involvement in her attack though Charles herself is Zemand.

Few have been questioned concerning Charles or the other four deceased victims, no arrest has been made to date and police say they're continuing investigations.

By Christine Davis.'

Wow!

I read the articles twice again and searched the crime data base for the location of the archived files.

L.D.O. great!

I wrote a request to the office for the files my optimism increased. There are so many questions about Catacá the ceremony, the law and the practitioners flooding my thoughts at the same time.

First thing, I ran a background check on Camielle Charles to no known crime. No listed current address, no details. I tried to find her daughter, there was no name. I zeroed in at the date of the second article to gage a possible birth date, June thirteenth...

"Funny, my birth date," I said aloud fixated on the screen.

CHAPTER EIGHTEEN

"Whose birth date?"

Eric frightened me.

I turn to his voice quickly holding my chest, steadying my heartbeat. The computer sloped on my lap. He stood behind the sofa with a white T-shirt, washed-out jeans and sneakers. Bemused, holding two full bags from the groceries and the keys bundled poking out his jeans. He ambles to the sofa, leaned over, kissed my hair. Then, went for the kitchen to put them down.

I hadn't noticed he left or returned, crap!

It was nearly four in the afternoon and the game finished at two. Nearly two hours he has been gone and I didn't notice. Screwing my eyes cursing at myself, I closed the laptop perching it on the coffee table, giving him all of my attention. He sneaked something out a bag hiding it behind his back.

Not this again!

I resisted rolling my eyes but couldn't hide my unenthused countenance. He sauntered to the back of the sofa. I rest my head back he leaned over. I admire his well-groomed face stroking it. We locked lips briefly.

I hope he isn't mad.

I cannot tell.

He put the bar at the back of the sofa. I tilted to the side seeing it.

"Chocolates." He's dry.

Moving it carefully to my lap. Immediately I tore the pack open, wolfed three blocks in less than a minute. The silk moisture is unbelievable, sweetened enough to savour. Not too hard to bite and strong enough to hold without melting in my hands.

Mmm, I hummed.

He came around the chair, eyes peers, an eyebrow up and a peculiar manifestation across his face. I am sighing inside, hoping that whatever comes out his mouth next isn't erupted into a fight.

He's come to sit next to me, throwing the keys on the table next to the laptop. I tilt my head to his shoulder. A silent apology and chance to whiff him. The scent confused me. His odour was unfamiliar, discomforting. I sat up, shifting with my forearms twisting in his direction. My mind strayed.

How long has he been gone?

Was I so engrossed?

Shit, he must be mad!

Out of the blue he confessed, "I got promoted Shana."

I blinked a couple times my heart skipped a beat and jaw dropped all at the same time.

"What?"

I crossed my feet under me, twisting to him expiating loudly gaping at him waiting, anticipated the other shoe to drop. After Sam's return, there were issues and he didn't quite get along with his new captain. The bias was neutral.

Is he the new captain of the D.P.F.

I didn't know how to feel.

His promotion to lieutenant was meant to be lifechanging but it was more of the same. Late nights, undercover with that bitch Aaliyah again, his frustration grew and the dissatisfaction with the job increased.

Maybe being captain would have a different effect. I am sceptical.

During the last police ball, the minister of defence claimed to have an eye on him. I wondered if the captain was removed.

Is that why he was on holidays?

Or is it more of the same?

A lie and he's telling me after the fact? Anticipation, I waited for details.

He didn't say anything.

Clasped his hands leaning forward with a shrug, I stare waiting.

Minutes past.

I didn't say anything.

… Shit!

I quickly corrected.

"That's great honey, congratulations." My tone is inadvertently condescending.

Crap! Hoping he doesn't realise. I leaned into the side of his shoulder hanging off his neck, "… So when are we going to celebrate?" *Better!*

"*This* is all part of the celebration." He shifts slightly to me.

"What do you mean?" I am confused.

"The five days off, being here with you."

He shrugs again crisscrossing his fingers into his lean forward. It feels wrong and I wait again.

Where's the other shoe?

He exasperated.

Maybe there isn't anything more Shana!

Crap! You need to fix it. "Is that what last night was about?"

I scoop his face with a grin. He relaxes into the couch but stares at his keys.

"No, not really but a bonus." I pierce my hazels tilting to catch his eyes. "… It was what this week, was meant to be."

"Oh," I say short.

"I am now an institution leader," he stated cautiously.

"Wow! More late nights," I blurted.

Shit, filter!

I bowed, gape my lap and I slapped my forehead. Then I folded my lips.

"Not really."

He finally turned to me. I expected 'yes', I still thinking of another reaction besides pouncing out of the chair bothered about it. I turned to him.

What does this mean for us?

I am not giving up my new career for this advancement.

I squint at him brewing. The potential argument where my views would surely fall on deaf ears; in my head, I'm already there. I listen intensively as he explained.

"… This new position has a lot of benefits; I will have a greater influence on decisions and policies.

"It would mean a change in lifestyle for our family. Home early and on weekends most days, it is the dream job, Shana… Some would say it is more a political position as I would have to remain neutral…"

His expression is serious in deep thought as he elaborates. Meantime, I search for the words taking a true interest in his passion.

"Just don't get involved in the politics, keep your nose clean."

I run my finger across his curved nose, bedazzled by his brown eyes clasping his neck around my arms.

"I have to keep most of what I am doing now secret."

I rolled my eyes. *What else is new?* I say inside, his expression impassive.

His thoughts as if I'm somewhere else, "… On the positive side, within the next eight to ten years, I would make such a massive difference to pension and our lifestyle.

"It can open a lot of opportunities, in the private sector or even options as national security minister.

"This job would be impressive on my resume coupled with my nearly twenty years policing experience."

He never spoke about his end game.

That's good, right?

It feels a bit morbid especially when I think of our thirteen-year age difference. I could see the pride of his achievement.

"I am so proud of you. I just wish you could teach me all you know." I pecked his lips.

"There's no need, you're a natural. I only wish I had acknowledged it sooner, or nurtured it." He gazed at me brooding on the past, I am sure.

I have waited so long to hear him utter those words. My heart swells and I fall even deeper in love with this man, my man, Eric Hall.

"Like when I accepted the assignment?" I simper still naughtily wanting him to admit the details personally.

"Even before that…" he trails.

My sudden retirement from D.P.F. comes to mind but I said nothing only gleaming at him. "… You would have been so far ahead now," he says with remorse in his tone and I know it's exactly what I thought.

What's done is done!

Don't go there… please.

"Let's not look back with regret." I shook my head wanting to forget the mistakes and heartaches. We're here now, happy. "... That's in the past. We're looking at our future, right?" He moves his eyes to me and I smile lustfully. "... We're celebrating."

He looked at me, his eyes brightened and his dimples sunk into his cheeks as he said,

"On the topic of future, when do you think you'll be ready for us to start a family?"

Whoa! Bemused I blinked a couple of times at him.

Wasn't the chocolate a truce?

There's the missing shoe.

I wagged my finger at myself inwardly.

"Uh... I thought we have a family?"

I try a quick diversion as he's ruined our disposition.

"I know that Danielle is legally your daughter. Yes, we are a family, but... do you really consider her to be yours?"

He's cornered me.

There's no right answer to this.

I have to think, carefully.

I folded my lips as he continued, "... I'm not trying to vigour you. I could have children twenty years from now." He jokes and I am not sure if I find that funny. "... I want you to be prepared, not surprised and fit the child into your schedule like you do Danielle."

My eyes opened and I am offended. Though true, I did forget she was by Elizabeth. I sigh at the truth, feeling guilty.

"I don't want you to feel bad about it. She loves you just as I do. We are both happy with the way our family dynamics are for the moment." He is tripping over his words and I grin at his attempt. Then he sighs before saying the most profound words of our relationship so far. "... I just want you, to be ready." He pointed at me with a smile, then it fades, his eyes still peeled to me and I am lost for words.

Wow!

It is a lot to think about, and I haven't really thought about it.

I parted my lips trying to articulate anything. My phone rang breaking our introspection.

Saved!

It is on the kitchen counter charging. I blinked long, then went for it. I heard his infuriated breathing. I quickly answered.

"Davis!"

"Shana it's Sam. I picked up the running suspect," she says ominous.

"What do you mean Sam?" I heard her groaning.

"Not my fault but… he's dead. I found him about an hour ago. *Yes, the scene is being processed by Paula and No, I don't think the media knows he's connected to our case.*"

The sarcasm always present, with a hint of mockery and assurance. *She confuses me at times.*

"Why didn't you call me before?"

Holding the phone between my shoulder and ear, I walked to the wardrobe, fished through the closet to find a clean suit, giving away my panic.

"No offence Davis but this will be your first dead body on a scene, usually it does not work out well for the newbies especially seeing the way he was killed."

Taking off my camisole, I pulled on a bra and I slid over my head, a white full slip in anticipation of a late return. The break in contact with the phone, I hear her exasperated breathing through the speakers. Found a maroon pencil skirt and danced into the skirt.

"How did he die? And is that what you call me behind my back?" I wait for a response.

"No Shana. He's been gagged, tied in his underwear, several fingers and toes hacked off."

The description made the pizza I ate earlier stir in my belly. But she continued I believe to deter me, "… Shot once to the head, tortured in his own kitchen, dusts of what seems to be drugs and brains are the new art painted on the walls," she describes graphically.

"I know what you're doing Sam," I called her out on it.

"What!" her innocent act is transparent.

"Send me the address," I command, throwing on a beige blouse and a maroon jacket. She went silent for a few seconds then my phone beeped. I view the text.

"Thanks!" I peered at the phone.

"You're welcome!" she teases.

"You done?" I roll my eyes at her slipping on my stilettoes.

"Possibly."

"Clean it up as fast as you can, call Paul. Be nice to the local police, but don't give them any details, only the basics if you have to… please, I'll be there in thirty minutes." *I think.*

"This isn't my first rodeo Davis," she says as a matter-of-fact.

"I know but your touch sometimes hurts."

I can tell she's rolling her eyes, and I know she knows I can hear her sucking her teeth.

"Just don't eat before you get here," Sam warned.

Too late!

I hang the phone up sticking my tongue out at it. In my jacket pocket, one of Danielle's small purses was left as a gift for me. I smiled at her thoughtfulness and stuck the phone in the other, ambled to the sofa. Eric stood up, moseyed around to the back of the chair, crossed his arms.

"I heard."

He got to the point placing his firm behind at the back of the sofa. I'm immobilised as he leaned in the way of the exit, my heart constricted. I don't want to choose and I hope he's not going to make me.

His manifestation indecipherable. I know he is displeased. He folded his lips inwardly his dimples sink into his unshaven beard, and his dark brown eyes fall in a daze. I close my eyes briefly with a sigh.

Please don't make me choose again!

I scowl inwardly, outwardly I say as if asking, "I-I'm not sure, w-what time… I'll be back."

I swallowed hard with a frown, dressed and ready to leave, ambling to him with his crossed arms. I stood between his legs leaning in and kissing him, his lips shut and I prolong, gauging his reaction. I defuse attempting to catch his glimpse.

"I understand." He finally looks into my eyes uncrossing his arms. "… We will pick this up later though Shana."

His dominating tone grabbing me into his embrace between his legs. I am sure just to feel his growing erection. I folded my lips inward blinking at him. He holds the back of my head with one hand, the other securing my midsection with his.

I gasp as the energy moves downwards releasing my lips with a deep throat groan. His mouth reaches mine opened, he immediately inserts his tongue into my mouth sucking and rolling sudden and deep to the back of my throat.

Just like that, stopping releasing me and standing, in position, mouth open, panting, waiting at an unspoken to-be-continued. I licked my lips tasting him, waiting and he's not reacting.

Hesitantly, I moved from him towards the exit. My heart pounds taking the keys off the side table next to the door lingering. Finally, unlocking the door, peeking at him from over my shoulder, I exit before anything more.

CHAPTER NINETEEN

It felt weird, we'd flipped the scripts. Leaving him hanging for work, it's not as glamourous as I saw it only from one side. I shook the thought driving out of the park heading to impromptu work.

My thoughts were far from the journey and the crime scene of a possible suspect to the rape and assault of Sharron Mall. One of her known associates was found dead in his kitchen. An execution Sam suspects, drugs dusted across the scene along with his brains. Configuring this in my head is causing some strange feelings.

I hope I don't throw up!

The lunch and snacks Eric fed me have not quite settled. His name in my thoughts reverberated along with the conversation in which I ran away from. Eric and I have never really talked about the future, children or anything at all. We live in the now.

Even finishing our wedding ceremony has always been a wish, an understanding, not an in-depth conversation. My hands began to sweat around the wheel. I'm becoming anxious about his motives and my pulse is racing at the gesture.

And that kiss…

I drove distracted along a narrow country lane trees and forest on either side. It is peaceful but has only calmed my turmoil a tad, becoming lost in the beauty. The road ends, my phone blinks, pausing the directions. I waited at the crossroads for it to change. A horn toot behind me. I turned left, then touching the phone to reactivate the directions, my battery is low.

I need this distraction. I try convincing myself.

An elevated pulse surely cannot be good. I should call Sam.

The phone rang three times before she answered.

"Yea."

Her abrupt decorum brings me back to the present. I squinted, irritated at her.

"I will be there soon."

"Shana... you're..."

The call ended.

Shit!

The reception has dropped at the same time my untamed tummy gaggled loudly. It has been an hour since the first phone call. The map on my phone had taken me through another thin road. I am exiting to a small town somewhere in Shadeyah, I hoped. I'm sold that my phone is just as lost as I am or...

This place was really hard to find.

Frustration builds, as what should have been forty-five-minute drive, has turned into a regrouping exercise.

Or maybe my mind is still on my husband...

I frown at the logic.

Focus Shana!

Then, I tried calling Sam again, straight to voice message.

Shit! I am late.

I scolded myself, driving slowly through the town to get my bearings, glancing at the map ever so often. It shows me to follow this road for another thirty minutes to my destination, which cements further my disposition.

I admit, I'm lost.

Moving along a street of maisonettes with some small shops below. A bank and what looks like a mini mall, food places and five storey apartments. The lack of traffic is causing a less convoluted search through my phone.

How far off am I anyway?

It appears to be the city edge with no outstanding landmark, then, a coffee shop.

Yes!

A small victory dance inside, and something familiar speaking to my appetite. Pulling the car on a curb, a little away from an open alleyway. It's between a food-place and a laundromat. I passed the coffee shop. I moan.

The open spaced alleyway appeared to be an entrance of some sort with huge garbage dumpsters. Maybe for the diner, or garbage truck. The neighbourhood just got dodgy as I spot a man collecting drugs from another man passing casually, discomfort grows.

Hunger turned into nausea followed by a bit light-headedness. The pizza and beer are not sitting well on my stomach. I pet my tummy, holding my mouth blowing in and out for a little in the running car. Swallowing my thickening spit, I turned off the engine taking a moment. Then, popped the door open sticking the keys in my jacket pocket.

Maybe I should get some directions.

I tried calling Sam. The reception is fading in and out.

"Sam. Sam, can you hear me... Sam, I am on my way," I unsatisfyingly yelled through the phone as it breaks in and out of her husky voice. So, at least one word will go through to her. The smell of the food cooking got stronger. I am positive it was the thing setting off the sickness.

That's new, but at least I sourced a cause, I think.

Still not a hundred percent sure myself that it is.

Covering my mouth and nose with one hand the smell enters the car. Quickly with my phone in the other, I exited the car slamming it. Trotting in the direction of the diner dialling her again.

A few persons walking about and a homeless man sitting in a box next to the dumpsters. The robust odours of garbage and pee brought back some unpleasant memories, adding to my heightened senses.

Two shops down the road I trotted to the red blinking neon sign. Pushing the red tinted glass door into a time portal it seems, my phone to my ear and one hand over my face.

Not that the chiming of the door wasn't enough to invoke stares. My staring at the red and white sixties themed coffee shop and diner with huge pictures of passed actors in black and white. Aaliyah's dad's picture is hung on the walls with pictures of antique cars and a splash of the Zeman canyons painted onto the walls. The theme fit perfect with the tone of this town.

Random and creepy.

Ashamed of the speculation, my hands fell slowly. The odorous frying oil, bacon and eggs being cooked did not help the cause either. I gagged slightly. My saliva has dried and I screwed my face. The food is at the back of my throat. I breathe slowly, gaining my footing, and called Sam again ambling inside.

The constant noise of the failed calls, and text messages of failed connectivity every two minutes, breaks the diner chatting. My business attire and stilettoes stuck out from the casual jeans, plaid and caps that are a trend around these parts.

Embarrassed, I slipped my phone into my jacket pocket as my high heels echoed. The glass counter displayed baked snacks. For a Saturday afternoon the store was nearly abandoned, few well acquainted customers friendly with the staff.

The customer assistant middle-aged blonde and grey hair twirled into a bun covered by a gold hairnet. A light-pink dress, and white apron, wrapped around her medium waist. Her name, 'Anne' on her name tag. Changes her attitude as she came to me. Not so friendly smile and crinkled eyebrows with her intense green eyes into my hazels. I grinned taking a deep breath.

"Hi, can I have an iced mocha and some of your doughnuts?"

My hunger spoke for me. My eyes widened at the order.

… And maybe something for the ladies as a peace offering?

"Can I also have two coffees and a green tea…" *For Lia, the diva!*
"… A doughnut and iced mocha."

Shit I already said that!

"Sorry, just one iced mocha and maybe two doughnuts…"

"Is that it?"

Her tone, sarcastic, shifts me. I folded my lips changing my mind about directions.

"Um-hum."

I squealed shook my head humming through my nose. She strummed the cash register the total eight-fifty came on the display and she looked at me. Checking my pockets finding the purse Danielle left for me a little pink zip bag with a purple butterfly on it. In my hurry I forgot my gun, badge, wallet and a handbag.

Shit! Running away from your husband!

My subconscious reared her ugly head. I squinted at myself. Luckily there was a ten note to pay. She gave me a few coins change and turned her back to me.

OK then!

I accepted her rude behaviour as a recompense to mine, walking away to an adjacent booth seat, sliding in. Waiting, I fiddled with my phone, I view Sam's first text message with the directions to see where I went wrong, my feet ached.

I should have worn flats.

Another admonishment thought slipped. I dialled her again and the phone died.

Ugh!

I shook my fist with the phone inside screaming at myself inwardly. Just then.

"Miss," the sales assistant called to me breaking my oncoming rant, giving me my order with another judgemental glare, her accent emphasising on the 'I'.

Strange accent, I hadn't noticed before, I noted.

The brown paper bag with my doughnuts folded and drinks in a carrier. Instantly I fished the doughnut out. I bite savouring the taste for a moment, chewing filling the dried saliva. My mood subsided and I sipped the mocha from a straw.

Balancing, the paper bag to my mouth, exiting nibbling vigorously with the drinks carrier in my hand, the grumpiness is fading. With a straw in the iced drink, I angle it to sip turning my back to push the door out to exit, it chimed and closed. I stepped out on the pavement with a smile of content, being fed. I turned towards my car with a positive strut, though I did not have directions.

Swiftly, the homeless man moved from the dumpster into my face. The smell hit me and I turned. The doughnut fell out my hand in the bag and I shifted the drinks steady to avoid a spill. Turning to retrieve the fallen happiness, he snatched the paper bag from the floor and took off in a sprint. My mouth fell open and I am stationary.

What the!

I am speechless blinking stupefied from the encounter.

Never has this ever happened.

Not in Ceda, a dense city with more than just this one homeless person.

Not living off and on the streets and looking for places to sleep for six months, in a dangerous city.

Not even in the few places I was allowed to patrol in my D.P.F. training.

Never!

I have never heard of an incident like this from anyone or experienced it.

"What kind of a place is this!" I had to voice my displeasure.

Of course, in this weird town, all I gained was stares as if I'm the strange one. Maybe I was. Sighing, I walked forward looking back at him go in disgust.

Shaking my head to gather my equipoise, I turned walking my shoulders into a pole. The four drinks, squished between me and the pole, giving me a second bath.

"Fuck!" I didn't hold in the built irritation and cursed aloud.

The mixture of warm and ice drinks across my chest, hot and cold. The brief shoulder ache does not compare to the slush that cascades down the front of my breast, soaking my jacket, shirt, skirt all the way to my shoes.

"Ah!"

I tantrum throw the cup holder, stomping, closing my eyes shaking my fist standing by the pole.

"… Great! Jus…"

I shouted aloud, gaining stares. Giving up, I throw my head up. The darkening sky and grey clouds grew quickly, breathing loudly. I try to prevent myself from going there, from being defeated by these few missteps today. Doing the only thing I remember from my past, to bring me back, to calm, I count.

Ten,

I breathe. In slowly through my nose and out measured with my mouth slightly opened.

Nine, I assess.

Only a sore shoulder and spilled drinks. No harm.

Then, I checked my pockets. My left, the phone is soaked.

"Aaahhhh!" Irritation won, groaning noticeably, loud. "…
Fantastic!"

I completed my yell and closed my eyes.

Eight… Breathe again, gain logic.

The other pocket had loose change. I gasp, enthusiasm is gone.

Where are my keys?

I pat both pockets frantically. Only left with the coins from my
purchase, I swallowed my panic and the tears threatening to fall from my
eyes with anger.

"Great!" Instead, I voiced aggressively.

That fucker lifted it. Concluding inside.

What kind of town is this? I am screaming in my head.

Inhale and exhale, in from the nose out through the mouth I try again
to calm trying to remember the number I have reached.

Instead, I made a fist, clench my teeth and stomp.

I stomp.

Stomp.

Stomp the cups flat, splashing what's left up my legs, yelling curses
and frustration in a growl that bruised my throat.

Seven? Positive reflection. Then, thunder rolled and the skies
darken.

Really? I frown.

You can't stand there all afternoon! I fight the urge to wallow,
whimpering.

Six… Reassess and regroup.

Still having an internal battle while standing next to a pole, drinks at
my feet, the scene has gotten more awkward and people walking have
now stopped to stare. Near my car I remembered a sign pointing into the
laundromat entrance.

Yes!

I stopped counting on reaching positivity.

The rain burst heavily through the clouds to finish wash whatever
pride away. My flattened hair is gaining springs as the water drips off
them.

Well done, Shana.

I want to tell myself to shut it, deciding to go there. I am too infuriated for any victory dance inside, on a messed-up afternoon. I stepped away from the pole and traipse in the direction of the alley slushing the mixture of coffee, tea and rain to my underwear.

I prayed it was open as I mosey in that direction. Between the sides of the diner pass the dumpsters. There were maisonettes tucked in an entrance past the fire escapes that hovered over the dumpsters.

My lucky but unlucky day.

With a sigh, I push the door. It didn't budge, I pushed it again, and it rattled. Then I pushed it again and again and again it only rattled. I shook it in anger only to see a sign that says, 'pull'.

I exhaled.

Pulling and clamber inside trailing water draining on the mat at the entrance slushing with every footstep.

The light blue walls, three rows of two washing machines back-to-back and a wall with six tumble driers: three at the bottom and three on top. The aroma is a mixture of fabric softener and dampness.

There weren't any customers inside but four machines tumbling clothes. A small sitting area with six light blue leatherette chairs and a table with magazines. I slushed to a machine second row down placed my coins in the slot carefully peeled my jacket, beige shirt and maroon skirt off, ringed them inside the drier.

The stained-tanned full slip will have to wait thanks to that fool.

Threw my clothes in and pressed start. An annoying buzz played. I pressed it again and it buzzed again.

What now!

I slapped it, again and again, and the same sound.

... Ten, nine, eight.

"Damn it! Work! Gah! Please, I just need you dry don't need to be clean."

I hit it hard yelling then realising.

I am talking to the machine!

Ten, nine...

Ugh, I can't count now this is driving me nuts!

"I gave you my last few coins damn it, now work!"

I slammed my fist into the machine on the brink of crying. Water fills my eyes and the lump in my throat is getting harder to swallow. Making an inventory of my situation inside.

I am in my slip and underwear with a machine that wouldn't work. The rain is pouring. The car is probably stolen... because I needed directions and didn't ask... and had to have a doughnut in a dodgy neighbourhood...

My nose starts to twitch, and I continued aloud.

"My phone is dead. I have no money. I was robbed and I am late! Excuse me, three hours late." I whimper. "... And I think I want to throw up."

I screamed putting my hands over my reddened face full-on sobbing.

"Do you want to wash your load with mine?"

The vibrating tone avulsed my thoughts as more blood rushed to my face. I peeked up through my fingers from the top to bottom at a gorgeous man. Beach-ready tan, with perfectly low black hair. A full neatly cut beard, soft smooth pink lips, white smile. Perfect teeth and his toned structure protruding through his light cotton shirt, soft black slimming jeans emphasising his package bulged to the left.

I can't believe I looked!

I was dumbfounded gazing at his beauty as my libido woke.

"W-what," I stuttered in a gawp.

"Do you want to wash your load with mine?"

He repeated but my eyes followed the words forming from his full lips surrounded by unshaven hair. A salacious need takes over electrifying my lower parts. I cross my legs, lips parted mouthing his words at him with a strange need to giggle.

Shit, I'm staring!

He was incredibly attractive. The door chimed, and someone entered inviting the cold air and blowing me back to reality.

"Shit!" I cursed, shivering.

"Do you need help?"

He asked with an amused smirk across his face. I shook the gawking recollecting my frustration and quarrelled at him.

"This stupid machine wouldn't work! I put all my clothes not to mention my money."

I hit the machine again and it beeped. I breathe hard rolling my eyes at it.

"It wouldn't go with so few clothes," he stated the obvious.

"*I know!*" I tensed my face at him continuing my rant, "... But it would be nice if I could get a refund." My sarcastic pitch is high and unintentional.

He laughed.

His hilarity is lost to me.

That's not funny!

I scowled at him, "Do you mind if I put some of my load with yours to help you out?"

His mood didn't shift to mine.

"To help me out?" I squinted at him crossing my arms.

"Yes."

His grin continued as he came over to me.

I narrowed my eyes at him. "Is this what you do to get free loads washed?"

"No, this is what I do to help a beautiful woman who looks like she's having a bad day."

He caught me off guard, and my cheeks redden.

He tried to hide his amusement at my discomfort.

A bad day? "Does that line usually work?" I am not impressed.

"I don't know... yet, it's my first time."

The humidity rises and the space between us thickened. My tummy tingled with the compliment. This only happened to me with one man, I married him. I stepped back.

"I'm flattered but I'm married."

Raising my hand pointing at my ring.

"Ah, newlyweds."

He points out the obvious, reminding me of Eric and my earlier conversation.

"Not really we've just been busy for nearly three years." *Why did I overshare?*

"Wow, that's a first..." His light brown eyes meet mine.

My mouth quivers a small smile and he's taking a step towards me. I am immobilised, and my heartbeat quickens.

"… So, when do you plan to end it?" He grins close to my face.

His words wake me.

"Excuse me?" He's presumptuous!

"… Or finish the ceremony and get your bands." He has corrected himself.

"That's a good question." *Really Shana!*

I pant, my mouth parts unwillingly to the rising room temperature.

"By law, you are not officially married… until the ceremony is finished."

I swallow hard immovable to him.

"We've been saying 'after this case' for years."

Again, TMI Shana!

My heartbeat in my ears thumping. I feel obligated to answer his invasive questioning with the truth.

"Lawyer," he asks.

"Not exactly," I whispered; he closes the gap between us.

"Police."

"Something like that." My words are limited, hard to articulate, his eyes are locked with mine.

"You have the eyes of someone driven for justice."

Is that all he's going to say about my eyes.

Really, Shana?

My cringy thinking brings me back. I moved away.

"I'm not sure whether to take that as a compliment or an insult." I sneezed.

"Do you need a towel?"

"I'm fine." I formed a cover around my mouth and nose with both hands turning away from him, I sneezed again.

"I insist."

I sneezed again.

He took a towel from a basket on the machine. His eyes never leave me, holding it out to me with a step towards me. He smooths the soft material across my face drying water falling from my hair to my face, electrifying our stance once again. The touch has me in a trance. I want to move but cannot. Holding my breath, the energy tingles through me.

"I live on the first floor of the next building. The first apartment. You can get dried and a hot drink."

"That's not a good idea. Besides, I am wearing hot drinks."

I stepped back again, he chuckles.

"Hum. What if, I put my load with yours in exchange for my hospitality?"

"I don't think so," I whisper aching for more.

"If it makes you feel better, I'll leave the door open and let you use my phone?"

"All right." I didn't hesitate.

CHAPTER TWENTY

"Is that a, yes?" he asked excitedly, smiling with broad and smooth lips.

"Yes," I repeat. He had me at 'phone'.

He gives me a large white towel to wrap over my shoulders. It was warm, fresh out the drier. I stood aside eyeing his movements curling the towel around me. There was a second plastic square basket on a machine next to me. With a sly movement and a grin, he takes his darker clothes out and puts them into the machine with my jacket and skirt. Cheerfully encouraging me, clearing his throat. I sigh, he separates my beige shirt from the maroon suit. He adds some of his light clothes to load another machine.

My day began with the warmth of my husband. The most in-depth conversation we've ever had and is ending with me being tardy for the third time for work. The walk of shame wouldn't be enough to describe me at this point.

My head fell to the floor and sees coins coming out of his tight jeans pocket. The act forces my eyes down where they shouldn't be.

Oh my gosh! I looked again!

I folded my lips, startled at my behaviour hearing the hum of amusement from this man. I know he's caught me. Admonishing inwardly, moving my eyes away. He added soap and fabric softener and pressed the play button, it buzzed. Irritating me once more, before beginning to spin. The hum is low, tumbling the clothes. He takes up his folded clothes basket and empty basket in his arms.

"If you would follow me."

He walked to the door, and I tailed. Wasting no time, he pushes the door open holding it with his back. I walked through to exit and then moved from the doorway. The rain has stopped but the evening is falling.

Alerted by a passing siren, I am looking up and down the alleyway, waywardly thinking I need to remain hidden. The unsettling cerebration went with the reality of the cold air and me, being half-dressed in public.

Hustling through puddles regrettably, with my loud stilettoes. He led me down the side of the alley to a building entrance tucked and hidden between two other buildings. At the front an old glass and red wooden door with a keypad to the side. He punched the code in pushing it first and waiting for me again. I trailed through before him up a dated stare case to a door in a narrow hallway.

He balanced the baskets on his hips, jiggled his hands in his slim jeans pocket pulled out two keys, stuck one in the lock and opened into a massive apartment. It was unbelievable.

Everything was so meticulously coordinated black, wood and chrome modern furniture like a show home, tidy as if out a magazine the aromas of oils are sensual. White walls with black and white photos of the canyons and ancient stone carvings.

From the entrance, two amazing, engraved bronze vases looked like they were of the Zeman origin. Two stairs down the living room, a black leather corner chair, the front of it facing the entrance covered with three black and white pillows. A black furry rug with white trimmings and a beautiful obtuse custom-made frosted glass table, a wooden base which stood in the centre of the room.

I stood in the doorway as he went up the curved stairs carrying the two baskets. Only gone for a minute, he sauntered downstairs holding a white T-shirt out for me.

"You can get out of those wet clothes if you'd like."

He signalled pointing from my head to my feet. I cling to the towel over my shoulders pointing at him with my chin.

"Thanks, but I don't know you."

And I will be wearing nothing but that…

"Where are my manners? We haven't introduced ourselves. Brian Kumal."

He reached his hands to me draping the jersey over his other hand.

"I'm Shannan Hall." *Did I just say that?*

Doubting the words that exited me I blinked a few times before returning the gesture, putting my cold hands out to shake his. Tough, firm, warm, smooth, there was some tenderness to his grip and his thumb moved along the outside of my hand. A moment, sending a strange sensation from the point of contact, that I couldn't pin and wouldn't say even in thought. "... I still don't know you." I stuck to professional.

He chuckled. "You can call someone if that would make you feel better."

"It would," I reply swiftly.

"... And you don't need to stand in the hallway." Brian's gawp remained.

"I think I might. Until I get my phone call, thank you." I stuck my nose in the air.

His face alights with humour turns on his heels and goes into the kitchen. Takes up a handset, and hands it to me, nodding. He is quite charming, and he knows it, standing with crossed arms bundling the T-shirt in his biceps. From memory, I dialled Sam turning my back to him standing in the hallway.

"Martinez," Sam answers after two rings.

"Sam it's me."

My voice is small and I'm expecting a complaint.

"Shana, where are you?" she begins just as Liz would. "... I've been calling you for the past three and a half hours." She gained traction.

I have lost track of the time and began to work in my head the events, all unfortunate before this.

"... I had to wrap things up here." She went on with her quarrel breaking my recollection.

I sigh, ignoring her challenging tone.

She hears me and quieted.

After a beat, I apologised automatically, "Sorry! I am fine and at..."

I turned around to face Brian, he keeps his posture and pleasant disposition. I lifted my chin to him edging a response. He's not moved, arms crossed, legs at shoulder width and the T-shirt bundled around his muscular arms. I rolled my eyes before asking, "... What's your address?" I pointed again with my chin impatient.

He shows his teeth almost as if sucking it before he answered.

"Twenty-four B 1218 Canyon Street, Shadeyah, Divinish."

He had such a mischievous ogle painted across his face that I hesitated. Then, he takes a step forward my heart skipped a beat. His amusement seemed to have increased. I frown at him but repeated.

"Twenty-four B 1218 Canyon Street, Shadeyah. I got lost, then my phone died. Someone's helping me," I summarised bullet point before questioning the relevance.

Should I offer some explanation?

I am not accountable to her.

But I know she heard him. She uses moments like these for her arsenal, not that there are any.

What would she do with this?

Nothing is happening. I rationalised.

He is helping. My subconscious arches an eyebrow. I shook the thought out my head.

Just don't be caught in his jersey with the door closed or look at his parts again. I talk myself into a defence.

"You're sounding as dubious as Aaliyah."

Funny how she mentions the one person that I hate being compared to, knowing how much I hate that. She likes to push buttons, but doesn't talk of her own motive. I know she's waiting for me to mess up to tell him.

I really hate them both!

"… As long as you don't do as she would. Are you doing as she would?"

Her voice stern, almost threatening. Just like when they all burst into my apartment the night after Eric showed up.

"*No!*" I shouted defending her suggestive tone.

How dare she!

I am not a ho, like Aaliyah.

"Look, I was robbed and had a little trouble." I stuck to my vague explanation. "… Is everything under control?" I moved off-topic to the reason I left my comfortable apartment with my husband.

I was not running away! Immediately, maintaining my stance about the in-depth conversation to my nagging subconscious popping up.

Focusing on the death of the suspect, the meeting on Monday and the implications, if they did not do this by the book.

I hope she's secured the scene, discretely.

She breathes loud into the phone. "I should be asking you that."

Excuse me?

She's not convinced and is mocking my tone.

Bitch! "I am fine by the way," I stated in irritation, sarcastically. "… Thanks for asking."

She's questioning my integrity.

Brian is clearing his throat.

I measured him from head to toe and toe to head. His eyes are fixed on me holding the jersey out, and he takes another measured step, shifting my comfort. My heart raced and guard is up, ready to step away but my feet are somehow planted.

"Can you send someone for me?" I pleaded.

Don't beg! I whine to myself.

"It'll take probably about an hour-ish." Her deep rustic voice is uncertain but level. I don't trust it.

Another hour! I whine inward!

My clothes should be dry by then.

I look at the positive, "OK… Bye," I whispered and hung up.

Brian is now in the doorway, a foot away from me with his hand out, raising his eyebrows at me.

"A deal is a deal," he is insisting,

I narrowed my eyes at him.

He is very arrogant, but I am wet and cold.

"Fine," I agreed with protest.

How is this going to work?

I lingered in the hallway thinking.

"The bathroom is the door to the left of the kitchen."

His brown eyes latch on to me through the doorframe in the hall. He's pointing behind him with his thumb over his shoulder, showing me the direction. I folded my lips, contemplating, biting my bottom lip from one end to the next. My heart is beating fast, unsure of if to trust this stranger who has offered to, and has somewhat helped.

He has kept his side of the agreement.

"This front door remains open," the answer flew out as a threat pointing at the doorframe before relinquishing to defeat.

"Sure Shannan."

I am caught off guard, he's calling me by my full name. No one does that.

Eric, only if he's mad. I am debating the sound of it out his mouth. Then again, only my friends call me Shana. Inwardly deliberating Brian's disposition: his tone was almost sarcastic and he's wearing a chortle.

I am offended.

"Mrs Hall," I squeal. *Again, really?* I started passing him. And he replies, "Maybe after you've finished Cáhilt." He's quick on the tongue.

I gasped widening my eyes, my mouth fell open. "Presumptuous much."

You shared.

I scoffed at myself yanking the T-shirt out his hands. Bundled it around mine stomping into his bathroom. His smile never faded with his staring. I locked the door behind me. It was a three-piece light marble, a huge mirror over the sink. I could have a full view of myself even at the other end of the bathroom. A delight, sleek and new.

A stray notion filtered taking off my shoes to clean them. I wiped my feet from the sticky drinks. Towel drying my now curling hair and detangling it with my fingers. It gains volumes and dry kinks by the second. I pout. Holding what I could together with a twist, it all into one tangled curl then wrapping it into a bun.

That will have to do!

Curious, does he live here alone?

Snooping in his cabinet, his after shave, perfume, shaver… nose clipper!

Gross, I've seen enough.

I accidentally slammed it. No mark of a woman…

What do I care anyway?

Dragging on his T-shirt over my head, my large bun snagged and loosen. The wet slip below, I shook my arms through, the T-shirt sleeves. It was massive, almost like a dress. Then, I lose the straps of my slip sliding it over my shoulders, keeping the jersey on just in case he came in.

He seems decent but I don't know him.

Folding my elbows through the arms of the shirt, and sliding my hand out the strap. Doing each one at a time, before I let it, fall to my feet. I undo my white lace bra repeating the process and added it to the pile.

I am not giving him my underwear.

I shook my head in agreement with myself. When I returned to the living area, he was sitting patiently on the couch deep in thought, I think. Cautiously, I ambled to him.

"Ahh... Yes!" he says almost as if he forgot I was still here but his tone carried something more with it. "... I will get these done for you," he says politely.

There, I stood next to the glass table, my feet bare, legs exposed at my thighs, handing a stranger my clothes. What Emily would have said being a fly on the wall.

He got up and nodded.

Peculiar! I squint, with a lost grin standing at least a foot or so, over me. "Thank you."

I nodded crossing my legs, taking in Brian's handsome deportment. Leaving the door opened as agreed, he left me, a stranger in his apartment, wearing his T-shirt.

I moved through the place. The wooden floors are smooth and quiet without shoes. A wooden bookshelf with a few books, scattered. A crystal bowl with clear pebbles and a few pictures in frames and trophies along a wall near the couch.

Across that wall a black and wooden heater. The red and orange light danced, dispersing heat. Next to a large flat screen TV on the wall leading to the hallway.

Should I sit, should I stand?

A virgin to this experience I am clueless to the protocols. I pace fascinated by the immaculate living space. The walls I examined displays trophies and medals and pictures of him playing football.

Impressive, I thought.

A few pictures and art hanging, then I spot it. One picture of a woman, hidden, tucked behind pictures and ornaments dusty. I zoned in. The woman strangely had features similar to Sharron Mall. Or maybe I am seeing her everywhere. Her hair was straight with a fringe. She, him and a cute boy, the child looked younger than Danielle.

"My family."

I gasped holding my chest and turning fast. He's standing behind me in the audit of his display. I strive to not show my surprise.

"Married?" I squeak.

Did I just get caught with my hands in the cookie jar? I shake my head at myself.

"Well, not exactly. Legally, yes. I've got the papers. I just haven't given up hope, yet."

He began the familiar brood, staring at me with a saddened expression, but his deportment I pick up, one of anxiousness.

"Is that your son?" I point at the picture.

He nods straying his eyes from mine and wavers.

"Do it for him then. You'll only make things worse, having him in the middle." I shrugged at him thinking of Danielle, Eric and Sam.

What two years ago, felt like an impossible, uncompromising and tough situation. I wouldn't want another child to live through.

"Damn... you do divorces too?" He smiles bright and contagious.

I returned a grin. "Not really." I shook my head folding my lips stifling the grin.

Moving away from him to the sofa, I modestly sat conscious of my lack of bra and hardening nipples. His quick glance turns my face red knowing he's seeing them but earlier, I also had a look.

Touché!

I grin, shifting and crossing my arms holding part of my boobs with my folding arm.

"Are you available to have a look at my papers?"

He trudges next to me. The T-shirt rides up, shifting around to make room for him on the couch. I am tempted to hold one of his pillows on my lap for better security but resist.

"You can't afford me." I shook my head emphasising.

It is not a good idea anyway!

The grim outcome of Eric and Sam's and the position I played in that has left me extra cautious. The air suddenly electrifies and I am having a strange attraction to him. He is somehow comforting me. This has never happened to me before. All of my pre-Eric relationships never had this type of chemistry.

Even with Kyle, whom I loved.

The admission feeds my guilt. Torn between wanting and avoiding this; he's definitely not making it easy with his charm and wit. Swallowing has become harder and the urge for a release is a foremost need.

Probably because Eric started me. I shifted on the chair in recollection of the amazing kiss we shared before leaving for work. Brian edges closer and I felt like we were almost horizontal.

Change direction, my thoughts warned.

"How did you find a place like this? From outside no one will guess."

Great safe topic. I high-five myself.

He sensed my rejection. Moving back a beat, then, retreating to the kitchen almost as if having a mental awareness. He broods shutting and opening cupboards and the kettle went on.

"Something hot as promised. What would you like Mrs Hall?" he calls from the kitchen. I turned to view him.

Calling me that still don't sound right!

His tone changed to polite and more businesslike.

OK then, "Tea, no milk, one sugar." My voice with a bit of remorse.

"Any specific flavour?" he said formally.

How many flavours are there? "Just tea…"

I say questioning and wait.

OK he's not going to answer.

"I don't quite remember," he voiced and I wasn't sure to what he referred. "… But I wanted to have something nice, for a family. To have my wife, raise a son and to be close enough to my family. A… real estate manager found this."

Brian has answered as if he heard me. He's glaring at the countertops as if seeing his life unfolds before him. His gaze reminds me of Eric's self-loathing daze.

Divert him!

"That's a deep confession for someone you just met." I try lightening the mood switching again but I didn't see his reaction.

Maybe I should have used my filter for that one.

He jaunts to me, sitting closer than needed causing an uneasy clench within me. Offering the cup handle. Our hands touched again and as before, we froze and the hairs on my skin rise. My heart pulsated at my neck. I inhale sharply unable to exhale. Something beeped. Snapping us both out of the trance, there was a moment of pause before he voiced,

"It's time to get the clothes."

He let go, sprung up and ready to leave me once again amongst his things. I am certain he cursed. Not loud enough for me to hear clearly but I was sure being around A.P.S. has inadvertently trained my ears to the sounds.

"Yeah, I have to be going myself."

I somewhat welcomed the interruption.

Sam might be close, don't want her seeing me dressed like this sitting to have tea.

My eyebrows went up at the thought that somehow felt natural when it shouldn't. He was mostly easy to talk to... *and I have an attraction to him.* Rolling my eyes at myself he said, "Sure... I'll be back." With a hidden simper.

It was weird. We were both thrown by the physical contact. I cling to my default.

"Thank you for your help, Mr Kumal."

I stood up, reminding myself of my professionalism, gave an assuring smile.

"Brian." He paused, correcting me ogling at my hazels.

Oh, we're back to this. "The clothes," I prompted him.

"Nice to have your company this afternoon Shannan." He nods again saying my full name.

I don't like it.

Then he went through the door and around the corner out of sight.

This has been an interesting day but it is time to get back to reality. I went to the bar stool to finish my tea. Finishing my inspection of his open plan, spread to the kitchen. Electric plate hobs, dark tiles and polished wooden floors, next to it a chrome staircase spiral around a pole. I admired the layout thinking what it would feel like to live here. When I feel a presence behind me.

Brian is standing in silence inspecting my legs curled around his bar stool, ogling. His expression is a mixture of fascination and I sense a need. My heart jumped at the sight. Holding a grey square basket folded with all his laundry, my cleaned suit perched at the top.

I hopped off accidentally pulling up the already thigh-high T-shirt, under the curve of my ass. Groaning with embarrassment, I hooked the hem down quick keeping my hazels on him shifting my weight from leg to leg.

He placed the basket on the sofa, moving straight to me, handing my cleaned suit to me. Our hands touched jolting the already thickened energy between us. We stayed in that moment like if in a bubble. The electric pull imminent, our breathing increased and shallow, he leans in to me. His breath touches my face.

No! My conscious woke me. I stepped back.

"Thank you."

My voice hoarse, soft and I folded my lips inwards for moisture. I stepped aside him, stepping back again holding the warm clothes then, turned to the bathroom breaking the thick charge. I flicked the light changing hurryingly.

Did he try to kiss me? The question lingered as I closed the door being sure it was locked.

Inhaling deep, then exhaling, I shook the lingering bits of the charge finally sensing something other than the strong need. I brought my suit to my nose sniffing the detergent and for a second thinking this is his scent.

Stop! My subconscious shouted at me waking me fully from what felt like a trance. I shook the suit realising he thoughtfully placed the bra in-between the clothes. *With that notion...* I dressed quick. My clothes crisp and fresh and unstained I am myself again.

Except for the afro.

Gaping myself in the mirror ashamed of the 'what ifs'. I tidied my hair as best as I can combing my fingers through the knots, shaking the curls to fluff the mane. Slipping my shoes onto my feet, finishing the business attire. I exited. He was in his kitchen ominous it seems. His front door still open, heating the hallways.

"Thanks for your help, Brian." I gait stretching my hand out to him.

"Leaving so soon?"

What is he doing? I tilted my head with a squint to him.

He's not returning my embrace.

"Yes Brian, I've got stuff to do," I verbalised my intention.

"With your case, huh?"

It feels like he's stalling.

"Actually, I do. See you around."

I say automatic, pulling my hands away. He grabs it, with both his trapping mine between his, just like the mayor, bidding to drag this out. Unlike mayor Mall, Brian's hands are not workman but not soft either.

This must be one of the customs the mayor may have been referring.

Still odd. I shook my head at myself.

"One would hope," Brian answers loaded, regret in his voice.

"Maybe…" I shrugged and gave him hope tugging slight on my hand.

"Possibly…" he almost whispers.

He is wringing this out.

The pulse around my neck thumps and the atmospheric zap gain in amps. I took my hand back.

"Good bye, Mr Kumal."

"Mrs Hall."

He nods again with his hands plastered to his side almost like he was bowing.

Yep, definitely a custom here.

I folded my lips inwards at his strange behaviour, suffocating my amusement and shock trying to focus on the fact that Mr Kumal was a good host and polite. I assessed, sauntered through the halls. My footsteps echoing as I leave, down the stairs and through the dirty door.

It was dark. I hadn't realised the time, it felt like minutes; forty-five for the most. It may be the time of the year, although this county does not snow like Ceda, I believed it would not get dark so early.

Sam should be here soon or I will be best to wait in the diner.

There was no light in the alleyway except for the entrance. I hadn't noticed if there were lights when I came in but…

It's strange to know there are residents living here without lights.

I made the observation. I could barely see my hand in front of my face just the light at end of the alley. I heard a garbage can turn over and a cat squealing which made me jump. Just then I remembered that homeless man, that thief from earlier and picked up my pace heading for the light hoping.

Maybe I should call Sam again.

A plan occurs and I turned to go back to Brian's. My heart trembles the memory surfaces, my meeting Eric. The urge to stay hidden returns. Hearing footsteps behind me coming fast I changed direction again and bumped into a man.

"Give me your money," he said, and I heard a flick of metal and he pointed a knife at me in the dim. His head was covered by a hoodie and his face hid with the darkness. I put one foot behind the other at a ninety degree angle the width of my skirt.

Polyester, pencil skirt! Shit!

I whine to myself.

Not wide enough!

Standing at an angle, same hand, same foot in front, fisting.

This will have to do.

Confident to make a move another set of footsteps behind me. A male: his arm slide around my neck, his elbow at my chin, throwing me off my stance. Winding an arm around my waist; pulling me into a waiting erection inducing angst and horror at the same time.

I swallowed hard, eyes bulged, breathing sharply and putting both hands in the air. The man behind breathes his cigarette on my neck with a strange accent accentuation on the 'I'.

"Didn't you just hear the man?"

Towing me back into the darkness, he tumbled me off my stance. My eyes dilate and dread rising higher as the seconds past.

"I –I would love to, but someone passed a little earlier than you guys, and took it all,"

I boldly explained, hoping to throw them off meantime trying to compose myself cleansing my lungs counting inwardly. Reciting my mantra.

Ten, Calm your breathing.

"That's OK, I was after something else anyway."

I yelp at his confession my mind now someplace else in full panic. He groaned deep in his throat and erection twitched at my back. My breathing became a pant and I cannot calm my mind. The first man with the knife closes the gap between us as the other step backwards towards the side of a dumpster. My eyes adjust slightly to the dark.

Eeek!

Cringing, for a second, I put my hands up, exhaled gaining my composure. The man slowly walked to me I countdown fast.

Ten, nine, eight, seven, six, five, four, three, two, one.

I am calm and my eyes burn. Bringing my hands to his arm around my neck, pressing my thumbs into the back of his palm turning the back of his hand winding it the wrong way around, and straightening his elbow. He yelled tipping to the side I am twisting, and he goes up on his toes. I held tighter.

The man with the knife swung. It made contact with my leg. Burning and warm liquid wet the side of my skirt. He cut me and my skirt partly freed my leg but not wide enough for an extended kick. I lean my weight on the man behind me to throw a kick to the man in front of me. Only, I made contact with his thigh using my stilettoes. I know it hurt.

Without letting go of the man behind me and twisting his arm. I squat under his extended arm moving out of his clinch as he screams. Making sure it has stretched all the way out and was straightened. Then, punched his elbow with all the force I gathered. The popping sound I confirmed me dislocating it. Letting him go, he disappeared cursing and screaming.

I held the wet slit he made of my skirt confirming I was cut. Then finish ripping the tear completely to free my legs and got into a stance. The man with the knife came towards me swiping the knife, I dodged it. He swiped again, the third time I caught his arm coming towards me with both hands and in that instant, using my elbow hit to his face and holding the arm tight and away from me.

Then turning to face him, I fisted and used my tilted wrist upwards into his face several times until it felt wet and I heard a crunch. I am satisfied feeling the warm blood and I knew I broke his nose. He dropped the knife, held his face and went off screaming into the dark.

Pleased with myself I nursed my wounded leg for a minute before I limped towards the light. I felt fingers through my hair and a palm at the back of my head grabbed my mane. Before I could turn around, I felt my head butt the wall and echoed the sound. An instant headache and loud ringing in my ears and darkness.

****

The lights moving over me in pulses woke me. My body flaccid and I'm too weak to speak. My vision, bleary my head aches with tinnitus.

My head really hurt.

Failing to hold my head, the muffled chatter escalates around me. Someone's touching me.

Why are you touching me?

I heard clearly.

"This woman is pregnant!"

What!

CHAPTER TWENTY-ONE

My eyes flickered to fuzz. I blinked profusely to clear them. Surrounded by bright lights in a white room, a steady beeping, something is clipped on to my finger. Everywhere hurts and my body is stiff, heavy, hard to move.

Ah, what is this in my nose?

A cool breeze blows into my nose as an uncomfortable drooping of plastic across my cheeks looping around my ears. Glancing down, with confusion I am covered, neatly, my arms outside of the sheet and I am wearing a white gown with blue spots.

My hands are hard to move with a prominent pricker at the back of my palm near my fingers. The beeping increased when I twitch.

My throat is dry. I attempt to swallow but groan from the pain in my head followed by the blaring sound in my ears. I recalled fighting, breaking someone's nose. I smile.

Smiling hurts.

In fact, my body hurts.

Where am I anyway?

I tilted to the right, there is a window and the beautiful sunrise. Attempting to raise my hands again that funny sensation at the back of my hand. It feels soft but sharp. A steady pounding consumes my head as everything gets louder. My breathing, my heartbeat, the pulsing sound of a monitor and darkness fogs me.

****

Awake again. Still sore everywhere, still confused. It's dark through the window. No stars just dark, my toes are cold and I shudder. There's a plastic sack over my head hanging from a thin metal pole trailing a plastic line leading to my hand with a sharp sensation where it touches my hands. The cool liquid forcing itself through my veins through the lines. I blinked tired again.

Footsteps and humming wake me; dressed in a white blouse and skirt, her broad behind to my face bending over, looking for something. I took a cleansing breath startling her. A nurse.

I must be in a hospital.

Attempting to open my mouth a seal of dried skin. No words came out, and the parched patches making it difficult to swallow. Fresh air enters my mouth suddenly aware of my grimy mouth.

With a rock, I try sitting up uncomfortably. Aching everywhere my head bobbed and the sudden urge to pee takes me. There was a funny sensation down there.

"Lay back, please," she assisted me gently.

I obeyed.

"Do you know where you are?" She shines light into my eyes burning my retina.

I try folding my lips to moisten them, the saliva too thick making no difference increasing the dehydration of my throat.

I groaned hoarse again.

"I am going to do some checks OK?" She sticks a thermometer into my mouth, "… Below your tongue please." Her silver watch clipped on upside down to my view: blue, black and red pens sequent in her pocket.

Some badges clipped on to her uniform, her voice experienced and stern and she doesn't smile. Her brown skin smooth and maroon lipstick perfect for her tone.

She turns a second. Wheels a tall machine close to my side, and adjusted the coupling around my arm securing the Velcro, presses a button and it tightens with a gruff sound.

I opened my mouth and no sound came out.

I need to pee… The need is urgent.

"Pee…" I finally got a word out painfully and barely audible.

"Don't worry you've got a catheter." There was care in her voice.

I gasped in horror. *Gross!* "Can I…"

My sound is as grainy as agony grips my throat. It is like I swallowed a sheet of sandpaper, talking hurts.

"Not until the doctor sees you." Her no-nonsense tone continued.

I feel a fraction of relief, which concerns me. I pout achingly.

"Lay back, I am going to examine your tummy."

I frown as she pulled the gown up and pushing down the covers. I am following her hands. The cold air reaches under me as I concluded my underwear was missing. Her face serious as she examines me and it hurts.

What an odd request.

"Do you remember what happened to you?" She plunged her cold fingers into my tummy with no remorse.

I wince looking up as if the roof can tell her what she needs. "Ah!"

I expressed the feeling of her examination. She took some notes then visibly relaxed, washing her hands at a nearby sink I hadn't noticed earlier.

"The doctor will be here shortly. He would be able to answer any questions you may have, OK."

Her voice is singsong with a hint of compassion. She has confused me on so many levels. Before I had the chance to ask a question, a tall slender man, clean shaven with a full head of black and grey short hair walked in. His white coat draped over his shoulder like Paula and his hands in the pockets. A stethoscope around his neck as he sauntered in. The nurse gave him the chart. After a quick scope he shook his head in agreement of the notes then focused on me with a pleasant grin.

"How are you tonight? I am Doctor Peter James."

"Hi," I held my throat as it ached.

"Nurse, can you get this patient some ice please?" he issued his command.

"Yes Doctor," The nurse promptly replied.

I hadn't notice she was still in the room. He strolled to the bed standing over me staring into my eyes making me a bit uneasy. The nurse handed him a glass with ice. He gave one to me cooling my lips easing my throat.

"A little at a time," he warns warmly. "… Can we start with your name?"

"Sh-shan-nan." My throat scrapes the word out shakingly.

Talking really hurts. I noted painfully.

"Good, the police will be informed that you are awake." I frown trying to recall but he continues, "… They would be able to help you."

I nod with some understanding.

"Do you know where you are?" he follows with another question.

"Hospital." This time I try softer, my throat still aches.

"That's right." He nods as if he's rewarding me for getting it right. "… Divinish North Hospital." My brain cannot connect so I listen. "… You had no identification. You've been unconscious for two days. You're here as a Jane Doe."

"What!" *That was clear! But still hurts.* I lift the hand without the needle to my neck guarding it as if that would help the pain.

"You were brought in unconscious, two nights ago. You've got a minor traumatic brain injury. Among other things," he said loaded and I wait for the details. "… I have stitched the adhesion on your head and leg."

The fight is starting to come back again. I must have been cut when he tore my skirt.

Someone pushed my head into a wall.

I shook my head painfully in agreement barely paying attention to the details of our conversation.

My eyes are tired and my body limp again.

"Get some rest and we will talk a bit later."

I shook my head again blinking long and relaxing.

****

The need to pee has woken me again with an unpleasant recollection of the catheter. Doctor James was standing over me peeping over his glasses at the sack of clear liquid on my arm. My movement was caught in his peripheral view.

"Good morning,"

He grinned finishing up his check. I looked up only viewing into his straight nose with some grey hairs turning swiftly at the sight.

"Hi," my nervous voice answered not as sore today.

"Shannan, right?"

He took his pen from his pocket pushing down the top with a click grasping the clipboard that sat on a wheeled drawer behind him. I shook my head at him.

"Are there any other names, Shannan?"

"Sorry, Shannan Christine Davis-Hall." I ached all my names for clarification and he writes on the clipboard.

"Missus, I assume. Your ring had to be removed. It's in the draw next to you. I didn't see your bands."

I gaped quickly at my hand, it was not there. I shook my head no to him.

"Can I ask how far I am from Shadeyah City?"

I blurted out, cutting him from his next question,

"Shadeyah counties are to the bottom of Divinish you are closer to Ceda which is to the top of the county."

My eyes widened.

"I am a little confused. What am I doing on the other side of Divinish?"

I rushed in my words demanding an answer, thinking of the last event, fighting. The gaps are making me nervous. His professional manner didn't shift.

"I still need you to answer some questions before I get into that. Is this your first pregnancy?"

"Sorry what?" My eyes widened. *Did I hear right?*

"… Have you e-ver been preg-nant before?"

He said slowly as if I cannot understand his language. I was sure that I spoke in the words he did. I frown.

I remember hearing that statement being brought in.

I thought that was a dream.

Or a nightmare, not real… my subconscious whimper in a corner.

"Mrs Davis-Hall."

He snapped me out of my musing, my heart rate increased.

"W-what do you mean pregnant before?" I am pale at the news.

"You're pregnant," he said factually with a grave expression.

I couldn't blink.

"… You didn't know?" he says almost judgementally and writes in his notes.

"What? How did this happen?"

This is the confirmation. Not the test Eric got me or the feeling that I am. It isn't because I was vomiting or that I have increased in my waist size. This was it. My palms begin to sweat. I groped the sheets covering me.

"Are you asking me?" he pointed at himself. "... So, I guess this is unplanned."

He wrote on the clipboard.

I can't see straight any more.

"This is not happening," I verbalised my thoughts putting my hands to my head accidentally touching the sore spot.

"You are about thirteen weeks by the measurements. That's why you were transferred to this hospital."

"Transferred?"

My eyes focused on the black pens in his pockets.

"Yes, you were transferred from Divinish Central Hospital. This hospital is better equipped for antenatal care; you were in and out of consciousness for three days. We believed you would have slipped into a coma. There was no swelling on your brain but you were unresponsive."

His strong blue eyes intensify squinting with every word as he continues but the sound of his voice muffles and fades. Panic filled me and a humming sound amplifies until he finishes.

"OK," a small voice barely escapes. A cold-chill flows through me. The reality hits me and tears flow down my face over the tubes going to my nose. I rest back unable to hold my composure sobbing uncontrollably.

Do I want to be a mother?

Danielle is great but... I never had to deal with poo and vomit except for myself and... Eric.

His name brings panic.

Shit, shit, shit!

"Do you want us to call your husband?"

I stopped breathing.

"Mrs Hall, are you all right?"

Minutes ticked and I stare. The beeping in the room loud, I concentrate on that.

"… Mrs Hall!" Doctor James called me snapping me out of the trance with Eric's name used to refer to me. It only lasted a moment or two.

"S-sure," I stutter in shock, then finally registered what he was asking.

He wants to call Eric?

No!

Not happening.

"Can I call him?" I try delaying this news for a day or two, at least until I can say it without cringing. My eyes close then open, I break contact with his pen in exchange for the sheets.

"You should rest. Give the nurse his number. She will contact him," he is insisting and I panic.

The urge to pee returns.

I tense, distracted. "Can I please use the bathroom?"

He grins impassive and I sense a 'no'.

"I will ask the nurse to help you with that."

For that second, I forgot. My face brightens red.

"Thank you." I keep my head down.

"You rest I'll be back to see you in the morning."

He exited I saw him through the window speaking to the nurse.

I can't sleep now, still in shock about this pregnancy probing my memory for the day it happened. I look down at my tummy, barely a bump.

How could you have lived with me for so long and I didn't know you were there.

The irresponsible drinking of beer and pizza surfaced. I gulped to hold the emotions in, ashamed of my behaviour.

What would Eric think?

CHAPTER TWENTY-TWO

I woke to humming and tightening of the Sphygmomanometers around my arm, it was still dark outside. She has put the thermometer under my arm this time administering and connecting another bag of fluid to flow through my arm. Exhausted, I let her, drifting to sleep again.

****

Awakened by movements and voices again in the room.

How often does she have to come in here?

I was limp and hadn't envisioned the quiescence of a hospital. Her consistent interruption is becoming an annoyance.

My eyes quivered forced by another disruption. Then opened in soft clouded figures, of the drowsiness that cleared to my husband standing in the doorway, exchanging whispered words with the nurse.

His hands in his washed-out jeans pocket, a white jersey and black shoes. His head and beard fuller than usual. He sees me. I am motionless. Unable to exhale, my heart quickens.

He dashes to me before I could think. Shining simper across his face, redden eyes narrowing with disquiet at me. With a great sigh, he sat on the bed. He grasped my hands and kisses it several times. Then leaning to my forehead, he pecks me and accidentally making contact with the bandage. I flinched painfully.

"Sorry, sorry," he apologised instantly. His eyes were glossy growing darker as he blinks at me holding my hand to his lips. His face crinkles about to cry.

"It's OK, I'm OK," I assured him but my tears slip away.

"Please, baby, don't cry."

His tone soft and broken, manifested the persistent flow of tears; he enfolds his arms around me rocking tenderly.

"I'm here."

Those two words softened the tensed expectation and folded me in the moment remembering the last time we shared.

****

The sunrise lit the room, naturally waking me. In view the top of Eric's lush head of curly hair. He sat on a chair leaning onto the bed. One hand under his head the other across my feet.

He is so peaceful when he sleeps.

The acknowledgement of the opposite once he's awake. I resist running my fingers through his wavy hair. I'd love to smooth the ridges. I don't want to wake to his inevitable interrogation. I enjoy the serenity and I was sated.

"Good morning."

Of course, the nurse came in.

I sulk in anticipation as he stirred. The nurse is sprightly; he sat up stretching his hands above his head with a big yawn, exposing his belly button and sculpted tummy and the trail of hair to his um.

He's got a grizzly-beard.

The lush black beard distracted my lusting. I chuckle inwardly.

"Hi," I whispered, hoarse again. My lips are dried. I cleared my throat and started again.

"Hey."

He beams bright and my mouth quivers. I folded my lips trying to hide the amused thoughts of his beard. He sat back sliding the chair away from the bed letting her through. Peeking around as she barks her commands to examine me and records them. She passes between us twisting and turning me to suit.

She removes the oxygen tubes from my nose. Takes empty liquid sacks off. It is difficult to hide the grin. I gazed everywhere else feeling his intense stare. My face brightens red with an inept laugh.

"The doctor will be here to check on you soon,"

the nurse informs as she leaves. I cross my arms waiting.

I wonder if he knows.

He sets the bed, so I am almost sitting. Fluffs my pillows and returns to his seat dragging it close enough so he can touch me.

"Where's your ring?"

His observation shifts me. I uncrossed my hand rubbing my ring finger.

"It's in the drawer."

I pointed next to him. He searches the small ones fiddling with pills. He looks into a bigger drawer taking out my suit in a sealed, large plastic bag with dried blood stains on the cloth and in the bag.

His glow grew serious. He searches another small drawer taking the three millimetres platinum, square five millimetres diamond ring and my platinum infinity diamond band out securing them into his jeans pocket.

More tensed than ever, he held the clothes. His eyes linked to my hazels resting it at the side of the chair leans back, one arm across his chest and the other under his chin and darkened glare as he sits upright.

"What happened Shannan?"

Calling me by my full name is never a good sign coupled with his judgemental tone, begins his grilling.

"My actual name, wow."

I didn't hesitate. A fight is on the horizon.

Filter if you don't want an argument, Shana.

"Why can't you just ask if I'm OK?" I moaned.

Does the filter need changing?

I rolled my eyes at myself and him.

"I am passed that Shana!"

He grinds through his teeth and I am ready to defend.

Oh, so where back to Shana, I huff inside saying. "What is that supposed to mean?"

"… Were you in an accident?"

… he doesn't know, I simmer a bit.

"… I thought you were…" His voiced cracked tentatively.

My heart sank.

A knocking at the door, we both looked across at the same time, subsided the looming explosion. He hissed through his teeth blinking long in frustration but like a gentleman, he went to greet the doctor.

"Hi, I am Eric, Shannan's husband."

He extended his hand to shake the doctor's, introducing himself.

Oh, so I'm Shannan again!

Irritated I crossed my arms.

"Mr Hall, yes."

"Doctor James." He also extended his hands to shake. "... She's been alert for just about two days. Can I see you outside for a bit?"

Dr James called him out into the hallway. I guess to explain my situation to him. It will fill in some gaps for him but that conversation will not end well for me. Eric has crossed one arm, his other over his mouth listening nodding occasionally. Suddenly he freezes. I guess upon the news of our bump. After a few seconds, Dr James left. Eric paused in the hall stroking his bearded chin.

Shit!

With a renewed spring in his step, he moseyed toward the bed. My heart rattling faster than his footsteps, I cover my face with both hands. Closing my eyes bracing knowing the only question would leave his mouth that I wish he wouldn't, but he can't resist.

"How long Shana?"

I don't want to open my eyes. I feel him over me. My tummy is cringing and head is spinning. Instantly I'm unwell.

"Shannan, look at me."

He grabs hold of my hands removing them from my face. Daintily, I fluttered my hazels at him.

"You knew?" he prosecuted me.

"I didn't know. I suspected."

He has a gawky grin. Then he stares. His puffy beard hides his expression or he's getting better at hiding it. He's retrieved the chair. I eyed his beard.

This grizzly beard, does not suit him.

"Before this case?" His volume increases, but his voice is excited.

"Does it matter?" I shrug sinking into the bed.

"Yes," he's insisting.

"Maybe..." I confess.

"Why didn't you tell me?"

I sighed. "Honestly, Eric the last time I told you I suspected you overreacted and the repercussions... weren't pleasant."

He paused contemplating a bit. I breathe in the memory gaping at his lost face. Seconds expand. He gapes down at me, his eyes alight.

"That's not an excuse, Shannan."

"Ugh!" This man could be so annoying!

"Why'd you do that?" He squints.

"What are you talking about?"

"Did you just growl at me?" his voice offended.

"Ironic."

"Really, why?"

"Your grizzly beard."

He touched his face, stood up glimpsing his reflection in the window. Dr James strolled in carrying a clipboard and a pen interrupting again.

Great timing, but I know this isn't over.

Doctor James stands at the foot of the bed squinting through his spectacles and questions.

"How are we feeling today?"

The acknowledgement of the human in my cervix is a little frustrating. He gapes at me tilting his head whilst checking my pulse. I sighed.

"OK I guess," I responded rolling my eyes.

"The nurse will take you for a scan in a while. Your husband is welcome."

The invitation causes Eric's goofy grin that's irritating.

"I will come," Eric's voice is enthusiastic.

"... Any dizziness or headaches?" The doctor continues his checks.

"Yes, dizziness. I feel nauseous," I admitted.

"Morning sickness, normal, but in light of your concussion, we will need to do more observations."

He's taking notes. I cross my arms, frowning.

"OK."

He lifts the covers and unwraps the bandage on my thigh.

"It is healing well." Shaking his head and writing on the clipboard. "... The nurse will dress that for you later."

My patience is at its end. I stared him dead in his eyes and said, "Oh, I do hope *you* have some better news! Maybe you can explain more to him."

"First?"

Doctor James asked he doesn't appear to be moved by my comment. Eric said 'no' and I said 'yes' at the same time. He looked a bit confused.

"His second. My first," I explained.

The doctor shook his head in understanding then crushed my hopes again.

"Everything seems to be moving along well. Your head is healing great and there isn't a big scar. The bandage on your leg can get fresh dressing today. Have you tried making your way to the toilet on your own?"

"No."

My face is red again, he smiles. Eric's expression is lost.

"I will ask the nurse to help you with that."

He points and I am embarrassed.

"I can help her to the toilet," Eric claims his stake and I frown at him.

"I have no problems with that. You can be moved out of ICU today and begin eating something other than ice. The nurse has taken off the fluids but we will keep the dialysis line in. Your blood pressure is a bit concerning though..." Eric's eyes are piercing through me. "... It could be due to this trauma... we will keep a close eye on you. Any pain or more dizziness, please let the nurse know."

"Then can I go home?"

'*No*'! Dr James and Eric said at the same time.

Rats!

I slouched emphasising my pout.

"I will transfer you to a hospital closer to your home."

"This hospital is actually closer to home. We live in Ceda," Eric confessed automatically,

"Oh," Dr James noted.

"I work in South Divinish. I've got an apartment there."

I quickly added. Eric has an unemotional glare. I don't trust it.

"… I will want to see you next four weeks for prenatal care. The nurse will make you an appointment. You will need to take at least the rest of the week off active duty and relax."

The doctor beheld me in a caring notation which made me want to hurt him.

"I'll be sure of that."

Eric owned like a good soldier pleased with himself.

CHAPTER TWENTY-THREE

We gaped at each other from a distance both absorbing the doctor's instructions. He began closing our distance with a breath cleansing his lungs.

"Shana, I uh."

"Mrs Hall."

The attendant, almost tall as Eric with dark khaki scrubs and green shoe protectors on his feet, a broad smile with a clipboard in hand. Eric's temples grew veins and his nose widened with temper.

I brace for the man who slid his narrow behind between the bed and Eric's chair. Eric's face a few inches from his butt, as he continued joyfully.

"I just need to confirm your name and date of birth."

I recited the information. Disturbed by Eric's dragging of the wooden chair feet on the white tiled floors giving the distance between his face and the man's butt cheeks. I stifle my grin peeking around this guy.

"I will be taking you downstairs to have a peek at the little bundle then I will take you to your new room."

His mouth opens as broad as his smile with each word he said. He pointed at himself when he said 'I' and at my tummy whilst talking.

"Would the daddy take the things?" he asked with a peculiar stare. I narrowed my eyes at him.

"Yea he's behind you."

He put his hand on his chest opening his mouth a second too long, unsure if it was surprised or in awe. Eric sucked his teeth long and hard with a huff rising from the chair. I couldn't contain my laughter. I busted out with spit from holding my lips tightly together. The attendant shared my giggles but Eric was not amused. His ego in fact, was bruised.

The attendant tilted my backrest and pulled up the rails. Unlocking the wheels with his feet going behind the bed and began pushing me.

"Are you coming *daddy?*" he called to Eric rolling his head making me chuckle again.

I guess it was in awe.

The ultrasound room was dark, the attendant waited outside while Eric came in. The sonographer helped me prep myself and expose my tummy. Then she squeezes the gel on my tummy, skimming the probe. There it was, an entire person the size of a peanut.

This is real!

Eric's eyes peeled to the monitor. I am filled with uncertainty. She moved the probe around several times pausing and taking pictures. It was becoming uncomfortable, when she gave me a tissue to wipe the gel off. Eric's silence brews me uneasy. He excuses himself, I guess the attendant rubbed him the wrong way.

Or was it me?

The attendant took me through the halls, into an elevator and up to another room. Eric wasn't waiting when I got there. I supposed he went for fresh air, a coffee or to freshen up. I dosed.

****

The sun sets on another day, in another room by the window, overlooking hills and greenery. I take a moment to reflect on the tiresome day. The nurse came in, waking me, to change the bandages on my leg. It wasn't as deep as I anticipated it looked like it was filled with clear gel to hold it together. Once she was done barking her commands she said,

"Ma'am the police are here. Do you feel up to talking to them?"

I froze a second, blinking. There are so many implications with that statement. I blink with my mantra inside.

Ten.

Eric may already have this under control.

The thought doesn't make it easy as I have a fair idea of the paths he will take.

But... if he knew the preceding events... he won't be too happy about that.

My subconscious warned.

I replay what felt like yesterday. His and my conversation of a family, getting lost and robbed.

What preceding events Shana, nothing!

They all seemed harmless until…

Strutting in Brian's apartment wearing his T-shirt. I groan at my judgement. My heart thumps and the monitor increased the noise.

I needed the help.

But did I need to give him my bra and walk around his remarkable apartment wearing my panties and his T-shirt?

I moan at myself recalling his warm hands in mine and looking at his package, twice. My subconscious crossed her arms and wagged her head at me.

That was innocent. I say to myself, *but stupid!* I admonished myself.

Then Eric's first words came back to me.

He asked me what happened.

Does that mean, he doesn't know?

Know what? I argue, recalling the men in the alley.

I don't want to have him hear me say that.

My heart gallops and I am going there. Back to our first meeting where he pulled a man from trying to force himself on me. I clench and feel sick. There is no way I am doing that again. Then it occurred.

If I give these officers the statement, he will have it off a report.

I wouldn't have to say…

"Yes, I am fine."

The better of the two options I take.

Something is still off. I need to know something.

"C-can I get a phone call before they come in?" It would be better to talk and be armed with information.

"This is not your office ma'am. I am not your personal assistant."

The nurse stands one hand on her broad hip, whilst she wags her index finger and syllabises the words.

Crap! My hands fall in my face. Then I clasp my hands together showing all my teeth as I say, "Please."

She rolled her eyes waddling out the room. I frown scolding myself. A few minutes later she returned with a phone.

"Thank you, thank you, thank you." I grinned as she gave it to me.

"Five minutes." She stood with her arms crossed. "Five!"

She curled her lips at me leaving. I called Noel quickly.

"Junior assistant Noel," she answers rehearsed.

"Hi, it's – um, Davis." I hesitate.

"Davis, are you all right?" her voice is excited and relieved at the same time.

I cut her next sentence. "Didn't Sam tell you I had some trouble?" I fished.

"We thought you were kidnapped or…"

I couldn't let her finish the sentence.

"I am fine, just had a little trouble." *Secondly,* I have to know what happened, what was the outcome of the articles, "… The meeting with the directors," I squirm thinking.

"Ah, that's been cancelled actually," she chirped.

Oh good! "What about the death of the suspect?" I winced, waiting.

"The media doesn't suspect anything," she says and I cannot remember having a discussion with her about the privacy of this case, though assuring, I sense something off. "… Sergeant Martinez and Lieutenant Paul are on that."

That's good they haven't stopped.

Is it? I began to unravel with a brief reflection on my career, and theirs, moaning about their methods and possibly having to clean up or…

"When are you coming back?" She cuts my oncoming tantrum. That question filled me with the hope I needed.

Realistically, would anything change?

I sigh with hope.

"Next week, I hope. Have to tie things up here," *In a manner of speaking.* "… Keep me in the loop, OK," I technically begged.

"Sure," she says apprehensively. "… But I have been assigned a side-project." She is wavery and her volume has reduced.

"What!" I shout through the phone.

"Agent Davis," she tried explaining softly, "… It is with the director."

"Oh!" I say, short with irritation.

He had time to meet her but not me…

The nurse returned putting her hand out for the phone stopping my rant as it began. I frown at her.

"Thanks Noel." I had to end my call.

"No problem," her reply is caring.

I hung up smiling at the nurse. I thanked her again.

As grumpy as she pretends to be, she likes me.

"The officers are outside."

Shit, I forgot about them, I pout again.

"I sure hope that baby doesn't get that frowny face."

The nurse smiled at me. I giggled at her leaning onto the bed.

****

Two uniformed officers rambled in. One tall, slim, blond with a moustache. The other, short round dark hair and his shirt two sizes too small. They were armed with large notepads and pens in hand. They stalked to the side of the bed watching over me as though I was a corpse or a science project.

"Good day ma'am, I am Officer Hugh, this is Officer Nubert." The round one introduces, the slim one waves. "… We're here to take a report on the incident that landed you here. Can I start with your name please?"

I should hurry them along,

I really don't want Eric here when I give the statement.

"I am Shannan Davis-Hall S.D.A.F. Special Agent. I got lost…" I ate my words.

"Ma'am…"

How old does he think I am? "Please, Agent Davis-Hall."

I have tolerated the nurse calling me ma'am, not them!

"Agent Davis-Hall, I prefer you answer the questions I ask please." Officer Hugh is snarling.

Great! I sigh.

"Where were you when you were attacked?"

Officer Hugh's accentuates the 'r's' with a slightly higher male pitch.

"*I don't know!* I got lost."

"Do you remember anything about where you were?"

215

"Near a coffee shop and a laundromat," I shrugged.

"Do you remember the names of those shops?"

He's talking to me syllabising each word as if I was five. His attitude has hit the nerve of my newly-found short temper.

"As pleasant as you are Officer Hugh, I don't have time for this and you are frankly, infuriating."

"Shannan."

Shit! Eric's back!

His deep voice echoed the disappointment beating in my heart. He braces the door with one arm scolding me with his eyes. I crossed my arms and mope at his suggestive motion.

I wonder how long he stood there.

"… Hi, I am Eric Hall, her husband."

He ambled to the officers, stretching his hands to embrace them. His tone is stern, deep and agreeable. I am not fooled by his manners.

"… My wife has just been transferred from ICU today. She will be giving a statement soon. Can we talk outside? Shannan, can you excuse us for a moment?"

He used my full name!

His whisper is like grumbles from where I lay. The officers were attentive. They exchange a few words back and forth. He takes a card from out his wallet and gave it to them. Then, came inside taking the ziplock bag with my clothes handing it to them. He shook their hands with smile of deceit, nodding softly.

He waved with one hand in his pocket until they were out of sight. His eyes blaze in fury quickening his stroll to me. My heart pounds harder as he enters the room. He pulls the door in behind him. I gulped. The click of the lock skips my heartbeat.

"What the fuck is wrong with you Shana? Why, would you do that?"

He growled at me.

"I-I…" The words unable to leave me, his warranted anger scares me.

Why do I feel guilty?

He's caught me, my eyes dilated. I am frozen, afraid to look at him afraid to look away from him.

"What were you doing before you were attacked?"

He walks closer to me, narrowed his brown eyes both hands in his jeans pocket. His height towered over the bed but he stands afar.

"I-I got lost."

My voice is trembling breathing harder and he doesn't ease off.

"Is that *all?*" His tone suggestive and sarcastic.

"Why are you interrogating me?"

My eyes fill and my voice soft with cracks.

I did nothing wrong!

"How did you get hurt?"

He is uncompromising standing away from the bed.

Is he really asking me?

A tear slips down my face. I hesitate to glower at him.

"I-I got lost, my phone was soaked, s-someone helped me… I called Sam."

Inhaling, I choke the tears flowing down my face, in recollection of the event. Only just realising, what had really happened in the dark alley. Saying it aloud would mean it is true. I didn't do anything wrong. So, why is he questioning me as if I did?

"What were you doing?" Eric asked again. I exhale seeing the events playing out in front of me but I don't want to say.

"… Two men attacked me; one grabbed me from behind, dragging me into the alley."

I did nothing wrong! My voice whispers in my head once more as my breath is forced in and out my body in a pant.

"Why were you in the alley Shana?"

He wants the details. I can't say.

"I was robbed, I got lost. Someone helped me!" *Please don't make me say it,* "… I called Sam… told her to come get me… She knew where I was."

He blinks long with fury in his eyes.

"I know you called Sam."

What?

And there it is. The accusation from his voice and the doubt in his eyes elevates the sniffle to a weep fest.

I can't believe that he would…

My heart constricts in disbelief, at his suggestion. I let it out for a minute swiping my tears with my palms. I inhale, then, exhale again. The distress manifested as anger.

"Fucking say what you're thinking Eric... but don't treat me like a suspect."

His silence and cold glare through me confirm it. Slowing my breathing, from my nose to my mouth I slowed my panic then, I regurgitated the words.

"... They tried to rape me," I said softly. My body shook in memory of his touch and breath that covered my face. Eric's eyes widened then, I turned away. Pausing, I turned away as my skin prickled describing the horrifying scene.

"I forgot my wallet, gun and badge hurrying to a crime scene in an unfamiliar city. My phone wasn't fully charged and I used it as my satnav and it died. Someone knocked into me, lifted my car keys.

"They came pretending to rob me. When I explained someone already had done that, he confessed he was not after that anyway. He and his friend dragged me further into the darkness by knifepoint.

"I dislocated the elbow of one who choked me and I broke his accomplice's nose... the one who cut my new pencil skirt... my thigh... they were... touching me..."

His accent reverberated in my head. The scene is too much. My nose starts to flare and my tears drop off as quickly as I wipe.

"... It was dark, I didn't see their faces... I won't be able to identify either of them... because it was really dark..."

I sniffled, snot running off my lips. I looked at him, his deportment hasn't shifted and the professional part of me comes out.

"... Best guess is to look in hospitals in Southern Divinish near the towns where I was, for anyone admitted with injuries that match the description I gave."

I breathe deep counting inwardly, calming until I stopped at one. He walks to the bed bringing the chair with him next to the bed.

"Don't, don't fucking come near me, Eric."

I shrugged the sheets aside, fluttering it close to his face sitting up. Then, dropped my feet off the bed my thigh bandage tightened. The hospital gown opened to the back and the breeze touches my behind.

"… I have lost four days lying here in the hospital."

My feet are shaking pins and needles running up my leg. I wince. As my feet touch the floor it slides.

"Where, are you going Shana?"

His voice still stern, I put my hand over my face. The glorious morning sickness lifts to my throat. I pressed my weight on my hands at my side. My arms tremble, I put my weight on my arms to lift my body finding my foothold.

He stands with me eyeing my movements. I raised my hand to gesture him to stand back my other hand buckled under my weight and felt his hands on my arms.

"Don't!" I pulled my arm away, trying to stand, my feet trembled sliding on the cold tiles.

"If you fall…" he warned with eyes tense.

"Don't, I said fucking no!" I shout pulling away off balancing. I put the weight in the injured leg. Both my legs buckled under the pressure, the pain surged my body and I tighten my muscles screaming to the pain. The soles of my feet skidded on the tile. Reaching for the bed my arms missed.

CHAPTER TWENTY-FOUR

One knee on the floor, he catches me scooping me bodily between the chair and the bed cradling me to his pecs. My body shakes from the near miss sending my heart into rapid pumping. It was nothing compared to the gravity of his betrayal. The initial adrenalin subsides giving my heart room to process what he's done.

"Don't touch me!"

I struggle out of his hold, shouting. The anger has taken me. He only secured me into his grip and stands. My nose flares and I huff. Turning with me in his arms, towards the entrance, he began a slow pace.

Where is he taking me?

"Put me down!"

My hand bounces off his firm chest. He squints momentarily at the assault, shaking me to a comfortable hold.

"Put me down, Eric."

He reaches the entrance and makes a surprising turn into an open door to a side room. The lights flicked on as he did, inside a toilet and shower room with a sink and bin. He walks in tilting me gently to the toilet cautiously releasing me on. I grip his shoulders steadying.

My weight shifted to thighs as I bend my knees sitting. With a gasp grinding, the tightening and discomfort under my thigh bandage, he puts me down onto the seat, shuddering. Turning his back to me facing the door he whispers, "I'm sorry."

I couldn't evaluate which stung more, his accusation, manhandling or the wound that has a bandage and blood stains. The thought of losing his respect and him questioning my trust, I burst into a cry.

His shadow disappeared and the door clicked softly and securely. An increasing pant grew as his voice echoed through me.

'Is that all? Why were you in that alley? I spoke to Sam'.

My face was engorged with tears and snot. I was not concerned by the volume, only that it was being unleashed. Eventually, I peed.

****

After five days of no flat ironing, the kinks tighten and my hair an untamed poof appearing shorter and frizzier. I pout at my reflection from the window as the sunsets on yet another day in the hospital.

I think I'm going to leave my hair like this for a while.

Really!

I sunk my fingers in the front of my afro combing through tangling it even more. Eric's image meshed with mine through the glass, he's returned. I am winded after a few hours and he's freshened, carrying flowers in a vase.

He glides slowly floating along the window. Anxious at his return, I shy from his gape swallowing the flooding emotions from his accusation. After the initial shock of my near miss and placing me, he picked me up from the toilet returning me to my bed without another word.

He just exited the room and has been absent for nearly half the day. He has had a haircut a beard trim and a shower by the smell, a crisp grey T-shirt and black jeans.

A baseless accusation that questioned my dignity.

Unusual choice for Eric which then, I recall, Mr Kumal's.

Is it?

Guilt shifts me following him through the threshold. He carries with him a duffel bag reminding me of training. I smile briefly. Emphasising my pout, he places the bouquet on the drawer at the side of me. He leans over, pecking my forehead another one of his ways to indicate an apology.

Apology not accepted!

My inner voice shouted. Although I don't want the tension, it thickens building my anger. The hope to pass this is unforeseeable.

"I brought you toiletries and clothes."

His voice is cautious. I twisted my head from his gape and folding my lips. There are no words I can conjure to express my emotions. He takes his place in the chair next to the bed.

I don't have the will to fight.

I know he would find a way of making me remorseful. Hurt from his evocative accusation neither of us acknowledging the events before sitting with the elephant in the room. I turned away.

I cannot look at him!

The nurse enters.

Thank God!

Making her rounds before it became more awkward. She checks my vitals, giving me some prenatal and sickness tablets. He eyed me quietly and I say nothing. I ate my dinner as he sits with me.

The next two days were the same; he sleeps in the chair, after my breakfast and morning check, he goes for a few hours and comes back freshened up. Returns in the evening before my supper with fresh flowers, I wake to the light flowing into the room and his head on the bed as he slept.

With some excitement, I limp to the showers. Today I finally get to leave the hospital. The bump on my head has been reduced but still discoloured. The bump, my tummy had grown slightly.

I slipped into a new lace underwear and a white bra under a light flowing summer dress. Brushing the knots from my hair for the first time in seven days, even wet, hurt and I didn't care. I did it with a grin, thankful that he hasn't brought me something that was not tight or that would snag my leg bandage or emphasise my fifteen-week bump. I stole a few minutes and felt the bump then limped to the bed.

Here we go!

Eric waits outside. The nurse came in as I came out the bathroom.

Perfect timing!

Eric was packing the bits into my bag. He stood aside. She led me to the bed taking my hand. She held my knuckles firm with the gloved hands carefully stripping the tape off bunching them together at the base of the splitter.

Below a bending plastic stuck in my vein between my middle and marriage finger. My blood steady in the line, she concentrates judiciously removing the dialysis line crawling out my skin.

That is one long needle.

I cringe seeing it coming out. She covers the bleeding hole with a plaster.

"Hold this steady," she instructs putting a ball of cotton on my bleeding wound. I press my index finger on it and she covers it with a piece of tape. "… Keep this on for at least an hour, OK?"

She throws the bloody line into a yellow bucket bin then winks at me.

She is a softy!

I reflect on my time here with her. She takes her bucket and carries it out the room. Eric sauntered next to me. My heart drums waiting for him to say anything. He chucks his hand into his pocket. I see him twirling my rings on his pinkie finger, closing our distance.

Doctor James enters postponing us. Secretly, I celebrate but frown that it would happen at some point. I breathe and Eric huffed. It never shifts the doctor's professional demeanour. He begins reading through the notes as he explains the discharge care to me.

"The cut on your right leg is healing incredibly quick, it is closed over. The incision was clean," according to the doctor. "… Your head only has a bruise. Your concussion has cleared, but if you get any headaches, please let us know."

Seven days were gone just like that. His lips continued to move but my focus was on the time missed off this assignment, the discussions Eric and I shared before all this and of course the one thing present that we won't say.

It would make this real and not a dream.

Occasionally nodding when Dr James' eyes moved in my direction, Eric's eyes never left me. Though he was attentive, sweet and supportive physically, it hasn't repaired the damage. I am still furious at him and Sam.

What did she say to him?

My imagination goes over the details I gave her and what she must have told him to induce that reaction. I frown at his actions. This has led me to believe that he doesn't trust me.

Not that I did anything wrong.

So why do I feel like I did?

The doctor handed Eric the documents and we set off. We were so close to Ceda, our home, our friends but he'd rather take the uncomfortable four hours' drive in silence back to the madness that waits in Divinish. Though not much dialogue was exchanged some things were just universal. Stopping for food and a potty break once.

I woke as he pulled into the parking of my apartment at dusk. Our last conversation flows back to me with some comfort. Finally, he's supporting my career choice. We're starting a family something that he wanted and his end game, new job…

Shit! His new job!

Only then realising his first week was spent with me in the hospital and he sat by my bedside.

I feel guilty.

The unpleasant conclusion troubles me.

What about my job? Crap!

A sudden stress unravels and I began writing a list in my head.

Sharron Mall is in the hospital, her one associate who died, mysteriously. My, to-do list, training.

"Shana!" Eric breaks my worrying. "… You're safe."

I don't know what expression there is across my face, but I exhaled. He turned off the engine and paused.

It is Saturday.

I nodded at myself, his expression softens a bit and I consider.

Work is not until Monday.

I have time to prepare.

I agree within and am tempted to call for an update. He still looks at me and his frown grows. I count to calm. Down to one and he's still staring.

I can't help it!

I sigh at myself popping the car door open. Looking at the entrance for the building and the beautifully hedged and flower walkway weighing my options. I heard his door opened followed by quick footsteps.

Although I have Eric's support…

Suddenly the garden view was blocked by Eric who widened the door and stands between me and the door. His expression I cannot read but undoubtedly.

He will definitely not understand.

My subconscious submerged. Putting his hands on the door frame, I moved my legs out the car. He stoops as I balanced my hands on his shoulder. He put his hands around my waist and stood and at the same time, he pulled me up shifting me to the side.

I lean against the back door and he goes to the trunk, taking the bag out. When we left the hospital, I was wheeled out in a chair and he lifted me into the car. For the stops, we went to the drive-through, my legs are like jell-O and it hurts to stand. The reasoning behind this whole ordeal comes to mind.

At some point, I will have to go in and give a statement.

This is one of the things I wished were not on my 'to-do list'. He has not pushed for it and I am not in a hurry either. The situation comes back to me like a flood, especially his inquisitorial. Then I am angry.

It would take some time to forgive him for what he did.

Slamming the car door in remembrance of his accusation, I hobble across the walkway eager to get away. He catches up in no time quietly walking to the apartment.

What happened to my car? I wondered.

Oh, and my phone. I need a phone! I thought of calling again.

I add more to the mental list. All the things that went wrong began to populate my head with the stroll. I shook the reflection away. I am eager to get back to work.

Just two days to Monday.

I repeated in my head.

He hasn't mentioned the baby since, nor have I reflected on having one since our pre-discussion of a baby. The dreaded day landed me in the hospital. The truth is, it all feels surreal to me. I will be someone's mother, something that I have never given much consideration to.

I don't want to think about it.

We got inside and he put the bags aside the door and the keys in a clear bowl on the side table near the door.

That is new!

On the breakfast bar ahead, there was a vase with mixed roses, perfectly between the stools. Next to it a new phone, car keys and my work laptop all lined up. I smiled at the gesture, cheerfully hopping towards them. Eric can be so sweet and maddening all at the same time.

"Look," he calls my attention, I turn to look at him. "… I have to go to the office."

Why did he have to choose maddening first?

I frown instantly outraged turning to the bed instead, slumping.

Wow, didn't see that one coming!

I am sarcastic with myself.

"OK," I verbalised softly folding my lips inwardly, and breathing loudly.

Not even a real conversation after four days of silence.

BAU: business as usual.

Ugh!

The sheets are silky, new and a neatly made bed, he added a comforter. He walks, gazing at me, his brown eyes reflecting my disappointment. Taking my left hand tenderly, he pulled the rings off his pinkie finger gliding my rings onto my finger. He's stooping at my feet peering at me.

"It would not take long," he assures me bringing my hand to his lips, gently kissing it. I shook my head.

No more late nights? Right. I thought.

"I know what you're thinking Shana." He is guarded.

"Do you, really?"

It flew out and I am not sorry scrunching my face at him.

There is always a trick!

"Look, I need to collect some things to work from home."

His job, I am ashamed. "… You need to stay off your feet and rest for the next week." He is uncompromising.

"A week," I whined unexpectedly.

"Were you listening to the doctor at all?" he raises his voice, annoyed.

"Yes," I whimper, *No!* I scold myself inwardly. He stares again.

"You can get me on my phone if you really need me." His voice is softer and I turn away.

"Fine!" A woman's tamed version of saying, 'fuck you' in one word.

This conversation isn't over!

I retreated temporally knowing with him gone I was free to catch up without his judgement. I grin inwardly. He kissed my hand again getting up with a groan. He walked to the bowl, took the keys, a quick glance at me, then left.

A few seconds passed, and I waited for him to return. Five minutes went past, I wobble to the glass doors, opening to the balcony overlooking the car park peeking to see if he was gone. I celebrate inside. The suitcase is sitting at the entrance and the dress is beginning to stifle my boobs. I changed into a pair of shorts and a camisole.

This should only be a few minutes.

I hopped to the breakfast bar and the laptop back to the bed. Stacking the pillows behind my back, I sat up crossed my ankles and opened it on my lap turning it on. Checking some emails, reading a few reports and added some to my research some Zeman words.

They've caught my attention. Though, we use some Zeman words for some things there are many I didn't realise were Zeman and meant something else.

I smell the iron minerals of blood as I run through the woods, barefoot. Only the moon as my light. The red eclipse is radiating the moon, dim, through the dark but guiding me. It is painful, and the soles of my feet are sore. My heart races as I sense a shift. A part of me knows but I am confused, lost and afraid.

My hair is naturally curled into a muddy afro. I hear her soft voice echoing to me, *stay hidden.* I am looking around, ever so often to find her. Instead, I can sense him, he's found me. I began panicking again.

I am stuck.

I feel it, touched my feet. Eek! I yelp.

A combination of trepidation and power imprisoned me. My heart thumps through my ears and I am breathless in panic. I feel the luring power moving ahead of the creature crawling. The creature was guided by the power. It's thick, heavy, slimy and cold.

Curled around my ankle, rising slowly, coiling making its way up my thighs leisurely. It's around my thighs, moving to my hips tightening, crawling around my back.

I can't move.

It's surging through every part of my body. It touches as if calling the static light to my skin, with pleasurable sensations I didn't know were possible. There was a deep rumble in the earth and I feel the heat burning my eyes.

"Please no, I'm pregnant," I shout in my pant.

I am paralysed by fear. I can't see... can't move... it's not stopping... it throws me forward and I'm about to fall.

"Shana!" Eric shakes me. "... You're safe. Wake up!"

Wheezing, my eyes flickered clearing to his caring brown eyes reflecting my panic. I swiftly felt my torso as he knelt on the bed over me, his large palms on my shoulder moist under the straps of my camisole. My face is distended with tears and my clothes are soaked, from sweat, the room is filled with a mist of condensation, the laptop at my side and I am sideways on the bed.

"It's just a bad dream, baby," he whispers in a reassuring tone laced with concern as he sits back on his heels bringing me into him and holding me. The room has begun clearing as my breathing steadies. I sat up and he sits beside me. Finally conceding to my fear, I wept over his shoulder.

Suddenly, the smell of what he's brought home hits me. It briskly raised the fast food we had earlier to my oesophagus filling my mouth completely. I gag, pushing him aside. Retreating for the bathroom with fewer steps than expected, I let it out. All the undigested meals I ate today, into the toilet bowl.

He followed me with haste as I curled over the bowl. I sat on the floor for a breath, hanging my hand around the bowl with my face inside, willing myself not to puke again. My over working sense of smell stands in full gear. A hand towel slips over my shoulder, my hair tightened and a clip, claws through my mane tying it away from my face.

"I thought I was over this part," in-between breaths, I mentioned.

"Have you read any of the literature Dr James gave you?"

Eric breathes disapprovingly from behind me, rhetorically breaking our silent stance for a fight.

Oh, my gosh! "I don't have the energy for this tonight, Eric."

I exhaled tiredly pressing the towel over my mouth. Reaching up I flushed the toilet. Balancing over the bowl, I push up with my hands. I limp past him who was sitting behind me on the floor. I rinsed my mouth and limp outside. His shadow behind me moves and he shouted.

"I am not trying to pick a fight, Shana." He follows me outside to the bed.

"Really, could have fooled me!" I turned wearingly at him.

"Are you picking one?" He pointed at me.

I rolled my eyes. "Ugh!" I plopped on the bed.

"We have to talk about this at some point."

True, I crossed my arms. "I know!" I muttered emphasising my exhale.

"Do you want to talk now?"

He made an unexpected move to the kitchen, slipping off his shoes, undoing his pants button, zipping his fly piece shaking his jeans loose down his leg. He takes each foot out one at a time, held up the jeans and folding it, placing it on the bar stool. His thick thighs fill the boxers.

"Please cover that thing you brought in here. I don't intend to be throwing up all night. I am sick of hospitals."

He laughs moving it to the fridge his chest shows through his white cotton T-shirt, just about covering his front bulges but shorter than the thigh-gripping boxers which outline his spank-able behind. I admire him as he glides around the tiny kitchen,

"What do you feel like tonight?" He breaks my drooling.

"Can I think about it?"

My breast nipples hardened pointing through my light-blue camisole and the lack of bra has given me salacious thoughts. His head stuck in the fridge and his bounce-off-the-hand slap-worthy ass sticking out as I stray into a memory of his touch. He closes the fridge displeased shaking the few bottles around breaking my concentration. In his hands a beer and a club soda.

"You need to have food at some point." He sighs placing the bottles on the countertop, "… Think you can manage this and I can have a beer?"

He is opening and closing all the drawers. The thought shifts me uneasy.

"Can I settle my stomach first?"

He sighs louder leaving them both on the countertop.

"You are starting to show."

"What?"

My head went straight for my midsection. I look bloated as my tummy seems compact under the filled comfortable jersey fabric. I am confused.

"You look pregnant," he says in delight.

"Are you calling me fat?" I sulk.

"I would never!"

He grins bright walking to the front door, takes off his socks, putting them in his shoes, placing them by the entrance of the apartment.

"Do you really think so?" I am worried.

"A little, for those who know you, particularly, your breasts."

He takes up his jeans passes me to the cupboards, places them into the closet and takes off his T-shirt. I twist my mouth admiring his saunter.

"Are you complaining?" I suck on my bottom lip.

"Just observing."

My camisole scarcely contains them even when I'm not wearing a bra. He stands near me, my heart races and palms get wet. He ambles to the bed sitting at the opposite end in his navy-blue cotton boxers and I am aroused.

"Have you thought about becoming a mother at all this past week?"

My libido went to zero and I sigh. I think for a moment.

I really don't want to think about that now! I whinge to myself.

"Are you ready to be a father again, especially with your new job?"

The impromptu work, shifts and the risks you said would not happen, although I know better. I summarised my protests, thankfully inward trying to keep my emotions in check but he answers right away.

"Right back at you."

Aw, he really wants to talk. I sulk inwardly.

"I really want you to be comfortable, with this. I know this is a surprise but..." He trailed with a sigh, his eyes reflecting and glossy. Then the silence grew, second by second.

Be honest. Reasoning edged me before it became tense and I took a deep inhale voicing,

"I am only just getting used to being your wife, Eric. We haven't finished our marriage ceremony, nor have we really had time for just the two of us, especially with the events of the past two years." Briefly, I reflected before I went on. "… Now, I feel like we're moving at a pace, that I'm not sure I can keep up with. I love you, Eric. But I am not sure if I am ready to be anyone's mother."

I took a pillow holding it across my lap gazing at his darkening deportment.

"You are so good with Danielle." He's tightening the gap between us, and I shrug.

"Yea, as a big sister. And honestly, I'm fine with that." I look down at the pillow thinking how true that statement is.

"Do you need some time?" Eric asks expectantly.

"I don't know Eric." I shrug again looking at the pillow across my midsection that mimics a pregnant belly saying even more truths. "I know you're ready, and you're a great father." I sigh acknowledging my immaturity and our age difference.

"So, what are you going to do?" He bows his head; his voice is low.

We sat in silence for a bit, his expression growing grim as the moment passed. Then it dawned.

Is he really asking me?

I hit him across the head with the pillow breaking his sulk. Speaking my thoughts aloud.

"I'm keeping the baby idiot! I know this isn't planned and we've both been preoccupied and I may have forgotten a pill or two."

"You what!" His two words sliced my oncoming rant and I realised the truth.

After the initial shock in his voice, I try explaining shakingly.

"I-I lost count, thought it became redundant. You were away, working. When you were back, I tried to track my period, to restart the pill. Only my period never came…"

He is not moving, only breathing, slowly.

"… I thought it was close… these past few weeks…" My voice trailed and he's quiet. Uncharacteristically.

I say for a response. "Being away for this job… I thought…"

His eyes fixed on my hands holding the pillow, and he said nothing. Silence.

My nose flared and the ball choked me, met with his stillness and quiet.

"… Say something…" I whisper begging, with heartache.

He moved his brown gape at me. Face expressionless, still, silent for moments too long. I can't bear it. It scares me, not knowing what he feels.

"Please! I'm sorry," I say quietly my eyes filling. "If you don't…"

He breaks his soundless conceive. Culling me wrapping his arms around me. Ravaging passed my lips coercing his tongue in my mouth, tasting me, sloping me to the bed. I have waited all afternoon to have him, making love, meaningfully and covertly.

CHAPTER TWENTY-FIVE

My head on his naked chest, his arm curved over me and around my back. I look up at his unshaven beard. I cull my fingers across it. He breathes deep turning on his side, a great big simper.

"Good morning," he said covering his mouth.

An 'A' for effort, but my stomach is not having it. I groan.

He gets out of the covers, strutting naked into the kitchen searching the cupboards taking a glass out. He bends over into the fridge taking a bottle of orange juice and brings it to me.

"Take a sip."

I blow out the sick feeling.

"Trust me!" he reassures.

I sip, took a moment for it to go down. The nausea slowly subsiding.

"… It is worse if you don't eat."

I eyed him.

"I read the books and have been through this already."

I narrowed my eyes sitting up as he reminds me of the sore topic of his ex.

Why does he feel the need to point that out? I sighed loudly.

"It worked, didn't it?" he boasted.

I grabbed a pillow from behind me hitting him over the head spilling some juice on the sheet.

"I just changed these!" he whinged.

I am satisfied. Placing the juice and glass on the side table.

"Ugh!" I came off the other side of the bed stumbling around the bed between the couch and the chest of drawers.

"Where are you going?"

He dives playfully swooping me by the waist pulling me on him to the bed.

"Eric, I need to pee!"

I giggled. He tilted us to the side of my injured leg; the laughing suddenly shifts to pain and he doesn't recognise. Continuing his leaning and tickling, adding pressure to my injured leg touching it by accident.

"Ahh!" I screamed.

He let me go. Cradling my leg in agony his face transformed instantly to regret.

"I'm sorry."

He tries examining the bandage.

"I'm fine," I hissed pushing his hand away nursing the wound.

He pounced off the bed with a three step haste to the bathroom. There was slight bleeding I examined it with tears. Upon his returned, he stooped, held on to my ankle with fresh bandages.

"Let me see," he said sternly.

"It's OK."

I pulled away. He held tighter.

"Just... let me see."

He holds me steady by the ankle his eyes troubled unwrapping the dressing. Wiping prudently the small amounts of blood from it, I dread. Moaning through my closed mouth I screw my eyes shut resigning to his care. Slowly he covers the wound wrapping it. Then, resting my leg tenderly on the bed his eyes gape me and he's impassive.

"Monday we've got to go in... you need to report this... incident."

His voice gave away his tension and anger. His tone in sync with his accusation and I defend.

"Why did you have to say it like that?"

"Like what?" He blinked at me a couple times shrugging.

"Ugh!" I growled at him, sitting up.

I need some space. Dragging myself off the right side of the bed I stand up, limping to the bathroom.

"Where are you going?" he questioned with a huff.

I sucked my teeth at him wanting to stomp through to the bathroom wishing I had something close to launch at his head, but instead pleasurably slamming the door behind me. It shook and vibrated. The sound of fluttering, flopping and a loud exasperating echoed through the door. I decide on a shower.

Why is he making such a big deal!

I washed my hair thinking.

The men are hurt and I am fine.

Am I fine?

I shake the doubt and exit the shower. It was quiet. Eric didn't come in. Wrapped the towel around me, I massaged the moisturiser in my hair and began to brush my large curls through. My hands are tired and I'm not half-done. I blow out.

Who was I kidding?

I took the straightener ploughing through my hair quickly tying my hair back into a ponytail. It has been nearly an hour and a half. Eric didn't interrupt me. Exiting cautiously, to orange juice spilled on the wooden floors, bedsheets were on the ground the mattress twisted. Eric was nowhere in sight. The balcony, couch, kitchen, and the front door was closed. I stopped breathing.

Ten, nine.

I closed my eyes. Recalling after he rescued me. I exhaled long. My phone sat on the countertop. I squint taking it to call him.

No!

My subconscious screamed. I opened the wardrobe his clothes were still there. An observation which calmed me. I pulled a vest and a pair of shorts tucking my phone in my back pocket.

Using the sheet to soak the juice off the floor, I bundled it together taking it to the bathroom and throwing it in the basket. My clothes from the hospital and the sheet fill the laundry basket.

I mopped the apartment floor slipping on a flipflops, limping downstairs to the laundry room. The four-machine room was empty. I put the clothes in and put it on to spin.

The memory of what caused this issue comes to mind. Unlocking the phone, I gripped it searching for numbers. Eric must have taken the SIM. All my numbers are in. I hugged myself content with his thoughtfulness. My overreacting may have caused him some discomfort. Liz is always my voice of reason. She answers on one ring.

"Shana, what's wrong?" Her words are irritating.

"Ugh… Liz, why can't you start a phone call with something else?" I whine at her.

"You haven't called me in nearly two weeks, and last time you called it was a thing with Eric."

I gasped, then defend. "There was no 'thing with Eric'."

"Really, all right, is there a thing with Eric now?"

Pausing with my mouth open, I have no words I eventually said, "I hate you!"

I hung up. A few minutes passed she's text:

I love you!

I smiled at it. Then she sent an emoji blowing a kiss, I texted:

I love you too!
Really missing you!

I sighed, put a timer into my phone, sticking it into my pocket. I waddle to the apartment, with a grin.

Eric was inside his phone to his ear pacing, raking his beard while he listens to the other person on the other side of the phone call. Our eyes met; he exhaled long blinking at me. He hung up the phone covering his mouth briefly removing his hand to say, "What in the actual fuck Shana!" Stunned I gaped at him shutting the door. "Where were you?" he growled at me.

"So, it is OK for you to walk out but not me?"

I respond to his aggression equally and quickly. He stilled.

"Walk out? Is that what you thought I was doing?"

"Weren't you?" I hobbled to the bathroom returning the laundry basket. He followed.

"I, I needed fresh air," he raised his voice slightly.

"So, did I!" I raised my voice marching out.

"Do you feel sick?" His tone softened with his demeanour.

"Ugh!" I groan frustrated. Why is everything suddenly about this pregnancy?

"Don't do that, it is not a word."

I widened my eyes at him heightened in irritation.

"That is the only way I could describe how annoyed I feel!"

I threw my hands up and stomped to the balcony leaning over the banister looking out to the parking and the distant rocks. He followed me leaning backwards, his elbows propped watching down at me, my phone beeped, then beeped again.

"Aren't you going to get that?" he huffs.

"Why?"

I shrug, he eyes me with anticipation. Shaking my head turned with a huff retreating inside and dropped to the sofa, turning the TV on. He sighed passing the sofa going into the kitchen without another word.

Is he retreating?

Silence brewed between us. He is noisy in the kitchen banging and moving things around. Intentional, I'm sure.

"Can you manage a cheese sandwich?" he calls from the kitchen. I didn't say anything only taking my phone from my pocket slapping upwards on the coffee table glancing at Liz's text emoji. It made me grin. Eric came across with the sandwich on a plate with more orange juice at the side. He peeked at my phone and the announcement of the finals football match starting in a few minutes.

"You need to eat, Shana!"

Aw, he's not going to stop!

I made sure he saw me rolling my eyes. Sitting up, seeing my midsection extremely bloating our future around me. My thought went to Sharron. She was fourteen weeks pregnant; her baby was fully formed and dead in the car with her.

This is an entire person sitting around my waist. A sickening feeling overthrew me and a sense of urgency to return to work.

I need to help her!

My work laptop is below the TV stand. Eric must have moved it. I dive for it. Eric blocked my way. I measured him with my eyes blinking a couple times.

"No!"

A simple directive with an impassive expression, that I dear not disobey. His view, I have seen once after an incident clubbing with Emily. I threw myself back into the couch and pout crossing my arms.

He shoved the plate in my face. I swiped the sandwich and bite. The white bread butter and cheese melted in my mouth. I took it from him nibbling. He visibly relaxed sitting next to me. The game starts.

I woke, confused, it was dark outside. I was in bed and Eric next to me. His naked chest to my back and one hand over my waist. The other under my head, his breathing on my neck. The body heat unwelcomed.

An urgent need for the toilet hits. I wriggled out carefully, creeping to the door. The laundry basket is in its place to the side of the sink, empty. The bathroom and toilet with a fresh flowery smell and the tiles are super white.

When did he clean in here?

A stray thought filtered. I pull down my underwear began to pee. He entered the room startling me, rubbing his eyes, with a yawn and stretch exposing his toned abs. His midsection stole a smile, finishing and wiping.

I hope he isn't going to ask me something stupid!

He went straight for the toilet and peed with a yawn. I washed my hands leaving him inside.

At times I forget he was a tidy bachelor.

My tummy began to argue waking Eric fully. "What would you like to eat?"

He stands behind me surprising me again.

Is that the only question he can ask?

I turned to him hunger pains hits. Quieting the noise by palming my bump in circles, ashamed of the noise. The offer of food has made my tummy louder.

I have a think, I can almost taste. "Something meaty, salty and fried."

I requested surprisingly vocal, the blood rushing to my cheeks as his strange stare is causing me to fold my lips in. I peeked through my eyelashes at him. His wide bright grin he walks to me pecking my cheek.

"OK."

He goes to the wardrobe next to me pulling on a pair of jeans and a white T-shirt.

"Where are you going?"

My eyes peered at his peculiar behaviour.

"Don't you want your, meaty, salty and fried food?"

I shook my head peeking at him again.

"I'm going to get it," he said as a matter-of-fact.

"Just like that?" I questioned, *Is this a trick?*

"Just like that," he repeated, with his contagious grin, his dimples at its deepest as his smile reaches his eyes.

"Can I come?" I peered at him, my cheeks growing redder.

"Sure but, you would want to change."

His observation accurate; I am in my underwear and a vest. Grinning wide, showing all my teeth at him, taking the dress he's brought me out of the hospital slipping it on with no bra. He takes out a denim jacket for me and a black leather one for him.

The last time I wore this jacket he asked me to marry him.

I am convinced he brought that on purpose folding my lips, shy. Slipped on a pair of ballerinas as he opened the door. Taking the keys out the bowl standing in the hallway, locking the door. He's secured my hand leading me across the hall and down the stairs.

Across the courtyard, there is some distant talking. Aaliyah is staggering, her hand hooked around a man's neck. He's holding her up fondling her breasts and smiling. Slightly hunched she is taller than him. The observation makes me giggle a bit.

I wonder if she'll be OK.

The thought made me uneasy.

"Should we help her?" I asked passing her. Her head was down and eyes dim.

"She's a big girl."

Eric dismisses. His mood darkens and he hurries me to the parking. Some of the stories Emily shared has been made true to my witnessing tonight.

We got into the car. I stare through at the scene.

"I hope he doesn't take advantage of her."

"Lia can take care of herself, trust me. Seat belt!" he orders clipping his. I clip mine. He turns over the engine, pulling from the parking quickly. His action brings me back to what Sam suggested when I called her.

What did she tell him?

CHAPTER TWENTY-SIX

Interrupted by my raging hunger pains again, followed by the heavy growling of my tummy. I patted my bump, Eric's amusement glows in his face.

"Looks like sleeping for nearly twenty-four hours has some negative side effects."

Whisking my head to him.

"What!" My eyes widened at him.

"You've slept for nearly twenty-four hours." he chuckles.

I don't share his humour.

"Did I?" I questioned in disbelief.

"Yes, you did." He smiles wide, his dimples sink into his cheeks.

"I don't believe you!" I am still in shock.

"Doctor James said this may happen."

I cannot remember hearing him say that, then again… I thought to myself.

"Why didn't you wake me?" I voiced.

"You were in a deep sleep, I tried."

He shrugs, pulling into the drive-through for a fried chicken restaurant. He makes an order.

I cannot believe I missed an entire day!

"It's OK Shana, you need the rest,"

Really, I huff at him in a squint.

He drives to the next window and pays.

"I don't believe I've missed nearly twenty-four hours, Eric. What did you do most of Sunday?"

"I spoke with Danielle, cleaned… cooked…"

"Well not enough, apparently!" I voiced unfiltered. He laughed aloud.

"I ate the same thing three times." He chuckled. "… I will remember for next time then."

"Waking me will be better."

He wagged his head. He collects the order putting it onto my lap. His expression suddenly darkens as he pulls away from the window and into the streets.

"Well, later today, because it is nearly four… you will have to report your incident." He inhales deep focusing on driving.

Don't remind me.

I frown for a moment crinkling the bag. The incredible smell escapes breaking my oncoming reviver. Fully exposing the bag opening, I savour the odours. Dipping into the box, my hand lays on a leg and I began munching. Chips and chicken went in less than fifteen minutes. Then the fizzy drink right after. The satisfaction was not as I hoped. I felt like a bottomless pit, I could eat more.

We drove through the city streets, aimlessly it seemed. It was beautiful, lights and people coming out from bars, even some carts with street food. Far different from Ceda, most nightlife is done contained, especially food. He parked the car on a curb near a tall wooden wall, alongside a construction site, I think. Then, opened the door for me to hobble out.

He takes the empty box and the paper bag it came in, scrunching it to a ball in his hands, putting his elbow out for me to hook my arm around his. Leading me along the pavement in a stroll.

It is livelier than I expected.

Being at the fringe of the suburbia doesn't aid my opinion anyway. The building site of a jade glass building opposite a mall appears ready to be opened. We walked across the front to a mall, my head on his arm along some cobbled streets.

The night was chilly and we went through the high street with sleeping stores. He threw the balled-up bag into the first bin he sees putting his arm around my back his palm on my backside.

Why haven't I seen these places?

As the thought left, I am reminded of the ladies on our first day here. The arguments and the time we've wasted. The fact that I have been here awake for just about a week.

The sun began to rise as we passed a beautiful high-rise apartment building. The sun gleams a beautiful orange and light pinks, painting the blue skies, starting a new day.

"Imagine waking up to this view, every day," Eric whispered in my ear then kissed my head.

"… Come on."

He tugs me forward as I balanced on him. We ambled around a corner finding ourselves at the front of the L.D.O.

Apprehension fills me and my breathing quickens. The night may have been calculated. Realisation clouts me. My subconscious is wagging her finger at me. My feet are shaking one ahead of the other and I swallow hard. We walked through the front door.

It was partly quiet, I supposed being early. He sits me on a bench at the front desk as he goes to the officer on duty, speaking with him briefly. I am reminded of our strange relationship. And once more of his law enforcement career. Then he comes back to me helping me up, leading me inside.

The wooden front desk was like a judge's bench. The duty officers' eyes follow me. Eric takes my arm, leading me to the oddly familiar precinct. I am anxious and his dragging me only adds to it.

His familiarity with the building is concerning. We turned two corners without direction and we stopped at a doorway at the end of a hall. My heart pounds and he opened the door.

The small square room, a tinted glass cut in the middle of the inner wall with four iron chairs around it. A long halogen light shone brightly over us illuminating the blue walls. He pulled out a chair for me, my face to the cut-out window. I know the reason not too far from the one on the day we met.

A lifetime ago.

But this was different.

Is it? I ask myself.

The cold iron chair slips under my dress as I glided my behind to sit. The line along his jaw moves under his beard and the vein in the centre of his forehead has formed. He drags a chair next to mine, bending his knees slowly to rest his behind at the edge. His legs widely opened and he's bringing his knees together and apart randomly.

His mien drives my disconcertment. Both silent, since entering the building. I take his hand, our fingers meshed tightly. The time passing, my ankles crossed with a small tap as the sweat on my palms increased.

My eyes wandered to a camera on a stand in the far end corner. My sweaty palms increased with moisture. The beat of my heart in my ears. The round officer, Nubert swings in with the door, startling me, my legs still.

"Do you want a coffee?"

He shrugs holding a cup himself up at us crisped in his dark uniform and shiny buttons. I shook my head, 'no'.

"No, she doesn't," Eric answered firmly.

His tone is a concern. I folded my lips thankful I was not the recipient of Eric's reply. Nubert's surprise to Eric's bark was brief but Eric's nonchalant manner worries me even more. Our reflection distant in the mirror.

"I apologise for the wait. My partner is on his way," Nubert explains hanging from the door.

Acknowledging him, Eric and I nod.

He pulls the door creaking it as he shuts it. Leaving us alone once more, to brew.

"It's OK Shana, just routine." Eric positions assuring me breaks our silence.

Though I am certain the statement is not for my calming.

My insides knot.

I breathe in my nose and exhale through my mouth.

I don't want to throw up. I repeated.

Breathing again. In through my nose. I feel his eyes. And I am sure he will ask.

"Are you nauseous?"

Huff out my mouth. *Ugh!*

He didn't even take a beat. Eric's probing aggravates me immediately. I crinkled my eyebrows at him, he sees that my mood shifts and his does as well. My hand slackens the grip enmeshing our fingers.

"I can tell you don't want to do this Shana, why?"

Eric whispers, stern.

Is he going to interrogate me… again?

He slips his hand from mine tilting to me. I crossed my arms under my breast and over my bloated midsection, with a purposeful frown. Eric is right, I don't want to be here. Everything about it exposes me as a damsel, which I am not.

Ten years ago, maybe but not today.

It just feels wrong! I protest to myself.

Officer Nubert waddles returning with his slim partner, Officer Hugh. They walked around the small table positioning to sit. Officer Nubert turns the camera on sliding into the chair next to his partner, with a notepad and pen.

There are some scribbles on the yellow notepad, that he looks over then he turns to a fresh page, as does his partner.

"Mrs Hall."

Hugh's thick moustache and Divinish accent irritates me further as he annunciates the 'I' and addresses me without my identity.

"Agent Davis-Hall, thank you," I correct him.

Eric's exhalations are loud.

"Pardon me, Agent Davis-Hall, do you feel much better to answer our questions today?"

Hugh's moustache twitches as his patronising tone together with Eric's questioning has me on the defence.

I shook my head folding my lips inward choking the oncoming attitude and rising chicken in my throat. Long intentional breathing calming my stormy insides taking my time to process before I reply.

"Do you mind Mr Hall, waiting outside?"

Hugh speaks to Eric off balancing me.

What! I whipped my head to my husband.

He squinted with a nod at me. The sign to assure that I've got this.

Dragging the chair along the concrete floor coming to stand. Says nothing to the officers, tidies his white T-shirt over his jeans and exits without protesting. Unlike him.

Why didn't he say anything? I sigh inward, eyeing him closing the door.

"Agent Davis-Hall," Nubert called my attention, my hazels move to him. "… You said you were lost, let's start from there. Where were you going?" he quotes, then asks.

"I was on the way to a field job."

I try being cooperative knowing Eric's eyes are on the other side of the mirror.

"Care to elaborate?" Hugh waves his pen, waiting to dictate.

"No! It is an active investigation, so I cannot." I am blunt.

"I understand. So, what happened, how you got lost?"

Ugh! His condescending tone is irritating!

I pause, filtering.

"I don't know. I am unfamiliar with this area. My phone lost connection and I more than likely took a wrong turn."

I answered truthfully but the sarcasm was an unforeseen side effect.

"OK, do you remember the place you were attacked?" He recognises and follows up with another stupid question.

"No, I was lost. I called a colleague of mine, giving her the address to pick me up." *What is his point?*

Does he think my answer would change?

"I thought you were lost."

Nubert cross and writes quickly. I squint.

"*I. Was. Lost!*" I clarify, "... I can't even tell you the name of the town."

"What is the name of the colleague?" Hugh cut to another question.

"Sergeant Samanther Martinez."

"At the hospital, you mentioned you were robbed, is that how you got your injuries?" Nubert asks.

"No, I stopped to get food and directions, whilst trying to call my colleague. A street man pushed the drinks I bought across my chest as a distraction to lift my car keys. I forgot my wallet, gun and badge at home rushing to the field job."

"Is that when you were the victim of this attack?"

Nubert interrupts.

That word used loosely and inaccurately on me. This thing that happened in the alley does not close me into a box.

If he would just let me finish! "I am not a victim!" my voiced raised slightly and I protest to that category. My eyes burned into Nubert for seconds and I really want to hit him.

Calm down Shana! Rationally, I reminded myself that he is only doing his job.

"You were attacked," he says as a matter-of-fact and it sends my annoyance and defence on another level.

"I was attacked, but not until later that evening. Look, it was a bad day all around. I had no money, no cards, no ID, no badge, no phone and no idea where in Divinish I was. Someone offered to help that was when I got a call through to my colleague."

"Who helped you?"

He cut my looming tantrum. I paused. A sense of guilt fell on me.

That's because you flirted!

"His name was Brian Kumal."

The name rolled off my tongue quietly. The sensation as if calling to him. The hairs at the back on my neck stood straight. I thought of his soft lips and his hand touching mine. We gazed at each other as if we were in a bubble and the heat of his body felt close to mine. The room temperature rose. I'm inhaling long.

"Do you think he attacked you?"

The officer broke my lust, deflating the bubble I memorised we sat in. I exhaled hurried. The assumed is uncomfortable.

"If his nose is broken or his elbow dislocated then yes, he attacked me."

I mocked his ridiculous notation.

Could it be? My subconscious poked.

"What does that mean?"

Nubert breaks my thinking with another obvious question.

"It means I broke one attacker's nose and dislocated his associate's elbow," I scoffed. They paused.

"How did you do that?"

Hugh throws a curve ball, changing direction. My skin prickled as I force myself to relive his breath on my neck, my stomach clenched. I begin to breathe slowly as the spit in my mouth thickened.

"It was time to meet my colleague. I walked through the alley towards where I was parked. One of them came from behind me dragging me into the dark. The other began touching me."

The tears filled my eyes. I can't regurgitate another word. The tears slip down my face.

"Can you describe your attackers?"

Don't go there Shana, I swallowed the spittle stuck in my tonsils.

"Mrs Hall," Hugh called me.

"It-it was dark. I didn't see their faces." My voice unexpectedly trembled, folded my lips right after.

Eric bursts through the doors. "I think she's given you more than enough gentlemen."

I covered my mouth.

He's saying something else to them but my ears are mute only my heartbeat thundering in echoes through my ears. He touches my shoulder I shudder whipping my head to a horrified expression painted on his face.

"Are you OK?" Eric whispered to me, stooped unconsciously handling the sore leg. His brown eyes reflecting my gloom and I stare pass his worried face taking even breaths, trying hard to swallow.

Then it erupted. Thrusting the table aside, I collapsed the chair as I flee. My stomach contents flow up and I gag. Retreating, confused through an unfamiliar hallway stopping the projectile with my palms. I spy the rescue of a common room bin tipped off the cover, throwing up the chicken, chips and carbonated drink. Covering the freshly lined bin with the contents of my stomach.

Ten. Nine. Eight. Seven. Six.

I exhaled. Then inhaled. The plastic-tar smell begins the build up again. Shallow breaths. I hover. *Five, four.*

"We're leaving."

Eric's baritone is a relief. He hulls my arm, removing me from my brief sanctuary, the bin, handing me a napkin. I inhale then exhale. I take it and he swung us one-eighty clutching my elbow rushing us through the now busy L.D.O. precinct.

Out the front doors we came, through to the streets and back to the car. He opens the front passenger door waiting for me to sit before he closed it behind me. Circling the car then sliding into the driver's seat starting the car. The disgusting aftertaste pools in my mouth.

I need to brush my teeth!

"You can rest today or whatever you like to do."

His tone was filled with regret. I think it's his way of apologising. He can be so sweet but all I feel is homesick and alone.

"I want to go home."

The forty-five minutes' drive he folded his lips, exposing his dimples, deep in thought. I texted Liz, she didn't answer. Emily is still deployed and who knows where Sue is. My three best friends, the younger versions of their disobedient, disrespectful and ruthless mothers, the A.P.S. Eric and I are the common factors bridging.

How would this affect my work or his?

And our baby? I need to know.

"Do you regret supporting me?"

I blurted out my thought because nothing else matters. He gapes briefly at me then at the road.

"I shouldn't have distracted you."

His honesty jolts me back to the evening both bitter and sweet moments.

"What!" I blinked at him a couple times recalling.

That to be continued kiss, my subconscious shook me.

"That day, I shouldn't have distracted you."

Was that what it was really meant to be?

Blood races to the lower parts of my body brewing on our bodies delayed gratification as he pulls up to the apartment parking, we walked towards my place.

Aaliyah's walking towards us, chiffon white sleeveless top and a navy light pants, fitted around her hips and firm behind. Her cinnamon face almost covered by her sunglasses her lips ruby and glossy.

She moved past us as if she didn't know us, not that we, that is me and her, know each other. It is almost ten. Her punctuality at least is consistent even without my supervision and I understand why now.

What was that about?

Eric does the same.

Those two, baffle me!

My eyes followed her making her way to her black Mercedes. She starts the car with a loud rev, skids out her parking and swiftly to the busy road.

Dare I ask?

I recalled his words last night.

"What would you like to eat?"

Ugh! I want to spit! And… "I would like a shower."

He grins. "That's a great idea."

His tone sings and is suggestive as he opens the door. I blush at him naughty thoughts fill me. After two years of marriage his words still have that effect on me. Hurried inside scooping my dress over my head and throwing it to the floor. He kicks his shoes off with his feet pulling his jersey over his head and I giggled skipping to the bathroom. We are both thinking the same thing. His phone interrupts the unbuttoning of his pants.

He answers, "Yep, uh huh…" He slows his entry, his jaw closes and he says something through his teeth, I frown turning the shower on, knowing how this ends. I pulled my hair back tying it up from the water. He comes in.

"Mind if I get in and out before you, I've got to go in for a meeting."

"Why not?"

I trundled my eyes at the disappointment standing in my underwear.

As expected, I woke to Eric crawling into the bed. He's managed to make it just passed midnight. How silly was I to believing this new job would be any different from before?

CHAPTER TWENTY-SEVEN

I did my part, went to occupational health and safety, saw a councillor and attended my weekly weapon training to be sure I will be ready for my return to work. The paperwork was done, the footwork was handled by the team, I hope. Eric though present at every appointment this past week, his distraction grew as the days for me to return to work came closer.

Uncertain if it is my job or his, I have been self-taught in our four-year relationship to stand clear when his silent frustration connects to work.

Every day he visits work for a few hours longer with sometimes a breath of scotch. Today, Friday, the final day of mandatory leave, I am making use of his day away, and invited my personal assistant Noel, to catch up.

He broke the corner at eight a.m. pulling out from the parking with my rental car. I watched as a routine from the balcony basking in the Divinish morning air. It is the coolest time of the day and one of the most beautiful sights to behold. The sunrise from the rocky red mountains.

My light cotton dressing gown draped over me exposing my favourite camisole and his boxers. Once the sun touches my face, it is time to go inside and shower, tame my mane and prepare for this brief at home. My bump has risen to the occasion, standing or sitting and I don't think I am ready for this part of my life to meet the work part of my life.

I need to gain focus.

I searched the wardrobe for a smart casual piece. Six pairs of suits I packed.

What was I thinking!

Reprimanding myself.

Thinking... I won't get pregnant.

Crinkling my eyebrows inwardly and sighed at my thinking. The flowing dress Eric brought to the hospital is the only option for this visit.

I hope I won't have to wear this everyday once I get back.

The reflection caused me to have a closer look. One slightly stretched skirt and a body-con dress. I sighed long. My phone beeped a message snapping me out the closet. An email of my upcoming work schedule came from Noel. She summarised two weeks' work and reports that she sent to the directors.

At least I didn't have to clean up before catching up!

Great news! Those ladies hadn't used their hurtful touch as far as the reports say. I danced in my head.

Getting three boisterous women to follow rules will always be the real challenge.

Noel has done well!

There was a booked meeting with the directors. My heart sank remembering the headlines and Sam-Sam's death, then my attack, I gulped.

I guess it hasn't blown over.

Most of the physical files were at the office. I reviewed the status of the case as from the day I went on leave. Completing more research, adding it usefully as a starting point to meet the directors. This is especially important knowing in the three weeks that we have been here, all we establish is; how much we don't like each other, and how little we know about this side of the country, the Zeman culture and that this isn't a simple rape.

****

Monday at last, the wound on my leg is a slither scar that hurts if I stand too long. I contemplate whether to bandage it. I showered making the mistake of washing my hair. Conditioning it one too many times to brush the curls smooth, then put a small bobble and held it into a bunny tail. My hair has grown a bit. The puff is past my shoulders. I examine in the mirror and catch the reflection of the curve under my tummy.

I don't want any focus on my growing bump.

I got a black cotton tailored dress with two white column stripes from my shoulders with a plunging neckline.

I don't know which is more obvious my bump or breasts, I sighed.

The zip almost didn't make it all the way up but I found a black jacket and draped it over.

That should do the trick. I winked at myself.

Eric fortunately had left for work an hour earlier so he wasn't around to witness my indecisive nervousness. He has been all over the place lately.

I am not sure if I want to ask.

A growing doubt creeps in.

I hope he didn't announce my pregnancy.

I'm not sure if I'm ready for anyone to know!

The scary thought surfaced.

Should I wear, my stilettoes?

I fished out black ballerinas.

Having this leg injury can be my excuse.

I slipped them in, getting my workbag and laptop.

God, I hope he hasn't done that!

Out the thought came again, now I am more nervous. I clipped my badges on the neck of my dress put my gun in the holster around my shoulders.

Now I feel like Sam.

Super conscious about my waistline, I checked myself in the mirror again. The seams of my dress display the thread that's fighting to keep it together and the zipper.

I hope I keep it together.

I ambled past Noel at her desk studiously taking notes as she talks on the phone.

"Yes sir... (she paused nodding and listening) no sir... (she looks up at me her green gaze meets my hazels) OK, sir... (she paused, nodding again) bye."

Who is she talking to?

I pass her nodding as if the person over the phone can see her actions. Her face red at the cheeks and her mouth slackened as if I was a ghost eyeing at me walking by. She hustled off the phone chasing after me through the halls.

"Agent Davis-Hall."

She's got it right this time!

She traipses with her moderately heeled court shoes echoing on the tiled floor a diary in one hand a pen in the other.

"… Agent Davis-Hall! Uh… you're back at work today?" She's pushing her pen clicking it.

"Yyyeesss."

I dragged the word turning in her direction for her to catch up. Her tiptoe prance fed my low tolerance. I blinked long to bring myself to calm, then replied, "… Didn't we have that conversation on Friday?"

I narrow my eyes looking up at her, she fiddles with the pen clicking the point in and out, the sound vibrates in my ear, my eyes twitch. Her grey pin-striped dress curving around her hips amplifying her round backside. I estimate her breast to hip ratio eyeing her up and down.

I am going to miss my waist these coming months.

I sighed not realising she's stopped talking, her mouth opened an O, painted with pink glossy lipstick. Her lips were thin, biscuit tone and powdered make-up and her cheeks flush from our conversation, maybe. She sees my stare and continued, "Oh, ah, I thought you meant next Monday." Her voice cracked and swayed.

"OK, that would have been the conversation a week ago, I'm back today. I don't see the problem."

I put my palms up shifting them as though they were scales. She lingered, one of my hands on my hip, the other loose with my workbag and laptop, measured her with my eyes and began to roll my head at her, her eyes opened, and she lifted the diary and blurted, "The meeting with the directors has been rescheduled for next week."

"You told me that on Friday." I squinted at her, my cheeks tightened and I inhaled.

"Oh, arr, there are interviews scheduled for this week as well as some transfers from other defence departments."

"*What!*" My arm fell off my hip.

Take it down a notch! I am reminded by my subconscious.

"… Sorry, when did this happen?" *Better!* I rolled my eyes at myself.

"Uh, I just came off the phone with the director." She sang her words.

"Who?"

"Um, yes, he has been ah, keeping things going here, as you were off... and."

"That's the director to whom we email the reports?" OK, I didn't expect things to be at a standstill.

"Uh, yea."

What is wrong with her? "Thanks Noel," I continued to my office.

"Can we go over your diary for this week?" She chased after me.

"After the meeting."

"Uh..."

"Is there anything I need to do now?"

"Uh, no."

"Is there anything I need to do before lunchtime?"

"Um, no... can I get you refreshments?"

I slow down.

What an odd question. "No, thank you I'll be fine."

She scurried back to her desk.

I sauntered across the workstations, Sam and Lia sat at their desks silent and busy at the computers. I supposed Paula is in the lab having her fun. I greeted them, they haven't acknowledged my presence. Not that they usually do but their seriousness concerns me.

At least they're not acting weird! Unlike Noel.

I noted walking to the door of my office.

There's a man in my office.

My eyes widen as I observed him on the phone reclined and swivelling in my chair. He was just as surprised as me. It was difficult to see who from the outside, but it is suspicious as I recall Sam and Lia sitting together working on their computers at nine in the morning.

I reached for the door and opened it. A slender, middle-aged man with mixtures of greys with his dark hair sat in a navy-blue suit on the phone. His right hand holding the phone wore a thick gold ring shaped like an oval with an inscription that is unreadable to me. A star with a diamond in the centre of the star.

His voice uniquely husky with an accent I don't recognise. He looked less than pleased that I entered the office, put his palm up signalling 'stop' as he continued his conversation.

"Yes sir, I know and understand this..." (He paused listening with a nod). "... We are working on a deadline..." (He paused with a frown). "... No sir..." (He sighs). "... I will keep you updated." (He listened again) ."... Thank you sir, good day," he threw the receiver in its place.

His brown eyes circled by a ring of grey intensely on me, wrinkles across his forehead, folds as he looks up at me tilting back on my chair.

"Good morning," his tone slightly vexed.

"Hi, um good morning." I was slightly lost for words.

"I understand you have claimed this office, but steaming into here was unnecessary, and a bit ill-mannered. Why didn't you knock? Did you not see I was on the phone?" His tone aggressive and low. "... Why are you here? Aren't you on sick leave?"

"My sick leave ended Friday. I am due back in today."

I was off balance by his reaction. The moment became awkward.

"I guess you want your office back, huh."

He shakes his head in agreement rocking the chair back and forth balancing by the desk preventing his spill.

"Uh, I have got, a lot of work." I am trying to be impassive as best as I can.

"Work?" He scoffed steadying himself in the chair. "... What work have you and those fastidious women done since your arrival?" he said in disgust. "... All you have done is pranced around, pulling rank and squandering resources since you've been here. Do you know what your actual job is?"

"Ah, sir?" I stood dumfounded, playing over his words searching for a defence.

"Director Kane!" He releases his position claiming his authority. "... Agent Davis-Hall." He syllabised my rank and name.

I blinked at his measuring posture and diplomatically defended my actions.

"Director Kane, it has been a bit challenging these past three weeks."

"Four!" he corrected harshly, erecting from the chair growing.

He must be at least six feet tall.

"Sorry sir?" I look up defending again.

"You and your team, have been here four weeks."

I try counting by incidents. "Yes sir, one week I was in hospital."

"Do you think because you weren't here, it doesn't count? Did you report your incident?"

His aggression causes my voice to flutter.

"I have sir."

"Did you follow up on its progress?"

Am I supposed to?

What is this really about? I asked myself, sensing his bitter undertone.

"Sir, I have only been in a few minutes." I had to defend myself.

He comes around the table turning his briefcase. Confronting, gazing down at me. I tilted my head upwards looking into his straight nose and two-coloured eyes. He is a bit shorter than Eric, narrow sloped shoulders and a bit of a bump like mine. My lack of heels means I am slightly above his shoulders but he's crushed me, lower than my height, continuing his cruelty.

"There have been three incidents since your investigation began." He put up his fingers briefly. "… None of which have had proper insight into. This means there are three open cases tied to this simple investigation." He simplified the complex and highly political investigation to his point and I reflect.

I can think of two including mine.

What did they do? My immediate thought to those untamed women.

"You women have been making a real mess of this," he stated again in abhorrence, I frown, wanting to interrupt but don't. "… And you are disrupting the balance of natives here, causing a whole host of work for me. I liaise with your P.A. your immediate duties for the next few days.

"A friendly warning. Keep your eyes on the prize and do your job. I don't want to be called back here. If I do, I'll be cleaning house, Agent Davis-Hall." He stepped back. "… I will leave you to it, but know that the clock is ticking.

"The longer you take is the messier things will get, for you. I look forward to our meeting next week. Oh and, thanks for letting me *borrow* your office, Agent. We'll be seeing each other soon."

He took a briefcase perched on the table and crawled out the door around me.

What did the ladies do?

What did I do?

I am frozen for a moment caught off guard by his abuse. I watched him through the glass digging his heel to the floor, then saluting the ladies outside. Noel with a diary and a notepad to her chest, giving him way following him with her eyes. I inhale suddenly the adrenalin slows through me and I shiver. Confused by the way I am to process this I can't breathe.

Ten.

Noel enters, breaking my counting.

"Agent Davis-Hall," she called with her singsong tone and Divinish accent.

I turned on my heels, retreating for the ladies' room. My breathing uncontrolled as I burst into a stall putting the cover down on the toilet sitting trying to bring my mind back to the task at hand.

Ten, nine, eight seven, six, five, four, three, two, one.

I ran through every part of the investigation so far. Inhaled and exhaled slowly gaining my focus.

Shit! The meeting!

CHAPTER TWENTY-EIGHT

Shaking him off, I washed my hands and face plotting my plan of attack. I chase to my office taking up the file folders and my laptop in one hand. Then, to the conference room to busy myself with the set up before the ladies. I opened the door to them seated in silence professionally dressed and waiting.

I didn't notice before Aaliyah without any flashy glittering jewellery or chunky bangles dangling, clinking and distracting everyone. Just a simple white sleeveless blouse and black pants. Her icy-blues piercing at me as I entered. I consciously tugged at my jacket shut.

Paula wore navy-blue pants and a blue striped cable knit jumper, ironed and her ample bosom covered tastefully. Sam, jeans tasteful with a light blue shirt her boots ankle height and below the table for a change. Both bemused and enthralled. I tried to be casual, to complement their professionalism, just in case this might be the last.

Still thinking of Director Kane's accusation wondering what happened in my absence. A soft touch is always the best to avoid an unnecessary argument. The vacant seat at the head of the table a bit troubling. I examined it before sitting, placing my laptop in the bag on the floor next to my feet. They laid out folders on the table waiting. I felt their eyes fixated on me as I shift to settle in the chair, resting the folders and leaned back.

Tension, not our usual explosive kind but the anticipative kind, it was very disconcerting. They followed my every move and didn't say anything. A stack of folders was left on the table for me. Taking one, I opened, and began reading quietly. Before finishing the first line of the report, I sense their eyes piercing through me.

"Where are we on your last assignments?" I shifted any preconceptions to work.

"I did not do anything beyond your request."

Paula shrieked, steaking her claim proudly. The other two tilted to look at her.

I guess it wasn't her but just as I expected.

"That's very reassuring Paula, but what *did* you do?" I squint at her.

"OK. When last we met, I had been working on the smaller pieces of evidence found on Ms Mall. Interesting though the gold thread embedded around her wrist is silk, guess where the silk comes from?"

Sam, Lia and me conjointly rolled our eyes she ignored it and continued,

"… Silkworms from a moth's cocoon; a very delicate material this was weaved into a rope. A strong one evident by the indentation on Ms Mall's arm. Attempts to find retailers or manufactures of this rope led only to ancient Zemand. It is found on ceremonial pieces of their robe. Only the elders possess this as a part of their traditional clothing and not the priest as I originally believed."

That's interesting.

"I have been researching the Zemand and saw two news clippings specifically about this ceremony, they call it Catacá." I voiced my thoughts.

"The only article that called it Catacá is the one about you."

Sam artfully pointed out with a hit of aggression using her pen.

Shana, don't! I warn myself gaping at her through my lashes from across the table. She leans on the folders, her eyes squinted almost daring me. I inhaled stopping at ten realising this is my forum and stared fiery. Aaliyah broke my burning attempt by the scratching of her pen taking notes in her diary.

Breathe Shana, breathe!

I attempt impassively softening my eyes. Paula continued,

"… This is all parts and parcel of the elders. They're the ones who perform or conduct the ceremonies. They're judges and executioners of their law. Well, that's what I read anyway.

"Since the evidence led to Zemand ceremonial conditions, I continued to look that way. The sticky stuff she was dowsed in is something called Cenæ. It is a substance only used for Cedérus' ceremonies, a mixture of honey, a red seed that is used as paint called rucoo and heroin."

"Drugs again?"

I snapped writing a note to myself. This time not sorry I blurted squinting slightly gaping at the other two deportments. They were busy dictating or I missed it looking up too soon. She shook her head only to take a breath to carry on,

"It keeps their victims hallucinating and unaware of anything. The Zeman say in a state to see the gods. Yeah! The red thread also a part of the ceremonial robe."

"That's great Torrez, you really did a thorough job," I complimented her intentionally.

"I'm not finished," Paula protests.

OK.

I am taken aback and shrugged. She went on, "... The Zeman caves are off limits to us. So, I am not sure if we may ever find the actual crime scene. Maybe if the law changes." She wavers partially dabbing in politics.

"... Charles 'Sam-Sam' Brown, age forty-four, he died from the single shot to the head spilling his brain throughout his kitchen wall. The evidence suggests, his murderer placed a sack of the drugs at the back of his head and shot him through the bag. Exploding the drugs and his brains across the kitchen.

"He unfortunately, was already dying. Autopsy revealed he had stage four cancer. He only had a few months to live anyway. The drugs scattered across his kitchen was heroin.

"His hands were bound behind his back, before he died, possibly tortured, all his fingernails were ripped out and bleeding. I don't know why they bothered. Living for him was probably just as bad.

"Ms Mall's car was also found with the same stuff at the same grade. So, I am maybe ninety percent sure she got the drugs from him or vice versa.

"Because of that connection, I ran his bloods and he was also a semen match for Ms Mall. So, I've got only two more samples to match her elicit day. I can bet that the last person is her boss. There is no physical evidence tying the wife to the crime scene."

I waited a few seconds, "Finished?"

I asked this time. She shook her head.

"Great work Torrez!" I phrased her consistency again. "… What about Sam-Sam's connection to this investigation Martinez?"

I looked across the table at Sam.

Be professional! I hummed to myself waiting for a response.

"I didn't get a chance to speak with him before he died, obviously."

She begins with sarcasm and I intentionally filled my lungs with air to give her, her third strike, but she belted faster than I could after that breath. "… Besides the rumours of him and Sharron Mall were friends and the semen sample, I don't know.

"I am not sure who was the supplier between him and Ms Mall, but we do know there is a third party involved, evidenced by his death.

"I did, however, speak to Sam-Sam's wife, Darline Shianne Brown. She said she didn't know about his terminal cancer, but she did say some men came by the house and he asked her to go with their kids to the neighbours.

"Apparently, that for their family was a regular occurrence. Whenever those particular guys show up, she knows to make herself and the kids scarce. She, by the way, has no interest in identifying any one of those particular guys.

"She says, and I quote, 'I would like to live in peace with my kids' end quote. She admits Sam-Sam would sometimes hold items but claims she doesn't know any of his suppliers or clients and she doesn't get involved.

"It made no sense holding her as an accessory with intent to sell as she doesn't look like she touches the stuff."

"Do you think she can help in any other way?" My filter has been lost again.

"Shana, this is a rape case. Illegal drugs are just a side dish. As far as I can tell, this little bite may be more than you would be able to chew."

I huffed. "What about his relationship with Sharron?" My irritation builds.

"It is funny you said his relationship, Sharron is his wife's sister."

"What?" I am shocked.

"Half-sister anyway; they share a mother."

"Great! This is even more twisted. I'll hand Sam-Sam's death over to the L.D.O."

"Wise!" Sam trolled her eyes with an obvious hint of criticism without a beat continued, "... She found his body. As Torrez says, there is no physical evidence linking her to the crime as well as financial ones.

"Classic case of he did it, she overlooked it. He was a hobo, he had no income and no purpose, as far as I am concerned. His debtor is rumoured to be Valentine Jason."

Her rustic voice bellowed Valentine Jason. I shook my head trying not to roll my eyes and hold expressionless.

"Him again... Did she have any more friends?"

This sounds like trouble and I need to steer her away.

"None as interesting as Valentine." Joy resonated from her voice.

She is really pushing it.

I need to make her change direction. I shook my head at myself.

"God, I hope you got something on Valentine, Paul," I begged, turning to Lia.

"Contact with him has proven to be quite difficult as he's constantly blocked by his lawyer. Whom only make statements on his behalf. Of which, denying any contact with Ms Mall and states he doesn't know Sam-Sam."

Aaliyah itemized on her fingers reading from her opened folder.

"His semen was inside of her!" I whined at her. *Didn't she tell his lawyer this?*

I exhaled loudly she blinked at me a couple of times then leaned into her chair to say,

"We can bring him in but I can guarantee his answers are all going to be as evasive as his relationship with her."

"Ugh! Our interest in him is strictly in the interest of Sharron's promiscuous day! Once we can prove he didn't rape her, we can move this evidence as well. It's not worth the stress! What about the necklace?" I raise my voice.

"You didn't specify," Aaliyah defends.

"I cannot believe that you took two weeks to get nothing!" I flew off. "... What are we doing here guys? What about Ms Mall? Someone needs to get the truth out of her. Can you get that Paul, without hitting her?"

Which is what I would like to do to her now, I turned to Sam.

"… Sam, I need you to interview all the 'semen sample' matches except for Valentine's. I don't think I need more stress."

I cannot tell between the two, they're equally infuriating!

"… Torrez, I need to see you in my office later. In the meantime, I would like the reports before six this afternoon ladies. We would meet again on Friday,"

They sat looking at me,

"Now, ladies!"

I scream after them. They scattered like roaches to light.

CHAPTER TWENTY-NINE

Why is every meeting so trying!

Do they always have to be assholes?

I am fuming. How stupid I was to believe they would have actually worked in my absence. The reports are flimsy and their assumptions manner are deplorable. My irritation is on high alert ringing in my tone. I slapped the files on the table frustrated.

Maybe Director Kane has a point.

We have wasted a lot of time bickering in the beginning.

We still are measuring and pushing one another's buttons.

I groan as his annoying voice echoed in my head.

Ugh! I took the folders putting it into my laptop bag with the laptop standing.

The door knocked. I looked up to Sarah Noel.

"Walk with me," I commanded setting off to my office.

"Agent Davis-Hall."

Yep, sounds like a mouthful. I shook the thought as it appeared.

"Call me that when Kane is around. When he's not, Davis is fine."

"Davis, we just need to go over some things…"

She trails hugging her notepads and other papers in her hands, still timid. I cut her quick wanting to get to the tasks quick, so I answered her possible reminder before she states.

"The interviews and transfers Director Kane mentioned that to me," I say dismissively. And she sings, "OK…"

I waited a moment for her to confirm, deny or move on.

She also paused before stuttering, "Uh, besides that…" She trailed off and my patience went to zero.

"Get to the point please!" I stomped expressing my irritation.

No wonder she was timid, I scolded myself.

I really can't stop myself today!

A.P.S are still boiling my blood, I am still angry at them. If I'm truthful, I am mostly mad at myself… *for getting hurt and being pregnant.*

Calm down Shana! I say to myself and took an inhale.

"There has been a follow-up article about Ms Mall two days ago and there are two more articles today about the progress of her case."

Fuck!

My heartbeat jumped and I exhaled like a deflated balloon. I am close to livid. Hearing the sound, I closed my eyes and took a breath to think. Recalling the last headline: *Officer Interviews Catacá Victim*, then opened my eyes to her green gaze. Reasoning with myself.

That was a small article in the middle of the newspaper. I nodded to myself.

They are gaining traction. Doubt surfaced.

"That's not good!" I say my worry aloud and followed by unfiltered panic. "… Which newspaper? Do they know I'm covering the investigation?"

Somehow, I feel targeted and the feeling to hide is returning, curling in my stomach. I count quickly, biting the inside of my cheeks. Noel eyes me strangely but answers, "They don't know your name. Nothing mentioned in the articles about our agency."

I sigh a relieved breath but know it is only a matter of time. I need to get ahead of this. "Keep an eye on it and get me copies of these articles."

I need to speak with the author or something.

I study staring before she broke my thoughts.

"Will do," she said, taking notes.

"Anything else, Noel?" I wait for good news.

"There are a couple of messages here for you, several emails and letters to be answered."

Breathe Shana breathe! "… I will check them in my office. Can you bring those letters for me, thanks?" I say tensely trying to get a handle on my emotions.

"Do you need me for anything else?" her tension has eased slightly.

There are so many things on my new 'to-do' list but more than ever I needed to wrap the one that would be pointed out in both personal and professional settings.

"Can you get Torrez in here for me?"

"Sure."

She handed me some letters and scurried away. I opened my office door, sat and began working. Emails were easy enough to go through then, requested moving the additional drug investigation to the D.P.F. finishing up with the letters, and making notes.

I glanced at my watch; it was lunchtime when Paula strolled in.

"You wanted to see me?"

She replaced her knitted sweater with a navy-blue camisole and a draped lab coat opened down the front. One hand in her pocket the other holding the door open.

"Yes, come in,"

I pointed to a wooden handled green cushioned chair directly in front of me with a pen. I had been mapping my diary with Noel's new 'to-do' list. She closed the door and plopped her behind without looking. The chair hissed releasing the trapped air in an instant.

I put my pen to the side crisscrossing my fingers on the desk pulling my chair in closer to the table. She tilted her head one way and then the other mimicking a snake, twisting her head and neck. I squinted, trying to figure out her composure but maintaining a businesslike tone,

"I have got another assignment for you."

"Oh," she says inquisitively sitting upright and placing her arms on the wooden rest.

"You have done a fantastic job on this case after an entire week. So, I have no reservations about your capabilities. There are two persons of interest that I would like you to look into. Both male, who would have been admitted into the hospital about two weeks ago, one with a broken nose and the other with a dislocated elbow."

"What is this for?" she questions,

"A connecting case."

One of her eyebrows rose,

"By chance is that the men who attacked you?"

How does she know? Shit! "Yes, would you be able to handle this discreetly?"

"Wow, Davis you are brutal."

I want to smile but kept a straight face. "Quietly, as in, between me and you only."

"Sure Davis…" She shrugs impassively.

"Great! Please if you find anything just get their information, *do not* approach them and the details stay between us."

She sat there while I untied my fingers and grabbed my pen.

"Anything else," I asked and she took another second before she realised.

"Oh, you mean now?"

I shook my head 'yes', she leapt up out of the chair scurrying out. She is a good soldier when she wants to be but I wondered if I should have asked her not to damage someone or property in the process.

My gaggling tummy reminded me of my increasing appetite. I saunter to the office kitchen following my nose to a savoury rice dish, fresh from the fire and maybe broccoli. The odours of garlic-flavoured baked chicken; I think. But I can taste the spices through the air it's causing my mouth to water.

I hope Noel has gotten an extra hot sauce as I can almost taste the seasoned flavours.

I rushed in anticipation and delight.

The kitchen was small and modern. White cupboards with silver trimmings, all equipment integrated with grey marble countertops. An under-counter fridge with a small square light wood dining table with two wooden red splashed art cushioned chairs that were opposite each other adjacent to the door but in the middle of the compact kitchen.

Sam sat casually, with her thick black square-framed spectacles, reading a newspaper, sipping daintily on a steaming mug of coffee, that frosts her eyeglass each time she sips. The double expresso is messing with the savoury aromas erupting in nausea. I swallowed hard, attempting to keep it in as I am slightly concerned about her reaction to mine and her ex-husband's news. But also, remembering our last one-to-one conversation and my heartbeat increased, I drew my jacket together before entering.

"Hi."

I stormed past her avoiding eye contact, scanning the countertops for the aromatic source. She paused with her coffee mid-air steaming the lenses as I bolted fast opening the cupboards behind her.

"Hey," Sam's rustic voice greets with no warmth.

"Do you know if Noel brought any food in here?"

"Am I the kitchen assistant?" she croaked.

Does she always need to be a bitch? "Do we have a kitchen assistant?"

"Hump." Her judgemental tone always prevalent.

Don't fall for it! "What's that supposed to mean?"

I stopped shifting the plates and cups in the cupboard, keeping my head in. The fresh wooden smell is not helping either.

"You are as bad as Lia!" she slurped the drink making my senses twitch.

Don't do it! "Is there something on your mind, Sam?"

My subconscious slapped her forehead.

"Not even a day back and already sneaking around."

I crinkled my eyebrows shaking my head, I am at a loss.

"What are you talking about?"

"I know you asked Paula to look into your 'incident'."

She stresses the last word putting her fingers up quoting.

Shit! I hope Paula didn't squeal.

I may have to put her back on that list.

Or maybe Sam was spying.

I'll play this one down.

"What are you talking about?" I say casually.

"I've seen Lia cover her tracks too."

Just then, I recalled Eric's initial reaction at the hospital and his admission that he spoke with her.

"What are you hoping to gain from this conversation?"

"I already did."

I scorned and laughed turning around and leaning my curved backside on the countertop. My hands supporting, gazing at the back of her dark shoulder-length hair fighting the temptation to slap the back of her head.

"You came to this conclusion based on what?" I dismissed her trawling. "... You have no idea what you're talking about. And what's interesting is, I never pegged you for a quidnunc."

"What's that supposed to mean?"

She swiftly slapped the newspaper to the table, twisting around with her hand at the back of the chair.

268

"Look it up."

"You are such a little twit."

Why does she feel she has the right to judge me?

I did nothing wrong...

Thinking about Brian and me sitting on his sofa with my legs exposed wearing his T-shirt makes me feel guilty though. I had some attraction to him.

Wait!

Then it hit me like a tonne of bricks.

Oh... my... God!

I didn't notice it before but.

My lips quivered and I folded them in stifling my amusement. She swiped her spectacles off her face banging them on the table.

Don't say it. "You're still in love with Eric!" My subconscious slapped her forehead again.

There was a moment of silence.

Then, I uproar my face is red. My laughter fills the kitchen. "... That's sweet." My eyes watered as I doubled over trying to catch my breath fanning myself with my hands. "... You really need to get over it." I pointed at her and then turned around to search the cupboards.

"Oh please, been there, *done* him... next chapter."

"Right."

I rolled my eyes with a sarcastic tone continuing to search for food giggling. I heard the chair screech across the white-tiled floor,

"You need to get over the fact that we share a child and doesn't matter what you do, *that* will never change."

She has abandoned the chair.

Is she trying to piss me off?

I pivot to her she is standing about three feet away. Her forehead wrinkled, her soft-blue eyes intensely squinted burning through me. I point in her direction as we faced off.

"Don't get it twisted, I love Danielle and she loves me, don't make her the object of our conversation."

I crossed my arms and our staring competition begins.

"She isn't yours and never will be."

Her voice rough and gaining volume, I step towards her closing the gap between us.

"That may be true, but you cannot deny that both she and her father love me. Doesn't matter what *you* do."

I uncrossed my arms propping a fist on my hip, effectively opening my jacket. Her eyes widen as she glanced at my bump. She pauses with her mouth opened and shut quickly. I stepped back quickly folding my jacket together. She sneered, grabbed the newspaper, folded it under her arms, picking up her reading glasses and coffee.

"You two deserve each other," she grunts pointing with her spectacles and storming out.

I'm muddled. *Did I win?*

CHAPTER THIRTY

Noel and I arranged meetings, and interviews, booked reminders and completed my daily report for Director Kane after lunch. I never expected one day to be so packed. I reflect on today's events and conversations whilst comparing them to the days ahead. Casting my eyes at my opened diary tapping my pen, as I gauge tomorrow's workload. My desk phone rang.

"Davis," I greeted shortly.

"I thought you changed your work name?" Eric's soft deep-tone, surprising me, mid-pondering and I grin at the phone.

"I did but I think saying Davis-Hall to answer a phone is a bit of a mouthful." I say with all honesty but not wanting to go into details for an argument or exhausting talk.

"Hall is one syllable." His voice is excited and I reflect his mood.

"You're Hall," I argue in a friendly manner still gawping at the phone.

"So are you." He pushes back lightly.

I pause, resonating on Eric's long-standing career and reputation. He is well-known in his field. I shook my head slightly, thinking of the reason behind keeping the only thing I remembered about myself and his absolute aspiring career and voiced low, "A big set of shoes to fill."

"Umm," he groans deep in his throat. "… Well, you know what they say about men with big feet." His statement is not proven but well established on his front. My skin prickles and the pulses began moving down.

"Not sure, what *do* they say?" Baiting him, I absently lick my lips.

"Hum, well, come outside and you will find out."

"You're here?" His statement did two things, made my heart flutter and carried the pulses lower. I am excited in more ways than one. Squirming in my chair.

"I am."

"Did you drive?" I thought of a plan.

"Taxi." Even better!

"I got the car," I moan, not looking forward to driving.

"I know. I'll drive."

I am beaming through the phone he has totally changed the ending I expected of today. The door knocks, I looked up. He's lingering in the doorway his head not too far from the top. Gracing me in a navy blue slim-fit jacket that suits his muscular frame peeks through, a white shirt with no tie the first button was undone, and he's had a haircut.

His hair was low enough to see his scalp and tidied around the edges, beard stubble wearing his gorgeous smile and dimples. One hand in his pocket the other holding the phone out to me as he leans on the frame balancing a foot on the tips of his brown dress shoe.

I hung up, my hand attached to the office phone still in excitement and the grin won't leave my face. His brown eyes twinkled at me. I feel an aroused buzz and my libido has awakened.

Oh, what this man does to me!

"Ready?" He smiles.

I am so!

We drove past the apartment, heading south on a highway joining the afterwork rush. His face pleasant but his thoughts seemed far away. He's concentrating face with his full lips folded in, pressed, tensing his jaw but revealing the deepest set of dimples through his finely cut beard. He's squinting and slowing at every sign we drive past. I think he's searching for someplace without a satnav. I am basking in his excitement, which is contagious.

"How was work?"

He breaks the silence, his eyes fixed on the road. I thought a minute or two recalling the events, Director Kane followed by the newspaper articles which I hope he never sees, and Sam...

"Uh... better when you were there."

He peeked at me for a brief moment.

"Have you decided who to tell first?"

"Tell what?"

He peeked again this time squinting.

"The baby."

Oh, shit forgot about you…

I passed my hand over the firm rise of my tummy taking it in.

"Oh yeah… Can I think about it?"

"I can clearly see the bump and it's not going to get smaller."

I sighed rolling my eyes. "Are you calling me fat?" I divert.

"Fat, never!"

We both giggled.

Then I recalled the near smackdown in the office break room. "I think Sam knows," I blurted the thought.

"What!" He chuckled with a cough and I see the smirk at the corner of his lips as he fixated his eyes on the road.

"My jacket came loose," I explained tilting to him.

"I'm surprised it remained closed." He laughs.

I gasped, "Are you calling me fat again?"

"I wouldn't dear." He shakes his head.

"So, you don't mind if she knows?" I am curious.

"I don't give a fuck what my ex-wife thinks!" his smile is growing.

"Eric!" I scold,

"I don't," he said with a nonchalant shrug. I huffed rolling my eyes.

"What about Aaliyah?" I blurted and his face grim.

"Why would you ask that?" His smile has dissipated and his tone is a bit rough.

"I mean, the bump will not remain, a bump."

Why am I apologetic?

He is quiet, his index finger brushing across his folded lips and moustache, his squint intensifies on the horizon.

"Lia and I have not been partners in over a year."

This is news! And it does explain the cold shoulder last week.

He's finally moved up and she hasn't followed.

I glow inside relieved that, she would not be close enough to him to touch him, using work as an excuse, particularly when I'm around. The notion makes me uncomfortable and I shift in my seat recalling the many, many examples.

"… We are moving on with our lives," he speaks, breaking my dwelling.

He takes a hand off the steering wheel and covers my midsection glancing at me with a partial quiver of his lips. I want to push him for more but I don't want to ruin the mood.

The traffic has subsided and busyness has calmed and so has he. I can get lost looking at him admiring his curved jawline, chestnut tone and naturally neat eyebrows.

My heighted sense of smell whiffs the fresh air and sea salts as we drive alongside a sandy shore, random white shells and seaweeds washed up the calm beachside traces of the receded tide. The seagulls sing loudly as they float through the cool breeze. I simper at him as he glimpses ever so often with failed attempts to keep his face passive.

He suddenly leaves the shore to a narrow countryside road, lined with trees, arching, pulsing sunshine through the arch branches and walls of dirt as we pass through. I frown at the narrow passage but he's small quivering at his mouth assures me ever, so often.

We're finally through to an open asphalt area and the end of the road. He says nothing as he parks the car close to a wooden double barrier overlooking a cliff. He turns off the ignition, opens the door and walks around to my door and opens it.

"Come."

The first word he says for the past half hour, gleaming at me, his hand out for mine he's bending with one hand behind his back. I swung my legs out rather unladylike releasing some of the bottled up excitement then gave him my hand. He pulls it to his lips kissing it, I blush as I stood amused at my man. He turns me around so my back is leaned against him I breathe sharp clenching inside. After three years he still has this effect on me, I am tingling.

"Cover your eyes."

I hesitate then obeyed in aching anticipation. He moves me a few steps forward then, let's go. I hear the car door shut and he placed his hands over my eyes leading me awkwardly. I feel his hands over my tummy stopping at something solid touching my thighs. The cool breeze blows across my head and I smell clean air. He moves his hands.

"Open them."

I opened my eyes to the view of the seashore cove, over the green hill in the distance, reflecting what's left of the blue skies. Further back, the city shining, glass buildings, all painted behind. The falling sun colouring the skies in orange and pinks, the sea between parting the two places. I admire the irony.

"This is amazing!"

I am in awe and tears filled my eyes. I am honoured that he found this place and would share this beauty with me. He's moved from behind me. I turned and he is on one knee holding open a red suede square box. Inside, a one-inch gold wristband with moonstones and aquamarine stones at the ends of the 'S' of the infinity band. I grin as tears pooled.

"Eric," I whispered.

"I love you, Shannan. You are everything I need. And more that I had hoped for. You give me so many reasons to be more, to want more. I don't want to lose you."

His voice is cracked with sincerity as he stares into the fibre of my soul. Tears skim without effort down my cheeks my voiced soft, cracked.

"Eric."

"Let me finish, please... I want you to officially be mine and I want to be wholly yours. Shannan Christine Davis, will you make me into an honest man and marry me here in two weeks?"

What! Two weeks! "I don't know what to say."

"Yes, for one." He waits then I caught myself answering quick.

"Of course, I will Eric but..." *Two weeks!*

"Don't worry babes, I got you."

"But..." I smiled, anxious.

"You don't have to do anything but get a dress."

"I love you, Eric Michael Hall."

I bend over, held his face between my hands and kissed him. A tear from him touched my fingers.

****

Sitting at my desk the next day recalling the night before... his mouth and tongue all over me. The feverish heat leading me back to the car like teenagers. I am almost having another orgasm.

How is that possible or is it the hormones?

I am swamped with interviews and I find myself shifting ever so often thinking about last night. It was amazing and something that ranks right up in the top three. Our wedding night, the night he ran out of condoms. I giggled to myself in memory and last night. I pulled my thighs together and squirm in the chair excited for tonight when he gets back.

Paula knocks breaking my reminisce waltzing in, shut the door and talks.

"Shana there have been two persons of interest with similar injuries."

I closed my laptop, wheeled my chair closer to the desk and crossed my fingers together leaning on the desk with my forearms. Her lips began moving, her eyes are on my exposed double Ds. I cannot seem to contain them. They've increased a size or two.

She says a lot but I am there again, under his knife, and being touched by the other. Fighting, being cut, then becoming complacent with injuring them, and not paying attention, then waking up in the hospital. Learning about... *you.* I flinch about to rub my bump but stopped myself in time.

If anyone of the three would ask me outright, it will be her.

I attempt to be interested in her medical facts, nodding between them and even opening my mouth once pretending to want to interrupt. But it is all another language to me.

"... Well, what do you think Shana?" She finishes her babbling.

"Err, how many hospitals did you check?" She gave me the folder and I moved it to the side of my computer keeping my interests on her.

"Two, close to your... mmm... 'incident'." She hesitates and ends.

Her apprehension and tone toils at me, particularly that new word that I am growing a massive dislike to.

"Why do you guys keep saying it like that?" I accidentally said it aloud.

Filter Shana! I warn myself.

"Like what?" She tilts her head squinting at me.

Unhappy that she didn't even realise, I dismissed. "... Never mind!" I shift clearing my throat. "... Are there any clinics close by?" I try another angle, just in case.

276

"Yeah, sure." She squinted taking a moment, looking over me tenderly. My heartbeat increased as she opened her mouth, but then said nothing. A quick relief, of her reprieve, I used the pause to throw her off and buy more time.

"Can you be sure that it was definitely them?"

She closed her folder, lifting from the chair and stormed out. The description is unfamiliar and makes me uneasy. I need to be sure.

"Thank you!" I shouted after her and she waved with her back turned.

Good, she didn't notice.

Eric is right, we do need to make the announcement.

… But I think Danielle should be the first.

I opened my laptop entering my password to continue working on the infamous 'to-do' that list Director Kane has so cleverly arranged with Noel. I rolled my eyes checking my emails and requests.

'Denied transfer of Charles Sam-Sam Brown's drug-related case'.

Huffing, I read the subject of a request for the shifting of the drug investigation to the L.D.O. The explanation:

'Please send to directors for review and reassignment'.

I'm gobsmacked. Having this added to my supervisory duties can be a nightmare.

Why do they want to stick us with this?

This would surely cause a brawl, especially if Sam is the only expert in this area. The numerous jurisdiction arguments are still being written for the powers that S.D.A.F. has. I rolled my eyes slapping the desk shifting the folder at the politics that would surely be named with this. Mayor Mall's warning comes to me, and I say a small prayer that it would not come back to bite me in the ass, forwarding it to the director to review.

The folder that Paula brought peers at me. I looked at it from the corner of my eyes and checked another email avoiding its stare.

Just do it!

Hesitantly opening the folders to see their faces, both men bruised and they used two different hospitals. Their injuries do marry. Marcus Whitely and Aaron Digby, their names aren't familiar but I try to memorise them. The pictures of their faces make my heart thump loud and all I hear is my breathing. I cannot tell if they are them, which makes me more worried about this situation.

Don't go there, Shana.

Shaking the thought, I began packing up for the next interview, placing all the folders on my desk into a pile, an article clipping fell out.

'Catacá Victim Dies'

The head line reads. I hold it for a while. There is something about this case that calls to me, as if I am drawn to it, to her, Camielle Charles, her life intrigued me. I have to be sure that it is purely based on the mystery, but it feels like more, and oddly familiar.

Taking my eyes off the picture in the newspaper clipping, I tried to find the other articles. I cannot remember seeing this headline. I recalled the headlines inwardly. Naming them from previous research. I recited them to myself.

Missing woman found,

Catacá victim gives birth.

I was right, there were only two, unless counting the recent ones, including myself. I squint in thought, annoyed that I went there and inside toiling about the upcoming directors meeting. I shudder at the thought, questioning the origin.

Where did this come from?

This third article seemed to have appeared out of thin air or discretely placed on my desk. Besides the interview details, I don't think Noel put these here.

Maybe Paula? It is definitely not her style, she doesn't have those layers, I think.

But, why?

I resolved to ask them both in the near future and read:

'Catacá Victim Dies

After suffering the Catacá fate surviving and giving birth Camielle Charles, twenty-eight, died.

Charles was found barely alive in a pool of her own blood after she had been reported missing for several days. She recovered in hospital unconscious and in intensive care for six weeks. She later discovered she had been made pregnant by her attacker. She gave birth to a healthy baby girl several months after celebrating life a week ago.

Yesterday she died mysteriously after being discharged. The cause of death is still unknown as investigations continue into her attack and death.

By Christine Davis.'

Wow!

I am sure this wasn't there before.

I began to research her on the S.D.A.F. database. There was a brief coroner's report with her name. Camielle Charles was found dead in a motel, here in Divinish. No signs of foul play. Bruises on her face from previous assault reported. No external leakage, no discolouration of limbs. Victim appears to be asleep or sleeping when death occurred. Further details in autopsy report.

Curious.

I searched for any other report. There was no mention of her baby, if she was with her and there was no autopsy report, nothing to indicate what happened to her, how she died.

How frustrating.

What happened to the child?

I searched for anything following her and Catacá. There was none.

Nothing!

This is making me even more curious. I looked at the coroner's name he is retired officer of the C.O.P.S. Sam's department. This makes me think there were also drugs involved but more than ever, question the authenticity of everything I read. She was born, raised and according to the article and coroner's report, all in Divinish.

But why are her case details in C.O.P.S. the capital's special police unit, in another state? The inconsistencies raised more questions, especially since her kidnapping and brutal rape was handled by the L.D.O. The same one unit on delay with Sharron Mall's. The ones that are hired by the mayor, which brought me back to his interest in courtesy while I was in Shadeyah, that really sounded like a threat.

How could there be only one page for this whole case?

Didn't I read that there was more than one victim?

Where are their reports?

This was basic information, a vague one-page note. I am deliberating if this was because this was almost twenty-six years ago, or maybe they are still updating the system…

Or something else? I ponder for a while.

Could this be a serial killer? I think of using Aaliyah, one of the best profilers in the country for a millisecond, before reminding myself of her trying attitude and pondered some more.

If so, where has he been all this time and what awoke him?

The memory of Eric's words after joining this department came back like a flood.

"… Honey those organizations are moulded in corruption, shaped by lies and cooked in conspiracies. I don't want you spending your whole career chasing after conspiracies trying to find the root of the problem and end up a part of the whole scandal."

Although most of what Eric said then, made no sense, I am regurgitating it.

Do I think this is a conspiracy?

I am not convinced. Though I can see some reasoning for the S.D.A.F. involvement and the call for transparency. The question that bugs me the most is.

What happened to her daughter?

There are three names that could possibly help me; her boyfriend, John Sommers, the journalist, Christine Davis and her daughter, who doesn't have a name. I doubt she will know anything about her mother, but finding out what happened after Camielle's death could be a great start. There are a lot of questions and how do I actually connect the two? My desk phone buzzed.

"Davis, your next interview is here."

Back to the now!

"Send them in, thank you Noel."

CHAPTER THIRTY-ONE

The department increased in members. Most of this week, I have been swamped. Deciding the balance of everyone's assignments, partnership and training, as more investigations started to filter in with staff. Tidying the Sharron Mall case with other connected cases became too complicated, though each team member did their part.

The commissioning of the S.D.A.F. Divinish office called the Jade, has made the week busier than I could keep up. I was glad though, the work distracted me from Eric's absence returning to work in Ceda.

Attended too many meetings and briefings to count.

Distributed assignments and training orders.

Wrote God knows how many stupid fucking reports for Director Kane.

I counted in my thoughts omitting those words from the report.

The drive to know more about Camielle Charles soon became less applicable. The game of hide the bump grew popular as the widening waistline and shrinking clothes continued like the tantalising cat versus mouse.

Eric went back home for a number of things which I supposed have some bearing on his promotion and to get Danielle from boarding school as the term was drawing to a close. Then it dawns.

How are we going to work this all out?

A moment of panic hits me walking up the long stairway into our suboffice.

Where are we going to live?

Not the conversation I should be having with myself on a Friday evening before possibly the most important meeting of my career, the Monday's directors meeting. Wearing the last of my loose-fitting clothing: a white, black pin-striped sleeveless blouse with a pleat at the V-neck flowing over my new favourite black stretched pencil skirt. The exhausted excused black flats and jacket that cannot button has not given the illusion at keeping the suspicious looks.

Or maybe I am paranoid!

Noel absent from the reception desk, her coffee nearly finished at half one in the afternoon. Training at the local police office, then attending the latter part of the opening ceremony of the Jade building took most of my morning. I didn't grasp the point of my attendance, so I didn't go. I spent another hour at the range.

A pit stop to the toilet, before the conference room. Vomiting ceased, but urinating increased. A cause to celebrate, especially for Eric who, mostly had to hold my hair back and clean the mess.

A quick look at my phone for messages from Eric. I huffed, leaving the toilet. Annoyed that none are from him. His contact since his trip is minimal and vague. I frown at my actions and ache for his attention.

The ladies were missing from their desks. The new staff members quieted as I entered, greeting me, the horrible word 'ma'am'. As if I was Aaliyah's age. I forced a smile, making a quick stop for my laptop in the office there; Noel has left a carrier cup of tea. I smile taking it to the conference room.

Surprised by a room filled with professionally dressed A.P.S. who sat having a civilised discussion in a soft tone. I blinked a couple of times being sure this was not me sleepwalking. I folded my lips with wishful thinking.

Maybe they are getting used to being in a team.

I narrowed my eyes at myself proudly.

I can add this to my list of achievements!

I am celebrating inwardly. My laptop across my centre and tea in a travel mug in the other. The room went silent when I entered. Their eyes followed me as I briskly went to the available chair at the head of the table, putting my laptop down and turning it on.

"Don't stop on my account."

The quiet uncomfortable tension is building and I don't like where it is leading. We are all moving our eyes from person to person like a standoff waiting for the first move. I leaned back gaping from blue to green to icy-blue to green to blue to green.

This is getting ridiculous!

I took a pen from the table and the notepad from in front of me then started to doodle. My pen fell to the floor. I leaned to the side to get it I can hear them gasping.

"All right!" I can't take this anymore! "... I'm pregnant!"

'What the fuck'! A sharp and quick ring entered my head with Aaliyah's voice, though her mouth didn't move.

Moaning, from the sound, I covered the side of my face holding from sharp pain at my temples, circling my fingers until it eased. Lia gasped, eyes widened and mouth opened. She shut it soon after, growing a straight-faced gape. Her icy-blues looked through me.

Sam initially choked, on what I would guess is her spit. Patting her chest while coughing. Then, clearing her throat to a stifled giggle. Bowing her head at the folders on the desk, crossing her arms. Paula smiled tilting her head slightly one hand on her large chest in awe.

"There, now that it's out!" I finished. "... Not that it is any of your business." A few more seconds passed in silence and I have just grasped what I did out of impatience.

Shit! What did I just do?

And I was worried about Eric? I held my mouth. *Filter!* Yelling at the runaway words that I cannot take back. I sighed still gaping the ladies' ogle.

"Congratulations!" Paula grins, breaking the uneasy silence with a caring gesture.

"Yea, congrats Shana." Sam giggles before I could reply to Paula. Her mischievous smirk across her face still choking as her cheeks are becoming red.

I would like to know what's so funny. I am fighting the urge to hit her in the throat. The thought though, pleases me.

"... Could you ladies please stop eyeing me as though I'm gonna *pop!* The seams can hold. Besides, you can barely even tell..."

I am rougher than I expected, Aaliyah's eyes fell on my chest.

"... Well, they're some exception."

I pull my shoulders and my plunging neckline across to cover my blossoming chest then I sat up pointing.

"... But you all have children so, *stop, now!*"

I can't believe how good that felt. There is a part of me that dreads Eric finding out about this.

They soaked it in for a bit but I don't want any Q and A or gossiping, though, if it were their daughters, I would have entertained the thought.

Professional is the way…

"… Are we ready to catch up?"

The rhetorical question was posed as a command to move on and they did. Aaliyah handed me a file and explained with a morbid expression, "Adam Jolee has been gallingly unpleasant where the nugget is concerned."

"Paul…" I anxiously edged a reply.

"Relax Shana. I didn't touch one grey hair on his annoying, little head. He sent his lawyer who was even more irritating! I have filed the paperwork."

"For?" I quizzed.

"Obstruction…" she said and her icy-blues widened at me but she did not add.

More paperwork. "Fine!" I wrote a reminder, with a groan.

"Valentine still has been uncooperative and shook his attorney after me. He was kind enough to stay with his mouthpiece this time, but still denies knowing Sam-Sam.

"He did however admit to knowing Ms Mall after I showed him the DNA results of her fortified semen samples…"

She handed out a card with some squares and a picture of a man next to it.

"Cute," Sam said it before me.

Lia narrowed her eyes at Sam but continued, "… They had a 'thing'. She was a close friend with benefits. "He claims to have an alibi to his time she went missing and the time she appears. He didn't miss her because she comes and goes as she pleases.

"Shana, I know you would want me to interview his witnesses but I am telling you now, that would be a waste of time. He is very sly, and well connected so even if he is guilty of this crime, which I doubt he is, unless there is irrefutable evidence, he is a slippery snake. He won't spend a day in jail and the backlash won't be pleasing either. Can I move on to another assignment?" she complained narrowing her eyes at me.

"Sure Paul." I jotted a note. "… I will need you to interview Ms Mall."

"You mean to take another statement?" Her words are suggestive, and condescending, correcting my technical terms.

Irritating bitch! I know she's done that purposefully.

"Yes…" I try not to fall for it. "… But we have to be careful of the way we deal with this."

"Do I need a set list of questions?"

I squinted at her, still attempting to be an ass.

"Will do." She took notes.

"Torrez, the evidence on Sam-Sam?" I tilted my chair towards Paula.

"The drugs are the same as what was found in Sharron Mall's car; same potency, ingredients everything as far as I could tell, came from the same source.

"Sam-Sam and maybe Valentine's connection to Ms Mall relates to the narcotics in her vehicle, not the hallucinogen in her veins."

"That is some good news. Our request to have Sam-Sam's case transferred has been denied. It has to remain in-house and reassigned," I shared. "… I can also give the assignment to another team if it would lead to Valentine, Sam, but you're my narcotic's expert." Sam rolled her eyes and I asked, "What is it with you and Valentine?"

Sam turned her face away from mine and Lia yelled, "History." The one word was loaded and I did not push. Then Paula continued, "Sharron Mall's follicle test came back clean. She was not an addict or had not been for some time. Only rumours about her drug use."

It only raised the question to why would she have drugs in her car? I thought but didn't ask, only noted. "Great. Send the report to me. I will pass this to another team, Sam. What about the other men on Miss Mall's 'day'?"

"Other semen samples…" Sam croaked, and I stopped her.

"Let's not refer to the men as 'samples' please," I corrected her.

"OK, let's start with the least complex story then. We would work our way to a timeline. John Sommers, middle-aged, criminal record, easy to find, he was just a means to an end…"

The name triggered something in my unreliable memory and I took a note to look at it later, while listening to her.

"… She wanted something, he was old, gross and wanted sex." Taking a moment with a fluttered eyes at the statement of 'old', I swallowed my words and try remaining emotionless for a bit to pay attention. "… He said she owed him five k, and the debt was to be paid on the last day he saw her, after their activities."

"Did he say what she wanted?" I asked.

"A favour, an extension on her borrowing and he thought she skipped town. They met and did the deeds around lunchtime early afternoon.

"Christopher Bailey, another criminal, was her regular customer when she was on the streets. He was just a customer seen her around eight that night.

"Terrance Jason was her current boyfriend who has a wife and two kids by the way; he spent the night at her apartment then went home around midday. They stayed in that morning.

"Mr Jason is the brother of her part-time boyfriend, Valentine who saw her sometime during the day. Two 'men' are still unaccounted for but we can assume that since Mr Bailey picked her up as a street girl maybe there is where she also picked up the other two samples?" Sam crinkled her face in disgust and so was I. But we've got a job to do.

"Are we sure she worked the streets?" I wanted proof before pointing a finger at her. Especially knowing what was done to her.

"Even if she didn't work the streets, we are all sure that she doesn't like condoms, and, is a ho." Sam closed her file staring me right in the face.

I stare at her for a moment in another face off wondering if the last few words are intended for me.

"Sam!" I warned.

"Prostitute," Aaliyah picked up and I almost giggled at her audacity. What is wrong with her filter?

"Call girl," Paula added and the three chuckled at their agreement for the first time since we arrived in Divinish.

I am glad that we are getting along but not at the victim's expense.

"Guys, stop now. That's not at all funny!" I warned playfully.

"You were thinking it!" Sam mocked and baited.

I was not! Really? I shook away thinking with a small pout.

"Plan of action?" I change direction ignoring their judgemental comments.

They all became quiet.

"… Now you guys stop talking? OK… I have a meeting on Monday with my directors. Then I will know how they want us to proceed."

They all gazed across the room, twirled in their chairs and wrote in their diaries, all shutting down, in light of this new information.

"I understand it would take some convincing to plead her case… knowing her lifestyle and the fact that she fabricated some parts of her story, but have you been around to the hospital to see what was done to her? It was worse than the photos."

I groaned and my insides tossed in recollection, but also the emotions washed over me again, bursting at my seams scratching my insides for vengeance.

Still, no answer.

They wrote notes not fully regarding me. Shaking my head, I took the pictures of her crime scene, throwing it at them.

"She has been hurt, messed up really bad, and she may be scared. More than the fact of us finding out about her promiscuous life. Adulterous choices and alternative career choice. She was forced to have sex, cut up like an animal, and dumped like garbage. Let's not get started on the loss of her child."

They paused with a stare at me then Aaliyah broke the ice, "We know that Davis, but… what would you like us to do? We know the system."

I sigh, having some idea being a subject in one case myself. Being forced to feel like I had to prove what was done was unwanted even with evidence and a witness. Sharron Mall's pictures were exposed and the articles slid out.

They all took a peek subtly.

Although, these are not a secret, it felt like one. Aaliyah maybe an asshole but she is good at what she does. Sam is a total dick but her instinct for the job is unmatched, and Paula, has an eye that picks up everything. They are all first-class cunts, but they are also, really good at their jobs.

I looked at it then them again, cleansing my lungs, I throw my thoughts to them, even though I hate their personal opinions, I respect their professional ones.

"I have found something… some articles, this resembles her attack and there were seven victims and one survivor. So…"

"You're thinking there may be more victims, other than Sharron?" Lia finished my sentence.

I nod then continued, "… Now we know of my suspicions…"

"This can be an isolated incident, Davis." Aaliyah pointed out. "… Maybe concentrate on Ms Mall for now." She uncharacteristically stared me away.

I think for a second. "… Sam the archive cases come from your department, maybe you can do some digging for me? It won't hurt to be certain Paul, and we can meet Tuesday?"

"Sure." Sam writes in her diary and I wrote in mine, Lia scoffs.

"Paul, can you verify that she may have been working the streets, and any other useful data about her street life?" She says nothing but takes notes.

"Torrez! Can you find and examine the evidence of the cold cases with Sam, if she finds anything? We can meet here Tuesday after lunch maybe around two."

They sat there with a perplexed expression.

Sam broke the silence, "Shana, discovering her… um… street credit, is really damaging. The accused can come up with so many simple reasons for hurting her. The most you may get out of this is an assault, misdemeanour or A.S.B.O."

"A juror can go either way, Davis. And given Ms Mall's background… it's best to quit while we are ahead," Lia expressed her opinion about the case, for the first time since we began.

"Are you guys serious?"

They stared at me with their shoulders shrugged accepting defeat.

"… Are we by any means saying this is OK?"

I held up a picture of her in the trunk of her car they didn't flinch, but I did. It was the one where her dead baby was still attached to her, covered in blood.

"… For someone to cut a woman up. The baby ripped out her gut and we do nothing because she is known to sleep around?" I yell at them.

"Those words never left Sam's mouth Davis." Aaliyah is defending her pointing at me.

"Then what are you saying?" My temper is getting the better of me.

"Are you willing to risk your career for this, on her?" Aaliyah's eyes squinted on me.

CHAPTER THIRTY-TWO

After much self-debate I completed the night's report still riveting the ladies' observation. With the absence of Eric, I finished my Friday night at eight missing the ball. Not that I would have gone. He hasn't called all week and I am not sure of the protocol for contact.

I could really use his advice on this one.

I tossed the idea of initiating communication as I strolled down the high street to fetch food before calling it a night. The fresh, cool Divinish air at night was something to experience. The skies are so well lit with amazing sunsets as autumn light stays until late evening. A far contrast of the cold, dark nights in Ceda.

No shorts needed.

My feet are unusually sore. I dragged them to the door approaching the empty apartment turning the key. It was time to exhale after stretching the seams of my favourite skirt. I came inside, locked the door placing the keys on their new resting place, a side table next to the door, my handbag exploded on contact with the sofa. I grumbled.

All the preparations slid across the double seat. I waved my hand at it thinking it could wait. I positioned the food on the breakfast area took my gun from behind my waist band and placed it in the safe. I peeled the skirt off and took the shirt off placing them in a basket and went for a shower.

So many things are overflowing in my head as the water flows over me. An odd sensation rises from inside my tummy, not the usual gaggling of hunger but the tiniest bubbles from my abdomen. I paused, it stopped.

After the shower I pulled up a shorts and camisole tidied the chair then sat to eat. I take a moment to celebrate that I am no longer prisoner to sickness in my pregnancy though my new fight is sleeping.

My best guess is hormones.

I sulk at the taboo.

I really should read that prenatal book or do some research.

I condemn my lack of interest in the books. Exhausted and restless, I cannot mentally shut down after today's arduous work playing over the team's shutdown from a win and the direction of this case. I texted Liz:

Hey, you up?

I waited a few minutes my phone pinged. She sent a sleeping emoji I texted:

Good, you're up,

I beamed at it then she sent a middle finger.
How rude!
Classic Liz, I texted:

Really missing you!

She texted:

Missing sleep and you!
Good night!

I giggled, took the remote from the coffee table and began flicking through the channels.
… The background noise might help.
The news was playing. I paid attention to the local announcements. Then, I heard a reporter mention Sharron's name and I raised the volume.

"It has been five weeks since Sharron Mall was found brutally attacked in the trunk of her car. Ms Mall, the daughter of our sitting mayor, Maynard Mall, who was first unidentifiable due to her severe injuries, has finally been discharged from the hospital.

"After five weeks recovering, there has been no word from lead investigator, Shannan Davis-Hall and the local police have not yet made any progress into finding out what really happened."

My eyes bulge and I held my breath covering my mouth while continuing to listen.

"Some anti-Zemands blame the Zeman culture and religion for this attack as it resembles a cleansing ceremony which they call Catacá. This has not been included in the bill to abolish human sacrificing ceremonies of the Zemand by parliament.

"This ceremony is not subjected to public knowledge because it is never really practiced and, is not included in the bill of abolishment for certain Zemands ceremonies as, it is not a sacrificial one and is part freedom of culture and religion.

"Some call for the ban of this culture and religion saying this is taking freedom of religion too far, and bordering on human rights. Though only recently, the Zeman have always been accepted in society, the history of persecution and hate are still prevalent in our memories.

"This delicate negotiation is still up for debate. Many Zeman still won't profess their culture openly due to persecution and hate crimes against their families, although the Zeman are the natives of this country.

"Most Zeman laws are still present in our daily lives for example, the marriage ceremonies. Conversely, Daver has been accepting the first world standards as we have been viewed by most as first world.

"However, Zemand claims only if you are born Zeman then you are bind by their laws until death.

"There is no official word from the mayor, though at this time, his office has released a statement asking for privacy for him and his family.

Melissa Terrance, Daver news."

Oh… My… Gosh!

I was frozen, stupefied beyond belief. Every emotion spiked but the most prominent one was anger. I wanted to hurt someone. The person that exposed us gave my name to the press. A few suspects immediately popped into mind but I needed to be sure. My phone rang. I hesitated as the number was blocked then gingerly answered,

"Davis."

"This is Paul Alex from the daily express, would you care to comment on the case of Sharron Mall."

I was relieved and hung up. Thinking.

I was restless, late news at eleven… how many people would have seen that?

I hoped that I was the only one using it as white noise.

Worry then overthrew me and my phone rang again without hesitation.

"Davis."

"Remember the discussion we had a few weeks back?" The mayor was pissed.

"Mr Mayor." *I don't know what to say.* "… It is late and I need to get my team on the line." Technically shooing him off the phone.

"Either you talk to me now or I'll be talking to your directors," he shouted with authority.

"Mr Mayor." I am apologetic. "… I understand your frustration but I will look into this. I assure you that we have been extremely discrete. If it is on my end it'll be dealt with. Can you be sure it is not from your end?"

Shit, Shana! I regretted instantly.

"Are you trying to insult me?" he screams into the phone.

"No sir, I am not." I closed my eyes and began pacing between the sofa and the breakfast bar. "… I am just covering all angles."

"Well do that." A dial tone followed.

Crap!

I cursed at the phone crushing it between my palms closing my eyes processing. Phone calls of authority are just beginning and my brain is on pause.

My phone rang again my heart is at my throat.

"Hello!" I am guarded.

"Good night, Agent Davis-Hall, I am Amy Welch," a woman sings from the other end of the phone as if I should know her, but her accent sounds Ceda.

"Hi yes," I kept my stance waiting for her to identify herself.

"I am the director's assistant." She sings again. "… He has brought forward Monday's meeting to tomorrow. At the Jade building tenth floor, nine-sharp," she explained and I dread.

"That won't be a problem, I'll be there," I said with my eyes closed, I am brave as another dial tone follows.

"Fuck!"

I screamed then blocking my mouth remembering the hour calming my infuriated breathing, I began thinking.

Ten, nine, eight, seven.

I dialled Sam.

"What the fuck Shana!" Sam's sleepy voice raged.

"There was a news clipping now there is trouble." I wasted no time.

"Huh?" Her voice cracked, not fully awakened.

"I need you to run proper checks on the transfers we had this week. Let me know what you get." My first thought went to the newbies.

"Now?" She groaned.

"My meeting on Monday is now, tomorrow, just got two calls and I am expecting more," I summarised.

"I warned you Shana." The sleep left her voice.

"Do you want to start with 'I told you so'?"

"Yeah, that might just wake me."

I hung up and dialled Noel.

"Two people I need you to find their sources, Melissa Terrance and Paul Alex, both reporters." I jotted the names into some notes for the follow up.

"I was about to call you. Director Kane called me and he asked me a few questions," she said cautiously.

"I don't expect you to lie Noel," I tell her.

"I didn't!" My eyebrows raised at her response, but I am happy for the transparency. "… Do you want me to come over?" she asked artfully sandwiching.

"That won't be necessary." The notion wasn't ever a second thought. "… Could you pass the information to Sam. She's the best to lead on this, but don't tell her I said that." I corrected my compliment.

"Are you ready for tomorrow?" she asks strangely but I have been prepping for the meeting since after meeting Director Kane.

"I will let you know after," I say honestly and unfiltered again. Then ending quick. "… Good night, thanks."

It was nearly midnight, now I really couldn't sleep. I went through the wardrobe to find anything that could make me look like I didn't just screw the whole case.

Who would do something like this!

All the women I work with each one can do something as damaging as this to me and each one had a reason. Sam sent me a few statements after an hour. Noel forward me more newspaper articles and the investigative reporters names. I began typing and researching.

The alarm woke me, six-thirty. I am a bit queasy and the funny fluttering in my torso started again. I pulled up my camisole and saw a flickering under my skin.

Is that my baby moving?

I put my hand over it but don't feel the touch. When I moved my hand, I saw it again.

My baby's moving!

I leapt from the bed with excitement, grinning from ear to ear wanting to shout it to the first person. Eric had missed this. I went for my phone which I turned off last night. The reasoning induced a frown.

Switching it on, I searched for his number remembering he didn't answer last night. Apprehensively holding it in my palms. Then, messages start popping in and my phone came alive. The reminder of the mess last night.

Shit!

I can't tell him now.

Annoyed at myself again, I review the messages. Four missed calls from Paula, Sarah and two from Sam. There are some numbers I do not recognise and some voice messages. My priority shifts.

First, the meeting.

I frown in a panic and empty my closet. Aggravated at my dosing.

I should have been putting together the report.

I unravel, arguing with myself. I texted the three:

Thanks!

Noel answered right away.

Need me there?

Would I? I question myself.

I sat on the edge of the bed, shifting the pile of clothes in an exhale to think. Absorbing the night growing angrier at myself. I let my fear out and weep a moment holding my phone rubbing my eyes with the heel of my wrist.

This is my fault.

I need to fix this.

I replied:

I'll be fine.

Thanks!

These hormones are really getting the better of me!

I blame my tears on my pregnancy.

What is the worse they can do to me?

A thought from my subconscious submerged.

I can get fired. She answered right away singsong in my head.

It was humorous and I laughed wiping the residual tears with the back of my hands.

I stood to my feet, viewing the mess I made on the bed. Folders covered mixed between clothes. The view was even more hilarious. I giggled even more placing my phone on the side table. All the worries went with the laughter.

I showered, straightened my curls. My dark, glossy hair flowed past my bra and covered my back. The tantalising game of hide the bump was over at my office, not that I can hide it anyway. My reservation lies with the skirt-suits I brought stifling me.

Opened the wardrobe, looking for the one thing that I can wear and breathe in. Eric had a slim fitting blue shirt calling me.

I grinned folding the very long sleeves under my elbow. The length fell right above the knees of my black trousers.

Could pass for a tunic!

The zipper couldn't go up without choking me. I open the fly, tucking it to the side of my exposed bump, it was snugged and covered my growing ass. I turned in the mirror.

It's almost as big as Aaliyah's.

My confidence boosted, my behind secured the movement of the black now tight-fitting pants. Eric's shirt covered the mess of my pants. I winked at myself comfortable and stress free. Ill-prepared but it didn't matter any more.

I drove myself to the tall glass Jade building in the midst of town. It was modern and new by the looks of the shining glass compared to the surrounding buildings. A bay park available at the front of the building I took viewing the glass.

The wide staircase narrowing at the top, I strode through the rotating glass doors to the reception. There wasn't any sign but the security and receptionist stood over a counter waiting as I entered.

They were both wearing dark blue suits and the men had earpieces hanging from their ears. I stopped going for the lift. The pleasant young blonde lady with a warm smile welcomed me, "Good morning. Do you have an appointment?"

The reception was closed off, small with glass doors. At the side of the reception there were three single entrances with security doors. Everything was silver or white. I approached the reception whilst gazing at the busyness behind the foyer.

"I am Agent Davis-Hall I've got an appointment with Director Kane."

"Yes, the directors. I need to see your S.D.A.F. badge."

I fished it from my handbag spilling some of the handbag's contents on the countertop and showed it to her.

"You will need to place it over the red light by the doors to get in and out of the building. Your badge should be visible throughout your visit to the headquarters."

"Headquarters?"

The question I thought I said to myself came out loud.

"Yes, Agent Davis-Hall. The walls have maps on every floor for direction. You are going to the tenth-floor conference room, 10.3.4 there will be a sign on the room, this gentleman will show you to the elevators."

Then it dawned of how clueless I've been. I retrieved the contents refilling my bag feeling a bit sheepish and becoming nervous about the vastness I didn't understand.

"OK then."

I shrugged almost as though I had been drinking before I arrived there. I put my badge over the red light of a closed passage with double glass doors and waited. The doors opened briefly and I walked through. Unimpressed, the man showed me to the elevators to the tenth-floor. I placed my badge around my neck.

I wished I had brought a belt.

I glance at my reflection my face became flush after the revelation of the headquarters. Knowing, I would have made yesterday's ball a priority.

The embarrassment may have been worse standing with Director Kane!

An unwanted fact rose from my subconscious and I squint at myself. My face is glowing and the lip gloss has enhanced my pink lips contrasting with my now greenish eyes changing as I am nervous.

I look really pregnant!

I am worried at the director thoughts since I have only been on the job for a short time. The doors open and I walked through the dark blue toned hallways with desks and busy staff pacing the office with folders and others typing at their desks. I saw the sign at the end of a copy machine.

The tinted glass made it difficult to see inside. I knocked, my face grew serious as I gathered my business attitude. Then turned the silver handle of the glass door pushing open and strode into well lit room with a large glass table to the end of the room.

My heart fluttered with apprehension looking at the five people seated to the top. I blinked several times sauntering in. A large television screen behind them, shaping their silhouette to the S.D.A.F. shield lit inside the screen.

Adjusting my eyes again, I hesitate making my way to the vacant chair at the far end of the long table.

Oh... my... God!

I blinked profusely and my heart raced at the sight, trying to articulate if it's a vision or I'm dreaming.

"... Honey those organizations are moulded in corruption, shaped by lies and cooked in conspiracies."

His famous words flooded back to me.

Conspiracy my ass!

Eric sat in the centre amongst the titans. My eyes widened and I am forcing my mouth to close, continuing my shocked amble. I tripped up on my feet, my mouth partly opened. He flinched at my stumble. I steady my footing fixing my eyes on him growing in rage at his actions. Counting slowly down from ten taking a breather, remembering where I was.

Ten, nine, eight, seven, six, five, four, three, two, one.

After the initial shock, I made my best endeavours to maintain professionalism. But the indignation was hard to calm. The panting ekes to reveal this added emotion of anger as a few chosen words surfaced. I argue inwardly.

He must think me a fool.

Ten, nine, I blew out.

Let's just get this over with.

"Good morning."

The loud greeting clear, with hints of aggression.

Not here Shana! Focus!

I warned myself standing next to the only chair at the end of the table before me.

"You can take a seat Mrs Davis-Hall," a dark woman with a powerful voice to the extreme left commanded. I swallowed hard as I feel the words, the four favourite chosen words, of A.P.S. choking me. I am shivering and my palms are clammy, the anger burns violently through my stare. I sat, crossed my legs at the ankles shaking the anger through it as the woman continues.

"Thank you for coming Agent Davis-Hall. Last night you missed our opening ceremony," she stated partly as if questioning but my gut says otherwise. I nod at her unable to show an expression at her tone and attempting to hide the surfaced emotion.

"So, I'd like to firstly and formally introduce you to the S.D.A.F. directors board.

"To your extreme right is Acting Director John Kane. I believe you two have met…" I squint and he nods with a strong gape at me. "… Next to him is Assistant Director, Jennifer Matthews. In the middle, the director in command, Director Eric Hall. To his right Director Jerome Franks, his second-in-command. Lastly, I am Acting Director, Stacy De Leon."

She introduced the board.

I couldn't accept as true.

I shook my head in denial of this betrayal. My eyes are pooling and reddening I'm sure as I am fuming.

He just didn't have the courtesy.

I nod as my lips twitched. I am mouthing my thoughts but acknowledging the board of directors.

You can be infuriated later.

I accepted this as foreplay to an eminent fight biting my lips to hold in the curses beneath. There was an awkward silence as my eyes burn through my husband then he broke the pause.

"Agent Hall…"

"Excuse me, sir, I'd prefer to be called Agent Davis-Hall thank you."

I corrected him promptly.

He's baiting you! Don't!

He shifts in his seat he cleared his throat with a small leer picking up his pen as he goes through a list.

"Agent Davis-Hall, the purpose of the scheduled meeting was to introduce you to the directors as well as to give you a broader perspective, to understand the chain of command.

"This was meant to be an overview of other departments, the beginning of the team's move into this building. But it has come to our attention that the progressive approach and stealth where Sharron Mall's case is concerned has been compromised, and that is no longer an option with your initial assignment.

"Especially when the media has named you personally as a responsible party for justice. This has presented us as the board that the problems indicated in your task force may be larger than we anticipated."

I couldn't hold my tongue.

"With all due respect sir, there have been problems from the beginning. Someone put together a team of women who frankly hate each other for good reasons too; maybe as a really bad joke that truthfully, I still can't understand the humour.

"We have worked far better than anyone projected and honestly, I don't believe the reporter's information came from us."

I turned the page of Sam's report.

"You have worked with the team reasonably well and there are no reported incidents connected to these ladies about this case or lawsuits that I know of. However, *as* the field agent assigned to that suboffice your duties were far beyond that one case.

"I have met with Assistant Director Kane about the surrounding issues with the team but there are some concerns, you seem to be adjusting with those."

"Thank you, sir."

A surprising compliment for flattery I ponder.

You're not marginally off the hook Hall!

"There are several things that you will have to complete before the team's move to headquarters materialises."

"Move?" I quizzed.

"That office is only used on basis of intimate cases that require some finesse. It was never a permanent base for work. The Jade is. Arrangements are being made.

"In light of the naming, you will make a press conference since, you are the face they know. We are asking that you squash the rumour of the unfounded Zeman's culture involvement."

"Sir," I am muddled.

He explains, "This is damaging the delicate negotiations and shedding a lot of unnecessary light on the Zeman lifestyle across the country. The government doesn't need it and since we work for the government, we don't need it either.

"There has been an increase in hate crimes against Zeman. We also need you to wrap this case up. Your team has three months to do so, with a conviction."

My eyes widened and I stifled a sneer wagging my head.

"Director Hall, that may not be a practical time frame as there are so many leads to follow as well as new assignments given to me. Though no one can deny the cruelty Ms Mall has been through, we can't get past the holes in her statement and the fact that she is promiscuous.

Convincing the court with these facts may require a special type of finesse and tact."

"I am certain you are capable, Agent Davis-Hall just by the way you have presented yourself today," Acting Director Kane comments condescending and mocking. Eric's eyes moved to him narrowing as if he gave away a secret. Kane shifted in his seat and adjusted his tie. Eric's brown eyes fell into my green and I shifted.

"You will be fine." Eric reassures me, "... Just don't repeat what you've just said about Ms Mall outside of this room or show up on any report. Your job is to find the responsible parties not to judge.

"You have your time frame and assignments. The media release is here at six tonight, feed the press what we want them to hear. Do not mention the Zemand. Acting Director Kane has been assigned to your division. It's called the special victim's unit, SPV.

"He will, if he hasn't already been directing you on assignments. All your other duties will be shifted to him provisionally. You are still the field agent in charge of the suboffice but he is your direct subordinate. He will issue your orders from here on."

He put his pen down.

"Are there any questions Agent Davis-Hall?"

I shook my head and still my feet ready to leave.

"That will be all then," he dismissed me.

CHAPTER THIRTY-THREE

I am in awe, my soiled hands grip the chair handles, he is distracted, my heartbeat quickens. I know his next move. Absorbing the past hour's meeting and what's to come.

Choking the fury, working his logic and understand his lucidity, inhaling deep. The blood rushed across my body. I fondled with my bag. A renewed motive, I pounced out the chair admonishing my sheepish tendencies.

Am I that blind?

Quickly exiting with a steady pace and purpose. I got to the elevator. Workbag thrown over my shoulders I am banging my frustration on the call button. Running the past four weeks through my head a lot now makes sense, which made me more angry.

The receptionist from downstairs pranced in my direction shouting my name, "Agent Davis-Hall,"

I scoffed loud straightening the wrinkle in my face preparing for a change in expression when she introduced herself.

"I am Amy, we spoke yesterday."

She put out her hand to shake mine. She was pretty, an asymmetrical shape, sandy blonde hair, soft, blue eyes. A small feminine shape and a tailored grey dress.

"Oh, hi!"

I waved at her rubbing my clammy palms on Eric's shirt and gripping my bag tighter under my arm to prevent it bobbing over me.

"I am Director Hall's personal assistant." My face went sour as the words left her. I locked my jaw. "… Sorry for the late call yesterday, he asked me not to say anything."

Of course he did! My smile faded adding to the list reasons to be mad. I inspected her perfectly smooth thin lips and soft milky skin as she spoke.

"Director Hall asked me to fetch you."

Fetch me! I grind inwardly.

This elevator wait is too long!

"Do you know where I can find the lady's room?"

I can probably slip her better than A.P.S.

The mischievous thought pleases me, tapping the impatient tick through my feet thinking of the words that *will* come out when I see him.

"I really need the lady's room."

Hairs prickled the back of my neck. I felt his stare turning slowly and still. His long strides marching towards me. I folded my lips grinding the words hoping that would be enough to hold them back.

"Thank you, Amy." She nodded stepping away. "… Sorry you had to find out this way Shana."

Wow! An actual apology!

He moved to my face effectively blocking the doors, forcing me to look up at him, but keeping a safe enough distance to remain professional. His volume only for my ears.

I moved my head around avoiding his dreamy gaze. He looks good in that suit.

My hormones aren't my friend, especially with a week away.

The tapping of my feet increased confused for a split second about which will win, hormones or anger.

Amy scurried away confirming annoyance. I began biting my lips and twisting my mouth left and right pounding the call button around him standing.

"Look at me, Shana!" His tone firm and deep.

My hazels meet his brown glossy eyes. I can't read his expression which irritates me further. "… Is that my shirt?" He's only just discerned. Breaking the anger bringing confusion.

"Really, that's the only observation you made?"

I pout really trying to keep my voice down.

"Let's go to my office."

He stepped back gesturing imprinting his strong thighs through his silver grey slim-fit pants and for a moment his jacket peeped through his broad chest under the white shirt distracting me. I wonder if it's purposefully. I shook it off.

"No! Thank you, sir."

"Shana!" his voice commanding,

"I'm fat and nothing fits! Your shirt is the only thing I can wear and breathe!" I change direction to avoid my explosion.

Smiling adorably in amusement at my comment, I squint at him. He took out his wallet holding a black card between his index and middle fingers to me. Replacing the wallet to his trouser pocket.

"There's a mall down the street, you can get what you like there."

I paused and my stare got deadly. "I think I need the toilet." I try a move to avoid this conversation and slip him.

"Take the card!" His insistent more like a directive and I know he sees my tactics.

I stare at him again, hard.

The elevator came up ringing and opened, my cue to run. I treaded in. Grinned stabbing it to close. But, it didn't. He followed as the doors closed. Looking down at me in contempt and shrugging at his jacket, forcing me to say it.

"Do you *want* to do this here?" I challenged.

"If you must." He breathes, sharply rolling his eyes.

"You made me to be a fool, Eric!" I growled the first words that came to mind.

"From my end you held it together, well." His compliment almost threw me off.

"You lied and undermined me." I turned to him pointing.

He keeps his stance. "I did not lie. You never asked for any details about my new job."

My jaw dropped, "A technicality? Really." I scoff and my voice went up a couple of octaves.

"Take the card... get something to wear." He grinds between his teeth.

I rolled my eyes grabbing it from his fingers tucking it into the shirt pocket then crossing my arms. He then leans on the glass inside with his hands in his pockets seeming to relax a fraction.

"Are you done?" He smiled slyly.

I growled! "Ugh!"

He just doesn't get it!

The double doors opened and I rushed out without looking back. Then around the revolving doors, down the widening stairs and into the car slamming the door behind me. I was livid.

Mad because of what was said in the meeting.

Mad at him for omitting his position.

But most of all, mad at myself for not seeing the signs before.

Tears stream effortlessly down my cheeks and I shake in anger, cross at everything.

After a few minutes the tears dried and my breathing slowed, I closed my eyes counting to ten slowly, to stay there and focus, calming me into the now, concentrating on the task ahead.

The press conference.

I dried my eyes, got out of the car, shutting the door and locking it. Crossed the streets and ambled into the mall Eric suggested, moving my feet without purpose. I need to replay the past few weeks.

The beginning of the case.

… His lies.

His visit.

… He lied

And his new job.

What a big, big liar!

I growled stomping now aching my leg that I believed was healed. I slowly thought about the conversation on the day this happened. He talked about his new position and even waited for me to say something.

The realisation hits. *I really wasn't listening, nor did I ask.* A smidgin of guilt covers me.

He should have told me! My subconscious reared her head and for once, I didn't want to smack her, I was giving her a high five.

Hunger hits me walking into the odours of a food court. All the savoury flavours remind me it is lunchtime. I bought lunch of spicy chicken and mashed potatoes throwing away the green peas, drinking a large cup of orange juice. Feeling dissatisfied, I bought and drank another one.

I am still angry.

Looking at my phone made it worse.

He hasn't called or texted me.

Sighing, I sat in the food court thinking about his actions and planning mine. The tapping began on my tummy again. The reminder that even though he has done some really messed-up-shit, I cannot stay in that place. I smiled at the gesture of the baby asking me to calm.

I really shouldn't be squeezing you.

I looked down at my growing bump. Then began a stroll through a few shops for something to wear. Bought a few work pieces of maternity suits a new pair of flat shoes and a bag. Spending his money didn't ease me but would surprise him. I got another juice just because he was sponsoring and because I really prefer buying food over clothes.

Changing into the one suit I bought for the return of work, and the beginning of what would be many press statements. The rest of the bags went to the car.

A crowd was gathering at the front of the building. Looking at the middle of the staircase where a flat area was, a stage built up with the national flag to one side, the S.D.A.F. flag on the other. The quote of arms on the podium with news team microphones waiting on it. Cementing the directive from the husband who holds my career in his hands, the same one that omitted the truth.

Just do it Shana, talk to him later. Reasoning annoyingly appeared.

I climbed the stairs, waiting at the safe distance at the podium, looking into the building. The mayor lingered inside talking to Eric. He nodded occasionally and posed for some pictures, Amy in the background with a black open folder, I guess taking notes. Our eyes met briefly, but it was different, cold and disconnected.

He whispered something to Amy and she left him temporarily descending to me. I walked with her to the reception. Only to hand me two drafted pieces of paper returning to his side. The words filtered that they prefer me to say.

My heart ached at the sheet of paper watching Eric in the background, distant. My nose pulsated and I wiped my sweaty palms in the new trousers wrinkling it. The mayor moved and Amy returned to Eric's side. Mayor Mall descended to the crowds, and began speaking filling the atmosphere with his baritone echoing through the waiting possibly fifty reporters.

This suddenly became very real.

Director Kane led me to the platform standing in the background as Mayor Mall finishes his statement. The nervousness and the flashes of the cameras synced. He has announced the Zemand festival of their creatures' opening to the public for the first time ever, this year and the launching of his campaign for re-election.

I truly wondered if he was a Zemand himself or if this was an attempt of securing re-election theatrics. I held my speech in tight waiting for my turn. He skilfully avoided any questions about his daughter and keeping only to his announcements. A true politician, something I can't be. He opened his arms pointing in my direction, proud it seemed.

Changing my pout to a smile, I nod, tug at my black jacket over the new maternity shirt and comfortable black maternity trousers, the jacket button couldn't close. I strolled towards the flashing lights, in the background Director Kane lurked.

Why is he here if they wanted me to do this?

My heart pounded as I moved my feet closer to the platform. Thankfully, the flashing blinded me to most faces in the crowd easing some nerves as I opened my mouth.

"Good evening,

"I am Special Agent Shannan Davis-Hall, lead investigator on the attack of Sharron Mall. The case is still under investigation so there isn't much I can share at this time. What I can say is that I am working with dedicated specialists in various fields and we have questioned several persons in relation to this case.

"This attack is not being condoned and we are working very hard to bring the person or persons responsible to justice. I will do my best to keep the media informed as best as and wherever I can, where it is possible.

"I do ask for the respect of privacy for Ms Mall and her family while she recovers from her injuries; and the opportunity to do my job.

"Thank you."

The first instinct to cover my face with the speech as the bright photography flashed. Kane pulled his hands down signalling for me to show my face swiftly I complied.

They all shouted questions and I smiled fading into the background as the mayor and Director Kane took the stage.

Eric was nowhere to be found. My heart constricts and I cannot begin to sort through my feelings about his revelation and his manner. My chest tightened and breathing became difficult. Everything around was closing in.

CHAPTER THIRTY- FOUR

Standing in the background, as Kane and Mayor Mall took the front entertaining questions. I looked on to the spectacle. The men's hands are locked in a handshake and have a bright grin. Waving and posing for the photos. I stepped backwards toward the building.

The political agenda is so clear for Kane and maybe Eric. The revelation of his job and the position he has placed me, it is unbelievable that he thinks it is OK. A pain grew from the pit of my belly rising to my throat forming a ball. I'm flooded by betrayal, disappointment and anger, guilty of stupidity. I count from ten.

He has clearly wedged Kane between us to protect himself.

I don't resent him for that.

I prefer not having direct contact with him in work at all. So, no one can accuse me of earning favours. The tension both sexual and irritation cannot be seen by our peers. Although, we've finished Shabráda for nearly three years, us not finishing Cáhilt makes us nothing more than an affair in the eyes of the law.

My ring means nothing and our relationship, cheap. I believe Acting Director Kane sees me that way and countless others will, once they know of our relationship. I frown.

Searching the crowd for my husband, the glimmer of some hope that he still supports me. That he has some remorse. My nose began to flare as I scan without success. My eyes are filling.

I need to get out of here.

Slipping into the building, I went past the reception. My badge dangling around my neck. I took the elevator to the underground parking, and out to the layby chasing to my car choking a cry that I've pooled. I left the Jade building on route to the apartment.

I need an explanation!

Fury increased thinking about his technical clarification as his voice replay in my head.

'I did not lie, you didn't ask.' I growled at his justification. I count again becoming madder at myself for doing it.

I parked and waddle with a limp up the stairs in the twilight. By then, counting wasn't enough. My chest tightened and the betrayal formed into rage as I ration my situation.

I can't believe Eric does not see the erroneousness to his actions.

He manipulated me and lied.

I stomped inside.

Of course, he is not here!

The empty apartment annoys me more. The uncertainty of emotions if he had been here swirls inside. I toss my workbag and all the other purchases on the sofa and paced. Then, picked it up retrieving my phone. There are some missed calls from unknown numbers.

Stupid reporters! I sulk.

Pacing again, waiting for him. Fifteen minutes feels like an hour ticking away and lately patience isn't my best quality. Blaming my short temper on the innocent child again, I closed my eyes admonishing myself. Watching my phone again and unlocking it this time.

Should I call him? I scroll through my contacts seeing his name after Emily's and sigh.

What would I say that I didn't before?

My fingers tremble hovering over his name wanting so badly to hear him. Eric is the one I usually turn for diplomacy and tact. Cracking my heart in two from the disappointment of hoping only in him.

No!

I shook my head putting the phone on the countertop, stopping myself right before I did it. Using my hands for something else, I opened the fridge. Food is the newest distraction and I sulk at the sight.

A cold beer was chilling on the door with scarcely anything else inside. The rising and fall of my chest intensifies and a tear finally slips. Eric and me, our default, though he would argue is not true of pizza and beer. There was no pizza in the fridge but there was beer. Images of us sitting in several settings having this aches me.

Emily is always the first I'd call in a situation like this. But she is still in the conflict zone, and I can't hear a note of her carefree voice cheering me. She can't come get me, take me out to party all night long, to get tipsy and drunk-dial Eric, not this time and possibly not in a very long time.

Retrieving the glass bottle from the fridge, I shut the door. Turning the cover, I put it to my lips and without thinking I tilted the bottle slightly opening my mouth. The cold liquid wet my lips, satisfying entering my mouth. But the smell reminded me of him. Removing it from my lips, I move towards the bed gaping at the beer.

Why did I just do that?

The baby woke with the tiniest taps from inside, I feel like its mocking me or telling me how horrible I am for tasting something that I craved in default. Suddenly, I felt like a trapped animal.

"Aahhh!" I screamed.

With one swift move, the bottle left my hand. The glass smashed and liquid bounced off the adjacent wall near the entrance. My heart raced but I was resentful. I snatched the lamp and it flew to the wall, shattering as it made contact.

My chest rose and fall as my breathing filled the silence after the shattering. I begin to swipe all the countertops throwing everything that's loose to the ground, not able to stop myself. All my feelings eased with each thing tossed.

I emptied the closet of my things and stuffed them into my suitcase. Swung my handbag over my shoulders tugging the rolling bag behind me. Eric's excuse for knowing where I stayed and getting a key.

'So, what are you saying, can't come by to see my wife... Well, I took some time off... we didn't really celebrate our anniversary this year... I called in a favour'.

"Lies!" I scream aloud wishing the images of his face away.

How could I be so stupid?

I scoffed at the thought.

I have had enough of this!

I drove an hour to the airport and bought a ticket at the counter. I need something to make me feel like myself again. The entire two-hour flight I brew thinking of my life and how we got here.

Passing through customs and collecting my bag quickly, a sudden loneliness came upon me. I missed my friends, my house and my life in Ceda. The baby taps wriggling around, I rubbed the bump.

I missed my husband.

A waiting taxi at the airport drove to the end of a peaceful cul-de-sac. A detached light-painted house. Immediately, I relaxed and the tension ebbed. The house is in darkness and the streets quiet.

I took my keys and opened the front door. The dancing light of TV and the background sound filled the room. A child's laughter and excitement filled my ear. The big head of curly hair I recognised before I saw her face. She turned to me prancing then ran out of the chair I replicate.

"Mum." She grabs me in the hallway wrapping her little arms around me.

"Danielle!" I was soothed by her welcome. "… Please don't call me that!" I warned cheerfully.

She got herself into the irritating habit of calling me Mum from time to time. I always have to remind her not to do that. It pisses off her mother, not that I care it does, but Sam will so eloquently quote; 'I am much closer to her age than I am to her father's'. In reality, I am fifteen years one way and thirteen the other. Though that's not the issue, it makes me uncomfortable. To me, it's just as bad as calling me ma'am or granny.

Her father condones and encourages it. They both know it annoys me but she obeys her father more than she does her mother or me. She loves to please her daddy. *Daddy's girl.* I mock.

"Oh, I missed you so much!"

Holding her at the moment, contented by her love, she rests her head on my chest. The small, hard, bump wedges between us. Though she is the first person I wanted to share the news, telling her without him is not why I am here. There are some obvious changes, I look a bit bloated around my waist and my boobs have grown significantly.

A smaller version of Elizabeth, with the forward talk and asking the hard questions I think of what I should say. The baby is introducing itself tap, tap tapping. The smell of popcorn enters my lungs. Danielle stepped back and I wonder if she feels the soft nudge. I tilted my head to her brushing her wild hair behind her ears, she looks up at me and rubs her small hands over my tummy. *Uh-oh!*

"It's really hard." She eyes my reaction and I try to remain impassive searching for the words that would not undermine Eric's and my agreement. "... But you don't really look pregnant."

She finishes and brushes her hair. Hiding my initial shock, I giggled trying to determine her source before dismissing her if she has discovered it on her own, instinct told me otherwise.

"Who told you?"

"Mum did." She shrugs and I breathe.

That bitch! Inside thankfully.

"... I didn't really believe her, but then Dad did," she sings innocently.

Opening my eyes to the widest, I bit my lips and then sighed.

Another 'thing' he neglected to discuss with me.

Fuelling my anger. "When?" My pitch is unnaturally high.

"A few weeks ago." She motions.

Jerk! "Trust me, there is someone in there." I am mad because he probably told her and God knows who else when we found out but opt to shift the conversation from her maddening father. "... Sweetheart, I missed you!"

Asshole! Curses still entered my thoughts and I held her tight absorbing the comfort and taking in her powdery scent. Emotions pooled. Further diverting before I popped.

"... It is really late for a school night." I sniffled wiping my eyes and struggling not to focus on him.

"It is school break," she complained putting her head on my chest again and arms around me in a matter-of-fact voice.

"Really, am I that out of touch?" Holding her close my chin is nearly at her head. "... Wow! You are getting taller or I'm shrinking."

"Yeah Mum, you are out of touch. I am taller now." She giggled.

My eyes twitched at that word again. "... Funny Danni. And you know Sam hates when you call me that." I remind her of a reason to stop.

"Yeah, I know." She comes out of my hold. "... But you are my step-mum, and I like calling you Mum and daddy says it's OK." She puts her hands on her waist.

"I will measure you in your room to be sure. That is too quick for one term, before long we would be shoulder to shoulder."

"You're not that tall anyway Mum." She made me twitch again, this time I rolled my eyes at her comment and then, smiled, looking around. "Where's Kayleigh?"

"Right here Shana." The part-time nanny pokes her head of blonde shoulder-length hair at me blinking her soft blue eyes that have darkened in the unlit room.

"Slacking off?" I joked at the teenager.

"No, getting popcorn for the movie, of course," she calls coming into the living room without offence.

She was only hired recently as the nanny. She tutored Danielle for nearly six months using her experience to help her with her degree in education. The neutral benefits us both and she is thankful for the travel and extra money, at least until the term restarts and Danielle goes back to boarding school.

I do feel some guilt not being the one to get Danielle from school and plan our holidays. I couldn't bear another minute as a mind-numbing trophy wife. Though I am sure that she is in glee about this impromptu visit.

"Come on Shana, this is a really good one."

Danielle led me to the sofa, my arms wrapped around her shoulder and she cuddles under my arm whilst she filled me in on the two months we've missed from school and the few days she stayed at Dave's.

Her intelligence is past her age and our conversations sometimes are mature and in-depth. She is truly a joy. Our bond is strong and her acceptance of me is worth every story she tells.

I began feeling remorse for leaving her to chase after my career and especially for letting Eric ship her to boarding school. I remembered being sent there by her father and feeling abandoned.

The thought scares me recalling some of the many attention seeking ventures Emily came up with.

She had Aaliyah on her toes. I shook my head in memory.

What worries me is Danielle is friends with Emily's sister, Melanie. I grin at the thought of one of my best friends. I would like to catch up with them if I can.

We fell asleep on the sofa. Waking up Sunday morning on the sofa, Danielle was probably in her room and Kayleigh in the guest room slash office.

I forgot once again that I don't have a waist and most of my clothes don't fit!

Sunday morning's complaint as I got dressed. Thank goodness I have a couple of maxi dresses but my favourite set of clothing is now Eric's boxers and jerseys. Particularly because my underwear is tight across my thickening thighs and his jerseys are usually like a dress.

We ordered food in, lounging, watching movies, chatting with Kayleigh. I enjoyed Danielle's company over the next two days. Watching her playing and enjoying being with her is a bit of a fantasy, in our own bubble.

So many memories in this house just calms me, but sleeping in our bed without Eric, doesn't feel right. The idea of him brought me back to the mess I couldn't stop myself from making.

Eric probably walked into that.

A part of me was a little concerned but a smile grew thinking of his reaction. I fell asleep happy.

****

Danielle jumped on the bed waking me. "... Shana, you have a visitor," she said, excited.

I was startled holding my tongue from cursing. "Oh, what."

I popped open my eyes she sat at the edge of the bed. A wide grin and puffed out hair reminding me to tidy it after my nap.

"Aw, it's too early for that Danielle!" I closed my eyes groaning surprised that I fell asleep in my bed.

"Mum!" She knows saying that will get a reaction, and I took the bait.

"Danielle," I whine looking at her innocent face, her bright-blues staring at me, I see the mischief written across her face.

"Someone is here to see you."

She gestures her hands waving them towards herself getting off the bed and standing at the door which was open.

I exhaled with a loud sigh, her footsteps stomping down the stairs for me to follow and I am too tired to chase her. Three days home has been great reconnecting with her but yesterday's water balloon fight has worn me out.

Ugh!

I rolled out the covers tossing them to the side, imagining the visitor that would get her excited and Kayleigh silent. My heartbeat increased.

Shit!

If it was Eric, he would have come into the bedroom. Logic taunts me, still upset that he hasn't made contact or apologised for his untruthful tongue.

I followed after her.

My hair curled naturally and flattened where my head lay from three days of no flat ironing. Dressed in Eric's spotty blue boxers and his white T-shirt wiping drool from my face. Across the hall and down the stairs. I rub at my eyes and yawn, checking my reflection in the mirror at the bottom of the stairs, combing my fingers through the knots in my hair.

I guess this would have to do!

Apprehensively sauntering, into the open living space, fuzz still in my eyes, I heard Danielle's voice talking to the mysterious visitor. Seeing Sam erected at five seven posing her usual torn up boyfriend jeans, black boots and white T-shirt tucked into her jeans. Underneath her black leather bike jacket and pair of Glocks poking through exasperated.

This is the last person I expected.

Actually, I didn't expect anyone but Eric and he still didn't show. She is narrowing her beautiful eyes at me with clear aggravation across her pretty face, I brace.

Here it comes.

"What. Are. You. Doing. Here?" She pointed at me in an annoyed tone saying each word, one at a time.

I rolled my eyes and sucked my teeth at her. "I live here Sam." I crinkled my eyebrows at her foolish question, correcting her.

"You live here." She scoffs. "... Think that is funny?" She shook her head. "... We thought you were in trouble... again."

Hum. Sam concerned? The notion faded as quick as it came.

Cute. "Did anyone think of calling my mobile?" I shrug.

"Who wouldn't think of doing that?" Her sarcasm is prevalent in her tone as she rolled her head, flopped her hands up then slapping her thighs.

"Ahh..." I remembered not picking it up on my way here. "... Oh well."

Her eyes widened but I shrugged, turned one-eighty, waved my hands and left the room.

"What!" Her jaw loose. "... Wow! Maybe that baby's scrambling your brains."

She points at me shaking her head. I rolled my eyes.

"Thanks for the visit, Sam."

Danielle came and hugged me from behind. I turned; she lay her head on my chest for a second. I brushed her hair with my hands. Then to her mother, looking at us both she may be waiting for the argument as she's sometimes the referee. Sam shook her head, a disappointed expression across her face as she sucked her teeth at me, I'm sure.

"Danni do you have all your things?"

"Where are you taking her?" My voice in a panic.

"What is truly wrong with you, Shana? Go on Danni." She shoos Danielle. "... I thought you were the one who demanded respect and who had balls bigger than your mansion?"

She shouts at me forcing me to reflect on her statement. Being professional is important to me to draw the line but Eric complicated this with his position and lies.

"I need time, a break, Sam. Time to think!"

My heart quickens as I recalled the news. The directors meeting. My new directive by my husband who hurt me, lied to me, and the humiliating press conference.

"You were running off on us."

Her volume increased as she pointed at me backing me into a corner.

"I was not." *Wasn't I?* "... I... I just needed time to think."

My anger increased thinking of it all. She continued her abuse.

"Think about what, Shana?" Sharron Mall lying to me on the hospital bed and Eric's excuse for not telling me.

I turned my face huffing through my nostrils.

"… Since that press conference reporters have flooded our office and we have been sent threats almost every day. You started something, and instead of standing with us, you ran away like a little bitch."

Is she seriously challenging me again?

I gaze into Danielle's beautiful blue eyes as her head moves from me to her mother. Restraining my tongue from foul words, I have to be heard.

"Sam, there are things happening that you do not understand."

"You made me trust you, and you left all of us to fry."

My breathing paused as her words cut into me. Her voice cracked and I believe her for the first time ever. I blinked at her a couple times to gain my countenance. Her cheeks flush as her innocent blue eyes burns through me. All true, and unexpected but that's no excuse for my behaviour towards my team.

This one you can't blame on Eric!

I sober my thoughts. The team who was least expected to succeed. I groomed and boasted that I achieved something that probably wasn't predictable.

"Are you two going to fight?"

Danielle disrupted us. She's always the one who can bring me true perspective.

"… Do I need to call Daddy again?"

Again?

The threat of Eric's intervention calmed us both aware of his temperament.

You can't continue to blame him for everything. My subconscious wagged her finger at me.

Though Eric had a huge part to play in my anger, all the blame was not his.

I wanted, the career.

I accepted the assignment.

I have something to prove.

At some point I need to take responsibility. Finally accepting the burden on my shoulders.

"No Danielle."

I held her face between my hands gazing into her beautiful blue eyes. My tone soft maybe impassive. I kissed her forehead.

"Go get ready to go with your mother, Danielle."

She grinned with a nod squeezing me then her mother, prancing out the room and up the stairs. Once she was out of the room and I was sure she was out of earshot, I exhaled with purpose, ready to spit some truth.

"Sam, I didn't! I wasn't quitting on you guys. I needed space, to think, to put things in perspective. As I said before, there are things happening…"

"Is this about you and Eric?" she grunts frustrated.

Why would she ask that?

This sounds like Elizabeth's influence. She never mentions Eric and me in the same sentence.

Because it usually is? I growled at myself for thinking it, took a deep breath before releasing more of Saturday's meeting.

"Do you know about the deadline?" I am compelled to regurgitate my fury.

"Yes, and your new boss, Kane told us!"

Asshole!

I am forced to list the new directives blinking long to reel in the betrayal.

"… And he boasts about being the new boss," she croaks.

He would.

"… The entire staffing has been moved to the headquarters," she shares the news said by the directors and I recall hearing it from Eric's mouth.

I try to rake in my anger. Kane doesn't seem to like me and I know why now.

Eric is his boss… and mine.

"… The Jade building!" she clarifies.

I still, knowing the next thing she would announce is Eric's promotion. I should, at least give her the courtesy.

"Do you know Eric is the director of S.D.A.F."

I threw up the words feeling ill. Aware of how his position will always shadow mine in a compromising manner. Sam sighed.

"Yes, Lia told us last week."

My eyes widened. *Bitch!*

Sam eyes my reaction but shrugs afterwards. It concerns me. I am overthrown into rage by the mention of Aaliyah's announcement prior to my knowledge. I grind my teeth.

How did she know and I didn't?

Exactly why I am *mad!*

He is always such a vault when it comes to their relationship. Though I remember their glacial meeting three weeks ago.

Or maybe she is just on another claim to fame statement, and it's not true. *Do you believe the previous one isn't true?* I asked myself.

When would I feel secure about their relationship?

Don't go there! Focus Shana!

"They want me to get the case to trial … in three months, Sam. A conviction." I summarised the meeting.

She inhaled sharp. "Did he actually say that?" She crossed her arms with a frown at me.

"In plain words, yes." I say exasperated.

"Hum."

Less vocal than I expected.

I see her mind going. She has her hand fisted into her chin and she's looking down.

"What?" I am impatient for an answer, an honest one. "… And please speak your mind, Sam,"

"Not that I need your permission to do that but, it appears as if they are throwing you under the bus, Shana."

Eric won't allow that! I gulped,

But… if he truly doesn't want me to work in law enforcement.

"Exactly." The filter came loose. I admonish myself filtering, "… But I am deliberating their reasoning? Why does this case need priority? Why is it so important that this should go to trial? Why would someone take that woman's dignity? And why would she, after three weeks' recuperating, lie to us about it?"

"Those are good questions Shana but the answers are not here, they're in Divinish. Let's go find out then." She is leading me out to the halls.

Uhh. "Can we go tomorrow?"

321

I whine suddenly conscious about my attire and cannot be asked to get dressed and squeeze into something uncomfortable for work.

"Get a shower and be here in thirty minutes!" she mocked me.

"Thanks, *mom* but I don't sound anything like that Sam."

"Twenty-nine minutes." She looked at her hand although she never wears a watch.

CHAPTER THIRTY-FIVE

Kayleigh took Danielle to Sam's apartment in a separate taxi. Sam and I made our way to the office and she called ahead.

"I want Sharron Mall in an interview room before I get there," she commands the person on the other end of the phone call.

I narrowed my eyes at her.

She sucked her teeth. "… Shana want's it done nicely."

She's shaking her head and rolling her neck at me listening to the voice on the other end of the phone.

"… Yes, Shana is with me." (She paused to listen again shaking her head in agreement). "So!" (She protests and was cut short, listening again). "… All right then, will do."

She squeezed the end button on her phone. Then tilts to me slightly as we shared the back of the taxi.

"I will suggest you give your husband a buzz," she states gaping at me through her long dark lashes pushing her phone to my face. I narrowed my eyes at her.

"You can use my phone if you like." She drags her alto tone.

I squinted even more.

"I will call him when I am done!" I crossed my arms focused on the journey through the traffic to the office.

She grinned naughtily.

"Keep doing that and you'd get wrinkles like Lia."

I ceased immediately rubbing the folds I created with the frown.

We both laughed.

****

Fifty minutes ride to the office, up the hallway to the foyer entering our pass code, Noel not at her new post, her desk appeared to be cleared out.

323

Though many questions filled my head, the task at hand is more important. Sam left me as I walked around the lab to Aaliyah in the interview room, she had already begun interrogating Sharron Mall like she was a suspect.

"Answer me!"

Her voice echoed high-pitched through the speakers in the observation area. Lia leaned to the table pounding it with a closed fist creasing her silky grey tailored suit. The material was exquisite and her perfect ass, firm and curved smoothly with the jacket compared to my only white maternity shirt, black maternity pants and loose black jacket. Stuck in the same thing I wore to the press conference the only maternity clothing I owned.

Sharron rubbed her thumb over her ruby polished nails looking at the table as her long brunette hair covers the scars on her face. Her camisole black straps exposed her red lace bra. She wasn't moved by Lia's tactics.

What is wrong with Sharron?

I gazed through the one-way glass waiting for Sam to recover what she needed from her desk. My anger builds as I think of Sharron Mall's attitude to the investigation. I remembered when I was brought into the police station after my encounter in the alley nearly nine years ago.

The photos of her badly bruised and bleeding. My visit to her in the hospital, her eyes and head so swollen, I couldn't tell if she was awake or asleep.

Why would she lie about this?

My role, the ethical and professional lines face me.

I need my questions to rest.

My feet began to move to the door. My chest pounding through my ears and palms are sweating. I took a deep breath feeling a change happening. I turned the knob. She wasn't to the least moved by my presence. Pulling my jacket together blocking the bump. I slid on the chair opposite her where the camera would have a view of us face-to-face.

"Hello."

My voice intensively chilled as I called her to look at me. She does for a second continuing her posture. One arm across her chest and the other propped as she ran her thumb across her ruby pedicure fingers staring at them. She has covered the restraint scars with a large bangle and leather armbands.

It took moments for Aaliyah's gaped at me blinking a couple times.

"Davis?" she questions my presence, shocked, I believe, then finally reacted to my invasion. "… What are you doing?"

Without altering my intention, I moved my hazels to Lia's icy-blues slowly without moving my head positioned face-to-face with Sharron's. Either by the expression on my face or something seen by her, Aaliyah's breath hitched. Then, I return my gaze to Sharron's, now fallen hazels in response to the same aspect. Her hazels appear brown in the light.

"I'll just be a few moments, with Ms Mall." I settle myself. "… Don't worry."

I say only for manners, condescending like Lia. My hazels burned into Sharron's.

A growl left Lia. She stormed out stomping her well balanced designer heels. The room door echoes behind her when she shut it. Mixed feelings began to flood me like at the hospital staring at Sharron as we face off. Although she doesn't appear to be intimidated by me, I need her to be.

In I breathe, slow and deep, calming the whirling storm. Deflecting the strange emotions I sense from Sharron. I concentrate on my breath out the nose until it becomes so quiet, it feels like I have built an invisible wall around myself and I count from one to ten. Focusing on the things that has got me tied into knots and using each number to put it all into perspective and untangle the emotion.

The news headlines. *Anger, mine.*

Anticipation, jealousy and curiosity. *Anxiousness, not mine.*

The possible political agenda exposed. *Hate, not mine.*

The timeline given to this case. *Hurt, mine.*

Her careless attitude presented today. *Fury, mine.*

Eric's lies and excuses. *Livid, all mine.*

Even as I see the peeking scars behind her dark hair, where she's cut a fringe to hide them. The tectonic plates lifted and I exhaled, *ten.* The confusion cleared.

"Ms Mall. I am Special Agent Davis-Hall. We met at the hospital a few weeks ago." I try reminding her of what she's escaped although, I hardly believe it is anything she would ever forget. She cringed a millisecond. I found my opening.

"... I just have a few follow up questions for you. Is that OK?" I begin formal reading her.

Her anxiousness is now hinted with a bit of fear, like tar, the scent hit me. The emotions that had weakened me, paralysing me after her first interview are pulling back, fast.

Then a second later, Sharron stills, her pulse below her skin at her neck, flickers quick and she bows at her ruby nail polish avoiding my stare, I believe. It didn't matter though. I was here with tonnes of built-up resentment and it was about to come out and Sharron Mall is the target.

"Sure," she answered still nonchalant in a stare away from my eyes.

Considering the person now and recalling a few weeks ago, I took another breath. Attempting to blow out the frustration of events and focus on her reasoning, attempting to keep my mood under control.

Maybe I am the one who need to remember. I cleared my throat hoping that will help the emotionless approach I feel the need to take.

Aaliyah's writing pad to me, I turned away from her graceful cursive to a blank page. Though this will be recorded, I would like to write so that *I* don't forget. Underneath the notepad the folders, the horrible ones that still raises bile to my throat and this was nothing in comparison to seeing her in person.

Carefully, I placed pictures of her across the table to face her. She flinched again, and moved her eyes away.

Good, she does remember.

"Ms Mall, I need for you to go over with me, the conversation we had a few weeks ago. I would like it if this time you begin from the start of the day. It will serve my team better, if we were to follow in your footsteps."

She caresses her nail polish slightly squirming.

My no nonsense stare burns at her. I feel the complete retreat of the waves drown me in emotion but sense some fear beneath the anxiousness. The room heats and I am losing my patience.

"… I would appreciate if you can stop fidgeting with your fingers and look at me."

I raised my voice growling at her.

She twists her head as though cracking her neck eyeing me intensely as if I annoyed her.

Breathe, Shana, breathe!

Slowly leaning back slapping her thighs on her short, thigh-high red, skirt sitting up with aggression.

"I already told you guys what happened."

I smirked and a giggle left me.

Nothing about this is funny, specifically, her attitude. I narrow my eyes at her, feeling the rise. Heat, going up from my feet moving, up my ankles to my thighs.

"I'm not sure whom you're referring to, but I need you to think, before you say anything else," I warned her.

She is starting to piss me off!

I really want to smack her.

"… Start from when you got up the morning you were attacked, even if that includes taking a piss." My voice is calm and I nod at her.

She sucked her teeth then started with an attitude.

"I woke up took a *piss!* And started to get ready for the day. Father called me, he wanted to talk. I told him not to call me again and hung up. I went to work, stayed for a couple hours and left."

She is rushing her words and I am almost at popping level. *She thinks I am kidding!*

"What time did your father call?" I interrupted her staying on professional course but my heart is picking up the pace. The heat is now at my thighs.

"I don't know but he woke me. He wanted to meet somewhere I didn't care anyway," she mumbled her words in irritation.

"What time did work start?" I am grinding my teeth, filtering my anger.

"I got there for nineish. I think it was inventory week, so I had to be there early." Her fidgeting is irritating and I can't take much more.

"Do you take drugs?" The filter has gone, and something has shattered warming me, completely.

"What?" she sounds wounded. "… No," she defends.

"I don't believe you," I just said it.

I don't care anymore!

My voice is gaining volume, growing to antagonism and something inside begins to stir.

"Do I care what you believe? I don't!" She continues to fidget and the room warms.

Does she really want to test me?

Her tone brings me to livid.

Lucky for her I have gained experience with attitude these past five weeks and I am ready to let my frustration out. Everything that irritated me this week, I brought to the surface. She starts to rub her arms and my eyes caught it.

"I can tell by those marks on your arms." She opened her mouth but I cut her. "… Don't say those are from the attack because some of those look fresh. The ways you are fidgeting with your fingers suggest you need a hit. Drugs were found in your car. Your blood was laden with heroin."

She shook her head from left to right.

"I used to!" She put her fingers to her lips and began to chew on her nails.

"You are lying!" I grunt through my teeth. "… How long ago was that?" I am poker-faced to maintain professional, boiling beneath as this room heats.

"Look I was gang raped." She moves her fingers only to growl the words then, began tapping her feet under the table.

"I find that hard to believe." I nodded calmly.

She looks up at me, stunned. "I was! Five of them…"

She trails, shrugs crossing her arms. The foot movement stopped and the rocking began.

"Look, stop wasting my time!"

My anger has kindled, the temperature of the room increased and my tone became dark, stern and uncompromising. A deep earth grumble begins. I crinkled the paper under my hand snapping the pen in two and my eyes change.

I can't take it any more!

I threw the pieces at my sides and pointed at her counting on my fingers.

"… I spent five weeks chasing your lies, looking for the fictional biker gang."

"No, it's true—" she defends and I counter.

"You lied about the way you were taken. You lied about the drugs. And you lied about being raped."

The words pained me as I sense her hurt, shame and something I cannot get a grip on, but my anger is in full force, focused on my past and the current disposition. Everything that I have put on the line believing her. I see only anger boiling from me shattering any empathy.

"No," her voice trembled and nose sniffled putting her polished fingers into her mouth biting, rocking and shaking her head left and right. Sweat glistens her forehead and condensation cover the viewing glass.

"For all I know this was all orchestrated. Isn't that what you do? You lie to get attention from your daddy. I have your juvenile rap sheet here with reports."

She gasped low, her eyes widened to me.

The strong wave of humiliation hits, shattering against the hardened rage at her as I went on. "Extortion. Bribes. You've staged your kidnapping before. Your father had to cash in on a lot of favours, just to keep you out of jail."

"Mayor Mall isn't as innocent as he makes everyone think. And, I could care less what Father says!"

She raises her anxious tone and rocks back. A fresh wave of fury washes over me seeing her resisting the truth. My breath increased the heat, her camisole soaks with sweat and I push.

"Really, then why are you so agitated by the mention of 'Daddy'? You are a liar. Attention seeking, spoilt brat! You did it time, and time again. To swindle money and to get anything you want.

"Why should I believe you?

"Why would anyone believe you?

"This is now under the eyes of the federal court.

"You want attention.

"Now you've got mine!"

The low earth rumbling gains volume and my eyes burned. I stand up leaning, over the table, looking down at her.

Suddenly, her movement stopped and she stands holding the table looking straight at me with her hair wet, sticking to her neck and shoulders.

"I… was… raped!"

She screamed each word one at a time hammering her fists at the table before sitting down. Something snapped in me.

The deep earth rumble ceased instantaneously and she catches her breath, dripping sweat leaned over the table.

Then she looks up through her long lashes with her head down at my furious stance. Her hazels glossy, red and staring into my brown eyes as the tears and perspiration fall onto the table and her hands. My eyes are still focused on her. Wrath still the forefront emotion, I was unsure of whom it came, equally we both were angry. The door opened.

Sam burst in leaning on the table, to wedge her face between Sharron and me.

"Davis, can I see you for a moment?"

Her rustic voice low and demanding. I am unmoved.

"Not now Sam!" I hissed. My eyes fixed on Sharron, hardly noticing her.

"Davis-Hall!" Sam yells and grabbed my arm, then letting go instantly. "… Ouch!" she voiced shaking her sore hand. "… Shannan!"

Sam never calls me by my full name, ever. It catches my attention but doesn't shift my intent. Satisfied with Sharron's now broken and remorseful stance, I can leave.

"You can take it from here," I snorted keeping her in my view before pushing past Sam.

Sam, watched the fogging room, nodded at Sharron who was now damp and whose face was now covered with tears. She closed in the door and chased after me.

"What is wrong with you? You can't gnaw her like that! Did I just say that?"

I avulse still capturing her words.

Wait!

"What did you just say?" I asked her.

330

We both paused.

The heat subsided slowing with my breathing.

"You were interrogating our victim!" Sam quarrelled at my handling of Sharron Mall. Sam left me to discover my queries of why and I growled at her questioning me.

"… You're late and she made a fool of me!" I am still mad.

But Sam's words lingered in the air snapping me back from rage.

Sam a voice of reason? I calm at the realisation.

"Welcome to law enforcement." She wagged her head at me dragging her alto tone. *She is never a voice of reason.* "… Why do you think I bang so many heads?"

"Because you enjoy doing it," I say without regret.

Oops! My filter is lost! Subconsciously I am looking for it.

"Yea but more than that, it's because of victims like these." She points into the room and I pace my irritation away. "… You OK, you're burning up?"

Samanther's concern stopped me, "Am I?"

I used the back of my hand to touch my forehead. I am sweating but not hot. I see the sweat marks on my shirt. "… I don't feel anything."

She prudently does the same thing then shrugs her shoulders.

"I should get in there whilst she is in this state. Maybe we might get the truth." She gives me the strangest look rubbing her palm.

"Maybe!" I am indecisive and suddenly tired.

"Wait out here, observe!" She winks opening the door.

"Are you…" I question with a squint knowing her tactics.

"Will be gentle, not like you." She narrows her eyes at me and walks through.

I gasped at her gesticulation.

She dashed in, pulled back the chair squatting to sit. She eyes the condensate in the room peculiarly. Carefully slapped the files on the table leaning back with one arm propped at the back of the chair. I observed through the glass tapping my foot rhythmically.

"Hi, I am Detective Sergeant Martinez I will be taking the interview from here, are you ready to start or do you need a moment?"

Sharron held on to the chair seat sniffling and shaking.

"Do you want a moment or can you continue?"

Sam slid her chair on the tiled floor causing a screech. Sharron tiredly raised her head.

"I am ready." A sorrowful voice leak.

"Well let's start a fresh here Sharron, tell me the truth even if you have an incline that you might be seen in a bad light. It is far better that we work from the truth.

"It is a miracle you survived this attack. My guess is who did this to you thought you would have died and you didn't. Give me the chance to catch this son of a bitch."

Hum, she is gentler than I was... for once!

Sharron sat with her hair cascaded over her face, tearing staring at the table. The camera fixed on her face, I wanted to comfort her but I didn't want to be taken for a fool again.

She knocked on the table as she was knocking her memory out. She locked her eyes on the smallest detail of the table raised her head to Sam again, then continues her death stare at the table.

"My father called me that morning asking me to meet him at the Little Meals Restaurant, for dinner that night. He wanted us to talk. It was the anniversary of my mother's death. It was her favourite restaurant.

"A place not too far from the canyons, good food not too fancy. A home away from home place. I cursed at him and hung up. She died because of him.

"She was sick, complications of the liver or so the doctors said. He was always too busy to see her, left us there to watch her die.

"Prick!"

Her eyes filled for a second and blew it out. Then filling her lungs without a prompt went on.

"I went to work early. It was payday. My boss Marlon Samuel wanted to fire me. I wasn't a good barkeep.

"Humm!

"The only reason I stuck around was the free booze, and he kept me for the sex. We had a good thing and I got paid twice. I've seen him peeping in the lady's room at me so, it wasn't that hard to get that arrangement started.

"I took the cash and he took his sex and I left. Anyway, I met Sam-Sam outside the restaurant that day he wanted to take me to see Valentine."

"J-Jason?" Sam stutters for clarification. Her face momentarily shifts but quickly recovers and tunes in.

"Yeah, we were having a thing, nothing serious. Just a bit of occasional fun. No strings attached, but that is not why he wanted to see me. I used the opportunity to commandeer merchandise. I was desperate, and he somehow realised what happened, and he demanded I return it."

"Merchandise? You mean drugs?" Sam stops her.

"You can say that." She shrugs.

"What kind?" Sam questions

"Lady H," she replies.

Sam stiffs, then prompted, "I need you to say it."

"I stole heroin from Valentine Jason OK!" She raised her voice and twisted her neck like a snake. "… I gave some to Sam-Sam, in exchange for telling Valentine he couldn't find me, he wanted sex instead. I did it and he snuck me to my boyfriend, Terrance Jason.

"I told Terry after sex that, I was pregnant…" She looked straight at me through the one-way glass. "… And I was keeping it." She cried those words out.

"… Weeks before, he spoke, of leaving his wife. Starting our own family. But when I told him, he got nasty, cursed at me and changed his mind.

"Jerk!

"Talking some crap about working things out with his wife. I think… it would be less complicated if he admits he's just afraid of his brother." She choked on her grief.

"… Sam-Sam didn't love, my sister." She whispered and shook her head.

I am shocked at her admission. She had sex with her sister's husband, knowing she was pregnant. They had an ongoing, sexual relationship. *That is really messed up,* I thought.

Before long, she looked into the glass ahead, straight at me and said almost as if answering my thoughts.

"I needed a solution. I wasn't in the best position." Then took a deep breath looking down again. "... I went to V hoping to pin the baby on him."

Sam scoffed, I guess is with whatever knowledge or history she shares with Valentine Jason, but I could bet on what a man in his position reaction will be.

"... He knew it wasn't his, dismissed me instantly. He also knew about me and Terry and he knew what I stole. He was not happy about that. I offered to work it off, sex, anything for taking his drugs. He took the sex. Then, gave me one day to get the money or his stuff."

Wow! That really was a hard position.

Agreeing with Sharron's assessment, I crossed my arms watching the small incline of my tummy wondering what I'd do to take care of it if Eric rejected me. I empathise.

"What happened to the drugs you took?" Sam confronts her.

She laughed scorned shaking her head from left to right, exhaling her answer.

"I sold it, paid my rent." She sighed, lost in thought fixated on a single object. "... I made a deal with two of V's employees, arranged an exchange of more products, promising to pay with the profits I would make on the streets. Selling it with myself. I made a little over three thousand that night... thinking I was home free. Three thousand five hundred was my mark.

"My debts would be paid off. One last packet, one more customer before I head home and it would be done." She paused with the shaking of her head again. "... Father rolled up on me." She scoffed. "... He knew exactly where to find me. I told him to beat it. He hung around chasing any potential customers. The last deed I would do for the night. I had no choice, I headed home instead.

"Father sometimes has his goons follow me. I thought... I thought, it'll be a terrible idea for him to find me at V's."

She is right, that would have been for both of them.

She bit her full lips at the corner like I would sometimes and then, let it go.

"... I got to the parking lot of my apartment with the tail. I was fuming by that time. I was about to get out and confront him, when...

When I saw this person, standing in a red robe ahead of my car, with the hood covering their face... almost like the Grim Reaper..."

Her description was vivid, erringly familiar. My breath was caught at my throat sensing more than she is saying, reaching for the image in my memories, lost in the fog. Tears began to flow down her cheeks and her stare became blank.

"... he just stared... not moving at all... Creepy..." The urge to hide floods through my system and a shiver crawled over my skin. I want to move my eyes from her but I can't.

"... Then, an old man came up to my car window knocking asking for a ride. He scared me, I told him to get lost! When I looked back the stranger in the robe was gone. I couldn't shake this feeling, I thought he was the freak with the robe," she murmured the last few words and Sam interrupts her.

"Can you describe this man?"

She hesitated, ticking seconds past. Her voice cracked. "... He was old, maybe around father's age, blue eyes, bright full of life when he looked at me." She is dazing towards the camera.

"Would you be able to describe him to a sketch artist?" Sam asked and she said nothing for a bit, then.

"I think I could." She looks at the table again.

"What happened after the man came knocking at your window?" Sam encouraged her.

"I turned the engine over and was about to drive away.

"I was afraid.

"He was too old to be someone father sent and I didn't want that freak following me inside. Then, he opened the front passenger door and sat inside my car. I didn't know the doors were unlocked. It may have opened when I turned off the car, I don't know." Her voice is cracked with her attempt to restrain her melancholy.

"... Before I could make a move, my head crashed through the window. I think that's when it broke..." She began to really tear up. "... The next thing I remembered, I was naked and bound like a star, in a cave on a stone alter.

335

"Everything was dark... red... it looked like blood... and shadows were painted on the walls. It stunk, really badly. One of them forced my mouth open, pouring a liquid down my throat..."

"Do you remember how many there were?" Sam cuts her.

Sam! Let her finish! There was a long break for her to catch her breath, and she answered,

"I don't know three, four around me could have been more. It was really dark. Hands were touching me. I am not sure what happened next, everything was blurred. Time was lost along with awareness. I only remembered feeling the blade, every cut. Each time I think they have finished torturing me I feel another.

"There were no voices but mine screaming to be freed, screaming from the pain and the sound of my blood dripping to the floor. On occasion when they spoke it was a different language. The caves moved. I must have been hallucinating. Everything I ever did; all the lies and pain came to life in front of me until, I couldn't take it any more. I was guilty. I did those things. I deserved it. I was, I was the monster."

She wept loudly soaking her face with tears and snot.

She paused blowing out to continue, "... Then they soaked me with something sticky and I felt his scaly, slimy, cold skin over me... I was too... I just couldn't scream..." She burst into a cry again. "... I was too exhausted... I couldn't... I couldn't scream..."

I turned away attempting to hold in the anguish by covering my mouth. Sam gave her some time to cry then pressed on.

"I understand but it would really help if you can remember anything at all especially about that person," Sam asked the very important but very hard question.

Sharron cried and cried, holding herself bending her head to the table staining it with her tears breathing hysterical and loudly. Sam offered her a tissue. Slowly she accepted it to dry her face. When her breathing was under control she finally said,

"He-he had, a feather, on a necklace." Sharron touches her neck as she described, "... I-I remember it brushing over my face as he..." She trailed, but Sam waiting, not adding nor taking away any details, giving Sharron time again to compose herself.

Then, Sharron laughed scorned, before saying, "... I guess I must have passed out or something, because, the next thing I remembered was seeing the guy who smashed my head into the window, hanging over me with bright lights behind him. I thought I was dead. Then I realised, I was in my car trunk, he tried to take the necklace."

"Describe him." Sam stops her for a profile.

"He was old grey hair, pale-blue eyes. Well-dressed."

I think I know who that is. I've looked through the folders so many times, I know who she means. I need to be sure. I began pacing as the interview room gets quiet and Sam was taking notes. Suddenly, my hands are around the door handle and I am inside the hot room again with both ladies. Taking the picture out of the folder that was left by Aaliyah, I think and pulled out the profile with the record of the man.

"Is this him?"

Sam startled at the sight of me again, disrupting her flow. Sitting back and putting the pen down she looks up at me leaning over her shoulder placing the item over Sharron's tears and pointing at the black and white profile. Sharon shook her head 'yes'.

"Davis!" Sam exclaimed.

"Would you be able to pick him out of a line up?" I put forward my proposal dismissing Sam.

Sharron hesitates.

"... Don't worry he won't be able to see you, we will protect you," I assured her.

"Davis!" Sam is calling again.

"I can try." Sharron voiced shakingly, slowing down her breathing. She looks at the photo and not at me. The room was silent and I was celebrating my victory as Sam stared shocked and annoyed at me. Just then Sharron claimed apprehensively.

"Oh, during some time when I was in and out of consciousness, I heard the voices talking about me possibly being a key. I heard them mention a name; Shala or something." She squints before correcting her pronunciation. "... No it was Shannan."

CHAPTER THIRTY-SIX

That moment, everything inside me froze, the room grew darker my breathing became louder I am terrified, having the urgent thought of hiding.

"Davis!"

Sam's shouting my name brings me back to now, standing next to me with a puzzled expression. Weather to me interrupting her interview or my reaction to Sharron hearing her attackers personally naming me, for what, I am too afraid to ask.

"T-Thank you."

I exhaled, and stuttered, escaping to the hallway.

Absconded leaning on the wall outside the interrogation room for a moment catching my breath. I closed my eyes and begin my count to ten. Vomit touched the back of my throat and trepidation filled me. I stop. About to retreat to the lady's room holding my mouth from a spill, when Sam came out seeing my panic.

"Don't go there Davis, breathe! She is trying to rattle you."

Sam didn't seem convinced by Sharron's words but I was genuinely afraid.

"If she wanted to scare me, she did a fine job."

The words I was thinking flew out before I could filter them.

"Half of what she described seems fictional and she definitely sounds delusional. This shouldn't mean anything. She heard me call your name."

"I am not sure," … I can't shake it…

Ten, nine, eight, seven, six, five, four, three, two, one… Am I calm?

"… Thanks Sam."

I know she is trying. I cleared my throat standing tall shrugging my blouse for some cool and to compose myself after the unexpected end to Sharron's new version of the events.

"… Reports later." I change in direction.

I don't want either of them in my head.

"After I wrap things up here?"

Sam's squint says otherwise.

Briskly, I made my way into my office. Acting Director Kane hadn't changed much more than my chair, which annoyed me each time I sat. Fidgeting with the adjustment levers in the middle of reviewing my diary, to bring calm from something familiar, exhaling the stress. I settle in the chair as best as I could and fired up my computer, there was a large brown envelope on my desk.

Wary of things being left for me, I breathe deep before turning it over. 'Catacá' was printed in bold across it. I let it go instantly wheeling back in my chair. My heart increased the beats.

This is not funny!

Scanning through the glass of the office, everyone was gone.

Who put it there?

Slowly pulling my chair into the table, I took the envelope into my hands and a letter opener ripping off the top and peeking inside. Pictures and a sheet of paper, I thought at first glance. I turned it over on my desk; a spill of graphic murder scenes. I swallow hard reviewing them each.

Describing the details to myself, all women bound and gagged laid in pools of blood. Horrified but curious, I went through all the photographs. Below were pictures of the first woman naked, bright sky-blue eyes now grey with no pupil.

Her mouth opened, slightly with blood inside spilling out, body taut in place. Her arms away from the body, elbows straight, hands in a fist. Her legs tense, knees straight with pointed toes, grey, moist skin with blood trailing across the torso. Oozing from the slight incisions, dark red clotted blood-marks ankles and wrists severely bruised with twisted patterns.

There were six women before their deaths all looking like they're in their early twenties: beautiful, dark hair, big curls of silky hair… they could be of mixed race… tawny skin tone or a really good tan… smooth naturally oiled skin all different colour eyes, intense, bright, piercing. Report was soiled, brown or old.

Where did these come from? Is it real?

There were reports typed from a typewriter with no author, I read the reports summarising:

Six victims of the serial murders Catacá; Each with five cuts along the torso. Two under the breast. One below the belly button. Two above the ovaries. Victims bleed out and had been found in various locations around the desert. No obvious links unique to another other than the attack.

Unsure if this is a medical report or just a note, I question everything.

What is this?

Shuffling through reports of the six women who died from attacks similar to Sharron Mall's, I went through, picture after picture. Then, I was stunned, and paused, seeing one of the victims in the pictures was of Camielle Charles, her attack before and after.

This picture, she resembles me a bit.

I twisted her picture for a better view. Around the eyes and the cheeks as she stared back at me posed in a bamboo chair with a scenic background. I put my hand into the envelope searching for anything more.

Empty.

Hum, that was unaccommodating.

Where are the rest of the reports?

Why is this coming to me one page at a time?

Who sent this?

Behind the pictures a stamp of the Divinish Police Station laid out my next stop.

OK then, but should I loop Sam?

My subconscious for once agrees we need more to bring it forward to the team. I was curious.

More research then?

I thought… I typed in the search engine… 'The Zemand ceremonies'.

The Zeman legend celebrates in threes. Every three years one of the creatures will be chosen by the reading of the skies and stars, a task given to the master priest of the Zemand.

There are seven first creatures of the Zemand religion. Berána and Sevínah, the mother and father creatures of the Zemand, the first creatures of the earth had five sons, each son given a gift for their talent and therefore became their charge.

The Zemand gods are not a reflection of man or animal but a mutated version of them both. Each god took on an animal form and an image has been made of them as their creature.

Ceremonies:

For Berána, his animal form: a bear. The men would dress as bears, hunt and sacrifice a bear in his honour, the Zemand believe this sacrifice will bring them strength.

For Sevínah, her animal form: an eagle. They would gather an eagle's feathers and plant crops for she brings them prosperity.

For Cedérus, his animal form: a cobra. Blood ceremonies for cleansing, beginning of wars and revival.

For Alena, the wolf, they would decorate their homes and stay three days in the wilderness, if they spot a wolf whilst they camp it is a sign of wealth and prosperity for three years.

Tajin, the tiger, a coming-of-age ceremony for warriors of the Zemand faith would be held, boys at twelve would take a leap of courage and be marked by a tiger's paw.

Saleen, the rabbit, he is known to be the wisest, they'll make paintings and crafts, document their lives.

Jikah, the pig, there would be another coming-of-age ceremony for young boys over age twelve. He is known to be the noble one, Zemand will need to complete a noble task to become a man, or they will honour their youth by playing games and celebrate the last of their youth.

Not quite what I was looking for.

I said to myself stacking the files and taking notes. My phone rang, I was plopped back into the now, holding my chest from the fright and broken thoughts I exhaled taking up the receiver.

"Davis!" I answered the desk phone without looking continuing my notes.

"What in the actual, *fuck*, Shana?" The sound of his voice like ice, sending chills though my spine, inducing palpitations, freezing me in place. "… Sam didn't tell you to call me?"

He growled loudly and angrily through the phone. It made my heart skip a beat. I was caught off guard.

Shit!

The four-day delayed fight has caught up to me. All the events of today and the forgotten call. Unprepared and muddled to a reply, lost is my fury and fear, now flooding is his. I took the moment to examine my actions versus his anger unable to sort the difference between us two.

Sam did offer her phone. My subconscious is back, and annoying.

I peeked over my laptop and there is no one sitting at their desks.

I have definitely lost track of time. Rational is also not helping.

My saliva thickened and I closed my eyes recollecting the way I left things; I was angry at him for lying to me, putting me into a compromising situation and making me feel like a fool.

Though that was sort of my fault too. My conscious is really, really not helping.

After the press conference he disappeared and I took the anger out on the... my breath hitched.

I messed up the apartment.

Double crap!

"Did you... did you fuck up the apartment, and leave?" he hesitates saying, with some hurt.

I swallowed hard, now understanding his reaction to the mess. The pleasant thoughts now gone, the delight I felt, lost. My throat instantly dried.

I couldn't reply.

My words gone at the ambush.

"What the fuck is going on with you!" he yelled again.

The wave of my anger returns in the moments of his pause.

I was made a fool.

All this time he lied to me. Inhaling to speak he said,

"If... If..." He's stammering with breaks in his voice. "... If Danielle... hadn't called me..."

Instantaneously, the vision of him sitting at the bedside with blotched eyes and a thickened beard came back to me. I shiver, forcing to relive the entire ordeal of being attacked. Guilt raised slightly.

What have I done?

"... Eric," I called his name apologetically finding my voice, the sadness gathered with a welt in my throat.

There was another pause between us.

I wiped my hand over my face looking down at the desk, the article in view. Sharron's picture and her new statement. Sharron's name calling comes back to frightened me. The instinct to hide comes back with a sense of someone spying. The sense of urgency filled me.

I see an impossible deadline he laid out for me with the files laid across my desk, the door with the opportunity to change and I want to walk through.

There is too much at stake for me.

I need to delay this fight.

"… I'm sorry!" I whisper to Eric, no remorse. *Not sorry!* My subconscious makes a face and the next few words left me. "… Can we do this later?" I try deferring the argument again or standing my professional ground.

"No. I'm on my way over…" he announced, uncompromising with no warmth.

My heartbeat increased.

Why is he doing this? "Eric, please."

"Today's your prenatal appointment…" he answered creepily and I shut my eyes raking my untamed mane.

Shit! I screamed inward.

"… And I know you forgot." He pointed out, his voice has gotten low and icy.

He's right. I did!

I cursed again at myself for forgetting.

It would be a long and uncomfortable ride to Divinish North, I thought.

There would be plenty of time to argue. I frown at the lost hope of delaying this argument.

Crap, crap, crap!

The photos stare at me and I at them. I need to help these women that have not had justice for twenty-five years. I need to delay him. I began scribbling, writing some questions and possible places to look.

"I am nearly finished with some paperwork…" I rush the research, but also begging his delay, squeezing the receiver between my ear and shoulder tapping the keyboard fast to finish today's report that I postponed for curiosity.

"I am your *director*…" He reminds me coldly and the masked calm hit me.

I gasped at his pulling rank. A rekindling of not only why I am annoyed at him, the reason I believe, Acting Director Kane has approached me with such contempt. Not to mention, others like Young and Aaliyah who are convinced our relationship is nothing more than superficial. My heart sunk along with the hard work I put in and the drive to solve this deepens.

Fuck! I mouth it.

"I understand." He has cemented the special treatment that I loathe and others will throw back at me. "… Get your stuff and meet me downstairs, *now*." He switches from icy to shouty.

"That's not fair." I choke my hurt shutting my eyes with a long exhale.

He's flaunting being director in my face!

"Is that paperwork more important than our baby?"

His tone softens washing a different wave of emotions over me that keeps a hold at my throat. I look down at the small rise of my belly.

Ouch! "That's not fair either Eric." My voice is laden with it croaking.

There is no winning.

"Hurry up. I am here." He seems to be back to a mixture of anxiousness and care.

"Fuck!" I slump my head in my hand.

"What did you say?" his voice echoed from the receiver.

Oh shit! I said that out loud!

I panicked the phone slipped from my shoulder bouncing on the table before I caught it and hung up. Keeping my hands on the receiver gazing at the streaks of sweat and dirt beneath, attempting to control my breathing.

Shit. Shit. *Shit.*

CHAPTER THIRTY-SEVEN

"Mrs Hall." I held my eyes still and even tried not to flinch at the name. The ride here, Eric voiced his concern, and so did I, loudly. Neither of us admitted to being wrong. The argument ended in stalemate as the two-hour drive came to an end. Both reserving to focus on the appointment, we entered, civil.

"… The baby looks good by the measurements, eighteen weeks. Your pregnancy is moving along as expected. Any headaches, dizziness or nausea?"

Doctor James scrutinised, the monitor pressing the transducer probe into my exposed lower abdomen glistened with gel. I shook my head.

"Umm mmm."

Mumbling, I cannot help but inspect Doctor James' fine head of black and grey hair and his eyeglasses pulled down on his nose as he looks over them.

What is the point of him wearing those!

I can tell the baby is not enjoying the invasion and, neither am I.

Eric's ear to ear grin and total focus on the screen is making me weary. All I see is a black and white blob, though the doctor is explaining it to me. My face is scrunched from the discomfort and confusion on the monitor. I hardly listen to the explanation that's causing my head to spin and grip the side of the examination table. My vision from the doctor to Eric to the monitor utterly baffled.

"Can we know the gender?"

My eyes widened.

Eric's patience lasted longer than I expected.

"I am not too sure how I feel about peeping at the baby's parts," I say and Eric squints.

"I would prefer to know." He is not backing down and neither am I.

"Doesn't it have to be decided by both parents to be revealed?"

I push back and Eric narrowed his eyes further. A fight is on the horizon.

"Maybe in a couple of weeks."

Doctor James breaks the argument pressing the eyeglasses higher up, his nose. I shake my head still with the idle thought of his glasses wearing etiquette. The baby is awake. I feel the tapping and resistance to the probe. My tummy shook with a ripple.

"Wow did you feel that? The baby turned its back," Doctor James asks.

"Yes, the baby isn't enjoying this either," I pouted and say my complaint loud, then changed to softer. "... But the kicks are a bit stronger now."

I noted the discomfort from that movement. Eric's grin faded. I folded my lips and avoided his eyes. Seeing only a pout from my view. I can't tell but I know his attempt to be emotionless. I crinkled my eyebrows with a sigh thinking I should explain.

"At first it felt like bubbles or someone is tapping me from the inside. Now, it's like an actual kick to say, 'don't bother me'."

Hopefully that will take an item off our looming fight list.

Doctor James chuckled, tilting to me with care in his pale-blue eyes. Doctor James insists on shortening my last name, maybe because of laziness, or because he only acknowledges me as a part of Eric.

"That's normal. The baby will get stronger."

The doctor chuckled again. I looked up at Eric whose mood has shifted. I am partly surprised he hadn't given me a stare for my comment. The doctor gives me tissues to wipe the gel off. Eric seems wounded and the doctor turns his back to wash his hands.

Eric's very quiet, this concerns me.

"When is the next visit?"

I try to recover the excitement unsuccessfully applying any in my voice.

"One month, Mrs Hall. You're progressing as expected and your concussion has cleared. Your blood pressure is down and there are no complications."

The doctor's list was all positive. Something I felt from the nagging that Eric would have leapt around the office hearing. But we both notice Eric's dreary expression.

"… You might be able to see the gender then if you'd like to know."

The doctor pleasantly touches Eric's shoulder.

"I'm not too sure how I feel about that though." I glare at Eric, expecting some resistance but he still hasn't recovered his sulk.

"Continue the prenatal vitamins and I'll see you in a month."

The doctor left the room. I cleared my tummy, pulling the tissue out from my pants waist rolling on my side to get up. I tidied my shirt and pulled on my jacket. Eric barely concedes my existence as we mutely made it to the car.

"Can we get some food?"

I try breaking his esoteric console. He opened the car door for me to get in but says nothing. I sat in and he closes the door.

No food then?

I concluded internally. He walked around the car his head bowed. Opened the door, sat, placing the keys into the cup holder pressing the ignition and ceased movements still looking at the ignition button.

"When did the baby start moving?"

His voice loaded with regret. My eyes widened and I brace choosing my words carefully. Tilting towards him I shrugged my shoulders.

"I don't know, about two, three weeks ago."

Is that what his mood was about?

He turns the engine over the soft humming in the background. He leaned over to drive then paused to ask,

"Were you going to tell me?" He is almost inaudible, his lips hesitantly parted.

"Is this a trick question?" The words flew out in disbelief.

His eyes begging for an answer and I am cornered. So, I gave the details.

"You weren't home. I felt it, a strange bubble inside," I explained touching the bump. "… I thought that was gas." I giggled. "… Until I felt it again." I shrug. "… Then you ambushed me at the director's meeting, disappeared at the press conference…"

I summarised the past three weeks pinching my straight nose bridge, weighing my temperament. I sense his sadness. I huff.

"I cannot be responsible for your absence, Eric. You wanted a baby, it's here."

I pulled his big hands over my bump. His palm completely covered my midsection. I placed my hand over his. The baby tapped us. His breath hitched and eyes alight with excitement whipping his head to me and then my tummy.

"… If you want to be a part of the journey, then, be here. You've promised me great things with this new job, keep them. Ideally, I would have waited until we finished Cáhilt to begin to talk about another child but…"

I trailed and released his hand. He kept it there until the baby stopped. He unbuckled his seat belt, leaned across the car surprising me with a passionate kiss. Caressing my face, I felt that magnetic pull between us. That pull that causes me to forget everything and become lost in him. I closed my eyes briefly to feel what I've missed for three weeks.

As he began moving his hands across my shoulders and down my arm, I opened my eyes and defused. I pleaded against his mouth.

"We're in the parking lot of a hospital!"

He closed his mouth still holding my lips inches away from his and snorted loudly. Moving his lips brushing up against mine cursing and temporarily retreated then buckled in.

"Seat belt Shana!" he admonishes cheerfully. "… What would you like to eat?" His voice once again in charge and excited.

"Something spicy and quick."

He beams at me pulling out from the park.

We drove into the city the tall buildings, bright lights shining through the car the busy streets reminded me of Ceda. I am gratified in the moment. His face concentrated folding his lips exposing his dimples through his light beard.

We drove past our new headquarters into what appears to be the middle of the city. He glanced at me. We're both ascertain each other as he made a surprise turn into an underground parking of a new building.

"Where are we going?"

I hope he doesn't want us to do it here!

I am anticipating the ways to tell him no, if I could. His smile and decorum sit like an aphrodisiac speaking to me deep into my loins. Inside, I clench as my heart quickens, pulling my knees together, both my hands clinging to the chair moist as I try holding the urges.

"Being director has some perks." He smiles and I can only think of pouncing.

"What do you mean?"

I am excited not paying full attention to his words only watching his full lips move between his neat moustache and beard. He pulls into a park up against a white wall. Few cars parked around us, he suspiciously looks around and stopped the engine.

Then, he comes out and opened my door. I closed my eyes a second remembering the afternoon drive and making love in the car like two teenagers. I smiled naughtily for a second then thought of the 'what ifs,

"No no."

I playfully refused. He stood with the door open waiting.

"We're not going to do anything here, at least not today."

He assures me with his grin I am a tad disappointed and relieved. I clamber out but cannot hide my smile. I feel my face changing colour. I am a bit embarrassed. He took my hand locking the car and leading me to an elevator. He presses twenty-three.

High!

An idle thought. He has his hands meshed with mine as we go up our gleaming reflection, my face noticeably rosy. I rest my head on his bulging biceps wrapping the other hand around his arm.

We look perfect!

I savoured the moment and the door chimes. In one swift move he swoops me off my feet, a shriek left me.

"Oh, Mrs Hall, packing on a few!" he groaned in emphasis.

I gasp. "Mr Hall, I think it's because someone is taking a free ride."

"Hum, well he's only there for the next four to five months."

"*He!*" I complained.

"Or she…" he corrected then pecked my lips.

It is a beautiful layout of a reception room with two two-seated couches, beige with red featherlike fur. Surrounded by a light wood and glass centre table facing a high light wood frame. A black electric fireplace with red and orange lights dancing in the dark. Above there was a light wood thirty-inch mirror perfectly blended the floor, walls and centre table.

A dim light lit the countertops of the modern kitchen with a built-in oven standing height. White cupboards with frosted glass and under cupboard lights. A Belfast sink, a breakfast bar, behind that a door and stairs next to the beginning of the kitchen. There was a large glass window overlooking the city and another door next to the window along a white wall. He flicked on the lights.

"Which room do you want to do it in first?" His eyes lit with excitement.

"Eric!"

I slapped his chest playful. He leers, I know he is serious.

"… Put me down and we can explore."

"Upstairs, there's the master bedroom the ensuite. All you need to know right now." He rushed his words.

"Are you in a hurry Mr Hall?"

"To make love to you… always."

He leans over to kiss me. I blush and tingled at the same time.

These damn hormones!

He walks with me cradled in his arms through the threshold his smile white and wide staring his brown soft eyes at me. My breathing increased and the memory of the foreplay in the car comes to mind and I grin at him.

He briskly passed a large window twinkling the view of the city at night it touches the top and bottom of the apartment between the lounge and the kitchen.

Amazing!

He kissed me hard sucking me in, exploring my mouth, our tongues dancing and my senses heighten in anticipation. He carries me up the stairs through the hallways into the softly decorated white wallpapered walls and pastel king-sized bed, gently laying me down, our mouths fused.

I lay in a dark room. The sound of something dripping gets louder. I called out a loud 'hello' for someone. I hear the breath of something deep and slow constant, in tune with the dripping sounds. I can feel the presence of someone. I called out again and something grabbed my hands. I hear my name in the distance.

I scream sitting up and pulling the sheets with me.

"Shana!" Eric is calling me.

I am sweating with enraged breathing. Confused, looking around at the strange room. A light coloured wall and wall papers.

"Shana, it's a dream!"

Eric is sitting up next to me with his hands engulfing my shoulders. I am breathing shallow scanning the room. *Where am I?* Partly worried but comforted that he is next to me.

"... Shana, you're OK."

He reminds me once again and my staring softens as he puts his arms around me. I flinch at first, then whinge. My tummy hardening by the second, stiffing and feeling very uncomfortable. I still don't have control over my breathing for a new reason now.

"It's OK... it's OK babes." Eric strokes my hair. "... Do you want to talk about it?"

I swiftly gape at him glancing the bright red time highlighted by the clock on the side table five past six.

My tummy still feels like rocks and I grind the agony on my teeth, rubbing the bump, breathing laboured.

"Is the baby, OK?" his voice alarmed,

I almost snapped.

"It's a bit uncomfortable," I confess in honesty.

"Do you want to go to the hospital?"

I shot him a look. "I'm not in labour. I think. The baby must have gotten frightened," I concluded.

He smirked. "Good thing he's in there then." He caressed my bump and it got softer. "... Magic hands can put him to sleep even when he's in there," Eric boasted.

I fluttered my eyes annoyed. "It'll be more useful once he's out."

"Oh, so we agree it's a boy then?"

I got out the bed taking a pillow with me then launching it at Eric's head. He caught it emphasising a groan.

"Dream on Hall!" I padded to the door inside the bedroom, assumed it was an ensuite.

"Where are you going?" he grabbed my wrist.

"It is still a workday. I have a busy schedule, and someone is squeezing my bladder."

He released my hand with a grin rolling flat on his back with his hands behind, his head his muscle taunting me. Wearing a black boxers peeping at me ambling to the bathroom with a sigh.

"I know, but if you feel uncomfortable again, call me. We will visit the doctor again."

I strategically sucked my teeth going into the ensuite. He goes on.

"… I've got to go back to Ceda for a few days, for work."

I heard him from inside the beautiful four-piece grey stoned bathroom. I sat on the toilet.

Relief!

The room smells new, the paint, grout and the tiles. But I am distracted by his confession and I try to be neutral and non-judgemental. This time listening attentively.

"Oh." The only words that I can conjure to fit the criteria.

The last time he went there he came back as my boss.

I am wary thinking.

"Assignment?" I asked this time waiting for the bomb or other shoe.

Getting up, flushing and washing my hands. He strode his long steps into the space, his boxers and bare back, standing next to me. Both his hands on either side of the sink, flexing unconsciously, his buff arms around me, staring at me through the mirror. I clench at his morning glory or just well-endowed form poking at me as he opened his legs to line himself with my ass.

"Mmm hum," he groans nuzzling my hair. "… Just a lot of … meetings." He shrugs kissing behind my ear. "… Not anything worth worrying about."

"OK," I nod looking into the sink trying to remain positive. *Is this how it will be?* I question his promise to myself.

Eric, hearing the disappointment layered with a lower tone though I am trying to be neutral. He held my shoulders turning me to his direction, bending so our faces are close.

"You should be able to get me if you need to…" I look away from him. "… but I'm supposed to be, unreachable." He cups my chin tilting my head upward to see his beautiful brown eyes, but I frown.

What is that supposed to mean?

"OK," I singsong with a sigh.

Shifting from my right to left to right foot. I want to ask more but instead I sighed, coming out of his hold to begin my morning routine. He stops me.

"We also have to discuss security."

There's the other shoe.

I scrunch my face. Opening my mouth, "What?" But he cut me quickly.

"Before you protest, I am not going to do anything, until we have a full discussion when I get back. But we may need to, assign you a bodyguard, given my position in the S.D.A.F. and the fact that you're my wife. Even though you are a federal agent. This has to happen."

I pout, wanting to object but appreciating his consideration, already plotting.

Taking a deep breath, I nod at him, as his reflective browns ogle into my hazels.

"Do you still have my card?"

He interrupts and I groan.

Where is he going with this? "Yes," I whisper.

"Good." He pecked my lips. "… I moved all of your remaining things from the apartment to here."

"You did what?" *He, moved my stuff?* My subconscious is standing in shock.

"This is where I want you to stay, especially when I am not in town and more so if you don't want a security detail."

His tone was condescending and I refrain from addressing his insulting statement to erupt from the looming fight, but I did emphasise rolling my eyes. He huffed.

"You need to get something for Friday,"

"Why?" I frown.

"I've been invited to the Zemand opening festival ceremony and ball… And, you're coming with me."

I recalled watching the ceremony with my best friends when we were teenagers and even seeing Emily attend, twice with her mother. The formal do has me nervous.

"… Plus, you can get more clothes. You're growing out of them anyway." He pointed out calling me fat technically.

Wanting to argue, I rational. *Don't fall into the trap.* I folded my lips only two words escaping.

"OK Hall." I ended as an answer to a command.

He peered at me for a second then we began to move around starting our morning routine. He got a toothbrush from a standing grey and white storage with a tube of toothpaste handing it to me as if creepily reading my mind.

"Are you OK getting something for our wedding on Sunday? It doesn't matter the cost," he says leaving the bathroom.

My face softens and my eyes widened.

Shit forgot about that!

"Is it this weekend already?" I accidentally say out loud and he knows I'm panicking. I turned my back to him.

"You forgot, didn't you?" he is saying returning to the bathroom and I avoid his gape.

I have no excuse but. "Baby brain!"

I heard that somewhere and tried it on as an excuse, bowed and knotted my fingers hearing his ruffling something behind me.

"Shana-brain." I turn ready to defend myself and I was taken aback. He was naked.

"Get out!"

I playfully resist this distracting man.

"What, I need a shower!" He is coy.

It only took that brief delay in answering for him to enfold his arms around me fusing our lips in a heated kiss.

CHAPTER THIRTY-EIGHT

Eric is the most distracting man, ever! He sure knows how to divert my anger. After he left me in his new loft, I took a few minutes wondering around the kitchen for something to eat before making my way to work.

I am beaming strolling into the suboffice thinking about our morning of shower sex instead of paying attention. It is unbelievably quiet. There's not usual rustling or anyone busying themselves at my entrance. Noticeably, no one has approached me shoving papers in my face or reminding me of my diary.

Where's Noel?

I squint pondering, with a pause ahead of my office. Boxes are everywhere, some half-opened others piled atop another and for a baffled second, I panicked before the answer came.

She must be at the Jade building.

Another directive awaits me, I exhaled measuredly. These along with the dreadful Acting Director Kane is Eric. The morning after glow leaves with the thought. Lazily, I crawled into the office. There are a few boxes left at the side for me from my assistant, I'm sure. Also, certain she is setting up my office as we speak.

Sam, I guess was out chasing Sharron Mall's new theory of the scaly rapist.

She is like a dog with a bone that one.

I shake my head appreciating her efforts despite our differences.

But that is what makes her the best at what she does.

She would never hear me say that... ever.

I strolled into the office wearing the last of my clothes that still fit, stretching one of my favourite skirts in the process. Though the top is loose and the skirt comfortably pulled over my tummy, I am fighting the need for maternity clothes, getting fatter and not looking or feeling like myself.

I fired up my laptop to check if anything is needed urgently. We are also expected to be moved by the end of the day, or so the detailed email from Amy Welch explains. I rolled my eyes picturing the words coming out from her.

It will be weird!

Seeing Amy looking after Eric's office needs and him in the top floor office, I assume. I shook the memory of my first directors meeting. I hope it'll be the last, seeing how I was ambushed and wondered if Eric has disclosed our personal relationship.

He must have, with the ridiculous talk about security detail.

I wagged my head thinking of the endless implications of who knows and who doesn't. I pray it never passes around as office gossip.

My diary isn't at its usual capacity but I am still busy. It is good though, otherwise, I would be forced to think of going to a strange new apartment without Danielle and Eric to keep me company. I thought about moving around my desk to reach for my diary.

I will need to contact Paula to see where she's got on the 'incidents', I quote the word in mockery taking a deep breath.

Acting Director Kane says there are three, I can name two. Sam-Sam's death, and my attack.

What is the third?

The thought passed then I glimpse those pictures again, still spread across my desk like a crime scene. My thinking has been shifted successfully.

There must be more to this.

I gathered the photos and reports into a folder packing them in a box with the rest of the case files and sealing them for moving. The reports were made by an officer of the L.D.O. There was a bit to complete before lunch.

I ambled through the mall during my lunch break. Parked on the curb of the Jade, leaving the boxes at the suboffice to be collected, touched base with Eric, who reminded me about shopping.

Honestly!

Whose husband reminds their wife about shopping, with, their credit card?

I argue as I stroll in cautiously to a bridal store, gaping at the dresses that mildly interest me hung on the manikins in the window.

They cannot fit!

I am shaking my head in disgust at every one of them.

"Shannan Davis!"

An unrecognisable voice called from behind me. I swerved around. Spotting the evenly tanned man, slim fitting shirt folded up to his elbows. Black straight-leg pants and shiny dress shoes.

Brian Kumal stood staring his amber eyes sparkling at mine. Handsome as ever, his hair longer than before at the top and low at the sides. His beard was in a-need-to-shave state and had spikes, just the way I like. The air intensifies. I suddenly lick my lips as my mouth goes dry.

"Hi."

My voice is soft and high-pitched. I am both startled and stirred, heat rose a centigrade or two. I am certain the glass condensate. Fine sweat marks engulfed my face. Its gloss reflected on the steaming store windows down my only white maternity shirt and the stretched black skirt I pulled over my bump, exposing more legs than I am used to.

He stepped a foot away from me leaning in for an embrace. I crossed my arms breathing and closed my eyes imagining someplace cooler. I opened, straight hair sticks to my neck curling in contact with the sweat.

"Shannan."

He wakes me with his smooth base tone. I cleared my throat.

"Brian, how are you?"

My voice is still a pitch too high.

"I can see you still haven't completed the ceremony."

I blinked a couple of times.

"Still forward I see." I took a step back feeling the polarity pull.

What is wrong with me? The moments shared this morning comes right back and the places Eric touched tingled again. I strive to pull my thighs together.

"Caught you at a bad time?"

"Always!" *Where are those words coming from?* "... Ah... no..." I clear my throat again. "... Now how can I help you Mr Kumal?"

"This is a pleasant surprise. I didn't expect to see you."

His smooth voice flows through the air and I watched his smooth pink lips move trying to avoid mouthing his words. I moved my eyes from his gaze clearing my throat again.

"Neither did I?" The octaves in my throat still aren't cooperating and I screeched.

"I heard a commotion in the alley that night you left…" He steps into my space lowering his voice and his smooth full lips mesmerise me. "… I didn't see anyone when I got out. I hoped you got to your 'case' safely."

My legs wobble and I want to move but he has caught me and a wave of desire tingled through me. I tilted my head back staring up into the amber highlights in his eyes.

"Maybe if you were a gentleman and walked me to my car, you would have been sure."

I smile and he is inches away from my face. My breathing enraged popping my bust up and down. I use all my will to keep my body in position. The warmth from his body radiates to mine and my cheeks flush.

"I should have." He feels regret. "I'm sorry."

"Is that what you are hoping to gain today, Brian?"

The now regular tap from my bump wakes me from his enthralling hold and my body relaxes. Hunger is growing. Brian steps back. With a sudden awareness in his gawp at the rise of my tummy.

"Well Agent Davis, the time we've been apart you've been busy."

I tug at the maternity shirt revealing the small bump underneath and smiled.

"Extremely!" My voice went high-pitch again.

He grins. "We must, uh, have coffee… sometime." His voice is laden with hope and I am squinting at him confused by his gawk.

"You do know I am married." I held up my hand showing him my wedding ring effectively bringing the shirt gathering at the top of my noticeable belly.

"Not legally… to him…" He smirks. "… Yes." He keeps his eyes in mine.

Humph… "And you are." I let my hands fall at my sides.

"Legally… but…" He trailed with a tense voice.

I step back again, his hold released. "Good day, Mr Kumal."

I turn on one-eighty, swiftly exiting the store without a dress before his lusting takes hold of me again. My heart beating out of my chest.

What is it with this guy?

I was able to catch my breath at a distant bench. Turning back, he was gone. My thoughts and reasoning are not quite what it should be around him. All I feel is a sexual drive, I cannot grasp as to why. I am in love with Eric and has been for more than seven years. But there is something different and unsettling about this man.

Arguing inward, about the strange reunion with Brian, I am rustling back to the office. Moving my thoughts away from Brian, I began making a to-do list.

First and foremost, the crime scene photos that awaits me hidden in my desk draws. Moving my feet quickly then, I find myself standing outside the L.D.O.

How did I get here?

Though, it is a short distance from the Jade building my body has carried me somewhere I thought.

I would have eventually gone but …

I huffed at myself.

Since I'm here.

I measured the significance of this building walking up to it. The tinted building with blue trimmings it was old and the moss residue along the stairs, reflected the care to this building.

Similar to my office the layout and smell of refurbished furniture and fresh paint. I walked pass a small waiting room with light blue paint large plant pots with palms trees. I couldn't tell if they were real.

The detail much more noticeable from my last visit. Advancing towards the front desk I identified myself to the duty sergeant. It grew decibels quieter instantly making me uncomfortable and eager to leave. But there is a need to gather whatever physical files from Camielle Charles and any other Catacá case to gain contentment.

"Most of the files should be in evidence lock up or in the archive somewhere."

The duty sergeant explains. I was guided in silence to an eerie room with one door entrance. I signed the clipboard form and the male officer pointed at a door down a corridor leaving before I could ask anything. It has been many years but it is still worth a try to know whether we were dealing with the same murderer.

The light from the hall lit the dark room. I placed my hands along the wall on the inside of the room turning on the light. After the click it flickered halogen soft light that flickered constantly to the end of the room.

Get the boxes and get out!

I have to remind myself feeling unnerving. I walked through ten isles of dusty boxes packed on iron shelving four rows taller than me but stacked randomly. After about an hour I recovered a small box. Hard to believe six murders, a possible seventh victim surviving this attack can produce such poor evidence.

Seven women lives ending in a small box.

I sigh discerning the one victim in my investigation and the brutal level of paperwork involved as it compared to this.

The door was hinged on the inside and I couldn't carry the box and open the door. I noticed a big book on a shelf closest to the door and concocted a brilliant plan.

I could use this to keep the door open.

I retrieved the book, opened the door to its widest and dropped the book on the inside of the metal door. The heavy door slid a bit then stopped.

Yes!

The lights began to flicker slowly.

There must be a shortage somewhere in the switch.

It has been glitchy since I came in, I try to ration for comfort. I went into the musty room again to quickly take the box. The light went out.

Stupid switch!

There was some light from the hall that shone in creating a guide. I put the box down again. I exhaled, wasting the moment. The light became smaller and I heard the book sliding. Eerie, creaking the iron hinges in the process.

Shit!

I ran towards the fading light reaching it only as it shut, the metal sheets covering the door echoed a loud vibrating sound that jumped me.

No, no, no!

I huffed slapping the metal door in anger. The sound of something fell off the shelved came from behind me. I scare automatically turning toward it knowing, I was not alone. In a panic.

My unsteady hand feeling for the handle through the dark, turning as my breathing increases. The hairs on my skin prickles.

I felt him behind, skimming his tough hand through the curls of my hair making a fist. Forcing my face forward against the door. Leaning his body weight against me blowing his cigarette breath on my exposed neck.

By instinct my hand went up to free my hair. I step forward to gain a footing but feeling the cold metal through the light cotton shirt. My other hand on the door in line with my chest needing to push away from the door and he grinds his hips into me.

"Ah!"

The only words I can conjure as my bump grazes the sheet of steel. Using all my strength, resisting his squeeze. He steps his feet shifting between mine spreading them apart, gyrating his erection on my ass tugging my hair tighter.

"Please!"

I beg between shallow breaths. The tears escape warming my cheek and pooling on the iron door. Barely able to swallow the building saliva. He is silent, but his other hand is making its way up my thigh with a handful of my stretched skirt. I shiver, he groans deep in his throat exhaling the smoky breath. Rubbing his nose against my neck and inhaling deeply against my hair.

"P-please, I."

I can't say anything else. My nose flares running as quickly as the tears and he pushes harder against me, then, he whispered against my ear.

"Don't scream, you hear?"

He breaks the silence revealing a funny accent; creepy, familiar like the man who attacked me in the alley. I dread. He tightened the hold in my hair tilting my head back to his lips. Opening his mouth again, breathing shallow, his tongue made contact with my neck.

"Eeek."

I cried as he licked from under my collar, up to behind my ear. My stomach and everything deep within clenched. I squealed softly squirming under duress. He paused, sucking on my earlobe. I still, not able to breathe as the deep chill took over my entire body. I trembled uncontrollably the tears cannot cease.

He reaches the end of my skirt his rough hand made contact with the scar across my upper thighs. I break into a cry. Then, he took a step backwards taking me slightly away from the door. Releasing my skirt snaking his hand across my belly, my baby moved.

"Feisty, just like mum eh!"

He tilts us pulling open the door. Taking another step, he slid through the crack. Not before gliding his tough hands over my breast. And releasing my hair on his way out. My hands in the air, frozen in terror. A few seconds pass. I stay in position one hand in my hair the other on the door tears dripping out my eyes holding my breath, withering.

CHAPTER THIRTY-NINE

Slowly I exhaled, the adrenalin slows. My hands flopped at my sides helpless. Not even on the day Eric and I met, I have felt so... powerless.

Ten... nine... eight... seven... six... five... four... three... two... one...

Counting down from ten twice. Finally, I gained feelings in my legs, my baby moving again. I caressed the movements trembling with one hand the other went over my mouth choking the scream.

My baby.

Doubling over thinking of all the 'what ifs' the weeping flowed out onto my hands. My chest tightens. I can't steady the shaking nor catch my breath.

What just happened?

I try to process and build the courage to leave that room. Counting from ten to one again. Fight or flight; I fled down the deserted halls covering my mouth. Into the first door I could find. The ladies room. Kicking in all three cubicles being certain I was alone. I screamed hoarse standing behind the main door crying. Thinking of his intentions made it worse, questioning mine motives for being there.

There was a push at the door. I dashed into a cubicle locking it stifling the flowing tears. The person came in, used the toilet, then left. Minutes later, I unlocked the door. Facing me, was a large mirror behind the sinks.

My hair slovenly, eyes tear marks, along my rosy cheeks and the corner of my eyes. The reflection of someone I do not recognise. The scar on my forehead a slither, red marks, of how firmly I had been pushed against the iron door.

This woman I don't know.

Another lady entered jumping me at the entrance.

"Oh, sorry, I didn't mean to scare you," she said by the way.

I shook my head, feeling the tightness of my chest increasing. I grinned at her, screaming in my head. She went into the toilet my eyes fell upon the glisten remains of this man's saliva tainted on my neck.

An oncoming weep-fest to follow when my phone rang, startling me. My speeding heartbeat passes quick, I glanced, Noel. I shut my eyes taking that moment. The woman exited and the call went to voicemail.

I don't ever want to feel like that ever again.

I decided as the victim reflected at me through the mirror.

That is why I learned to fight damn it!

I shout at myself inwardly gaping at my sorrowful self. The reflection irritated me. The reddened face, tears and bruises. Anger surfaced and I couldn't breathe. My phone rang again. It was Eric.

I exhaled the fear as the call ended.

Vengeance surfaced over the fear.

After a few seconds it rang again. I answered.

"Sorry, I uh, was in the toilet." My voice wavered with emotions.

"Shana," he answered, then asks. "What's wrong?" He reads me like a book. I blew out attempting to steady my voice.

"I-I, I'm…" The ball grew with trepidation. My nose burns and heat covered my face. I want so badly for him to be here, to rescue and protect me.

Stop now Shana! My subconscious made her way to the top boiling with anger.

This is why you pursued law enforcement. You're not a victim Shana!

"Shannan, what happened?"

Eric asks more forcefully breathing into the phone. I hear his waiting and I know calling me by my full name usually precedes a command.

Tread carefully, my subconscious warns. "I- I, I'm not feeling so good."

Sort of true… I fight the truth.

"Sickness?"

The first thing he thinks? "Why does it always have to be about this pregnancy?"

The anger fell on him. *Shit!*

"OK." He breathes, loudly into the phone somewhat waving a white flag.

"Sorry, sorry…" I exhaled choking the terror.

"Just checking in," he says softly into the phone. His impassive tone is waiting and I take a breather to calm, trying not to give anything away.

"Thanks, I'll be OK." I speak into what would be.

You will be.

Saying with some confidence to convince myself.

"I'll be home soon." He listens to my excessive shuddering breathing before adding, "… Call you later?" His words wavering and pauses with at least ten seconds of silence. "… I love you," he says, waiting again.

I cover my mouth whimpering in the memory of my assault replying quick, "Love you too."

And hung up, putting my phone face down on the sink. I put both my hands on either side of the face basin glancing in the mirror unhappy with what I see. My eyebrows crinkle, I squeeze my eyes shut wringing out the last of the tears I will shed today. I rake in all the professional façade I can and began thinking.

Paula!

I dial.

"Shana!"

She answered after the second ring. I exhaled spilling the words quickly.

"Hey, can you come meet me in the L.D.O.?"

"I am actually here. You asked me to get the evidence from the cold cases."

She reminds me of my lapse and the cause of my emit distress. I nodded as if she can see me turning the speakers upward my cheek for a brief squeal. Then I went back to professional holding the phone correctly.

"Do you have your kit with you? I am in the ladies' room, ground floor."

She paused.

"Are you OK?"

I exhaled truthfully. "Not really…"

I hung up.

A few minutes later Paula entered, her white coat draped over her light blue camisole and a silver case in her hand.

"Shana!"

She sees my terror. I put my palm up to her greeting her at the door. Gripping the professionalism by the nails, I watched as her expression shifted as she sees the distress across my face. I swallowed hard.

This cannot leave this room. I agree with my subconscious.

"I need you to do something for me." Shakingly, I make my request gathering thoughts to the place where I function best.

"What?" Her tone exhausted.

"Um, this is to stay in this room." I hesitated softly, as a fresh batch of sadness pooled.

"Shana, I don't like secrets."

"Please!" I gulp, the damn is wavering and my vision is cloudy from the tears.

"What is it, Shana?"

Her blue eyes popped at me. She steps closer to me lifting her hand to rest hers on mine. I pulled away raking some confidence with it. I need her word.

"Please!" The desperation groans in my voice.

"Sure," she singsongs with a sulk.

"Um, the incident I asked you to look into."

I shook the terrible memory vaguely remembering the names of the men she found, if at all, they are the correct ones.

"Yea." She nodded. "… The men who…"

I put my hand up to stop her from speaking and she did.

"His. His." I folded my lips stuttering. "His… His DNA is on me."

I finally got the words out. Her eyes widened and the horror on her face shifts me to swallow and I began shivering.

"Shana!"

She pleaded my name. I closed my eyes for a second shutting her pitiful gaze from me. Then, putting my hand up again then pounded my fist on the sink.

"Paula…" I shook my head 'no' at her begging again, "… Please!"

"Oh honey."

Her tone and crinkled face got to me. She folded her lips with empathy stooping to open her kit on the floor. Taking out her gloves and swabs. I stretched my moisten neck to her shutting my eyes.

"Shana, where on your body?" she whines for an answer.

I shook my head no and a tear escaped.

"Shana!" Her voice is forceful for the first time towards me.

"No, um." I exhaled, *ten*... "... He... he licked my... my neck... and ear."

I groaned the words, shut my eyes clenching in memory.

"Shana!" Her eyes became glossy as she watched at me squirm.

"It's OK, Paula."

I swallowed again and paused waiting for her to collect the evidence off me. Paula skimmed the swab over my neck and ear. I shudder each time she touched and moved the swabs across my skin.

"He's got a funny accent, like the village outside the town where I got lost," I added and she tilted her head for a second before asking.

"OK, I've got it. What's next?"

Her asking me to lead gives me the confidence to subdue my emotions and it guided my thoughts to logical which is where I function the best. I take her lead inwardly saying, '*nine*' then moving my hazels to her greens.

"I was in the evidence lock up, the lights went out and the door shut. I am not sure how much footage you can get. Any problems let me know."

I am almost back to field manager. She was silent securing the samples and I can see her brain going on overdrive.

"You don't have to do this alone Shana."

"I'm not." There was a pregnant pause and her gaze soften. "... Thank you, Paula."

I asked you!

We paused momentarily and I was enlightened.

Our history is the least complicated. She has always been a mentor. At school, training and even right now, mothering. The one thing that cannot be denied about Paula is that she is always present, and supportive, in her own way. My heart warms.

Not too sure if I would say that out loud to her.

"You want me to walk out with you?"

I am winded and apprehensive. Instead, my eyes begged and my thoughts were: *please!* "Thank you." I shook my head and reminded myself out loud. "… I am fine."

Paula clicks her kit shut. Eyes dilated and I shudder at the noise stationary.

"I was already on my way out."

She smiles sweet at me opening the door for me to exit before her. My legs wobble and I scan the scarce halls fawning her lead. She kept a few inches from me and my feet are a few inches from hers. My eyes move from person to person memorising their faces as I leave.

"The evidence or lack thereof is in my car."

Paula attempts to distract me. I nod my sense of touch increased absorbing all the static in the air.

"I was headed for the apartment after taking these to the Jade to ensure the chain of custody isn't broken."

Paula starts her random rattling an included some professionalism.

I turned to her in a squint.

"Yes Shana, I am aware of your whininess."

My face darts to her and I am a tad insulted. "Whiney?" I shook my head, offended.

"It is for good reason. *I know!*"

She emphasises her last two words, teasing. She somehow managed to distract me.

"I walked here," I tell her as we exit the building and I try to recall the journey and the reasoning. It was not worth what happened.

"You can have a lift then." Paula walked with me down the stairs to the pavement keeping her eyes on me.

"Sure." I acknowledge her moving dazedly in public.

"Suzanne has met someone," she said snapping me out of the trance of regret. To news of one of my best friends and her daughter.

I whipped my head to her, almost in a giggle. "What!"

Her distraction of gossip worked but surfaced another emotion. Guilt.

I haven't contacted her since I started in Divinish.

But neither has she. My subconscious awakes.

I understand that she may be busy finishing her nearly three-year rebranding project and as friends, we never dwell on absences but the present.

"She thinks it is serious, she might actually kill me for saying."

We got into the car and I resonate on her words. Suzanne is such a romantic. We were partners in crime whilst in boarding school and university. She often gets caught up in the idea and gestures of romance, evidenced by her many ex-boyfriends.

I beam inwardly in memory of the many times I had to be the shoulder she cried on, after all her heartbreaks. Bitterly, it also reminded me of the minimal contact we kept the two nearly three years Eric and I have been married.

"For her sake, I hope it is though."

I smiled entering the car. Paula smiled taking her dirty lab coat off throwing it into the backseat. She sat her ample breast jiggle as she reached and shimmy the seat belt across them.

"Is Eric around?"

Her heart is in the right place but.

"Let's not, Paula." I put my hand up as she simmered.

She darted into the Jade quickly and I locked myself in the car taking that moment to analyse but not before long she reappeared. I unlocked the door upon her return.

The ride ended in silence as she pulled into the park. The sound of voices walking across the courtyard coming towards the few cars in the lot. One voice familiar as the shadows enters the open space and the bodies come to light. Aaliyah and a male companion, her hand draped on his shoulder.

"Doesn't she know she's getting too old for that shit?"

Paula bursts with honesty and disgust. It makes me laugh. Paula glanced at me rupturing with laughter as well. We pushed the doors opened going down the path to the rooms. Hesitantly, I remember the mess I made in the apartment and Eric's reaction. I also recalled his conversation this morning about security and me staying at his new high-rise. My eyes widened at the thought.

We passed Lia and there was a thud. Paula and I pivot an instant one-eighty. The man was on the floor. Lia paused in a stance. Paula shook her head yanking my arms.

"Wait!" I urged Paula. "… She might need some help."

Paula scoffed.

"Lia can handle herself and, the guy *is*, on the floor."

I blinked at her a couple of times.

What! Baffled at her answer I try reasoning again. "That's your sister."

Paula cringed at the remark and frown not looking in the direction.

"And, a highly skilled black belt."

She singsongs with a squint; the guy got up.

Lia flinched shouting at the man. "Move on!" Waving her hands at him.

She somehow always manages to look stunning even when drunk and staggering. She saw us looking on at her scene.

Then, pointing at us. "… That includes you two."

Who does she think she's talking to?

"Excuse me." I began to walk in her direction.

"Shana!" Paula called yanking my arm, "… She's not worth it, she's drunk."

The man opened her car door clambering in. She hopped in after him yelling. With a huff, I turned to the courtyard Paula hooked her arm around mine leading me away from the pair in the direction of my apartment.

The same one Eric scolded me a few days ago for vandalising and, the fact that he told me to stay in his new apartment. I pale at the thought of him knowing the details of what happened since he left me. At the same time, I don't want her there. The judgement in her eyes alone would not be worth it. I need an excuse, fast.

"Paula, wait." She paused exasperating, *I can't go in there,* "… I, uh, I left my car at the Jade." *Good one.*

She haled and narrowed her eyes at me with a counter.

"You can get it in the morning." She says,

Crap! I need to move away from this place.

"Are you going to take me?" I firmly insisted.

Why did I say that? Her eyes darken.

I don't want to go back there either.

Say no, say no, I beg inside and my eyes widened looking at her.

"Sure." She tilted her head to the side and grows a strange look.

Damn! Think she's on to me. "I can't go in there Paula." I decide on some truth.

"Why?" She waited before heading in my direction.

Keep the mess to yourself. "*No,* no, it's just, uh, Eric has an apartment, in the city."

"Do you really want to drive back there tonight?"

Not really, but... "Please." *I can't face what I did in there.* I clasped my hands together at her showing all my teeth.

"I am too tired, and you should try and rest," she quarrelled.

I sulk, and further explain, "He's moved most of my stuff there."

"Well." She walked past my door towards hers settling two doors after. She fished out her keys and unlock the door. "… Come in, sleep, you can find something of mine to fit that small bump."

"Small?"

My eyes widened at her suggestion. I tucked one hand at the top of my tummy and the other below for her to view the extra weight, that is a child around my waist.

"The only thing that shows you're pregnant are those." She pointed at my breasts. I attempt to covered them, somewhat agreeing with her. "… They're nearly my size, hiding the tummy."

I pulled the shirt flat across my tummy with a crinkled face at her exposing all of the bump roundness.

"Really."

"That looks like you've eaten too many burgers."

My mouth loosened with a gasp at her suggestion. She lingered at her apartment door. The same time my phone beeped, Eric texting goodnight with an emoji blowing a kiss.

"Is that him?" Paula asked.

I beam at the phone. Feeling his comfort from far away, one more day until he returns.

"Are you going to tell him?"

CHAPTER FORTY

Turning my mood instantly, I almost forgot the stain of the strange man with his intention in the alleyway and then in the evidence lock-up. His saliva germinates on my neck and ear. I shudder inside and for a moment taken back to the pitiful victim I viewed in the mirror after. Angry at the recollection of the image reflected at me watching the glistened spit on me, I grew angry.

"Not now!"

My foul disposition echoed with my words.

I heard a shriek from across the courtyard. Both Paula and I faces moved in that direction surprised at the sound. The screaming of a familiar voice of a child; Danielle is playing with her mother. Her voice vibrates through the door and across the courtyard. She once again brings me relaxation and stability.

"I will catch up with you later."

My head went in the direction, a welcomed comfort after today to see her.

"You can knock if you want, company tonight."

Paula reminds me once again switching my mode pushing buttons that will have a negative effect for her.

"I'm fine."

I growl rougher than expected. Taking a short walk around the open hall across to Sam's room and knocked. Sam is shouting at Danielle to quiet as she walks towards the door with a playful voice. The door opened and her blue eyes pierced at me strangely.

"Shana," Sam said abruptly with her usual warmth.

"Mum!"

Danielle shouted from behind her. Sam threw her head backwards whilst I tilted looking around Sam as we both squinted at her. She knows that nickname she's given me annoys both me and her mother.

Danielle pushed past Sam putting her arms around me. She is at the right height for a cuddle. Right under my chin and her puff of hair curly and opened to the wind. Giving me exactly what I needed to end this horrible day. I hung on to her long then kissed her puffy hair. Suddenly she bends over surprising me by greeting the bump emotionally tears began pooling.

"What do you want Shana?"

Sam's usual couth behaviour kicks in. She sometimes read me better than I'd like.

"Paula, um, helped me with something today but I left my car at the Jade. Can I get a ride back?"

The story conjured and the half-truth rolled off my tongue as if practiced.

"To get your car?"

Her tone drags, she squints at the dark behind me but her morphed expression said it all but I say.

"Yes," squeaking showing my teeth with a tilt at my head.

"No!"

She exhaled in a millisecond, as expected, but I want to be sure questioning.

"No?"

"Yes. No Shana. You can get a lift with one of us tomorrow."

She has a curious and judgemental expression. Her alto tone exasperated. I know she believes I was doing something shady. Just like with my phone call to her at Brian's.

Although I was wearing his T-shirt and my underwear. My subconscious pokes her head reminding me of the compromising situation.

Danielle began pulling me into the messy apartment. The same lay out as mine but the toilet on the other side as is the main entrance to the apartment. There are food boxes and some clothes on the bed. Boxes and wrappers from Danielle I'm sure on the floor.

Sam doesn't have a view of the red rocks but a pleasant one of the flowered gardens and the courtyard. She has two wooden short back stools at the breakfast bar, navy-blue sofa and chair.

The apartment reeked of pizza, igniting an increase of saliva that gathered in my mouth. My untamed tummy grumble, the baby danced. The source of the odour is perched on her grey and black countertop.

"Mummy..." Danielle breaks my lustful upcoming drool. "... Can Shana stay for the movie?"

Danielle began her line of questioning with whining standing in the view of Sam with her bright-blue eyes and untamed hair. Sam knows our ten-year-old logic is usually sound and the chances of Sam having her way is slim.

"Ugh... sure."

Sam groan accepting defeat early avoiding the list of questions which would eventuality follow if she had said no.

"Can we share some of our popcorn?" Danielle continues.

"Why not."

Sam gives up letting the door close and us pass by.

"Oh, and she can have some of the gummy bears."

Danielle grows excited, I smile but I must say for manners of course.

"I don't want to intrude, Sam." *I really cannot be alone tonight!* My inner thoughts shouted.

"You're not!"

Danielle answered my musing and her mother, being a great host as Sam annoyingly would say. It is not so much fun being on the adult side when she gets started as she would in the past to me for Sam.

Inwardly gloating as she pulled me to the two-seat sofa to sit with her under a blanket. Eventually, Sam moved from guarding the door and closed it conceding to the defeat of our ten-year-old.

The place darkened for a second. I closed my eyes, his breath stained with smoke covers me, he's pushing me into the door and I feel his tongue on my neck. I popped up, throwing a pillow standing at the image. A blanket fell off me and Sam jumped off her bed.

"What the f, Shana?"

She croaked disturbed from resting. Danielle groaned turning on the bed finding a comfortable position. My breathing unstable and loud, my eyes dilated. I shiver recalling the entire encounter covering my bump from being crushed. Fear fills me. The ball grows in my throat. I folded my lips.

"Shana,"

Sam called again, snapping my oncoming tears, bringing me back to realising where I stood.

"I'm OK, sorry!"

I scolded myself counting in my head looking to the nearest exit to leave.

"Wait, it's three in the morning, Shana."

I exhaled long fighting the sob.

"I know," I whispered. "... I shouldn't have fallen asleep like that..."

My voice cracked as I forced the words exhaling long and hard at the end. Sam walks to the couch standing a few feet from me. Her blue eyes soft piercing through me.

"There is a trick, to carrying your weapon on you, whilst pregnant."

I twisted my head back at her she changed direction throwing me off.

"What."

"I know Shana. You think you cannot put the weapon on your person, but thigh holsters are the best." She slaps her thighs demonstrating on her shorts. "... Outer thigh that is... especially wearing all those waistless, flowing clothes you have to when pregnant..."

She points and waves at me squishing her face and making it hard to take her seriously but I know she is.

"... I should have at least one from Danielle's pregnancy..." I sometimes forget what she used to be, and she continued to explain, "... In close combat, there are also ways of protecting your centre."

Although half of what she's saying makes no sense to me, I could see some passion and care although we both would never say that to each other's face.

"Oookay."

I nodded narrowing my eyes.

Why is she being nice!

"Look, tomorrow is training, right? Or may I say in about four hours!" She huffed.

She had to point that out!

Rolling her eyes and neck at me the gesture is comical. I try not to laugh, though her effort to be nice is hilarious and she's making me uncomfortable.

"I should get going." I stick my thumb over my shoulder partly pointing at the door.

"What you're going to do, is wake Danielle to her twenty questions." She growls at me.

"True…" *She's weirding me out!* My subconscious points out.

"I am actually the trainer this week."

She's still doing it!

"… Something about mandatory training or some crap like that."

Ah, there's Sam! "Humm!" I try impassive.

"Sit… rest… on the pillows. They're not for throwing."

Upon following her instructions, I wondered if Paula spoke with her. She went for the pillow throwing it at the chair walking to the bed.

Nope! Her behaviour says otherwise. I got up quickly.

"What are you doing?" Sam scolds me.

"I need to pee."

"Oh, right, don't flush, you will wake Dani."

I frown at the thought of the smell. Sam waited for me at the door reminding me not to flush.

She is so weird sometimes!

Leaning on the sofa handle, I snuggled with the pillow throwing the blanket over my shoulder. My eyes closed, but I cannot sleep. Too many scenarios playing over in my head and the feel of his tongue on my skin.

I really want to wash it off!

Alerted, my eyes opened to a slightly differently decorated apartment. My breath hitched and my senses piqued the room filled with the aroma of the brewing coffee, it woke me completely.

"Good morning."

Samanther Martinez's alto tone somewhat greeting me from behind. Her tone coarse unpleasant and startling me. Turning towards the noise of her speaking, she holds a newspaper folded in half, in one hand and a cup in the other hand. Her spectacles on her face slightly sloped on her nose something that really grinds me; looking over your spectacles.

Why bother wearing them? "Hey," I whispered grinding my thoughts which seem to have found a filter today. Sitting up I tilted leaning into the sofa. Peeking over my shoulder to Sam perched on a bar stool at the breakfast bar. Struggling to avoid spending more time than necessary, in thought over this moment, or make her hospitality... more awkward.

"You can shower... or actually go back to your place."

She drags her voice saying. I rolled my eyes with a huff.

She couldn't help herself.

And at the same time, I artfully raise my shoulders shifting my nose to my shoulder deeply inhaling at her suggestion. My shirt slightly crinkled but still filled with the starch from the store.

I'm good to go.

I raised my eyebrows at myself.

"I should go."

Go is most urgent on my thought. Danielle groans whilst stretching and shifting mine and her mother's attention. Spreading, her whole body like a star on the bed.

She looks like her dad.

A sobering thought penetrated as she opened her mouth with a yawn as wide as she can. Her large head of hair pillowed behind her. Her eyes caught me ogling.

"Shana, you stayed!"

She shouts sitting up and pouncing from the bed with excitement as her big blues lit. She sets in motion to greet me.

"Well good morning to you too."

Sam squints slightly wounded at Danielle's enthuse stopping her prancing in my direction.

"Good morning."

Danielle giggles, with some brightness in her cheeks. A broad white smile at her mother, she throws her arms open matching to Sam for a quick cuddle crinkling her newspaper. She giggles knowing what she had done. Sam huffs shaking the newspaper, putting it aside but after a second. She springs with a few steps wrapping her arms around me.

Then she kisses the bump, and began a conversation almost like I do not exist. For a few minutes she mumbles against my tummy. I lifted my arms at the back of the sofa, sliding my bottom to the edge of the chair and arching my back. Making this whole strange moment comfortable for me.

"Daddy says the baby hears everything."

"Oh, are you talking to me now?" I beam at her innocence.

"Yes, Mum."

Ugh! Sam and I were exasperated at the same time. I try ignoring it this time, looked at Sam.

"Yes..." Sam answered.

Really, hum. "Sometimes the baby wriggles. Right now, the baby isn't moving when it does, I will call you."

Her eyes brighten. "Is it supposed to feel hard?"

"Yes Danielle, before you ask anything more, I really need you to brush your teeth. It makes me sick remember. I am sure Sam doesn't want me to throw up in here."

"No, Sam does not..." Sam talked slurping into her drink.

I squinted at her getting up.

Danielle covers her mouth muffling. "Sorry."

"It's OK." I assured her stroking her hair.

She skips to the bathroom. Sam continued slurping the only sound in the room when Danielle was gone. I got off the couch, folded the blanket and placed it on the pillow, stacking it at the far end of the couch. My shoes were together, neatly at the side of the chair, and my phone on a side table above.

The time Illuminated after taking hold of my phone it was nearly seven thirty. Quickly checking to see if there are any messages there was none. I texted Paula good morning. She replied almost instantly:

Ready to leave?

Rude! But... Excellent timing.

Turning to Sam, I threw my hand up sticking a thumbs up over my shoulder.

"Ah, I'm heading out."

Sam scarcely acknowledging me lazily moved her hand from the coffee cup, her nose stuck to her newspapers, reading, shaking it to turn the page.

All right then. "... Bye Danielle."

I yelled in the direction of the toilet. Slipping on my shoes, holding my phone walking to the doors quickly. Danielle shouted muffled from the bathroom. I supposed she was in the middle of brushing her teeth. I went through the doors shutting it behind me. The sun rising behind the building lighting the flowered pathway of the courtyard.

CHAPTER FORTY-ONE

A short stroll to the parking Paula was sitting in her car, waiting. She eyed me as I closed the distance between us, leaned across the front seat popping the door open for me.

"You're wearing the same clothes," she exclaimed. "... And it is crinkled." Then she pointed out.

Those words bursting out with the door. My eyes widened and my mouth loosed, blinking a couple times at the irony.

Is she... referring to me?

The words fail me catching the door as it swung to me. Conscious, I tug at the hem of my blouse all around smoothing some creases then sliding into the chair. She pulls on her seat belt across her body and starts the engine hardly waiting for me to close the door. I pulled the seat belt rolling my eyes away from her view. I saw her reflection in the window.

"This is the only thing I owned that could fit me right now." Excusing myself aloud for us both.

That's not the only reason. My subconscious woke I puffed at my inner thought.

"Yea..." She shook her head in agreement. "... Maybe you can borrow something of mine."

What is it with these women today?

I crinkled my eyebrow.

What would make her think I could fit into her clothes even pregnant?

A flash memory of parent conference where Paula wore a tight black mini skirt and a bright pink strapped vest, her neon bra, popped through the vest. Mr Blackman stared at her boobs the whole meeting. The guys in the school teased Sue and Ian about their *milf*, my eyes dilated thinking.

Why would she think I would wear anything she does?

"Uh, I'm OK."

That was as pleasant as I could regurgitate a positive remark concerning her offer. She pulled out the park beginning our forty-minute journey into the city.

"So, what? Are you going to wear this every day?"

Why isn't she letting this go?

"Uh, Eric gave me his card to buy some new stuff."

Why am I explaining this to her?

Hopefully, that will get her off my back.

Gazing through the window at the passing cars, I enjoyed a brief silence.

"Yea, I know you hate shopping," Paula said as a matter-of-fact with a swift gape at me.

Ugh! "I do not!"

I try really hard to not sound whiney blinking two seconds too long, saying a prayer.

Oh, please don't continue the story!

Ten years ago…

Apprehensive to leave the alley with a man claiming to be the police dressed in dirty stained clothes. There was something about him. He convinced me to go into the hospital to get the bruises checked. The ride was short. We moved through to a side room.

Eric paced back and forth. My clothes were torn and smelly but so was he. Nothing about his decorum was shining and *I can* say.

He sat on a chair while I was on the hospital bed the curtains pulled, the female doctor came. Two bruised ribs, bruises across my face and a black eye, the result of sleeping in the alleyway at the back of a bar and a perverted man pouncing on a homeless teenager. It was late night, early morning. Eric leaned back on a chair next to the bed, taking another chair to put up his feet.

I heard a female voice on the other side of the curtain calling for him, waking us both. It was morning. I looked over at him who rose to his feet with a stretch exposing his sculpted lower abs and dark hairs on his belly. He yawns. A slight relief on his face hearing the voice, he pulled back the curtain, answering.

She was almost his height. Dark, lush mid-length hair, straight and glossy. Her odour came before she did. A flowery sweet smell, calf-length glossy boots and tight leather pants. Navy tight top and a leather coat, the most piercing pale-blue eyes and a contrast of a cinnamon complexion. She squints at me, then at him.

"What happened?" She crossed her arms. "… Are you drunk?" She inhales and frowns.

"Lia, come on!" he whines. "… I am a bit tipsy," he further explains.

She raises one perfectly shaped eyebrow.

"Step outside," commanding him tossing the curtain behind her. He follows. He says something to her. His baritone too low for me to follow but I heard her.

"You shouldn't be involved in any of this Eric."

He said something mumbling under his baritone and she replied,

"Shana, Shala or whatever!" she screams angrily at him. "… You are in no condition to do this." She continues her rant.

"I am not going to leave her," he grunts aggressively and clear. She sighs loudly, pausing.

"Then go get a coffee," she conceded. "… I will stay with her until you get back." She sighs again.

"You're the best." The shadow of him hugging her. Then, I heard a kiss.

"Yes, I know," she singsongs with a shrug.

The curtain is pulled back and she eyes me strangely for a bit.

"Shana," she is calling my name inaccurately but I do not correct her. She is very sure of her position and radiates intimidating. I cannot read her emotion as I usually can which makes me uneasy. "… I am detective Hall's partner, Aaliyah Paul. The doctors will be with you soon. In the meantime, I would like to take some of your information."

A small writing pad and a pen appeared out of thin air. She clicked the top and began writing as she asked,

"How old are you, Shana?" She is doing it again with a huff, eyeing me again.

"It's Shannan. Fifteen."

I stated soft and shy. She paused a beat blinking a few times observing me again following with another question.

"When did you turn fifteen?" She asks again, dismissive of the correct pronunciation to what's she's calling me.

"June thirteen," I answered clear.

"Where are your parents?"

I try hard to remember but there was nothing. No faces, no names, no familiar smell or place, only fog and a need to hide. I scan the curtain covered cubicles behind her and to my sides. It appeared to be safe. I shrug.

"I-I don't know."

She stared strangely then covertly looked around as I did.

"Did you leave them or did they leave you?" she asks squinting at me.

I raised my shoulders up and down and flinched in-between what should have been a cleansing breath.

"I don't know."

"You don't know?" she questioned with hints of irritation. "… Why don't you know?"

"I can't remember," I shout at her suggestive tone.

"OK." She put one hand up her palm to the floor waving at me whilst saying, "… Calm down Shana." I exhale holding my side and she observed me. "… How long have you been sleeping in the alley?"

"I don't know. Could have been last night."

"This was your first time living there?"

I moved my shoulders again. "I. Don't. Know." *She is starting to annoy me.*

"What about yesterday? Where were you?"

I think, but it doesn't come. "The first thing I remember was a man's body over me and another rescuing me, and you."

She squints. "Your accent, it's from Divinish right?"

I don't hear an accent. I squint at her offensive gesture to my speech.

"I-don't-know."

"All right. You know your parents' name?" Does she think the answers will change?

"Um mmm." I shook my head in disagreement.

"OK, once Detective Hall gets back, we will take you into the station have your fingerprints done. We'll see what we can find, OK?"

Her tone was more professional than sympathetic. I shrug. Food came and I ate while Aaliyah watched.

Eric returned with two hot drinks. Aaliyah smiled as he kissed her forehead thanking her for waiting with me. She got up with her drink and they went out of the curtain, Eric followed her outside in a whispered argument with her.

"Today is my day off, Hall. I was out with my daughter," she argues again.

"I know, I'm sorry."

He put his hands in his jeans' pocket gaping at his shoes.

"You're not drunk?"

"No, not really." He shook his head in agreement. "... I have been keeping watch over Shannan and trying to find her a safe place... Just until we can locate her parents or at least a foster home."

She rolled her eyes.

"That is very admirable of you Eric, but you are searching in the wrong county and she can stay in a holdover."

"I know Lia, but I was not sure if taking her with me was a good idea."

Lia crinkled her face in protest. "You're right, it's not."

She pauses and he says nothing. Then, it hits her.

"So, what, you were just calling to see if I could?"

He nodded not looking into her face. "Yes."

"Eric it is almost the Zemand festival and the new year, Emily is only here with me for a few days until she goes back to school. Then Ben is being his usual asshole self and doesn't want to take Melanie.

"We're not on an assignment so it is the perfect time for me to take some leave. I've got my two girls with me for the holidays. I am not going to spend it with a stranger in my home. I can't take another one even temporarily. Not to say the least a girl you found on the streets!"

"She has no one!" He is defending me.

"That you know of!"

Aaliyah answers quick then inhales deep shutting her eyes and opening them again. Then she glanced outside the hallway. I see a dark girl around my age pacing bored, distracted and ever-so often, glancing at Aaliyah as the girl does her.

The girl resembles Aaliyah but with dark brown eyes and skin slightly darker than hers. She had a beautiful brown tone.

"Here's what. Emily has to go shopping for gifts for the festival. There's a shopping centre down the street. She can go with Emily and we can get her out of those awful clothes and maybe she can get a proper winter coat. I can make a few calls and we can see from there."

"Thank you, Lia!" He held her close and squeezed her a bit.

"Don't thank me just yet. It is the holiday season and winter."

She called her daughter from loitering through the halls to her side and explained a task. I got dressed and walked outside the room while Eric and Aaliyah continued their conversation. Standing outside with Emily.

Emily looks a bit like her mother, but a chestnut tone and tighter curls. A single long plait falling to the centre of her back and a pair of amazingly dark eyes. Her skin was a flawlessly smooth chocolate colour with full lips and a great sense of style. She emitted confidence and self-assurance. She looked at me with a questioning expression tilting her head to one side.

"Take off that repugnant coat."

She came close to me shaking my coat off my shoulders exposing a battered sleeveless cotton dress. With a squint she walked to the closest bin disposing it. I folded my lips, embarrassed. She shimmied out of her coat and handed it to me.

"Here. Put this on."

She held her hand out nodding at me. Waiting in a light pink cashmere sweater. The material looked soft and comfortable. She moved her hands closer to me. I hesitated unable to read her then the cold breeze blew in with a door. A nurse walked past. I shiver slowly holding it. She uses both hands to pull at the hem of her top revealing beneath a white vest peeking a few inches past the pink sweater. Then she tidied her scarf.

"Much better. Shana, is it?" She smiled turn on her heals.

"Shannan!" I prompt.

"Shana is much better."

I shrug, curious about this kind girl.

"Come on. My mum gave me her card."

We settled into what Emily described as a trendy clothing store. She began trying clothes and handing me some as we made our way around the racks. She found something that she thought was cute leaving me with her handbag.

I walked around the store looking at clothes I find acceptable and not some of the more revealing or trendy clothing Emily likes for me. A sale's assistant began following me at every stop. She was not asking me anything but heavily eyeing my movements. I became nervous and sat at a stool used for trying shoes and decided a pair of sneakers will do just right and not the many high heels Emily has shown me.

I rested Emily's bag next to the bench, I sat and turned to retrieve a pair I liked. The sales assistants stood with the bag and the security when I returned accusing me of stealing. Emily was nowhere in sight and I was lost in words reverting to a language they don't understand.

The security handled me roughly aggravating my injuries taking me out the store into a holding area, calling the police.

CHAPTER FORTY-TWO

Paula interrupts my recollecting…

"A man doesn't usually let a woman loose with their credit card…" I saw Paula's reflection in the window gaping at my bad behaviour as she ignores continuing. "… I could understand, Sue told me about your incident shopping."

What! I screamed in my head my cheeks reddening fast.

"Uh…"

Why do they like this word, 'incident'? There must be another word to describe the humiliation.

"Eric was right to have her fired!"

Paula broke my reminiscing.

He had her fired?

"It doesn't matter though," I voiced then thinking of the unpleasant memory and I sulk.

"Oh, great, I can go with you then," she insisted.

What! "Excuse me?" *When did I invite her?* My eyes popped waiting for the view of humour across her face. There was none.

"Zeliah grew up with our father's money." Paula instead shares, "… Aaliyah is living with it but neither she nor I had it easy before…" her stare intensifies as her mind seems to have gone back to the moments that she lived. "… This is different…" She instead changed the topic. "… It'll be fun." She squeaked her excitement.

Her definition of fun maybe. "Is it really?" I narrowed my eyes at her, my voice whined.

"Yes…" she moaned assumingly.

I doubt it! Nervously, I smirked at her as she began her endless babbling.

Thankfully I saw the building and my car in the distance. She dropped me on the curb near to my car.

Waiting for me a parking ticket stuck on the window of my rental car.

Shit! I cursed inside assessing.

"Those things go to the directors," Paula with her obvious remarks irritating me, thinking of the unpleasantries once Eric or Kane gets a copy. Turned to her, grinning.

"Yes, thank you Paula." I swiped it off the glass crinkle it in my hand.

Opening the car door throwing it into the front passenger seat before I sat. Paula tooted her horn as she drove away.

Great!

Lucky, they didn't put a lock on my tyre. That would have been even harder to explain without telling him what really happened last night, though I cannot fully comprehend it myself. The feeling I thought went away returned, that helplessness and fear with the mounting of weeping.

Not here Shana!

Reminding myself of another thing I wanted so badly to forget. That his saliva is germinating on my neck and ear. I cringe inside urgently needing to wash it off. I pulled out from the curb and into the morning traffic. A short drive from the office to the loft, I am in dire need of a shower and a change of clothes.

The elevator doors open. I froze momentarily reminded of the unacquainted place Eric has insisted I stay whilst he is not here; all a part of the perks of being the director of the highest form of policing in the country.

The light sofa and the fluffy cushions show house clean, tidy with a light, sweet fragrance of a new home. I plop my shoes off taking up the sensation of the polished wooden floors, allowing myself the thought something besides my neck. A floor to ceiling window lit the room reflecting the skyscrapers in the distance. The morning sunshine and the bustling streets. Eric's position of authority is surreal like this place.

I breathe in. Standing so close to the edge of Divinish. Looking down at the city filled with people lively, retelling the many places this man can hide. The way he made me feel and what would happen to my career. My child and my marriage if Eric get wind of this. I frown swallowing hard. Triggering by the fact that Eric was scheduled to return from his trip later today.

I need to let this out before he gets back!

Taking a few more seconds in view of the city bare feet from a distance on high. I climbed the winding stairs from the kitchen opening the door at the top, into the hallway gliding into the master bedroom. The tears began.

Taking each button out, one at a time, sliding the shirt off my shoulders letting it fall to the floor. Whining out my skirt revealing the scar of my first attack. Reliving his rough hands snaking up my thighs I choke the helplessness. Crying stuttered out kicking the skirt away falling to my knees sniffling and bawling, cuddling my tummy for a long time.

Eventually I got up, fully undressed and had a shower washing attentively and hard at my neck and ear. It still didn't feel clean or wash away the sickening feeling that he left behind.

There isn't much more I can do from inside this bathroom.

With a sigh, I reasoned, exited into the bedroom. Only then paying some attention to the detail of this room, it is much bigger than our bedroom in Ceda. The walk-in cupboards with large, mirrored doors, a chest of drawers tucked in a corner and a dresser.

In the first drawer were Eric's underwear, socks and white T-shirts. I pulled on a pair of his boxers. It is looser than I expected, given my bump. Unsure if it was a positive thing feeling the extra room. Either way, suddenly and pleasantly I am distracted by my husband's crotch. Folding my lips in memory of his touch. My baby began the morning wriggle.

A direct result of his touch.

Regardless of which is the greater factor being with Eric, having the most distracting man will be welcoming. I smile, pulled the second drawer, filled with some of my camisoles and shorts. I giggled at the thoughtfulness but reminded by his domineering tendencies. I circled my eyes not wanting another reminder.

Exploring inside the mirrored doors, I found some of my suits. The aubergine one which I am sure cannot fit into, the one I wore for my interview. There was a black sleeveless dress, knee-high, jersey material.

Over my head it went slightly roomier than I remembered, shifting the jacket, the inside was slightly different.

He must have thrown it away.

Instantly shaking the thought, I began straightening my curly hair and adding make-up for work but first making a pit stop for a snack from the kitchen. My phone beeped.

Hey, are you at work?
Tenth floor.

My faithful personal assistant, Noel prompts me back to now. Viewing my watch, ten-fifteen.

Shit! Late again!

Admonishing myself for another tardy day, I still cannot live what I preached to A.P.S. This though, is a really understandable excuse. *I can't share it, not yet.* I needed the shower to wash off the unprovoked touch. Thinking of it only makes me frightened and clench.

Office set up.

Noel sent another text, jolting the pity thoughts. Thankful it was her and not a call from Eric, in this condition, I will release the truth.

Work is a good distraction.

I prepped my things and began listing my tasks. The mystery mail left on my desk was the first thought. The thing that led me to the L.D.O., to the unprovoked and befuddled attack. My phone pinged again, the preview shows Amy Welch, I shudder.

My report this week for Acting Director Kane is due.

I cursed before a reply text:

On my way!

Leaving quickly to the Jade building, taking my handbag with me and stopping for food at the drive-through that Eric took me to a few days ago.

It was already eleven when I got in. It almost felt like the excuses the women gave had reversed. Pacing with the hope that the others won't notice; Noel greeted me at the elevator and none of the ladies were in the area of their assigned desks.

Expected.

Noel gave me a quick tour, updated me with the ladies' whereabouts and left me some instructions that the acting director left with her.

"Paula is on the lab floor," explained Noel leading me through an open space of desk where other staff worked. At the end, there was a wall with windows and white blinds. A narrow walkway and a glass door.

Further along the doors is where my team should be seated. I huffed, opened the door and skip to my desk. The room had improvements to the last time. There are now three chairs in front of the desk, a television on a side table to my left under file cabinets. A clock near the TV and a larger table with three drawers inside waiting for me.

Setting up my desktop computer and the folders the ladies left waiting to begin the late report. Noel has found a desk outside the office and begins her work and I try making myself comfortable. My lower arm balanced on the edge of the desk and my fingers hovered over the keyboard.

Daily report first, then Sharron's new statement. Plenty to keep me occupied. I breathe deep gaining some focus. Fuel by my persistence with incognito photos and some attribution to the pregnancy hormones.

Sharron's vivid description of her attacker and her description of events finally marries with the evidence, although some of what she claims, if true, is terrifying. I don't know where to begin summarising where we are at the moment. As the thought left me, the office door burst open, startling me in the process. Aaliyah poured in washing her strong perfume into the room, filling the larger office.

"Davis!"

She whooshed in, breathless. Her large bangles clapped and jingled. Wearing a closely fitted shirt pulled tighter at the waist with a belt, to emphasise her envied tiny waist at age forty-one after two children and three pregnancies. With a black, slim-fitted sharply seamed trousers. Her voice in an urgent tone. I looked up quickly, slightly jealous of her ability to pull off business, sophisticated, effortlessly.

"How can I help you?"

She quickly shifted my mood.

"Uh, Ray is fine, if you must know."

She waved her hands around creating a distracting sound then placed them on her hips after painting the picture of her words. I squinted,

"Who?" I'm Confused.

"The guy."

She air-painted again with a jingle, I crinkled my face.

What is she on about?

"The guy from last night," she further explains.

"Oh." I shook my head understanding but wondering... *Why is she explaining this to me?* I continued my squint at her. "... OK."

I bobbed my head a bit and zoned into the computer gazing at the blank document, and deciding what to put on paper. Gathering my thoughts, I feel her glaring at me I moved my head slowly to her occasionally gaping at my screen. She shrugs her shoulders, pausing, I supposed, for a response,

"Yeeessss," I hissed emphasising my clear annoyance at her presence.

"I don't get you Davis," *What does Eric sees in her?* she says in thought. I scoffed losing my chain of thought throwing my hands up in defeat. Her voice filled with aggression and I am ready to defend.

"What now? What do you want me to say?" I grunt my irritation.

"A thank you will be nice."

I squint, shaking my head, baffled. "... Thank you for beating the guy, not beating the guy? What makes you think you deserve that?" *Honestly!*

I throw my hands up again, this time tracing my eyebrows with the tips of my fingers at the same time. Then shook my head 'no' sitting up in the chair to have a good look at her, crinkling my eyebrows at her.

"What would make you think you deserve your education funded?" She sniped.

I blinked a couple times rocking back into my chair, crossing my fingers into a knit over my baby bump, and a deep inhale. Her eyes rise and fell many times at my growing midsection. Her motivation is amiss and I am tired of her games.

"What do you want Lia?" I shrug. "... I had a scholarship. That's what they are used for?" I replied, defending her claim.

"Is that what he's telling you? Humph!" she scorned.

"Excuse me?" What is she talking about?

Now she has my attention, she grinned, knowing it.

"Later Davis." She stomps out.

What was that about?

I can't deal with her today!

I stop for a while.

Does she mean Eric?

She always does this.

Ugh!

I really hate her!

Now I was really distracted. She sure has a way of planting these little seeds of doubt. I try shaking her off beginning the report.

I can possibly blame the delay on the move.

Excusing my missed report from yesterday and the demands from the directors... *Eric!* I exhaled playing through the reasoning I could have used if he wasn't my husband. Then I typed:

To: Director Kane
From: Agent Davis-Hall

My curser blinked for a while as I ogled the computer. I listened to Sharron's statement in parts.

Ugh! I really loathe Aaliyah!

The additional perk of a television set that came with this office perched at the left of my desk. I turned it on. News played in the background with talks of Mayor Mall's.

Alerted at the allusion of his name he was standing on a podium surrounded by campaign decoration of colours, the national flag, pictures of himself and balloons. Lurking was his daughter modestly covering her usual tempting bits with lighter make-up contrasting from her usual dress code. Some of her bruises and scars partially covered by her hair, her hazels dazzled like pale blue. You can actually see her.

She resembles me a bit.

Could be the way she's dressed.

A stray observation on my part, as the reporter reads her report, I increased the volume:

'A typical underdog story has been gaining traction and everyone wants a piece. Mayor Mall has made up with his estranged daughter; after she suffered at the hands of a merciless monster, Sharron Mall has been branded the prodigal daughter and she's come home.

She has taken a day's break, from her rehabilitation, to attend this very special occasion. Today she supports her father with his campaign. Sources say she disconnected herself from the bad boys in her life and moved into her father's mansion.

She appears to be accepted and supported by the wider community taking on several charity projects of her father's. She mastered the smiling and waving princess routine. Investigations into her rape are still ongoing.'

Shit! I hope her traction has not brought fire to my doors. The mayor's threat and phone call come to mind. I sighed listening.

'… Today Mayor Mall as a Zemand high priest has the honour of announcing the Zemand festival's key god celebration. Zemand from all over the country will come for the next week to prepare and implement the ceremony chosen.'

A high priest? This make some sense and is now edging at my unreliable memory and I try to connect. The fog rose and my thoughts are gone.

So many questions.

As much as we would like to do things quietly, with the necessary press conferences, it definitely isn't an option any more. I lowered the volume and then began my report:

To: Director Kane
From: Agent Davis-Hall

Sharron Mall has retracted her first statement producing a new one. We are attempting to place a name with the description of her initial attacker. Sketch artist has produced a detailed description of her initial attacker. Detective Sergeant Martinez is currently chasing the leads on this.

Surveillance at her apartment has been retrieved but to no avail. The description of the figure in the recordings and sketch to some degree resembles Mr Adam Jolee, the man whose necklace was found around her neck when she had been retrieved.

Attempts had been made for Mr Jolee to be interviewed but his attorney points insist the evidence is circumstantial and there isn't anything but obstruction of justice at this time we can charge him with.

There hasn't been any real progress in the case other than Sharron Mall finally admitting to her fabrication of the first statement and this statement has mostly line up with the physical evidence but includes some unusual details.

I have also made links to a serial killer many years ago but the evidence is also circumstantial or coincidental. If more time is put into the connection with the two cases I am certain there will be a greater chance to supply a conviction.

With this in mind what shall I pursue sir?

Agent Davis-Hall S
S.D.A.F.

My hand hovered at the send button cut short by the mayor's announcement of the ceremony I increased the volume again.

'This year we are going to honour Cedérus… his power and revival will encourage us in this time of change, he will bring us prosperity.'

Unconventional choice.

I shook my head in disgust as I know he is milking his daughter's pain for his own advancement as well as masking any biased connection to the religion. I lower the volume again hovering at the send button.

Anomalous choice.

I hope he is wise not to nudge a peaceful serpent.

CHAPTER FORTY-THREE

Did you go shopping yet?

Eric texted. The sound avulsed me.

Shit! I held my chest from the fright. Eric nagging me, also displays the time of four-thirty.

Crap!

The workday is over and I am thrilling, anticipating at the return of Eric. A long week, of many snaking events. Ending with our move to the same building as Eric. I shake my head to think of the last time that happened.

Don't go there Shana!

Being in his arms is all I need now to end this emotional roller coaster.

Not just the sex?

My subconscious popped her head at me. With his prompt, I finished my day work and started my weekend.

Of course, sex!

I gave you, my card.

Why didn't you use it?

Is he ever going to let up? I sigh.

He can be so damn maddening.

I sent him an emoji with its eyes as the shape of an x. Giggling afterwards as I know he would have no idea what that means. I sent another:

Sorry, lost track of time.

At work.

He sent some blowing kisses.

He won't admit he doesn't know what it means. I giggled excited for his return determined to leave work on time. The lecherous ideas took over. My lower parts clench. I bite my lips imagining his lips touching every inch of my body. I grin pulling into the underground parking below the building. His car was not in his spot.

Hum… he's probably finishing up paperwork,

I, of all people, know about getting lost in a report or research. A little disappointed, I ordered my regular, Chinese. The food arrived before him.

I ate slowly, waiting.

Showered, waited.

Turned on the television, waiting.

I am a child in a room with a white chest, full of stuffed animals playing with them. The curtains light blowing in breeze, I was having such a great time. I hear a woman and a man's voice around me. Their words are muffled, nor can I see them. The male voice is telling me a story. I am giggling happy.

Eric's weight on the bed woke me. I gasp wrenched from a peaceful dream disoriented with the unfamiliar surroundings. Adjusted my eyes to his beautiful smirk white teeth pink gums leaned across to me.

I beam smirking, grasping his face in both my hands. His beard is soft, thick and low, and his brown eyes shine at me. With a sharp inhale, I pulled his face to me our lips touched and I sucked him in parting his lips. Playing all my anticipation into it our tongues swirling breathing heated wanton. He pulls off catching his breath.

"Missed me?" he says rhetorically. Invoking the automatic reaction of me rolling my eyes. Setting him free lying on my back.

"Maybe."

Grinning coy, he sat up and I only realised he's dressed in a white shirt black bowtie a black vest coat and his tuxedo pants, my thinking is in overdrive.

Shit! Did I forget our wedding day?

My eyes enlarged and I began a short fright. He is watching me in a strange way. I can't tell if he's pissed or happy.

"Did you forget something?" His voice was stern.

Crap! What do I say?

He's sat on my left taking his right hand up. I flinch breathing sharp. His eyes lock on mine making me uneasy, brings the hem of my vest below my breast. Then, he pulls the waist of the boxers pulling it to my hips.

My midsection exposed. Leaning slowly, he brushes his palm over my exposed skin. Not quite the touch I hoped for. I am fractionally disenchanted. Still alarmed at his words, I eye his movements. He leans over my belly and kisses the small rise.

"Don't you, Mrs Hall, have a ball to attend?"

Oh, is he mad that I forgot?

I shook my head 'yes'. I am waiting to be scolded.

"Well?"

Change direction?

I remember looking at the ceremony on the television when I was younger. It used to be so intriguing. I am not sure how I feel about it especially attending with the mayor and his family after this week.

"I am not sure." I shook my head.

"I have been invited. You are my wife and by proxy you need to be there…" I huff thinking of my current wardrobe and the clothes I did not buy. "… You know… as my arm candy."

He caught me off guard moving his eyebrows up and down. My giggle exploded I covered my mouth.

He's being cute and funny.

His excitement is contagious.

"… So why aren't you dressed?"

He insisted on lying on the bed next to me in his tailored tuxedo with his arms supporting his head. I groaned frowning then rubbed my belly.

"Your baby has once again squeezed me out of my clothes."

"And of course, you didn't go shopping…" Automatic reaction of rolling my eyes again. "… I am so lucky my wife hates shopping." His voice was slightly sarcastic.

Is he, mad again? "I don't hate shopping!"

"Really."

He lifted his naturally fine-shaped eyebrows creating wrinkles across his forehead. I sat up gazing everywhere else but him. Exhaled exasperating, he rolled over sitting on the bed with me I knotted my fingers looking down at them.

"I find shopping depressing…" Then whispered, "… Because I am fat!"

Partial truth felt great!

"You hated shopping before that."

Not him too!

Please don't make me relive that story again today!

He chuckled and then sprung out of the bed holding three bags that was on the drawers for me.

I must be really off today! I blushed.

"What's in it?"

Tittering with expectation like a child at Christmas I opened the first bag. There was a short, straight velvet crème dress.

"Wow, it's beautiful and doesn't look maternity like."

"There are some things which are maternity that are not flowing dresses, Shana."

I scowl at him, he placed the second bag next to me. There was a maternity silk nightgown.

"Is this a non-subtle hint?" I am bashful folding my lips at my current dress code.

His underwear.

"I would like the use of my underwear Shana,"

I scoffed at him. "I don't mind if you don't wear any." I smiled suggestively.

He cleared his throat. "Tempting."

Then shifted his pants. He put the nightie into my hands. The material was soft, smooth and exquisite. The third bag had two boxes. A shoe box, small square gift box and a pair of matching set of underwear below the two items, loose in the bag. My face flushed and sweat piled across my face.

At this rate, I would not have a need for blush make-up.

I opened the first box there was a pair of white slippers with a short-wedged heel. I dropped the bag and hugged him with tears.

Damn hormones!

He held my chin-between his thumb and index finger.

"It's not over yet."

Pecked my lips then, gave me the last bag with the box inside. Hesitant to open it, when I did there was another box, wine red suede. I opened to a pair of diamond earrings and a silver necklace with a crystal heart engraved with my name. I began crying he hugged me.

"Don't cry, babes."

He held my chin up to look at his handsome face. Emotions fill me and I smile. Thankful for him more than these gifts. He brushed the stray hairs behind my ears.

"I can't help it," I confessed.

"Hormones…" He trailed annoying me.

He just had to!

"You're not allowed to say that."

"Joy," he corrected in a high-pitch.

A chuckle escaped me.

"Now you're making me laugh and I am confused."

"You're allowed to feel, whatever you like, babes."

I simpered, unable to stare at anything else. He pulled a red rose from behind his back. Presenting it near my face. The beautiful odour reaches my nose. I took a hold of it, a card dangled from it.

To the one I love,

For the most loving and

Caring person in the world,

Thank you for loving me.

Taking care of our family,

Love forever,

Eric.

He regularly reminds me of why I love him. I am the luckiest woman alive. I wanted him right there. I folded my lips inward gauging him ready to pounce on him. He stood slipping into his jacket holding his hand out to me like a well-mannered gentleman. He is so handsome, sweet and caring.

"You really do clean up well Hall." I winked at him giving my hands to him.

"Let's go to the ball!"

CHAPTER FORTY-FOUR

We arrived after the procession. Although some reporters lay in wait, outside in the warm Divinish air, of lazy breeze and humidity. My hair survived four and a half months here and the straightening is holding quite well behind a white elastic band around my head. A braid tied in with glittered silver strings and diamond studs exposed my neckline and natural light make-up and pale pink glossy lipstick.

Eric pulled up on the curb, the valet opened my door and another greeted him opening his door. He glances at me with a small quiver in the corner of his lips rushing out and around the car to meet me.

I waited. He seems to be thriving in this atmosphere and enjoying a private joke. I fiddled with my wrap delaying my exit and giving him time to help me out. I raised my hand in anticipation. He takes it and I gave him a reassuring smirk. Putting his elbow up, I hooked my arm in his.

We walked the short path of gold carpet and up three stairs to the entrance of the queerly shaped canopy with funny-shaped pillars the ridges appeared to be scales in patterned. Like a snake's body. The tall white double doors crackled as they lay open for guests.

The moon's full, closer than usual standing at the top of the stairs I only just conceived. Eric is in his element. We gaze into the busy lit halls as the music of a live-stringed band hums in filling us as we enter.

The open floor crowd of ladies dressed in evening gown colours mixed with the men in black ties, lit room of detailed gold, abstract tiles glistening in the chandelier light. The idea of late arrival to avoid stares has now dawned as silly.

Heads are turning fast reminding me of the places my attacker has hidden. I carefully place my feet down the three steps gaping at my exposed legs as the loose cowl cream dress sits above my knees and the gorgeous, strapped wedge slippers that my husband bought me.

Mentally I check my shaved legs, securing the wrap around my arms, holding the light clutch in front of me. I breathe shallowly raising my head at the bottom of the stairs and catching the not-so-friendly eyes of the guests, my stomach cringed.

This looked a lot friendlier on TV.

Maybe too much wonton soup amongst other things…

Introspectively, as Eric's grin takes over, the mark along my neck is a subtle way Eric claims his territory or reminds me of the soreness of his intimate touch. I shake my head both pleased and ashamed of our events before this ball. The thought comforts me a bit.

I am on edge in the crowd. Knowing he is out there, the one who touched me, cornered me at the L.D.O. I didn't see his face but his voice haunts me. Plagued by the thoughts, my eyes moved around, power or paranoia?

He could be anywhere, anyone. The love bites, now rubbing them, I recoil at the memory of the assaulter's tongue. I see some of the mayor's officers around and I wonder if the culprit can be one of them.

Should I let Eric know?

Eric seemed comfortable placing his hand above my behind leading me to chaos. The eerie feel of eyes following our every move and piercing through the smile that I have painted. The hairs on my arms spiked sensitive to everyone and everything. I feel the static in the air, all coming towards me.

Being here, in the open, only increased the urge to hide. I feel exposed and the empathic wave of emotions mixed in the crowd, has definitely not centred my unease. I feel it, eyes focused on me and a hunger growing with the unwanted peering.

Feeling the blood rushing through to my skin, I scan the room with dilated eyes and my skin prickles. It isn't pleasant. It is unwelcoming as the mumbling conversations grew louder in the pause of changing songs.

I cannot control my breathing. Small groups of ladies and gents converse with Eric as he introduced me with a smile. I stood back avoiding everyone as they barely acknowledging me there.

My feet are getting tired.

My eyes look towards the seating area where some are enjoying finger foods and cocktails. Eric's signalling a waiter as they swoon past with champagne and orange juice flutes on their shoulders without luck.

Mayor Mall makes his way across the room, his black tuxedo tailored to his height precisely, an impassive expression. Curiously, a large gold rope necklace with a pendent that looks very similar to the one his daughter was recovered with after her assault.

His not-too-subtle bodyguards lurk closely behind as he is making small conversations through the crowd and I am struggling to avoid gazing.

"Are you, all right?"

Eric breaks my observing. I shook my head sinking my fingers deeper into my clutch bag. The sweat makes fingerprints on the silk, beige material. We find a table finally. Eric takes the bag from me, putting it on the table pulling my face to his.

"Sunday, you would officially be my wife."

Wow, after three years our Cáhilt is here.

Eric distracts my worrying with something else, I smile at him excited to be his. Relaxing slightly, I was dazed at his brown glowing eyes. My moist fingers knot between us. He took my sweaty palms knotted together between us, and brings them to his face, his stare focused on me kissing them. His breath tickles cooling them marginally and I blush.

"Let's practice our first dance."

He smiles, leading me to the crowd of dancing guests. As we walk, a song ends and another with a deep baseline begins.

"Maybe this can be our song."

I squint. He strolls slower.

"Do we actually have a song?" I grinned at him.

"Of course. Every couple has a song."

He leads me to the edge of the crowd bridging my arms around his neck and cupping his around my disappearing waistline.

"You're just making that up…" I giggle at him.

"Maybe, but our song would say so much more than just instrumentals."

I chuckle resting my head on his shoulder as we sway slowly to the live band. There was a strange statue behind the band, an image of a man but an animal. The strange pull of disaster tangles my insides as my heartbeat increases.

"Are you sure you can handle this?"

He sees right through me. I shook my head to reassure him.

"If you've had enough, we *can* get out of here."

His tone is suggestive and seductive as he whispers in my ear. His beard brushed against my face then pecks my cheek raising my pores but not enough to shake this vibe. I want to say yes, but instead, I deflect.

"I can use a drink."

Knowing Eric, he will not easily let this go either. I am not sure at this point whether I should tell him. Especially since I don't understand what happened or what the man wanted from me. Besides, I don't want to leave and ruin this for him.

"OK." His voice full of doubt. "… Maybe we can dance to another song?"

The tenseness has reflected in my dancing as we continued to sway. A beautiful piece filled with strings and humming begins. I feel his smile over my head. He pulls away. I stare at him unable to hide my grin. He surprises me with a dip and spin. It reminds me of my graduation.

"This brings back memories," he suddenly admits breaking my reminiscing.

We were thinking the same thing.

I squint pulling my head back to gauge his expression.

"… Our first dance," he says.

"My graduation," I finished confirming we were thinking the same thing. I hold him closer as I remembered.

We danced without any song…

"What was that guy's name again?" He's gawk is broad, filled with pride.

"Don't pretend you don't remember Kevin," I cackled.

"He ditched you at your dance." His voice still seems annoyed. I am lucky he doesn't know the actual story behind that. I scoffed.

"He didn't really ditch me. You scared him off." Partly true. *And he knows it.*

"I only reveal the eminent ending."

"Really…"

"Yes… Us…"

We paused gazing at each other as the song continues. Then he placed his lips against mine a few seconds before parting my lips with his. Holding the back of my head, pulling me into him sucking surprising me in the process; taking my breath with it.

I returned the favour kissing him standing in the middle of the dancing crowd. Only our heads move, filling each other's mouths. The music stopped and we took a few more seconds fused to each other.

"Thank you, ladies and gentlemen, honoured guest."

Mayor Mall calls the crowd to his attention on the stage. Eric and I defuse our lips turning to the stage. I tidied my lipstick with my fingers smiling. He cleared his throat. With a pair of rosy cheeks folding my lips as my husband stands behind me opening his legs so our midsection meets.

He pulls my curved ass, against his erection cradling both his hands under my tiny bump. His unsteady breathing falling over my hair, I am satisfied.

I am not the only one whose breath was taken away by that kiss.

I am pleased with myself. Mayor Mall continues, "This week is the beginning of the week-long celebration of Cedérus. For all those who don't know, Cedérus is the third most powerful Zemand god. He represents power, revival and forgiveness.

"I know everyone thought this might have been a really queer choice but as a Zemand high priest we study the moon. In light of what happened to my daughter, I was forced to revisit religion and look at the skies. Can someone help me with this?"

Mayor Mall stops and begins waving his hands and there is a loud metallic rumble that shook the floor. The statue has disappeared and the wall is opening to a very full moon that looks yellow. I instantly feel faint. He continues, "This year, the moon has become blood. A lot of us believe that is Cedérus calling to us for forgiveness and to show his power. We have answered. So, let the three years of Cedérus begin."

He has spread his arms open and the crowd uproar in applause.

Is he serious?

Eric has not changed his position. I try to shake this feeling but I can't more so. The overpowering strange sensation that has every hair on my body on high alert. A sixth sense, in tune with movements beyond my eyes. The moonbeams are charging something that's raising inside me. I swallow hard. My heartbeat increases and the sounds are quieting tuning into an invisible wave. My body tingles receptive of what I cannot see.

"What do you say we wrap this up and go?"

Eric shifts me, the music returns and I welcome the gesture. Suddenly, the weight of the baby on my bladder. I shook my head repelling the trance.

"I think I need the bathroom first."

Cold water on my face may help. I agree internally.

Eric released me taking me away from the crowd, my hands in his strolling with me.

"You're not coming."

I stopped him at the entrance. He squinted at me.

"Do you still want that drink?"

"Sure." I shrug.

"I'll meet you back at the table?"

I have managed impassive. He pecked my cheek looking at me going in.

Just a little while longer; A failed attempt to calm myself inwardly. I patted water on my face and used the toilet.

Moving through the crowd I only just notice Sharron Mall. Our eyes meet briefly she turns as soon as our hazels connect.

I don't think she forgives me for badgering her.

The explanation I gave myself. She is beautiful. The tasteful sapphire princess line, cap sleeve dress suits her. A far contrast to the things I have seen her wear. Although her thick foundation lightens her skin, the blue really brings out the clear and brightness of her eyes, she looks, pure.

After I returned, Mayor Mall has come off the stage and is socialising once more. I try to avoid his gaze. His stare pierces me. I hastily sprinted toward the table. Eric hasn't returned.

I grabbed hold of my bag again ready to leave. My palms are sweating again as the discomfort in my tummy returns. Anxiousness is beginning to overthrow me.

"Agent Davis-Hall."

What the…

The familiar but unfamiliar voice calls to me from the crowd of the dance floor. An unwelcomed magnetic pull quickens with my heartbeat of trouble as Brian Kumal sauntering.

My breathing thickens, misting smoke into the room. He skilfully swoops two drinks from the waitress passing by with a mischievous grin offering one to me.

"Mr Kumal."

I sneer at his optimistic and audacious gull clutching my bag in my hands over my tummy. He leans into me to give me the drink. Eric takes the drink before it reaches me with a perplexed expression.

Where did he come from?

Brian gawked at me locking his brown eyes to mine hypnotising me seemingly exultant and amused. The room grew quieter like we were caught someplace else.

It was an odd sensation; a tightness grew around my waist I felt my shawl loosen cascading down my shoulders. My hands fell at my side gliding over the baby bump. Eric cleared his throat catching the shawl before it dropped covering my shoulders successfully avulsing me.

"Um, Brian Kumal this is my husband, Eric. Eric, Brian." I introduced softly.

Brian stood eyes fixed on me as Eric stretched his hand forward with an unusual but pleasant grin, exposing his dimples on his lightly shaved beard.

A few seconds passed, Eric was about to pull his hand back then, Brian snatched his hand making a smacking sound, trapping Eric's hand with both his hands, firmly shaking.

"You're very, very lucky… she is…" Brian trailed, on what seemed to be him searching for a word. "… Precious," he said after a few seconds between a standoff of the men. "… Very special." Brian grinds through his teeth.

"Thanks for saying, but I already knew that."

Eric's words were swift with a squint. I grinned at their sombre faces. The moment became awkward as neither would let go.

"Can I get a non-alcoholic drink?" I fit between them and turned towards Eric, they let go.

"Would you like a juice?" Eric said fishing his wallet out his jacket pocket.

"This is an open bar." Brian pointed out slyly.

Eric shook the wallet into his pocket paused with an impassive icy stare.

"I'll be back." Eric sounded like he was warning, before walking away. Before though, he pecked my cheeks, eyes fixed on Brian.

When Eric was out of earshot, I asked,

"Are you following me?" I narrowed my eyes in irritation at Brian.

He put his one hand in his pocket, looked at the floor briefly before turning his eyes back at me.

"Believe it or not, I had no choice in being here," he says with a bitter undertone.

I frown at his gesture. "Is that so?" I crossed my arms showing off my small bump.

He eyes it briefly then moved his brown eyes back into my hazels, my heart leapt.

"Last week was a coincidence." He is defending himself with an amused grin.

I sulked even more, annoyed at his unspoken amusement. "I find that really hard to believe," I argued.

"Why is that? I shop, Agent Davis." He carries on with a grin wide and white.

"For wedding dresses?" I narrowed my eyes emphasising my exasperation at him.

He chuckled. "Shannan, I saw you... and thought I should, say hi."

"Humm," I groaned. "You are..." I am lost for words. "... Unbelievable! You know that." Grinding my frustration finishing my sentence finally.

He gasped, taking a measured step towards me. Too close, for me and the very ignorant Eric, who will; physically express his view, and is somewhere, around the room. Brian's minty breath blew on me.

"I don't believe that's an appropriate comment." He leered.

I stepped back. I can hear flashes of cameras around me and he sneered.

"Something funny Mr Kumal?" I asked waiting on a reply when I heard another voice.

"Brian..." Mayor Mall called. I turned seeing a small group of reporters following him. I squint at the flashes.

"Father." Brian was abrupt.

What in the...

"The story of the prodigal son continues." Brian exhales putting his hands into his pockets turning towards the mayor.

His jaws tensed imprinting the jawbones and he clenched his teeth. I can hear a hiss resounding from the 'S'.

"I know you're the faithful one Brian. Ah, I see you have been keeping Agent Davis company." The mayor looked at me quizzing me. I am just as baffled.

"I am here with my husband," I blurted putting my hands up.

I am just clearing the air.

Intensely gazing at Mayor Mall's deportment, who moves his head up and down with the same inquisitive expression at me. I hear the noise from the crowd increase as a jazzy, instrumental finishes, a slow tune starts.

"My husband is Eric Hall." My pitch is a bit high and defensive.

Why did I do that again?

"Husband?" Mayor Mall questioned in contempt with a stern stare at Brian. Brian flinch moving his eyes away from the flashes then the mayor nodded to say, "Ahh, the S.D.A.F. director." His poker face still painted before he showed some teeth for a photo.

Shit they've met!

Brian has slipped away in the conversation.

"Your son?" I want confirmation.

"The faithful one," Mayor Mall confirmed.

"Why did I believe Sharron to be an only child." I voiced my thinking, recalling her profile.

"She is not. She has siblings … you agent Davis-Hall." Mayor Mall's voice penetrates my reviver. "… Any progress with the assailant, my daughter?"

The way he structures his sentences and deceitful smile irritates me. Distracted by curiosity, I vow to revisit anything that may have been overlooked. One of the things that haunts me though is her insistent in the interview about being gang raped and her first story.

She lied, why?

A strange emotion waved. I am sensing something, peeking through, that is veiled, but quickly the curtain is closed.

Mayor Mall paused and his eyes move over me strangely. Not the first time tonight, and still creepy. The air electrifies all static feeds through the hair over my skin.

Photographers take pictures of us burning my retina with the flash and pausing the unnamed stance between us. I strolled away wording from the prying eyes wearing smiles, both of us as if rehearsed or natural.

"I am not at liberty to discuss an ongoing investigation with anyone, you understand." The professional comes out with a surprise of diplomacy. The mayor smiles genuinely and I sense his pride.

"I understand but, Sharron, my daughter, I need to know that you're doing everything you can, to get this. That you're watching over her, as a sister."

His tone is earnest, but his half sentences are disturbing. He almost had me believe that he cared deeply, feeling some compassion emanating from him.

Is he for real? This is the second time he has said something like that. This time, I need to be clear.

"With all due respect Mayor Mall, I don't take my work home with me. I am doing my best to bring all those offended, in this case to justice."

His head fell as he wagged it from left to right with his right hand in his tuxedo saying disapprovingly,

"Well Shannan, that's unfortunate."

He drew a golden pendent the length of a large key from his jacket pocket. The serpent Cedérus erected, puffs out, hissed at me. Its mouth opened with the body coiled beneath it.

The eyes were sapphires, flashed for a second to jade and ruby stones in the opened puffs swinging on a chain its gaze on mine. My heart palpitated chest tightened. I felt light-headed and almost lost my footing.

"Why?"

Stumbling I pushed his hand away from me, knots clenched in my stomach. The need to throw up comes. I moved towards the crowd to find sanctuary my mouth is suddenly filled with saliva, my vision blurred. I feel ill.

The room shook as I doubled over, everyone around seemed unaffected. I searched for my husband.

"Eric." His name barely sounded off my lips.

My face transformed in sorrow and I cradled my bump trying to protect the baby from this unprovoked act by the mayor. I called for Eric again only this time louder grasping at any and everything.

I looked up only to realise I am surrounded and everyone has a Cedérus' power form key like pendant around their necks, even Sharron Mall.

Breathing became difficult, I felt clustered, dizzy and surrounded by hate. My tummy tightened, stiffed and heavy. All surrounded movements slowed and slurred. I searched for an exit from this mob. I shout for my husband again with all the air in my lungs.

"Eric."

It is difficult to breathe. I crouch to the uncomfortable atmosphere everyone is looking on without helping. The laughter is clear, but the words muffled.

I try to get up.

"You want, to rise …" A voice shouted from the crowd.

"This is the door. Get up! Rise." Another clear set of words jeer from the crowd.

"Why are you doing this to me?" I whimper.

The masks of Cedérus' enclosed around me I hold my chest, weakened.

"Please stop!"

I saw Eric appeared through the horde he is mouthing but the laughter and mocking faded into my quickened heartbeat through my ears as the room tilts and I see feet around me.

A man stood outside of the chaos, he was wearing a red robe, with a gold rope around his waist as I was falling to the floor. His face shrouded by the hood but turns to me and I watch the figure unable to tear my gaze away.

Eric is on the floor and I am in his arms. The veins on his neck raised I could tell he's screaming. I was frozen by the very presence of the image outside the brawl. Then my vision went dark.

CHAPTER FORTY-FIVE

Gasping with a sit up to the immense pain, my tummy tightens with another one. Sweat streamed my face, Eric's hands in mine, trepidation surrounds us both. He tries to comfort me as my wet face comes close to his and I squeezed the air out with a harsh exhale.

"It's OK babes."

He says with reddened eyes moving the moist hair away from my vision. I held his hand, tight. His muscle flexed staying in position as I let all the pain out in the scream, gritted my teeth. Staggered and scared I reason within.

I shouldn't be in labour!

Please, please, please!

At only twenty weeks pregnant, this journey is just beginning and I am only now getting used to becoming a mother. I rebuked myself for every negative thought I had the two months knowing I was having a baby. Finally, I have accepted this new life and parenting. I cry begging God.

Please, please!

Please, baby, please, don't come yet.

I need to see you when you're ready, God please.

Clenching my teeth, grinding the pain I feel cheated.

I don't want it to be over.

Not yet.

My face soaked in tears I lay back on the hospital bed with a momentary release as a contraction subsided. The confusion of the monitors around me and the dialysis line where the midwife is injecting something into the line.

Catching my breath and I feel the tightness building in my cervix sitting me up again and I continued to weep with a yell.

"Gah."

I shout it out gaggling the pooling saliva feeling the intensity throughout my entire body. The sobs are ceaseless, and Eric comes to rest his forehead on my sweat filled head staring into my eyes. I felt another one. Crushing Eric's hand. The medicine has reached my arm with a weird cooling sensation flowing through my veins and up my arm. I lay back, relax, looking up at the lights over my bed.

I pray again.

****

The echoed thumping sound woke me. I welcomed the noise with a smile. The baby's heartbeat, I presume. Strong and steady, seemingly untouched by the events. My eyes are crusted by the tears from last night. I try opening them slowly because they ache. Joy fills me. Attempting to lift my stiff arms to stroke the bump.

Though plagued, with pain and discomfort with sealed eyelashes by the stains of crying and eyes sore, my smile grew. Blinking a couple times then flickering them to adjust my eyes to the morning light, I phrase.

Thank you, God!

What seems like a private room all to myself, a door to the end of my feet and a small wall structure near the exit. A bathroom I believe. Observing the strange environment, noting. I am hooked up to several chords and machines. Across my tummy, on my finger and I even feel the pricker of my hand where the dialysis, line pumps a clear liquid through my veins.

The laboured pain was gone, along with Eric. I try scanning again to see if he may have just stepped out before I woke. Trying not to worry I focus on this little bundle under my fingers, behind the walls of my tummy and protected inside of me. I sigh in relief.

I am not in labour. Thanking again for the miracle.

Sorting through the day that felt like an attack, I wonder what the mayor did to me and why. We were having a casual conversation and he spoke as he usually does in strange riddles. Then, unprovoked he shoved something into my face that made me … ill. My breathing increased again at the thought and the monitors spiked and a soft bell chimed.

This cannot be just about Sharron.

My mind rations the cause but I do not stay focus on that. I think of my baby and my husband having to spend the night with me crying from the pain.

The night would have been just as bad for him.

I excuse his absence again though, it concerned me. Comparing his actions to another situation where this part is familiar. The disappearing and returning with alcohol drenched breath.

I hope he's not self-loathing again! I sigh.

It would have been pleasing to wake up to him. I frown. But at the same time caressing my tummy delighted that the baby is all right. A memory of him staggering out of a bar, drunk walking through an alleyway come to immediate thought, with a rolling of my very tired eyes.

Or doing anything stupid! I begin a checklist of Eric's usual behaviour.

Like approach the mayor. If he knows it was him...

Was it really him? I question my own recollection of the ball, in echoes the only clear words I heard.

'You want to rise. This is the door. Get up! Rise.'

Something stirred inside me. Though the words strangely put together, they mean something. Focused on the phrases, I feel a strange shift and slight burning of my eyes. I opened my mouth. Words are right on the tip of my tongue. My throat bubbled to erupt something when the nurse came in.

She is just as she was before, professionally presented, pleasant deportment and the maroon lipstick contrasting her dark skin. Nurse Grumpy form Divinish North. She nodded once, with her hands at her side almost like a bow, strange. Offering me some water and medication with a singsong Divinish accent and a smile.

"How are you feeling today?" she asks giving me the small paper cup.

I nod rubbing my tummy. "Much better than last night."

Her expression says it all, a pity stare, followed by a stretched of silence.

She hummed before saying.

"… Doctor James will come to see you soon."

Then she took the cups and disposed of them, walking out the room. Did he take me to Divinish North again?

I worry that I may have been close to giving birth. The tolerant Doctor James saunters in not too long after, with the usual friendly demeanour.

"Good morning, Mrs Hall." He calls me incorrectly again and I twitch. Focused on the baby, I didn't dwell, paying close attention to what he has to say. "… How do we feel today?" He singsongs playing with the bed controls bringing my back slightly up.

"I am OK I guess." I mentally tick the boxes.

He's reviewing his clipboard of notes ticking, signing reading and nodding.

"Is my baby, OK?" I start the dialogue, impatient to know clutching the small rise of my baby bump holding my breath.

"Mrs Hall," he says it again, but I am too stressed to flinch. "… Yesterday you had a panic attack. It was not pregnancy related."

I released my breath shallow as Doctor James explain, meaningless to my expertise, and it does nothing to subside the anxiety towards my baby.

It was real! I felt it! My subconscious argues the point of early labour.

"OK… what does that mean?" Apprehensively I asked not hiding the concern for the threat of this pregnancy.

"Have you ever had a panic attack?" the good doctor asked.

Trolling through my memories for a place and a time. There was only the fog covering every moment. I shook my head. "… I don't know," I whispered.

"There is no need for worry Mrs Hall." *He is insisting on calling me that way.* I conceded listening. "… There are ways to deal with anxiety."

"I-I'm not…" I defend, the occurrence induced by the mayor.

The doctor looked at me with his head tilted and sigh. "You needed the rest. The panic attack aside, I am concerned about your elevated blood pressure."

"Blood pressure?" I frown. *What is he on about?*

"Yes. You seem to be developing gestational hypertension. This in itself is not as worrying because, there are ways to control this especially, if it is during your pregnancy.

"But I am concerned that this may develop into Preeclampsia. Only because this condition usually develops later in pregnancies, unless, you had hypertension before. Did you?"

He looks at me questioning.

I pout as a child would a father and protested, "No!" Shaking my head, appalled by his accusation.

"Do you have hypertension in your family?" he asked, innocently.

This question I am used to when meeting anyone new. They usually start with one, with a follow-up then, will reach to three questions tops, about my past. It wouldn't go any further, but with him, I'm afraid it would. It doesn't usually bother me because, it is part of me. But asking a question about something tangible, for the first time, I am sad at the loaded question and quiet.

Just say it!

Then I voiced low. "I don't know."

After eight years of trying, I simply lost the desire to continue the search for persons that birthed me. They are no longer in my forethought. I never conceived their unknown could affect any part of my life. I stare in silence rationalising.

"Can you ask your parents?" He pushes to question two. I know he means well, but something is brewing inside.

I hesitate. "I don't..." I exhaled. "... Know my parents." I ended loud and angry. The emotion just flushed to the surface for no apparent reason. I don't give them any consideration in my daily life.

Why do I need to now?

Resentment that I didn't know was there came through my subconscious, I am angry at them for abandoning me.

I watch the small rise of my tummy and vowed to protect this child always, the same promise I made to Danielle two years ago. I almost kept that promise. Resonating on the fact, that I would protect my children with my life, a question formed.

Why didn't my parents do the same for me?

Unless... they did.

The thought came and an urge to search came with a possible reason for my failure but it went in the same moment.

I have tried for so long.

I don't know if I could do it again.

Doctor James paused.

I crossed my arms bowing my head, waiting to see if there's a third.

"I have to do some more tests," he conceded and quietly continued his checks.

Annoyed at me, for taking the fury out on him, I just want to leave. Go home and forget any of this ever happened. Forget my feeling of being abandoned by them leaving me in a vulnerable state to be living on the streets, lost, attacked and almost raped at fifteen.

Avoiding the rabbit hole, I asked, "How long are the tests going to take?" I avoid his stare, patience on edge.

He clears his throat and he went on as professional as always.

"We have done a few tests already, and designed a special diet for you while you are here."

I breathe deep wanting the best but still ready to leave. "OK so what does that mean for me, and when am I going home?" My patience at the end and anger comes out again.

Doctor James stopped writing, put his hands at his sides, sighed before saying.

"Preeclampsia affects the placenta, which is essential for your baby. It is where the baby gets food and oxygen. If you continue on the path of not looking after yourself you can stop the oxygen flowing to your baby's placenta. Which would cause you to either give birth early or deliver a dead baby."

A chill pass through me and my heart swell with regret. He wasn't gentle this time and I took a moment to examine his words.

Eric.

"D-did you talk to my husband?"

I stuttered in fear of what Eric might do with the information and now, understanding his possible absence. Even I need a moment to absorb the information, my throat welted. Then the doctor answered me with more care in his tone.

"Yes." That confirmation made my heart leap and uneasiness escalate. "… I saw him before you woke up. You need to take some time to think about the options. The nurse will give you a few things to read, about panic attacks and high blood pressure in pregnancy.

"You will be in here for another few days just to be sure that your blood pressure is at a manageable state. Then, you'll need to perhaps get active, change your diet, put your feet up whenever you can. But most of all, rest as much as possible."

Doctor James completed more checks, signed the chart, then left. Whilst the doctor exited, Eric entered. My heart jumped. They shared a look upon passing one another and Doctor James tapped his shoulder and the men paused, spiking my anxiety observing me impassively. Then, they moved in opposite directions.

In one hand, Eric holds a double carrier and cups of hot drinks, lush not yet grizzly beard. He appears to have changed from his tuxedo to a pair of jeans, jersey and sneakers, quietly squeaking to the tiled floor as he enters handsomely tortured. *The beard seems to grow with his stress.*

One stray thought filter and I hoped it not to be true.

I wish I knew what he was thinking. He looks at me with caution entering.

I don't want to start a conversation that would lead to an unfavourable outcome.

He placed it gently at the side table, parted his lips. Then, exhaled closing his lips again, closing his eyes for a few seconds. His beautiful dimples sunk into his bearded face as he folded his lips inward in thought, I believe. Sitting on the edge of the bed, his eyes soften and glassy filled with regret, he leaned over me pecking my forehead.

"Good morning." The words he chose voicing softly.

Stroking my hair away from my face, over my forehead gazing at me. I'm still unable to gauge his mood. I opened my mouth.

"Hey!" I start low and we're both ready taking a deep breath voicing a distorted word together. There was a small quiver at his lips and I inhale again.

"Good morning." Sam careered in with a bouquet of flowers tall and obscure.

I squinted at her.

Eric groaned and clenched his teeth.

"What are you doing here?" Baffled at Sam's gesture, I voiced.

Eric exhaled loudly with an obvious groan getting up and turning to her.

I widened my eyes holding his hand, his back to my face.

Her expression upshifted as she stares at me avoiding his gaze. Briefly, he turned to me then took back his hands, placing them into his pockets.

"Sam…" Eric curt, turned to me I see the bones in his jaw working.

She squinted in his direction. "Good morning to you too." She answered his call, then asked me. "… How are you, and the little one?" She jeers.

"Sam," Eric warns through his teeth turning to her.

He is standing out of my reach. I try getting his attention blocked by the ridiculously huge vase of sunflowers she brought in.

Why sunflowers?

"Well, I had a lovely interrogation from Danielle this morning. Where she comes up with these questions, I don't know." She rolled her eyes I believe recalling the conversation our daughter usually carries, far beyond her age but is always entertaining. "… Somehow, she was not satisfied that I already gave her a sibling, could be because she is your age." Sam rolled her eyes again and Eric's jaw worked.

"Eric!" I called his name and he looked at me, thoughts broken for a moment of what he was about to do.

Honestly, I think she should know this man by now. I question her story and hope she gets to the point before his anger is at its fullest. His back is turned to me again and I cannot reach him to stop an outburst. Sam ignores whatever his face reads, I'm sure, icy expression or deathly stare to go on.

"… Today Danni finally let up from the annoying questions of 'mummy can I have a baby sister or brother' because it has been answered by you… so, thank you."

She grinned wide touching her eyes with a weird movement that looks like she wants to jump on me or worse, hug me, pointing at my tummy. Her pretty face is highlighted by the excitement in her eyes. Her twitching is reminding me of Danielle.

"Gee thanks!" I narrow my eyes at her.

"Besides I've done it twice, *not* doing it again!" she expresses with her hands widening her bright blue eyes making a comical scene.

I couldn't contain it any more, I laughed.

Sam finds herself between Eric and the bed, pushed aside the hot drinks rest her bouquet on the table. Seeming proud of her achievements and pulled a chair, as if we were girlfriends, barely acknowledging Eric. He stepped aside letting her through.

"… I brought you a visitor," she said landing her behind on the chair and crossing her long legs at the knees, smiling again.

Knowing Danielle has spent part of the Zemand week with her, surprised she had been so patient though. Wondering about the authenticity of her statement. But she is also weirding me out, again, being nice. Her heavy voice had cracked so many times it was strange to me. Danielle ran in the room pushing between her parents. She began her queries with the first question.

"So mum is the baby coming?" she asks with her big bright blues.

The title that she calls me both Sam and me flinch. I have to scold, "Danielle!" I warned playfully.

Why does she insist on calling me that!

Eric smiles.

I roll my eyes.

Sam stands to the corner watches her shoes briefly then back to Danielle.

"Oh no I remember, that's when your tummy gets really, really big." She expresses her sentence with her hands.

Hopefully, not! I consider my post baby body in fear.

"Oh, hi Daddy…" She turns to Eric wrapping her hands around his waist.

He responds, patting her head and kissing her wild hair. She hopped on the bed. Taking a deep breath, I am bracing the twenty intrusive questions. Looking and absorbing her excitement as she moved on to question two.

"Whoa your tummy has gotten really bigger since I last saw you."

I giggled and stroked her opened brown curly hair with an automatic answer.

"I saw you Thursday."

Eric's eyes widened.

Accidentally, I exposed something I delay telling and I hesitate.

"… I think it's the way I'm sitting Danielle," I try explaining and Eric's eyes moved to Sam with a squint, then to me. I gulp.

Danielle shrugs then shoots her next question. "Is it a boy or a girl?"

Eric grinned at her and I answer, "I don't know. I didn't ask." I folded my lips feeding on the happy emotions from Danielle.

"So, what is Mummy, gonna be?"

Something that Danielle and her sister are really good at, is asking the awkward questions.

The three of us breath hitched at the same time.

Everyone was quiet for a while. I took a few seconds to think and remembered my promise to always be honest with her.

"What do you mean?" I try to clarify buying some time for an appropriate answer.

"Um… to the baby?" She hits four and waits.

Sam and I looked at each other. Sam shrugged I hesitated. "A… a big aunt."

Sam moved her shoulders up and down squinting at me.

There was nothing she could add, I think. I shook my head awaiting at least five more questions from Danielle.

"So, what will that make me?"

I see her brain working the connections and I pause giving her a minute to ponder admiring her cute face. The thinking posture that is the spitting image of Eric. The way she frowns, crinkles her eyebrows and scrunches her nose, all him.

I hope that our baby gets that, that look.

I put both my hands over my tummy moving it up and down at the woken bump, maybe to all the voices or maybe just to Danielle and the warm feeling that emanates off her.

"This baby will always be your brother or sister," I say putting her out of her misery.

Her eyebrow went up just like her dad's when he is disarrayed.

"… Don't confuse yourself baby." I can see the muddle expression across her face. "Just like Auntie Paula and Auntie Lia are sisters; they share the same dad, you and this baby share your dad."

Looking at him who has a big smile towards me.

"OK," she took a moment drawing all logic, I'm sure. "… I have a surprise for you, close your eyes."

I obeyed.

"… No peeking," she singsongs.

"I wouldn't." I am playful.

I felt her move off the bed. "… All right, you can open your eyes… now."

Her excitement is contagious.

I opened my eyes and jump, to the surprise of my best friend Elizabeth and her Shabrada, Ian. We shrieked with delight. Eric came away from the bed getting out of the way.

"Elizabeth!" I am sure by my shrieking.

She's pregnant!

She didn't tell me.

I observed with widened eyes slightly disappointed. Numerous conversations we shared since I've been in Divinish, there wasn't even a hint.

She kept that quiet.

Wanting to pout and protest my subconscious pointed validly in song.

I didn't tell her that I was pregnant either. I checked myself thinking.

Shit! I only grinned at her grinning at me.

How did Paula keep becoming a grandma to me? Another question came to me and an answer.

No more babies from Sam made sense now. I chuckle internally.

She leaned over hugging me. Her warm ivory tone has gotten a shade darker with pregnancy. Her blue eyes bright with enthusiasm complimented her white cotton baby doll dress highlighted with the blue and green leaf pattern.

Her cherry shampoo hasn't changed or maybe it might be something she ate.

I viewed coming to me with a broad smile.

"Elizabeth Martinez, wow!" I say to her in shock.

My best friend, Elizabeth Martinez… yes, Martinez. Liz is Sam's older daughter and she resembles her mum and Danielle but paler. Although Eric has known Liz as long as he has known me, he didn't know Sam had another daughter until she returned from the dead almost three years ago.

She was well hidden.

Liz grew up with her grandmother. Sam never played an active role in the upbringing of her choice. There was no indication of her or her dad's existence. Like me, she was an orphan and mama Marts mothered us. I am comforted by the surprise of my best friend's visit. She comes in for a hug and I find words.

"Oh wow! How far along are you?" I asked hesitantly.

Liz grinned wide. "I'm about twenty-five weeks, due in April."

"That's great!" I stared at her rosy cheeks and fuller face as she explained. "Ian and I didn't want to say anything until after the twenty-week mark," she explains apologetically.

I have no excuse.

But I think, she may believe the same for me, given, um, history. My eyes still widened absorbing the shock of her news. Her face is full and cheeks rosy, her bump obvious pointed under her dress.

My best friend is pregnant, the same time as me! I am excited.

She pierced her big blues into me.

The way I found out and the days in the hospital as well as this case has filled my time, I couldn't tell her.

I excused myself slightly disappointed by her delay in news, and I also checked myself.

"I'm due in May." I felt prompted and know she has a lot of questions like her sister as do I. "… How's the Cahilt plans coming along?" I shifted the conversation to her to let the elephant out the room. She paused with a squint knowing me well.

"We've set a few dates. Two months from now… I haven't really set an exact date just yet." She begins her quarrelsome tone dragging the chair next to the bed to sit.

"The end of March?" I asked for clarification.

"And yes." She circled her sapphires at me. "… I know that's cutting it close to giving birth with a due date the second week in April. Sam has already made her concerns known."

She pointed at her mother who has put her hands up, making her black leather jacket flutter exposing her pistols in their shoulder holsters, hung below her breast and her white round neck T-shirt. Sam's bowing her head then shaking it.

"Yeah, aren't you afraid you'll give birth while walking up the aisle?" I squinted at her.

"Ian and I have completed Shabráda about nine months and we're finishing our ceremony next two months."

Her tone changes to argument and I know where she is heading. She seems to have gotten worse pregnant. I fluttered my eyes under my eyelids, leaning my head back, slapping my forehead.

"Oh my gosh Liz!" *Please stop!* Instead, she went on.

"The way I look at it, it's either that or wait until the baby is born. And, I don't know what might happen after that. I don't want to postpone and something comes up. Next thing it's three years later with the threat of dissolvement." The summarized version of my marriage.

Mine and Eric's eyes widened accepting the needed criticism.

"Ouch Liz!"

I say softly, looking down at my sheets creasing it between my fingers. Liz has managed to use herself as an example to drive her point. Sam circled her eyes looking away as she knows from experience to never get between Liz and my correction.

"The next few months, your marriage will become insolvent and illegal."

She never minces on her words; my second wake-up call today. Prompting me that my ceremony is due to take place tomorrow. Disappointed as I figure I will not be leaving the hospital on time and we once again have to delay completing our marriage ceremony.

"Thanks for reminding me, Liz and making me feel bad," I protest at the truth.

"You two made too many excuses…"

True.

She points at him who's face unmoved by her judgement.

"... except this time, I know it was planned for tomorrow. I'm sorry..."

She watches me laying back on the bed and pouts rubbing my shoulder. To have Liz here, truly revealed the lengths Eric has gone for us. Guilt is taking me. He doesn't appear to be moved by Liz as usual, but I cannot allow her to openly disapprove Eric's efforts. The delay has always been me.

Change direction... "Thanks Liz. What about yours? How is the planning?" I am crossing my fingers that she's taken the bait.

"It would have been epic, Eric."

She shows Eric the thumbs up with an apologetic tone and he nodded at her as they share a rare bonding moment. I crinkled the sheets again.

She doesn't seem like she's taking the bait.

"You're forgiven only if you will be my matron of honour."

I giggled. *Yes!* "I'm honoured Liz!"

Suddenly tears filled my eyes and I cannot stop it.

"... Even if they have to drag me out there in a wheelchair, I'm coming."

What is wrong with me? Even my subconscious weeps.

Elizabeth tilted her head to one side and her eyes watered then I started to really sob.

"Damn, I still haven't gotten use to the hormone spikes." I ration.

"Me too!" Liz's face reddens and she sniffles, a few seconds passed then we both ruptured with laughter.

CHAPTER FORTY-SIX

By then, Eric covertly eased himself out of the room. Ian soon followed him as they both knew they weren't going to get the chance to offer a word. Ian strode his tall, slender frame towards the wall, his extended lush goatee and bald head shining from the hall light.

He examined the wall before leaning his khaki chinos and short sleeve festive white shirt against it. Eric exhaled long and deep throwing his back on the wall leaning with him.

They're outside the door leaned up against the wall, their eyes inside at us as we continued chatting.

I am contented that he has another male to converse with at times. Besides his school friend Dave, who lives in Ceda, Ian is the closest friend that I know of, besides Lia. Which I disapprove of their relationship. Ian said to Eric.

"When you put those two together, they'll talk for hours,"

"Hum, I know what you mean."

Eric is short as he broods throwing his head against the wall creating a hollow knock. Lifting his moss-green jersey, Eric shoves both his hands into the pockets of his dark-blue loose-fitting jeans. Bending his knee and propping the sole of his black trainers on the wall.

"Liz and I have decided to have our wedding in March. Pending of course, Liz changing her mind."

Ian tries to break the oncoming self-loathing deliberation of Eric.

"Good for you, congratulations." Eric is clipped with Ian.

"I'd like you to be my best man." Ian once again is assessing him,

"No problem, just tell me when."

Eric exhaled again his foot slips to the floor and began staring at his feet still lean into the wall.

The hurried hollow trot of Lia's thick black heals filled the noiseless hallway. She's crossed her hands across her tucked in silk navy sleeveless blouse, beneath her bouncing full breasts. The balance of her matching single strapped small navy handbag on her shoulder.

Several gold bracelets clinked when she moved her hands to her sides, stroking her tight black jeans. She glanced at them, nodded slowly walking pass the door without stopping, as if covertly signalling Eric's attention.

Eric still raising his head sluggishly following her with his eyes until she was out of sight, an uncomfortable silence passed with her, between Eric and Ian. Ian closely observed Eric's reaction.

Eric waited a minute or two then went towards the vending machine, a clear vision from the hallway. She resurfaced as he jiggled in his back pocket fishing out his wallet.

She's on the other side of him being blocked by his body and says something only for his ears. He says something under his baritone inaudible whilst continuing his actions. She says something again and their whispering is gaining volume and becoming aggressive.

She smooths her hand from his back to his shoulders moving in a circular motion. He shrugged her off turned to her and shouted.

"Not now!"

She reached for him. He moves out of her reach putting his hands up, turning with a grunt he stomps enraged an unfamiliar cold expression across his face. He returned to stand with Ian again. Without whatever he intended to have at the machine, if at all that's the true reasoning behind his visit there.

Aaliyah scoffed turning on her heels sauntering towards the elevator. Hitting the call button repeatedly and loudly until it opened. She leapt in pressing a button crossing her arms jiggling the bangles as the door closed.

Eric resumed his position on the wall of the room opposite Ian. Leaning his head on the wall, facing Ian. Leaving a small passageway between them, Ian watches the frustration growing on Eric's face. He's waiting for the right moment to come.

He peeks at his wife glowing as she scolds me. My conservative actions to her invasive drilling about Eric and my evermore delaying nuptials he couldn't contain his concern any further.

"What's up with you and Aaliyah?" Scrunching his thick eyebrows and narrowing his green eyes at Eric.

"What are you talking about?" Eric dodged.

"Say that to someone who didn't see what I did. She's the only one who doesn't see it."

Ian pointed in my direction his annoyance clear in his tone and expression.

"It's a long story." Eric avoids it.

"Long story or not, you shouldn't be doing what you're doing. She is a smart girl, sooner than later she's going to put all the pieces together just as I did, and when she does… its better it comes from you than anyone else."

Eric breathes deeply, exhaling through his tightened jaw.

"I can't believe, how fucked up this thing has gotten."

"That's what this is all about? You should know that she's grown. She is no longer that scared girl you rescued; she has never been scared of anything."

Eric squinted at Ian hooking his thumbs in his pockets.

"Don't I know it?" He shakes his head a little as if thinking of a single moment then continues. "… She always leaves me room to wonder why about a lot of things."

"She does that to make you know she can stand on her own… Make this right."

Eric's and my eyes met as he peeked at Liz and me chatting. He bowed his head gazing at his shoes a bit, he released his pockets, came inside his eyes red glossy and an expression I have never seen on him before.

It made me nervous. Anxious of what to make of it then he parted the crowd of visitors leaning over me and kissed my forehead tenderly. Pausing a while spiking my disquiet further.

What was that for?

Sam called, "Kids say goodbye to Shana, she needs her rest." She seemed to understand that signal. It makes me a bit jealous, and uncomfortable. She continued, "… See you when you get back to the office Shana." Eric tensed with hardened eyes at her. She flinched eyeing him before continuing, "… Don't worry about the things there. Focus on that little one."

She hurried her words taking Danielle's hand guiding her off the bed, moving quickly to the door.

Eric whispered something to her. Being a passenger to their synced emotion detector is never fun. She puts her hand up waving. Danielle ran back, hugged me, I pecked her full head of hair.

"I will see you soon," I tell her.

She shook her head with a slight worry across her face then skipped to Sam. Elizabeth and Ian kissed me good bye. Then Ian slapped Eric's shoulder shaking his head. Whispering, 'good luck', I think is what I heard leaving me curious as to the upcoming events.

The blood rushes to my cheeks as my skin prickles. I am ready to accept. Sam eyed Aaliyah as she lurked outside the room. They exchange words loudly, thankfully without obscenities.

I think that may be because Danielle was there.

Clearly, I heard Sam urging her to leave us be. Sam, Liz, Danielle and Ian made their way to the elevator. Aaliyah continued peeking into the room partially distracting me from Eric's questionable foul mood. Eric seemed so shady.

"What's wrong?"

I couldn't wait any longer. I hoped that Doctor James' diagnosis hasn't made him mad or self-loathing. He tilts his head putting his hands in his pockets waltzing towards the bed.

I shift uncomfortably gazing at him softly. Aaliyah's shadow behind him distracts me. She's still in the hallway looking inside trying to listen in, I think. It is a bit annoying and I wished there was an actual door to lock her out but a strange thought filled me.

This doesn't feel right.

She is cautiously assessing outside but not entering, pacing a short distance to the door and back. She seemed to be walking on eggshells around Eric today. A few weeks ago, he completely ignored her in the parking of the apartment building. Their interaction concerns me. Usually, in a setting like this, she would come in with the crowd, rest her hands across his shoulder, intentionally touch him for me to see and joke about our age difference or something about Eric and my relationship. She thinks us openly as a joke.

He told me they weren't partners any more which is understandable, he's the director of the highest form of policing in the country, he has other directors and somehow, this time she was not able to follow him in this career path as she has done in the past.

Maybe because of her rising assault accusations that she racked up this past year.

This fact I read on the proposal to have her dismissed. *What is going on with them?*

My mind stray... *like he would tell me anyway.* I scoffed at myself crossing my arms as he forced a smile.

"I'm sorry..." He stands at the end of the bed watching down at me, not his usual stare with his big brown eyes.

"What for?" I am troubled and baffled at the same time.

Wow he's apologising?

He takes a cleansing breath before he explains, "... For not trusting you to make your choice... and for, a lot of other things."

What other things?

"I so badly wished I could sweep you out of this bed take you to those cliffs or marry you right here," he said earnestly swooping his hands to express himself.

I giggle at his actions wishing the same.

Then he was quiet again and the brooding built with his continued words. "I want you to know that you are... what makes me better, and the reason for me to be, better... you have my heart... my body, my life, my... everything. I love you..."

His eyes are glassy he is looking at me but it seems seeing something else. He comes closer, sitting in line with my hips. For a moment, I feel sadness, anxiety and shame as the air electrifies. This is not him. His voice was soft and a bit hoarse. I took a breath saying,

"I love you too honey but..."

He put his index finger on my lips, tilting closer to me. Taking my hand in his, under the IV lines and kisses it. His expression unfamiliar to me a bit of sadness and regret I think, locking his gaze deeply trying to conjure the words. Charting into undiscovered waters, I part my lips about to speak unable to imagine his concern or fear maybe. I need to smooth things out.

"No, I need to say this." He stops me. I folded my lips inwardly bemused by him. "… I have done…"

"Hi, how are you?" The voice came from behind, stopping Eric's sentence.

I leaned around Eric to see Aaliyah pounce louder than usual, dark jeans slim-fitted accentuating her already curvy behind. Her icy-blues focused on Eric with some threat or caution. She entered the room clicking her heels, lengthening her legs as though being six feet with those heels wasn't enough. She's holding a bouquet of random wild flowers with her political smile painted. Natural lip glossed in the light. Everything about her irritated me.

"What… do you want?" I blurted.

"Well, my new partner is sick so…" Her singsong tone gives away her ulterior motives to be disruptive.

"Partner? Really?"

I should have made clearer the chain of command. My inner thoughts raised with her suggestions that we are on the same level.

I look up at Eric gauging his manner before I continued. "… Since when do you give a shit?" The unfiltered words slipped quick, and I want to punch her in the throat.

"I don't want you to think that I'm a heartless bitch."

Since when does she care about how I feel?

There is nothing in her actions in the past or even recently that we work together which indicates care. She sways around the bedside table brushing closely to Eric and revels in my displeased gaze. Then, pushing the flowers Sam and Danielle bought for me, placing hers into my clear view. I scoffed.

"Too late." The words were like a knee-jerk movement.

She sucked her teeth and placed one hand on her hip pointing to me.

"Look, I'm trying…"

"Get out Aaliyah."

Eric startled me turning to her. His voice raised, steady and reverberated through the room cutting her short. My eyes widen and jaw dropped along with hers. He stood up with his eyebrows crinkled and eyes narrowed across my bed.

"What?" Her tone preventive and slightly surprised just as I was, only I did not say it.

Did he just... My jaw still couldn't shut.

I was gobsmacked beyond belief. Barely made eye contact but his expression firm and sure. A large vein popped across his forehead his eyes were bloodshot. All his muscles tensed, and still for what feels like a minute.

Silence is in the room.

She blinks once, twice then a few times more absorbing his shocking words. With a few more awkward moments uncertain of her next move like me.

"I-I was only..." she tried to explain.

"Only what: only going to insult my wife?" He is louder.

Oh, snap!

Aaliyah and I gasped at the same time.

"I have had enough of you and that shit. Don't you ever, disrespect her again." Eric grows out from sitting, turns to her face, pointed to her then to me, towering over the tall woman. "... Do you understand me?"

His eyes cold and voice a scary calm daring her next move.

She stills her eyes submissive but unapologetic an unspoken stance between them urging her to thread carefully. I lay between their tensions unable to leave as she absorbs his declaration of war.

"Can I talk to you outside?" She urged him softly in a secretive tone reaching for him.

"*No!*" he echoed again frightening me and astonishing her. "I think it's time you leave."

He pointed at the door behind her, his stare dangerous and tone I don't recognise, I am terrified.

"Eric..." She urges him again.

"Get the fuck out. *Leave!*"

My eyes widened and heart races as the words left his mouth.

She seems just as confused as me.

I have never, in our four-year relationship, heard him speak to her like that, ever.

It has been a long time coming. For years he stood by while she insulted and belittled me without defending me. I pinch my leg under the sheet because it didn't feel real.

I have to know that was real.

She slowly and unwillingly let the shock lead her out the room.

He exhaled his frustration putting his head in his hands, then on his hips, paced a bit then pulled a chair close to the bed. He sat again with my hands in his building the moment again, the doctor came in.

"Fuck!" he growled pulling the little hair he's got on his head.

Stood up, his politeness takes over welcoming him and being tentative to the results and checks. Walking outside as the doctor did his cervical check. He paced feverously he appeared to be making a conversation with himself.

I wish I knew what was wrong or what he was thinking so that I could help. What is it that he needs to tell me that could be so difficult? My senses tell me it is about her or about their 'partnership' but in the pit of my stomach I don't want to go there, not now.

… But when would be right?

****

Two days after, I was discharged from the hospital. Eric and I never continued the 'important' conversation and I didn't have any other visitors since Aaliyah.

I was excited to get out of there. I couldn't wait to eat real food instead of the rabbit food they were feeding me.

My hands were still sore at the removal of the IV lines Eric carried my two bags.

I cradled his firm biceps walking through the halls and calling the elevator.

"I have this sudden craving for that fried chicken we had in the drive-through."

I requested a craving tasting the awesome saltiness from my three days' lack of salt. The baby agreed tapping me from the inside. He smiled leaning across and kissed my hair.

"Do you want a regular bed here? Doctor James will be happy to keep you."

I narrowed my eyes at him and frown knowing is true but as always coming with a clever way of rebounding.

"I can't tell the baby no," I singsong with the fluttering of my eyelids.

"But I *can,* tell you no," he counters. I pout.

Rats! "Can you really." I looked up fluttering my eyelashes at him.

His full lips curved at the side then grew serious almost instantly. The elevator doors opened and two ladies poured out, we got in.

"What's wrong?"

He exhaled not looking at me giving me a half smile.

"We really need to talk about somethings…"

My imagination went to him and Aaliyah. Thinking about this is unpleasant. My subconscious crosses her arms.

The rumours are unfounded.

Then I thought of his job, then my job and our baby.

"… This is not the right scene." He broke my oncoming worry. "Let's just get you home. I want you to relax."

"You're not making me relax," I say my thoughts aloud then added playfully. "… I already said yes to marrying you and I am already having your baby… what else is it that you need to say? If it's that important why not right now? Cease the moment!"

The lift doors opened into the underground parking. The white musty room with soft lights spiked my senses I held him tight.

I never told him about what happened in the evidence room.

I wondered if he found out.

Or maybe he found the one who attacked me in the alley.

Or maybe he found out about Brian…

There's nothing going on there…

Still, why do I feel so… guilty?

My imagination went free.

Feeling of guilt, stupidity and inadequacy flooded me at the same time.

I should confess.

He paid for the parking and we strolled in silence. My arm around his biceps, my head resting on his upper arm, I contemplate the bad choices.

Then, the thought of him and his ex-partner the many untold stories between them coupled with the gossips. I am still baffled about our current mood.

A car screeched up the turns to another level and my senses spiked again. The dim lights set the scene for a chill in the air. Remembering the scene of my attack and the void of his motives, my heart palpitated.

He could be anywhere. My subconscious annoyingly reminded me.

Eric unlocked the car as we approached it. I swiftly got in hoping to calm my oncoming panic. Eric, dubious, took the bags to the trunk shifting and slamming it. He came around opened the driver's door and sat. Another van went screeching out its park adding to my disquiet, my heart raced.

"Honey did you get the plate on that van?"

I am trying to cover the basics.

He squints at me. "You don't need to be paranoid babe, I'm here."

He closed the door tilting at me.

He doesn't know!

A bright smile and his beard a bit unruly for my liking. I was genuinely terrified.

I should tell him. My subconscious whispered to me. I scare, thankfully he didn't see, leaning to the button, pushed it, the engine turns over.

Eric leaned towards me pulling my face with his massive hand under my chin, pecking me on the lips. Then, placing his forehead on mine. For a second, it calmed me. He let go, leaning into his chair and pulling his seat belt from the side.

"Seat belt"

He pointed to me waiting to pull out of the park. Then he sets the car in drive. I reached for it. The car shook. The sound of iron crumpling and tyres burning. Slowly I turned to Eric. His wing mirror and most of the car furrowed toward him.

The back of a white panel van backed into his window. Completely reversed crumpling the door, pushing back into us then, shattering his window and cracking the windscreen bringing the staring wheel to Eric's chest. My eyes bulge at the sight as I heard him groan.

"Oh, my God! Eric."

I scream as Eric's head began bleeding and his shoulder trapped beneath the crumpled metal and covered in glass. I turned to help, looking on the horrible scene. He leaned slightly to me moving sluggishly.

"Eric," I panicked, my mind went blank and breathing escalated. I don't know what to do.

Then his eyes opened wide with horror. A gust of wind entered the car. My door opens hands wrapped around my chest pulling me out.

"No," I try to shrug the person off reaching for him. "Eric."

I screamed watching the blood flow from his head. Turning to see the rescuer, I was blocked by a rag with a funny smell over my mouth and nose. Hearing Eric, call for me and seeing him in blurred vision struggle to stop them, then nothing.

CHAPTER FORTY-SEVEN

Jolting, I came to consciousness with the feel of a restraint falling forward. My vision cleared to a cockroach scurrying across the floor to an empty chip container next to an overturned dustbin. I shrieked muffled.

My mouth is bound.

Terror filled me. Startled I jerked feeling the tightness of the restraints around my wrists, chest and feet tied at the ankles apart. I panicked remembering the event before. My heartbeat increased. Anguish came. The awful memory of my husband sloped over the staring wheel. A van deliberately reversed into him.

Don't cry!

I stifle them.

Scanning the mildew cream walls, I am near a window cater-corner the door. In my view a dark coloured iron bed to the left. An off-white sheet, covers the bed explaining the reek of urine. My heightened sense of smell also picked up moulded cheese and wet carpet.

The red dust from the nearby argillite stone canyon formations flew in with the breeze to my right. Throwing dust around, in my hair, and eyes and tickling my nostrils. I twitch my nose.

It appeared to be a motel.

The old tube television on a three-drawer brown chipped wooden chest of drawers sitting on top gave it away. The window a few feet from the door only gives away the roofing and the red rocks.

Super senses aren't helping.

My gagging stopped by the duct tape covering my mouth. The taste of vomit is at the back of my throat. My legs are numbing they are secured and open, one ballerina's missing, my dress thankfully covering my legs, conscious that I have been taken.

… But for how long…

An unpleasant thought surfaced.

The opened glass windowpane brings a light warm breeze. But it often circulates the powerful odours. The running water I hear coming from behind me, I guess is the toilet. I bring my knees as close as possible together.

I need to pee.

I am twitching.

Then, the precious cargo I carry began a stretch. My baby moved also waking my appetite. The small but visible bump through my patterned maxi dress tapped a bit stronger converting my thoughts.

I whimper, muffled, barely able to breathe, unable to rationalise.

Ten, nine, eight, seven, six, five, four…

Closing my eyes, counting again but can't get to one.

Voices nearby, an argument between a man and woman whispered,

"… Why the fuck did you take her?" the woman whispered.

"She needs to know… playing with fire," I heard bits as he replies.

Ugh! I can't make out the words!

A shadow of a female, I think, with dark short hair flew into the room with the lace curtains.

"… What do you think she'll say uh? … think this through." Her words soft, missing bits.

"… Warned about this… dangerous…"

Dangerous.

Opened my eyes concocting an escape.

"… Do something now or I will…" Her threat, loud and clear.

"I'll fix this but…" He was muffled again.

"OK! … but… warned." There was nothing again.

Shifting in the chair, a slight groan left me a bit louder than expected. Their conversation paused, and I did also.

Shit! What do I do?

Footsteps gained volume to the door I wriggled frantically in the chair. At the window, the two shadowed images disappeared.

The door handles quivered, my eyes widened and breathing amplified as the irrational Shannan took over. The door burst in; I squealed muffled under the duct tape. He inhaled long and deep then shut the door behind him.

"Are you, all right?"

That familiar weird Divinish accent again. Slightly familiar but too scared to trace my memory from where I heard it before. I inhaled leaning back into the chair tensely deflating my lungs.

A slender man wearing a moss-green mechanic's jumper with a whitish nametag written 'Marcus' and worn out, light-coloured shoes.

I sniff the machine oil, cigarette and dirt as he came closer to me from the distance. He secures the door then strides to me. Once again, amplifying odours, heightened my steroid senses that had only just settled.

Standing in my full view, he raised his palms. My eyes widened. I whimper, clenching deep inside, shallowing my breathing. He brings his hand to my face I pulled as far away as I can but he still manages to reach me.

Carefully, he brushed the debris off my face with the back of his tough hand, bruising me. He does it several times clearing my face. I screwed my eyes shut tensing to his touch until his hand left me marginally relaxing.

"Don't be afraid all right," he says with his thick accent.

Moments after he removes his hand. I exhaled peeking at him.

He stills, swiftly gaping through the open window then walked to it and paused, watched outside slowly then moved his eyes to me.

I flinch. He patrolled along the window rubbing his hands together staring in thought as he paces back and forth twice. Paused then stared back through the window and at me again.

He crouched in front of me. My knees twisted to one another but did not quite meet. He regarded them oddly then locked his soft blue eyes into my green. I couldn't help but notice the dirt and grease in his hair and along his face. His blue eyes were actually pretty and he seemed to have some twisted care for me.

Then, he placed his hands on my knees. I bawled under the duct tape. Parting my knees as I resisted, he hisses blowing his smoky breath and closing his eyes as he did.

I can't win I am too tired.

My legs open and he stoops between them.

"Stay like this," he commands surprising me as he licks his lips folding them slowly as if tasting something. This time placing his rough hands over mine tied to the chair. I clinch the chair and stopped breathing.

He stood up suddenly as if alerted. I exhaled. He nervously viewed through the window and then moved his eyes to me. He paced along the window rubbing his hands together back and forth staring aimlessly again twice. Each time he gets to the other end of the window he glances through, pause, then looked at me and back through the window and at me again.

"I'm sorry, I'm sorry." He weeps. "… You might be hungry," he says with purpose.

His behaviour is confusing, creepy, frightening and making me nervous all at the same time. I eyed him closely.

He fearfully paced glancing through the window, paced along the window rubbing his hands together then back at me again. The motion mimicked a fly. He explained,

"I'm sorry… but this is the only way that I could talk to you, without them knowing."

I am perplexed.

You took me whilst with my husband.

What would make him think no one would know about this?

I answered him inwardly.

… Unless he… he didn't.

The thought pains me.

He leaned over and carefully peeled the duct tape off my lips taking a layer of my skin with it. I twisted my mouth and then moisten my lips from the dryness. It only made the nausea worse.

Keeping his face close enough, to breathe his cigarette after breath over my lips. He leans in further. I retreat to the furthest corner of the chair.

I tasted all the odours and struggle to inhale. It's at the back of my throat and I cannot hold it any longer.

Tilting my shoulders to the side I vomited. He jumped back, startled. I inhaled again and again vomited wetting part of my forearm. Gasping after it was over.

It's been a while since I did that.

The relief is partially satisfying but reminds me of the little person I carry. I gathered all the excess vomit with as much saliva as I could pool inside my mouth. With a long drag vibrating my throat clearing the last bits, I spat.

The man hurried behind me to the left and I hear movements adding to my nervousness. He came around me from the other side, and I flinch.

"I'm sorry, I'm sorry," he apologised and takes up the chair physically moving me over the vomit closer to the window. Shoving toilet paper at my face I didn't see it in his hands before then. I flinch turning away as he wipes my mouth and forearm.

"... This was the only way. I'm sorry but it was the only way... I'm really... really sorry that I had to do this... but there was no other way."

He bows his head over my lap stooping between my legs. I tense. His crying mystifies me.

"What do you want with me?"

The words flew out. His gaze was dark, intensified and his hands touched my knees. I groan. He's tugging at my dress. I pale with a small groan before begging.

"Please... untie me."

He stopped.

"I'm running out of time..."

My heartbeat increased and screwed my face stifling the fear.

"... I'm already a dead man for doing this... but... you need to know."

His voice cracks and he's tearful and I am baffled.

Abruptly, he gets up. My dress slid down my legs. Apprehensively, he paced again glancing through the window, paced along it rubbing his hands together then, back at me again.

"Please... untie me."

I tug at the restraints around my hands. The relief was momentary.

"I'm sorry..." He weeps again making a fist to graze his cheek with the inside of his wrist.

"... You don't understand how... precious... you are. How much you mean to..."

"Please... I don't feel well."

The contents of my stomach creep up my oesophagus and I swallow hard.

"I'm sorry but you are so important... you were hidden..." He is cheerful and says in a singsong. "... You don't know, but I knew the second I saw you..." He groans deep in his throat sauntering towards me slowly with a salacious smirk across his face. "... Your beauty... glowed... your eyes... and I recognised you." He stoops between my legs again, this time slowly pulling my dress to my knees,

"Please..." I try to remain calm.

"At first, I just wanted to see you..."

"Please," I whisper, trying not to focus on the need in his eyes as he sits between my legs pulling up my dress.

"... Then, I needed to touch you... then." He pauses with deep thought. The confession sends my heart racing as I think.

There is a third...

My thoughts are fearful but some bits clicked and I had to know.

"Did you attack me?" My mouth goes dry. I know the answer. He paused his action.

"Hum. Spilling your coffee was an accident..."

He reminisces between my legs his arms balancing on my naked knees. My eyes widened. The dress tail sloped between my legs his eyes looked up to the left.

Oh, fuck! It was him...

My eyes widened further.

This is not what I thought he did!

I squirm inward but try to remain impassive in light of this information.

"I just needed to touch you."

He moved his hands covering mine with a greedy smirk. He closed his eyes for seconds exhaling slowly. Blowing into my dress I folded my lips inward endeavouring not to alarm him. There was no saliva in my mouth.

"... Then, you dislocated my elbow."

I smiled inside, he sing-sang disapprovingly.

"Why?" My voice was soft, filled with disgust.

"You are…" He opens his mouth and nothing comes out but he did seem in pain, choking on something. The veins on his neck raised and his face reddens. Then he closed his mouth and his face returns to its natural colour. With a deep breath, he closes his eyes again then opened them with purpose. "… You need to know." He is back to urgency in his voice.

"Need to know what?" I am losing my grip.

"You have to stop the investigation," he says and I am confused.

"Why?" I asked.

"You can't continue to…" He began to weep bitterly I sat back into the chair, eyebrows raised, and I was still, lost in his sorrow. He wipes his face and I gain some confidence.

"Did you attack me… at the L.D.O.?"

The memory haunts me. I have to know. He dried his eyes and paused the stared at me.

"I didn't get there in time." He takes a deep regretful breath, "… You need to stop digging up those files, *stop investigating.*"

He starts soft and ends loud, standing and pointing at me.

"Why, what do you know about my investigation?"

I became curious. He sighs narrowing his eyes at me.

"This is not all about your investigation. What you're doing is awakening, rising."

"What the hell are you talking about?"

"You were hidden so well. Now… you're exposed… they know where you are… what they'll do with you…"

He is irate again. Some of what he says feels true. I sense his anxiousness and fear flowing through me as certain as he feels, I keep it at bay. I want to believe him but.

"You are not making sense… at all."

"Have you ever stopped to ask why our government would send a specialised team to investigate a simple rape?"

The words left his mouth and I try thinking but came up blank, the words leave my mouth.

"What do you mean?"

"The forensic specialist, an analyst drug officer, a profiler and you, the key. It was not just about diversity…"

I squint but there is only one word stuck in what he claims. "Key, what do you mean key?"

"They were sure this would have drawn you, the key... the key this." He laughs scorned. "... The key to his walk on earth."

I was almost sold until he said the crazy.

"I think that you might have inhaled a little too much canyon dust." I jeer automatically.

"Don't mock me!" he shouted raking back any confidence I gained. "... I can tell you don't know about your heritage, your value, your purpose or what you are."

His eyes darkened standing over me. His blue eyes gaze deeper at me, seeing into me. The hairs at the back of my neck stood up.

"... For an intelligent woman, you made a lot of stupid mistakes. He lured you here."

He's making sense to himself but not to me!

"Who, who are you talking about?"

He smirked looking away, suspiciously paced glancing through the window paced along the window rubbing his hands together then back at me again my eyes caught his missing three fingers index, middle and ring finger all gone on his right hand. He caught me looking.

"This is the beginning of my torture... stop looking, please. Let this one go. He hasn't found you... yet. Get away while you can. You are his key, the last piece that he needs."

He dangled his hand by my face and began pacing again. His emotion hits me again fuelled by fear and certainty. *But he doesn't make sense!*

"There goes this key thing again."

He pauses with a peculiar expression tilting his head to one side with dilated eyes widened at me.

"You really don't remember... do you?"

I ponder on his words and the abyss of darkness through my memory fills, resulting in frustration.

"Of course, I don't! Just tell me."

I yelled at him.

"I wish I could..." He weeps pacing near the window. Taking a deep breath. "... Your family..."

There was a loud bang that echoed through the halls. The insides of his head exploded across the TV, to the opposite wall and parts of me. Afraid to look up, my eyes remain where they were, at the window. Dark, freshly cut hair blew in with the curtains and an interesting ring on the killer's finger pointed across the barrel of the Glock.

I gasp in fright, as the sound shattered the quiet throughout the motel. His body bobbed before lying at rest at my feet, his blue eyes staring at me with pupils dilated. The air won't leave my lungs as I waited for another sound from that direction and the pain that would follow.

A high pitch monotone buzzed in my ear. His final thud triggers a massive shiver, that I could not stop. I screwed my eyes shut waiting, trembling, counting with a prayer.

Ten, nine, eight…

I heard footsteps fleeing.

… Seven… six… five…

A car burning tires and the engine sound fading away.

… Four… three.

A woman screamed. My eyes filled coming to the realisation of today's events.

… Two… one.

Boots stomping, increasing in volume close by. Then, the door burst open. I felt arms around me, his comforting smell and his voice calling my name.

"Shana…"

The relief in his voice was enough for me to finally exhale but insufficient to stop shuddering.

A preview of the author's next work

Eric

Ian was right. I fucked up. I should have fixed this shit, a long time ago. Something was off about her. I can tell. Shannan is jumpy and distant. Her thoughts are all over the place. She believes she must have done something wrong. It's not her, it's me. I have done this shit.

"Is everything alright?" Her multi-coloured hazels peer up at me, expectant.

She waits. For a reply?

I don't know.

The hum of the elevator descending grunts in the space. I don't dare move my eyes. Only guilty fucks do that. My pan hardens, and she look away.

Most do, at that look.

Getting this shit-fest out is what's going to happen, but she's not going to make me here.

This is not the right place.

"We can talk, when we get home." I suggest and I can see her eagerness for knowledge.

Shana's impatience's can be something that is loved or loathe.

Presently I loathe.

"This is not the right place." I muttered, aloud this time.

The elevator door's part and we got out into the basement parking at the hospital. She clutches my arm tighter. Something has her on edge.

Her thoughts move to Sam, why?

She is not intimidated by my ex, so what is it?

"It's okay." I try to relieve her.

A car screeches around a corner moving fast through the parking.

"Did you get the plate on that car?" She voiced her anxiousness.

Of course, I did. But I am not going to add to her mood. That'll give me a fucking migraine. Especially when my own thoughts are muddled. I simply raised an eyebrow. She simmers getting into the car as I take the bag to the trunk.

Another vehicle goes by just as fast and her eyes dart to it then to me when I got into the car. I try shutting down a connection that would lead a growing headache.

Not wearing a seatbelt, as usual, I scolded her while clicking mine. Her eyes widen in my direction of the incomplete action.

"Oh my gosh!" she squeaks, trying not to curse.

Turning quick, the steering wheel, wing mirror, glass window and front panel closed into me. Hard and fast. The noise registered in my thoughts seconds after the car shook from the impact. I can't move my feet. My hips stayed in position twisted to the left and my right hand is stuck across my chest, almost bending pinned by the steering wheel. I'm trapped. Caught in the motion of securing the seatbelt. Which, fucking secures me.

"Eric!"

She's crying out my name and the glass shatters. The van went forward then, reversed into my side further, scaring her into a shriek. My forehead burns as the windscreen touches it, warm liquid wets my face and I am blinded by the blood flowing down into my eyes.

I closed it.

Focused on me, her door opened. She doesn't find it suspicious. She is arguing with someone, whose voice is a mumble to me. All I hear is her yelling for me. Asking if I'm all right, telling him he needs to help me.

"I'm fine."

She hisses at him, penetrating what I thought was a blink. My head was resting on the steering wheel. Her back to him and she is moving back to me, pointing while saying incoherent words. A blank moment, succumbing to the injury. My vision blurring for a flash.

Then, I see his face. The fucker. Bending over, behind her, to look at me. A fucking wily smile grew. He wanted me to know it was him. His arm went across her chest and another went over her mouth. She kicked up, caught off guard fighting him. Then, she went limp, being dragged away.

Shit!

Fuck! A second to assess.

Shit! I am shocked.

Fuck! The other, she's taken.

Blood slowing it's dripping out my head. I don't know how long I have been here. I am sure, I just blinked. My thoughts pooled quick.

Shana is gone.

That fucker took my wife.

That motherfucker, kidnapped my wife.

Overthrown by anger. I concentrate. Stilling everything inside. Blocking out Shannan's cry. The car speeding away. All my anxiousness. Building the energy from my blood, the rights of my rise. Pooled from my ancestors, the house of Berána, the bear. First gods of the Zemand. The energy stirs, swirls, moves inside me. The air travels lazily to me. The sting of her fear and mine meets my nose, fast and foul. It doesn't work.

Damn-it! Fuck! I snarl.

The strength I called did not come. I fidgeted in my seat to find a way of freeing myself, realising then, the numbness of my feet has faded. My hip isn't hurt. The rise possibly made it half way.

"Fuck!" I growled aloud another F-bomb.

Cussing the Zemand gods for a half gift.

Cussing myself for trusting the Cáyî-Zeman and believing they, would not fucking collect.

Fucking helpless, I had no choice but, to wait.

I am sure there was someone coming out the white van backed into the car, but the person never passes in my view. Only footsteps fleeing the scene.

Shannan has been taken.

He took her, all for me to see, like it was some fucking joke, he smiled. My heart rattles through my ribs and I try to rational my next move. I try not to dwell on the loss, because I know he is as good as fucking dead. I am angry.

The next car coming around the corner a few minutes later, stops. Agitated, I barked instructions seeing a woman peeking through Shannan's open door.

"Call the S.D.A.F. office ask for Jerome Franks, get the fire services to get me out."

The flabbergasted woman, "Oh my God! Oh my God, oh my God, you need help!"

Of course! Fuck woman!

I shut my mouth tight biting those words, presently regretting as she repeats OMG doing nothing.

Irritation out with the exhale, "We're in a hospital." I gather all the calm in saying. "…Just find someone from the emergency department."

"Where is that?"

I would have slapped my forehead if my hand was not trapped.

Forty-five minutes later, I am still in the car. Franks is not here and the fucking woman is still confused. The crooked L.D.O. officers are delaying, I am sure of it, while the firemen are using the jaws of life to get me out of this tin trap.

Fuck!

I don't bother telling them about Shana because I know they would tell *him*. Once free, I feel it. Ribs, shoulder, elbow arm and leg all painful. The stretcher meets the car and the medical officers help me onto the bed.

"Can you tell me your emergency contact?" Someone asked.

"Jerome Franks!" I say rattling the phone number.

He knows once he is called with that title what that code means. Sadly, that maniac is too in love to hurt her, I pray. Not at all dismissing anything else that he could not do. Vowing silently to kill him myself for even touching her.

Thirty more minutes pass and Franks was in the examination room with me after processing the crime scene, having the teams prowling and updating me on possible locations. Though it was a small measure of comfort, I will be leading this myself once the X-rays and other tests come back.

Whitley is desperate, but he should know better.

I want to murder him even more.

The painkillers should hold up long enough to get this done.

Nothing else mattered.

Tactical change of suit and the APB on both escape vehicles led us to a motel. Broken down and disgusting just like him. SWAT is setting up. I need to be the first, just in case.

Bang!

A pistol echoed through the canyons and my legs just went towards it. Tyres burned. One team went after the car and the others followed me running with my gun.

Any thoughts other than the object was not allowed to penetrate. Holding the handgun in front of me, I leaned back and kicked without thinking about any injuries.

I was the first to see her, shivering, breathing, stained with his blood. He is at her feet, as he should be.

Happy it wasn't me, again.

Another inquiry would not be wise, given my position as director.

Disgruntled that I hadn't at least had, one punch to his fucking face. I breathe relieved taking her into my arms.

"Shana."

****

I want them to fucking stop touching her. She hasn't stopped shaking. I see the frightened girl again, but there needs to be transparency.

I hate that fucking word when it comes to her.

She's mine to guard, to keep from harm, to love.

I gritted my teeth watching the medical team, take swabs, pictures and undress her bagging it all as evidence. After the insistent internal swabs, that was it.

"That's more than enough," I commanded the team.

An hour of examination, down to a hospital gown. Prodded for more than a baby check made me ill and when she didn't react, it broke me. Showing me my failure. It is my responsibility to take care of her and keep her from harm.

My nails dug into my palms. I wanted to punch something. Cleared my throat, I swallowed my regret focusing on her. She is what matters.

Took her hand and she flinch. Retreating to a corner. I still not wanting to alarm her further.

Fucking flinch, at me!

Raking my anger, for those responsible careful to direct it correctly, I dragged my throat again. She looked through me. Her hazels like a canopy of leaves, darken. If he wasn't dead, I would have killed him, again. Him and his partner.

From review of the tapes, one person trapped me and the other took her. Whitley betrayed his partner to have her all to himself.

When I get my hands on that little shit, I'll do to him what I couldn't to his partner.

I need her to calm. Though her default blue eyes, hasn't shown itself, there is no way any explosion from her would be gentle.

There is a blue blanket on the bed. I grabbed it to cover her. Her hair is partly straight with debris. I clench my jaw taking a breath first.

We ambled ever so slow out of the room. Bailey and Samuels, my personal security stayed out of sight and we landed in an open bathroom with a few showers.

"Get me a towel. Let no one pass."

I issued my orders passing through. I bent to grab her glance, she moved her eyes slightly with a little life, then to the floors again. Without consideration, I undressed. Her eyes fall to my stomach.

Good girl.

Bailey put the towel, soap and wash cloth on the small wall. I added my tactical vest. Unbuttoned my pants and twitch at her gawk at me. I locked my jaw needing to control it.

Then, I took the boots and socks off, followed by my pants, throwing them over the wall. Her eyes moved up measuring me, the bruised ribs deep red and purple, under my dark skin caught her eyes and they grew glassy.

I turned the shower on removing the gown. The cold water doesn't move her. I turned to the side taking the washcloth and soap, walking into the weak flow with her that has now warmed.

Tilted her head back to wash over her hair. Pieces of leaves, dust and brain splatter fall to the floor. I keep her head up so she doesn't look at anything else. Even if she watches straight through me, I want her eyes to meet me.

The natural form of her hair springs into barrels, stretching at the weight of the water, waving to its curly form. She doesn't react. I know she hates getting her hair wet.

Fuck! I grunt underneath.

All the lack of response, she is protecting her centre, blocking my hands from touching my unborn son. I don't stop her, and regret looms between us.

I underestimated those fuckers.

Never, again.